Di Morrissey is one of Australia's most successful writers. She began writing as a young woman, training and working as a journalist for Australian Consolidated Press in Sydney and Northcliffe Newspapers in London. She has worked in television in Australia and in the USA as a presenter, reporter, producer and actress. After her marriage to a US diplomat, Peter Morrissey, she lived in Singapore, Japan, Thailand, South America and Washington. Returning to Australia, Di continued to work in television before publishing her first novel in 1991.

Di has a daughter, Dr Gabrielle Morrissey Hansen, a human sexuality and relationship expert and academic. Di's son, Dr Nicolas Morrissey, is a lecturer in South East Asian Art History and Buddhist Studies at the University of Georgia, USA. Di has three grandchildren: Sonoma Grace and Everton Peter Hansen and William James Bodhi Morrissey.

Di and her partner, Boris Janjic, live in the Manning Valley in New South Wales when not travelling to research her novels, which are all inspired by a particular landscape.

www.dimorrissey.com

# Di Morrissey

# The Golden Land

MACMILLAN
Pan Macmillan Australia

First published in Macmillan in 2012 by Pan Macmillan Australia Pty Limited
1 Market Street, Sydney

National Library of Australia
Cataloguing-in-Publication data:

Morrissey, Di

The golden land / Di Morrissey.

9781742611358 (pbk.)

A823.3

Internal photographs by Di Morrissey
Typeset in 12.5/15 pt Sabon by Post Pre-press Group
Printed in Australia by McPherson's Printing Group

Papers used by Pan Macmillan Australia Pty Ltd are natural, recyclable products
made from wood grown in sustainable forests. The manufacturing processes
conform to the environmental regulations of the country of origin.

*To Daw Aung San Suu Kyi for her steadfast and moral leadership that has inspired the world.*

*And to the people of Myanmar as they begin their journey towards their dream of freedom and democracy for their beautiful country.*

# Acknowledgements

To my beautiful grandchildren in the hope they will one day visit the Golden Land and discover a peaceful, democratic country.

To my adorable daughter-in-law Mimi and my son Dr Nicolas Morrissey. Thanks Nick for your help and knowledge, and the wonderful time you and I shared in Myanmar.

To my loving partner Boris Janjic for holding the fort, and for making my life so comfortable and such fun! Thank you, darling.

To my caring daughter Dr Gabrielle Morrissey Hansen, a fantastic mom, a dedicated educator and academic, and loving wife to dear Barrie. Thank you for your support and input. I'm very proud of you.

Very special thanks to my dear friend Janelle Saffin MP.

Thank you to my amazing editor and friend Liz Adams, whose valuable input challenges and pushes me, and who wrestles my hazy thoughts into focus and shares the daily battle of the book.

And to my friends: Australian Ambassador to Myanmar Bronte Moules (and Jantima); U Win Htein and Chit Suu, Eugene Quah and Wai Wai Kyaw, U Myo Thant, Gill Pattison, Ko Nay Dun Mya; Venerable monks Sayadaw Agga Nya and Sayadaw Vijja Nanda (Wiza); U Nay Oke; Thomas Soe and the Burmese community in Sydney; the well-travelled Greg Wisbey; Don M. Stadtner; Robert L. Brown, Professor of Art History at UCLA and Curator of South and Southeast Asian Art at LACMA (Los Angeles County Museum of Art).

To my family at Pan Macmillan: Ross Gibb, Kate Nash, Samantha Sainsbury, Danielle Walker, Jane Hayes, Hayley Crandell and special thanks to Rowena Lennox for her attentive copy editing.

While this book is a work of fiction, it is inspired
by actual events and people in Burma such as
Aung San Suu Kyi; her father, the late General Aung San;
members of the former royal family, King Thibaw
and Queen Supayalat and the military leader,
General Ne Win.

# I

## 1885 – Burma

IN THE COOL SHADOWS of the high-ceilinged wooden monastery the young monk sat with bowed head, chewing his bottom lip as he painstakingly drew his stylus over the lacquered red square that lay on the floor in front of him. Occasionally he hitched his cotton robe back onto his shoulder, draping the folds over his lap, his bare brown feet protruding from the robe as he worked. He sat cross-legged, his brow furrowed in concentration. Chosen by the abbot of the monastery because of his exceptional artistic skills, he had been given the chance to decorate the sacred text of a kammavaca that was to be presented to the king himself.

Ye Aung's talents had been discovered not long after his arrival at the monastery as an eight-year-old boy. His impoverished family had entrusted him into the care of the monastery in the hope that he would become a respected and learned monk. They, in return, could expect to gain merit for their sacrifice.

Ye Aung joined the long classes with other novice monks, learning to chant by heart the Buddhist canon in Pali, the ancient language that Buddha spoke. Many hours were also spent in prayer and meditation and reading the old texts held in the monastery. Through these texts Ye Aung learned about the life of the Buddha and legends and tales of the spirit world that hovered between myth and belief, as well as the history of the great kings of Burma.

Ye Aung was a quiet boy who was happy in his own company. When the other young monks played, chasing woven bamboo balls behind the long dining hall or flinging off their robes to dive and splash in the silky brown waters of the Irrawaddy River, Ye Aung would sit in the shade of a tree, gazing at the old monastery with its spacious corridors and high heavy doors, its sweeping tiered roof and tall, ornately carved spires held aloft by carved mythical creatures.

The teak of the buildings had turned dark grey over the century or more that the monastery had stood in the quiet, remote jungle clearing. The courtyard between the main building and the two smaller ones was made of fine white earth and was swept daily by the monks, whether the courtyard was sun-warmed or contained puddles shining in the monsoon rain. The buildings had a weathered, friendly appearance and a softness quite unlike the gilded pagodas and stupas that were scattered near the local villages and in the city of Mandalay.

This place was so peaceful that it might have appeared deserted if it weren't for the constant flutter of deep red robes, draped over a line in the courtyard or from railings and windows to dry, or the low rumbling hum of chanted prayers that droned from within the monastery like a swarm of earnest bees.

Ye Aung had always seen pictures in his head and he wanted to transcribe the rich tapestry of stories from his lessons into delicate, detailed illustrations. He shyly told his teacher, Sayadaw, his ambition, and Sayadaw began to encourage him. Even though he had not had formal lessons, Ye Aung loved nothing better than to draw with a brush or stylus.

He shared his dormitory with other young monks. Each had a mat on the floor and a coverlet and used their folded robes as a pillow. A small box held their few personal items, which included a writing slate and copies of the Pali texts they learned to chant by heart.

Ye Aung liked to sit alone in his corner while the other boisterous boys let off steam outside. He enjoyed his solitude in the quiet room where the open wooden window shutters let in the warm breeze from the river. Here he drew tiny images adapted from all he saw around him: fantastic creatures, glorious flora, the beautiful birds and even the monks themselves. Sometimes he drew pictures of the spirit-world creatures, or the animals representing the different birth days.

Eventually Ye Aung graduated to creating kammavacas, sacred Buddhist texts written on treated palm leaves. The leaves were smoothed and smoked before the texts were written on them, with spaces left between some of the lines for intricate illustrations. When complete the leaves would be carefully joined together with silk cords and folded between lacquered pieces of bark. Sometimes the teak-bark covers were decorated with gold leaf.

Frequently kammavacas were commissioned by families and given to the monastery when a son entered the Buddhist order. The special palm-leaf manuscripts were then stacked in decorated boxes or wrapped in cloth and stored in the ornate library chest in the abbot's quarters in the dim reaches of the inner sanctum of the monastery. Ye Aung's family had

3

been too poor to commission a kammavaca and the young boy hoped that by illustrating them for others as well as he could, he would be able to bring merit to his parents.

One day, Sayadaw called Ye Aung into the private sanctuary used by the senior monks. Here the older monks meditated and prayed, surrounded by relics, thangka hangings, figures of the Buddha and library chests holding palm-leaf manuscripts so old that few could still read the ancient script in which they were written.

Ye Aung was awed to be in this sanctuary and stood quietly, his head bowed, hands clasped beneath his robes as his teacher took a monk's robe from a chest. Ye Aung knew the cloth was old the moment Sayadaw put it into his hands. His teacher then told the young boy that the robe had belonged to one of the monastery's most respected and honoured monks. He explained that instead of using the usual palm leaf, pieces of this robe were sometimes used to make special kammavacas. First, the cloth would be covered with lacquer to become a smooth but pliant surface and then it would be cut into sections on which the monks would inscribe sacred texts. These cloth sections would then be joined together by narrow ribs of split and polished bamboo. Ye Aung would then illustrate the work with his drawings, using boiled black lacquer as ink.

'May I ask to whom this special kammavaca is to be given?' said Ye Aung.

Sayadaw smiled. 'It is to be presented to King Thibaw.'

Being asked to work on this particular project weighed heavily on the shoulders of Ye Aung. As he worked he began to have an inkling that there was more in the text than simply Buddhist teachings. He asked Sayadaw to translate the meaning of the ancient Pali script but Sayadaw shook his head.

'The old monks have special knowledge that they occasionally pass on, hoping that someone, somewhere, will be able to decipher what is hidden in the text. It's a means of safekeeping.'

'Like a secret?'

Sayadaw shrugged. 'Yes, such as where certain relics, riches or objects to be venerated are hidden. Perhaps monastic traditions. Whoever can decipher the text will acquire special status, karma and enrichment.'

'Can you read what's written in this kammavaca?' Ye Aung asked.

Sayadaw shook his head. 'The senior monks each write only a part of the story. No-one is allowed to read all of the manuscript.'

'Who knows the whole story?' asked Ye Aung.

'I cannot tell you,' said Sayadaw.

Ye Aung did not know whether his learned teacher did not know the answer or simply would not tell him, so the young man asked if he could draw some white elephants in this kammavaca like the carved elephant figures at the base of the monastery steps.

Sayadaw smiled. 'I'm sure the king would like that very much. The white elephants are sacred indeed.'


Ye Aung was worried that he had displeased the abbot when he was called to stand before the senior monk. But seeing the pleased expression on Sayadaw's face as he stood nearby, he was reassured. Indeed, so pleased was the abbot with Ye Aung's work that he gave his permission for the young monk to accompany the senior monks to Mandalay to present the completed kammavaca to the king.


In the cool of the early morning, led by the most senior monks, the holy men filed solemnly from the monastery, carrying their alms bowls. In his cotton shoulder bag the abbot carried the gift to the king that Ye Aung had spent many months helping to create. When Ye Aung saw the bag he smiled to himself, knowing what was in it and remembering his drawings of white elephants wearing jewelled necklaces and richly embroidered cloths with bands of gold around their tusks, walking beneath a gold-tasselled white canopy, escorted by musicians and magicians.

The monks walked for days through villages, pausing at food stalls and houses where they were given water and food. Once they passed the bodies of two dacoits who had been crucified on a hillside as punishment for raiding a local village. Ye Aung shuddered when he saw them and quickly averted his eyes, although he admitted to himself that the villagers had the right to protect themselves from such bandits. Knowing that lawlessness abounded in the countryside, he felt safer when the monks arrived on the outskirts of Mandalay.

The closer they got to the royal palace, the more crowded the roads became, not just with people but also with dozens of pigs jostling around them.

'King Mindon, who came before King Thibaw, fed a thousand pigs each day to earn merit but when he died they were abandoned,' Sayadaw explained to Ye Aung.

The monks arrived at the expansive palace, crossed the wide moat on the fifth bridge, walked in single file through the grounds, past the watchtower, and were led to a beautiful, large pavilion. Inside, a carved wooden partition divided the cool and airy space into several reception rooms. The monks went into a small room to await the arrival of the king.

Ye Aung couldn't stop looking at the throne, heavily decorated with intricate carvings, which sat at the end of the room, while, high above, the ceiling was painted with lavish scenes and spectacles from the life of King Mindon, who'd built the splendid palace.

When King Thibaw arrived, he did so modestly, without Queen Supayalat or any attendants but accompanied only by two of his young daughters. The princesses were dressed in silk longyi, full-length sarongs in brilliant colours with tight-fitting, long-sleeved silk blouses and jewelled flowers pinned at the side of their long, smooth hair. Ye Aung thought they looked like a pair of beautiful butterflies and he tried not to feel too prideful when the younger princess held the kammavaca for a moment before returning it to her father.

It was a short and formal meeting and, if not for the presence of the two princesses, a very dull event. After it was over, Ye Aung followed the older monks to the central shrine of the palace to offer appropriate prayers. He couldn't help wondering if the king would study the pages of the kammavaca and notice his illustrations or if it would simply be placed in the royal library and forgotten. Nevertheless, he said a prayer for the wellbeing of the king and his family.


Within a month, there were dramatic changes in Mandalay that affected even the quiet life of the monastery. British troops had moved in from the coastal regions of Burma and travelled up the Irrawaddy River, marching through the villages and markets on their way to Mandalay Palace.

The novice monks were ordered to stay indoors while the senior monks spread out through the countryside to protect their shrines and relics. The invaders had no respect for the Burmese culture and took what they pleased. In the marketplaces, supplies of rice and staples were stretched and there were greatly reduced offerings for the monks on their daily rounds to the food stalls, shopkeepers and houses of devout townspeople. When they returned to the monastery their alms bowls were often empty.

7

Ye Aung asked Sayadaw about the welfare of the king and the royal court, especially the princesses. Sayadaw told him that the British had taken them away from the palace in bullock carts and sent them to live somewhere in India. The British were now in control of all Burma.

Eventually the abbot decided to find out for himself exactly what was happening in the city. But when he returned from Mandalay he was greatly distressed. He said that he had heard that the palace was now called Fort Dufferin after the Viceroy of India, and that the British officers were using it as their private club. Jewels had been plundered from it and the largest gemstones had been sent to Queen Victoria. The lavish Burmese throne was now in a museum in Calcutta.

Just before dawn several days later, a small fishing boat pulled into the landing below the monastery and a figure wrapped in monk's robes hurried up the steps and along the path to the clearing where the monastery stood in the dark shadows.

Ye Aung stirred. Lying on his mat on the dormitory floor, he'd heard the splashing of an oar in the river, and now the soft brushing of footsteps hurrying up the stairs and the creak of the teak boards as the visitor walked swiftly along the outer corridor. Whispers were exchanged. Then Ye Aung heard the sounds of several more monks as they followed the visitor to the zayat, the pavilion in the grounds of the monastery that was used by the monks for meditation during the day and where visitors rested.

Ye Aung, now wide awake, was curious and he rose and walked quietly past the other sleeping boys and through the darkened rooms, slipping between the pillars of the main corridor, out through the tall carved doors and down the stone steps at the rear of the monastery.

He knew that eavesdropping was wrong but he also knew the monks were worried about the British. In the moonlight he saw senior monks sitting in a close circle on the floor of the pavilion, speaking softly. He didn't dare go any closer so he turned and crept back to his place on the dormitory floor and hoped he'd learn more later.

Sayadaw didn't disappoint him, taking him aside after morning meditation that day. From the look in his teacher's eyes, Ye Aung suspected that he had either been heard or spotted creeping about the monastery the previous night.

Sayadaw looked serious as he began to explain. 'There is much trouble in the city. Everyone is very distressed. The British soldiers burned the royal treasury.'

'So are all the money and jewels gone?' asked Ye Aung.

'I believe that only some money was left. A lot has already been looted and the king took as much as he could in the short time he had before leaving Burma. It is said that he also arranged to have much of it hidden.' Sayadaw shook his head. 'But no, Ye Aung, that is not what has upset the monks so much. In the treasury were kept all the genealogical records of the hereditary nobility. These important records were inscribed on gold-bound palm-leaf manuscripts and wrapped in embroidered silk cloths.'

'As beautiful as my one?' said Ye Aung and Sayadaw gave a small smile.

'Perhaps, but none would have the devotion and imagination you put into your work. And, sadly, the royal library has also been looted and many precious books and records of our culture have also been destroyed.'

Ye Aung could only stare at Sayadaw in shock, imagining the thousands of manuscripts, many hundreds of years old, that must have been burned. 'Why would the British soldiers do this?' he whispered.

Sayadaw shrugged. 'They want to impose their law. But they will not be here forever. We have been here for centuries, and one day these British will be forced to leave and we will again be ruled by our own wise and peaceful men.'

Ye Aung tried to remember the teachings of the Buddha and to forgive the ignorant soldiers who had caused such destruction, but he feared that the kamma-vaca he'd illustrated for the king had now been turned to ash. Suddenly he said, 'If there was a secret in the script on the king's kammavaca, it might be gone forever!'

'Then its secret wasn't meant to be found,' said Sayadaw philosophically.

Ye Aung heard the chanting of the lessons begin as he scampered across the compound. He touched the carved elephant at the bottom of the steps to the monastery and whispered a swift prayer in the hope that by some blessed chance his special manuscript had survived.

## 1913

The late afternoon colours melted over the slick brown surface of the Irrawaddy. The tranquillity of the still river was broken by the chugging of the engine driving the large paddlewheels of the laden steamer as it churned towards Mandalay. On the polished teak open-air upper deck, in the section reserved for first-class passengers, pre-dinner drinks were being served. The dark-skinned Bengali boat crew of the Irrawaddy Flotilla Company waited on the passengers, all of whom seemed to be British, as they reclined in their planters' chairs, screened by tubs of palms, sipping their sundowners. The men, dressed in crisp whites, were discussing trading prices, the formation of a new British teak company, the continued growth of the Yenangyaung oilfields, their successful rice crops and news from home. In more subdued tones, they discussed the latest rumours of the continuing machinations of the exiled King Thibaw and his queen, still languishing in Ratnagiri in India.

'They have to be watched like hawks. They're always plotting to get back to Burma,' said a planter.

'She's the one to watch. You know she was behind the massacre of most of the king's relatives, even some half brothers and sisters, and anyone else she thought might have challenged his succession,' said another.

'Beaten to death in red velvet sacks,' shuddered his companion.

'I was told by a British officer whose friend was present at the executions that it was all very ceremonial. Indeed, quite respectful and calculated to be swift since the blows were judiciously placed,' responded the first planter.

'The people didn't like Thibaw much, either. Blood-thirsty, even if the chap did play cricket,' said his friend laughing.

'Damned primitive lot if you ask me,' commented another of the group. 'Thank god we've annexed the country now. They should consider themselves fortunate not to all be stuffed in a velvet bag.'

'If it wasn't for loyalty to the flag and the opportunities out here I wonder how many of us would stick it out,' mused a retired colonel.

'I think those ruby mines, oilfields and teak forests are rather attractive,' said the paddlesteamer's captain with a slight smile. 'As are the Burmese ladies. I think the rewards of Burma are well worth putting up with a bit of discomfort.'

A little apart from this group of men, Andrew Hancock sat quietly while the drinks and Chinese savouries were being served by the stewards. He listened half-heartedly to the conversations nearby. Staring out over the river to the thickly forested bank, Andrew thought of how incredible it was to be here in Burma. Travelling and adventure was not the life he had expected. His father worked in a bank in Brighton, and Andrew assumed he would do the same, even though he was passionate about photography. He thought it was wonderful to capture something or someone in a photograph and make that moment last forever. Unfortunately, he could see no way of earning a living taking photographs. Then he had a marvellous piece of luck. A distant uncle died and left everything in his will to Andrew. While it was not a fortune, it gave Andrew the time and opportunity to see if it was possible to become a professional photographer.

Andrew quickly found that photographing Brighton was quite dull and he realised that what he really wanted to do was to combine photography with adventure, so he sailed for India. He travelled throughout the country, mainly taking photos of village life, although he did get to the durbar in New Delhi where he saw George V crowned emperor of India. Then he started to write stories to accompany his photos and found that several magazines were interested in buying his work. This meant that he could stay out in the east even longer.

One morning, as Andrew was having breakfast in Calcutta, he heard some men talking about Burma and their discussion piqued Andrew's interest. So he decided to see for himself and now, here he was, as Mr Kipling would say, 'On the road to Mandalay'.

As he sat dreaming to himself on a chair on the deck of the steamer, he was joined by a small, plump Scot wearing tropical whites who peered at him through a pince-nez as he introduced himself.

'Good evening. I'm Ian Ferguson. I don't think I've seen you before. Is this your first trip to Mandalay?'

Andrew rose from his chair and offered Ferguson his hand. 'First time in Burma at all, actually. It looks to be a wonderful country. All those temples. I don't expect that there is another place in the world that has so many.'

'Ah, yes,' replied Ferguson. 'The Burmese are devout Buddhists. What brings you to Burma? Civil service? Trade?'

'Neither,' said Andrew. 'I'm a photographer. I sell my work to magazines back home. May I ask what it is that you do in Burma, Mr Ferguson?'

The little Scot beamed. 'I'm an art expert. In fact, I would go so far as to say that I am *the* expert on Burmese culture and Burmese artefacts.'

Andrew Hancock was impressed. 'So you travel the country, learning the culture of the people?'

'Well, laddie, the thing is the Burmese don't really value their culture. Their temples are packed with arte-facts that the monks don't bother to look after. You can buy any number of beautiful things at the markets for a pittance. The Burmese would rather have the money than their religious objects.'

'Perhaps they do care but they really need the money,' Andrew suggested.

'Nonsense, laddie. When you've been here for a while like I have you'll realise that we British place a far higher value on the local culture than the Burmese do.'

'So are you preserving it?' asked Andrew.

'I certainly am. I collect the best of it and send it back to Britain.'

'Into museums?'

'And to private collectors who appreciate Burmese art.' The man gave a short laugh.

After Ian Ferguson moved away to join another group, Andrew reflected on their conversation. He had not been in Burma long and was certainly not the expert that Ferguson claimed to be but he thought it odd that the Burmese should be so casual about their art and culture.

He had observed quite a different attitude in India where the pomp of the rajahs had suggested to him that Indian culture was highly esteemed by its people. He found himself questioning why the same would not be true of Burma. Perhaps he would find out for himself how correct Ferguson's pronouncements were.

The Irrawaddy was now a mile wide, the banks a distant blur. Occasionally the ship steered a course into a deeper channel to avoid the tangled roots of vegetation. Once or twice Andrew saw a small craft being paddled by fishermen, and once the sight of several dolphins leaping from the water brought many of the other passengers to the side of the vessel to exclaim in excitement. Andrew wished that he could photograph the small dark-grey, snub-nosed creatures, but they moved too quickly.

Then the river narrowed and steep volcanic hills smothered in lush jungle rose up beside them. The riverbank was no longer soft brown mud but solidified lava, shining in the afternoon light. At the river's edge, large pools had formed and were surrounded by sheltered clearings backed by high cliffs. The captain told Andrew that elephants sometimes bathed in these pools but now, as they passed, all looked deserted.

Suddenly a small island of thick overgrowth divided the river. To one side was a sheer cliff face, which the water rushed past. The steamer took the calmer reach around the island, giving Andrew a view of a monastery perched on top of a cliff, seemingly abandoned and in some disrepair, yet still imposing and breathtaking.

As they nosed further along, Andrew's attention was caught by a flash of light high in the hills. It took a moment for him to realise that the fiery gold light was the setting sun glinting off the roof of a pagoda which clung to the edge of a precipice. How on earth, wondered Andrew, were people able to ascend to it? It looked impossible.

And how much gold leaf had been applied to the pagoda for it to glow so richly? Moments later he caught sight of another temple, or stupa as he now understood some were called, its distinctive rounded bell shape also shining brightly.

All he had read and heard seemed to be coming to life: stories of chambers of perfumed sandalwood and eaglewood leading to the legendary House of Gold. Its walls were plated in sheets of gold, while a carved vine encrusted with fruit and leaves of emeralds and rubies the size of large eggs embellished its columns; inside a golden casket on a gold table was filled with precious gems; guarded by solid gold idols studded with glittering stones. How much was myth, how much reality?

Now he knew why Burma was the Golden Land – a country, it was said, resplendent in more pagodas, temples and shrines than anywhere else in the world. A country rich in Buddhist culture, rich in natural resources and rich in colourful history. And here he was, ready to explore and photograph it.

## 1926 – Rangoon

Andrew turned off the Strand, the road that ran beside the river, down a small lane between the solid colonial edifices of the post office, the courthouse and the shipping companies that serviced the busy port of Rangoon. He passed street vendors and their tiny food stalls where the appetising odours of frying noodles and savoury pancakes reminded him that it had been some time since he'd had breakfast. A row of narrow doorways led into cluttered dark cubicles that sold everything from bicycle spare parts to cooking utensils and handmade straw brooms. Halfway down the lane was an entrance marked by fluttering magazines, postcards and an array of coloured pencils. Andrew stepped through the door and into a little shop. The Scottish proprietor was dressed in a white shirt tucked into a traditional checked green and magenta cotton longyi, knotted at the waist. He didn't look up from where he sat, cross-legged on a short stool, reading a book.

Andrew glanced at the used books on the shelves, some well-worn English novels and textbooks written in both English and curling Burmese calligraphy. He turned to the shop owner.

'Good morning, Mr Watt.'

The owner peered over his glasses at him, then stood hurriedly and extended his hand.

'Mr Hancock. This is a surprise. I haven't seen you in some time.'

'It certainly has been many years, hasn't it? I was told that I would still find you here. It's good to see you again, Mr Watt.'

'Yes. Not since the outbreak of the war, I think. Pull up a stool or a cushion.' Mr Watt clapped his hands and a young Indian assistant appeared from behind the rows of books. 'Vinay, this is an old acquaintance of mine. Please go straight to the tea shop and fetch us tea. Now tell me, Mr Hancock, what have you been doing with yourself all this time? I thought you might have married and settled down by now.'

'No; perhaps I'm not that type. Things have been uncertain for me. I sailed home when war broke out and spent the next four years in the trenches on the Western Front.'

'Not a pleasant experience for you.'

'It certainly wasn't, although at least I came out of it relatively unscathed, which is more than I can say for others. I was luckier than most. When the war finished I was at a bit of a loose end. My father had died and my only sister, Florence, married an Australian soldier she'd

16

met when he was on leave in Brighton and they moved to Australia. I didn't like to leave my mother alone so I managed to get work with Lord Beaverbrook's newspapers as a photographer. I tried to write a novel, but it wasn't very good and no-one would publish it. When my mother passed away, I decided that there was nothing to keep me in England, and I thought that I would like to come back to the east, and so here I am, looking for more stories about this wonderful land and its people.'

'I heard that your magazine articles were very well received in London along with your excellent photographs.'

'Yes. That work really interested me. Can't say the same about being a London newspaper hack though. But what about you? How have you been all these years?'

'Still happily married to Moe,' said Mr Watt, referring to his Burmese wife. 'I don't think we'll ever get back to the old country. Both of us would find the cold unbearable.'

Andrew concurred, knowing that it was probably the frosty reception that Mrs Watt would receive in Scotland, rather than the weather, that kept the bookshop owner anchored in Rangoon. As Vinay returned to the room with the tea, Andrew asked, 'And your business is doing well?'

'Well enough. What are your plans?'

'I'm planning to be a wanderer again, trusting in the goodness and generosity of others, specifically several London magazines. But instead of an alms bowl, I will carry a camera and a notebook,' Andrew said smiling. 'But I'm not just looking for travellers' tales to send to these publications. I'm trying to get beneath the surface of this country. In Britain there's a lot of ignorance about Burma and its people.'

The bookshop owner nodded gravely. 'Yes, the British really have very little idea what is happening to their empire in the east. Changes are afoot. There are anti-British rumblings, even here in Burma. The Burmese are patient people. But for how long? The young ones are becoming restless. There has been a rebellion at the university.'

'I can't help feeling that our country exploits Burma,' said Andrew, gently.

'I may be from Scotland, but I have thrown my lot in with the Burmese. I have begun to despise the arrogance of our soldiers and civil servants who consider themselves so superior to the people they are ruling, and about whom they know very little. They like to play lord and master in Burma, when the same people would have very little social standing at home. Sometimes I am ashamed to say that I'm British,' Mr Watt burst out.

Andrew nodded thoughtfully. His attention was then caught by several beautiful photographs hanging on one of the walls. One was of Burma's most famous pagoda, the Shwedagon. The beautiful monument with its golden dome and jewelled spires was Rangoon's pre-eminent landmark – as spectacular as any edifice in India or Istanbul. Not only the people of Burma but also foreigners came to pay their respects there. Another photograph was of George V. Next to it was a formal portrait of the late King Thibaw and Queen Supayalat taken in a lavish throne room. The final photograph was of a distant monastery, somewhere near a lake, whose golden bell-shaped stupa was surrounded by misty mountains.

'This one is very fine,' said Andrew, taking the picture down from the wall to look at it more closely.

'Yes, it is beautiful, isn't it? I'm not surprised that you noticed it. It was taken by Philip Klier,' said Mr Watt. 'He also took the one of the old royal family.'

'Ah, yes.' Andrew studied the stoic faces of the royal family, their frozen expressions waiting for the time exposure on the camera to be completed. 'He was an excellent photographer. Tell me, Mr Watt, do you know what happened to the royal family after they were banished to India? I remember hearing some stories but maybe they were all rumours.'

'Poor Thibaw. Rather an ignominious end being sent into exile so far away. I hear they led a lonely existence. You know that the queen came back to Burma a few years ago, after the king died, although she was never allowed to return to Mandalay.' Mr Watt took the photograph from Andrew and put it back on the wall. 'She died last year. At least she was given a suitable funeral in Rangoon. She's buried at the Shwedagon pagoda.'

'And his daughters? What happened to them?' asked Andrew.

'One of them married a commoner, which upset the king and queen. They live in the hills – Darjeeling, I think. The other princesses also had to make their own way, especially after the family money and jewels ran out.'

'Did you ever meet the king and queen?' Andrew nodded at the photograph.

Mr Watt peered at Andrew over the top of his spectacles. 'I'm not that old. The king was deposed more than forty years ago. Though I have been in Burma a long time.'

'Which is why you know so much about Burmese life and culture and history,' said Andrew.

'I know because I want to find out about it, unlike so many of our countrymen who are closed to all ideas except their own,' Mr Watt said. 'When I first came to Burma I was part of the Indian civil service but when I was working in Mandalay I fell in love with a Burmese girl. The choice came down to my beautiful Moe or the ICS. And here I am, still in Burma and still learning about this country and about Buddhism, and still in love with my wife. My life is simple and I like it that way.'

Mr Watt gestured at the photo of the royal family. 'For them it was difficult to change their ways. They really didn't adjust, which I suppose was understandable. The king always hoped to return, however that was not to be. One of his half sisters lives near here although her life is far from what it used to be.'

'I didn't realise that. Do you know her?' Andrew asked.

The bookshop owner picked up several books and placed them back on a shelf. 'Yes, I know Princess Tipi Si. She came back to Burma with the old queen. Now she comes in here occasionally to borrow books. She lives very simply. Being Buddhist, she accepts her different circumstances, perhaps not with grace, but with fortitude.'

'Did she never marry?'

'Oh, yes, when she lived in India. She's had a colourful life! I haven't seen her in person for a while; she sends her retainer in for books. I rather miss our conversations, although she's challenging company,' he added with a raised eyebrow and small smile.

'I'd very much like to meet her. Do you think she'd see me?' asked Andrew. 'It would make a great story for one of my magazines, especially if she would let me take her photograph. Do you think she would agree? I would pay her a sitting fee, of course.'

'Why are you interested in her? That is the old Burma. Burma has changed. The monarchy is gone. No-one misses the excesses of the royal dynasties.'

'I believe people always like to read about interesting lives. Lives of people who were once powerful, but are now very different.' Andrew was going to add that perhaps people felt better about their own circumstances when they could read about another's misfortune, but instead he said, 'I'd like to know about the last years in exile and the old queen's final years in Rangoon. It seems very few people know about her and I'm sure my English readers would enjoy reading about her.'

'I'll ask next time I see Tipi Si, but she may not agree,' said Mr Watt. 'Where are you putting up while you're here?'

'The Strand Hotel,' said Andrew. 'A bit of an indulgence until I decide where I'm going next. Or you can leave a message for me at Bourne and Shepherd here in Rangoon.'

'The photographic studio. I know them.'

'I will be doing occasional work for them while I'm here.'

Mr Watt nodded. 'You mean photographing those whites-only functions? I'm pleased that you're planning to get out of Rangoon. For those who wish to see beneath the golden stupas, there are hidden treasures in Burma.'

Andrew wasn't sure exactly what was meant by this oblique comment, but he was excited by the adventures that might lie ahead. He thanked Mr Watt, promising to call by again, and bought a well-thumbed novel by Somerset Maugham before he left the shop.

Andrew walked around Fytche Square where Queen Victoria's statue gazed severely at the passersby, and then strolled down towards the busy waterfront. He decided that he needed a pot of English tea and turned under the portico of the Strand Hotel.

He sat at a small rattan table and glanced through the novel he'd bought but he was really thinking about what Mr Watt had said about the exiled princess. He tried to imagine what her life had been like and what it must be like now. She sounded as exotic as a character in one of Maugham's novels. Andrew was sure that if he had the chance to interview her, he'd have no difficulty in selling his pictures along with a brief story to a London magazine.

So he was pleased and delighted when, a few days later, a note was handed to him by the tall and burly Sikh hotel doorman.

*Tipi Si has agreed to see you. Here's the address*, wrote Mr Watt. *She is a surprising lady. Quite a character. She might expect something in return.*

Andrew settled himself into a trishaw, steadying his camera box beside him on the seat as a wiry driver pedalled past crowded markets, busy tea shops, noodle stalls and a jumble of leaning shophouses. They made their way through narrow lanes interspersed by grander colonial streets, which were filled with business houses. The trishaw rattled over cobblestone squares, and Andrew caught glimpses of some of the city's pagodas and temples, all of which were overshadowed by the magnificence of the Shwedagon Pagoda.

The driver turned down University Avenue and then into a street lined with mature trees and large residences that had been built for the British years earlier. The street also contained the homes of wealthy Indian, Chinese, Burmese and European businessmen. The houses of former ambassadors and employees of the deposed royal family sat among rambling gardens overlooking Inya Lake.

Andrew was taken aback by all these grand houses and for a moment he thought Mr Watt must have been mistaken in describing the reduced circumstances of the princess. But then the driver stopped outside one of the mansions and pointed to a small house beside it, no more than a couple of rooms, set amid an overgrown garden.

Carrying his camera equipment, Andrew opened the gate and walked beneath dank, overgrown trees and across the decaying lawn covered by swarms of mosquitoes. In the distance he glimpsed the white portico of the big house. A second look at the huge home gave him the impression that it was unoccupied. Shutters, their paint peeling, leaned crookedly at some of the upstairs windows. There were moss and leaves on the steps, and birds had nested under the guttering, in which luxuriant

grass had sprouted. The small house, which had presumably belonged to the gatekeeper, looked equally
dishevelled.

Andrew knocked on the door of the small house and
it seemed an interminable length of time before he finally
heard shuffling footsteps. The door was opened by a tall
young man, dressed in a longyi and a formal white shirt.
Andrew guessed from his light skin that he was a Shan
from the northern hill country. The boy's dark eyes were
friendly but he looked surprised to see Andrew.

In halting Burmese, Andrew said, 'Good afternoon.
I am Andrew Hancock. I am here to see Princess Tipi Si.
Mr Watt arranged it.'

The young man nodded and replied in careful English, 'Yes. The princess is expecting you to visit. Please
come in.' He held the door open as Andrew removed his
shoes, slung his camera box over his shoulder and entered
the shadowy house. Andrew assumed that the man he was
following was not just a house boy, for he was obviously
educated and had a poised air about him rather than the
acquiescent shyness customary of servants.

The house was small, though it had high ceilings and,
being bereft of furniture, seemed bigger than it was. It
smelled musty, looked dusty and felt forlorn. When they
stepped into the reception room, Andrew took in the bare
tiled floor and a slowly turning ceiling fan. The room contained little furniture, just two chairs, a low table, a carved
mirror and a wooden screen that sectioned off a corner.
Through the rear door Andrew could see a lean-to, which
was clearly the cooking area, next to the bath house. In
the reception room, sitting on some large embroidered
cushions, sat an elderly Burmese woman.

She sat straight backed, her hands folded in her lap,
her chin lifted, her gaze directed at Andrew although she
made no effort to greet him by nod or gesture. She was

23

dressed in a silk longyi and a tightly fitted, long-sleeved lavender silk blouse. Her only adornment was an elaborate hair comb that glittered in her smoothly coiled but faded black hair.

Andrew bowed his head slightly but before he could speak the princess finally acknowledged his presence.

'Good afternoon. Mr Watt informed me that you would like to meet me. As he is an old acquaintance, I agreed.' Her English was accented and formal.

'Thank you. I am honoured.'

'There is no need to be. I am no longer a royal princess. Please, sit down.'

She waved towards the other chair and when Andrew sat down, she adjusted her position slightly so she could face him squarely. Now that Andrew could see the princess more clearly, he was impressed by how regal she looked with her cool, imperious expression. Her skin had the soft creases of overripe fruit, but her dark eyes glittered keenly as she looked at the man before her. She did not seem embarrassed or worried about her impoverished circumstances.

'What do you wish to speak to me about?'

'Your story intrigues me. Mr Watt may have explained that I write stories and take photographs of interesting places and people in the east, which I sell to English magazines. When Mr Watt told me about you, I wondered if you would allow me to write a magazine article about your life.'

'I am no longer interesting, Mr Hancock.'

Andrew smiled politely. 'I don't think that is true. May I ask in what way were you related to the late king?'

'I am, or rather was, his half sister. We had the same father, but we had different mothers.'

'Is that why you went with him to India?'

'Yes, when all the royal family were forced into exile.'

'That must have been difficult for you.'

'For the king and his chief queen, yes. I was more bored than anything. Ratnagiri was a backwater. The king quickly became involved in the construction of his new palace, which did not interest me, so I disguised myself as a servant and wandered the city. There I discovered there were Indians who liked the British no more than I did. I went to meetings to hear them speak. I became very involved with their plans to rid India of British rule, for I could not respect the British after their treatment of my family.' She paused and added accusingly, 'And my feelings against them have multiplied.'

Andrew felt embarrassed by her vehemence and tried to keep her to her personal story. 'I believe that you went to England at one point?'

'I wanted to learn more about my enemy, so I sold what little jewellery and possessions I had and I went to England with a charismatic Indian who was a poet, a philosopher and a fighter for India's independence. He made me realise just how much we in Burma had been exploited by the British. But I did not stay long. Two years later I married a saopha from the Shan hill tribes.'

'A Shan prince. That seems appropriate,' said Andrew.

The princess shrugged. 'We were minor royalty, but we were invited to attend the durbar in Delhi in 1903, which was held to celebrate the accession of Edward VII as emperor of India. King Thibaw wished to attend but the British refused his request. But I rode at the head of the Shan chiefs in a golden howdah on a white elephant decorated with jewels and peacock feathers.'

'That sounds very impressive,' said Andrew politely.

'It might have been if I'd had more money, but my husband was mean and, as you know, my family had nothing.'

'What did you do? How were you able to live?'

'I went into trade. First with elephants and then I expanded into other business opportunities. I enjoyed it and I was quite successful but my husband did not approve and said that what I did was not worthy of a Burmese princess. So I divorced him.'

'When did you come back to Burma?' Andrew tried not to show impatience with her bald summary of what seemed to be quite major events. He longed for all the details.

'As you may know, when the king finally died in India, the queen and other members of his family were allowed to return to Burma. Although the queen was not permitted into Mandalay, I was allowed to take up residence there. I knew it well and had friends who could help me. I went into the logging business. I also traded ivory with the Chinese. Opium, too. But I found it was better for me to be in Rangoon. I could make more money here. I bought property. I managed to acquire some lucrative contracts, building roads and supplying teak logs to the British. The British did not like me because I drove a very hard bargain with them.' The princess smiled for the first time and paused, then she reached across to the little table and struck a small gong sitting on it.

The young man swiftly and silently appeared and the princess spoke to him in a dialect that Andrew didn't understand.

'I have ordered tea,' she explained.

'May I ask you, the young man, is he a Shan?'

'Yes. The Shan are a very proud people. They have always been independent, never under the rule of the Burmese kings. His father was a friend of mine but he was murdered. Now I care for his son who helps me. So, while he is not of my blood, he is all the family I need.'

The young man returned with a pot of smoky Burmese tea, poured a cup for each of them and then silently left the room. Andrew gazed around as he sipped his tea and wondered to himself how it was that a successful businesswoman could end up in such reduced circumstances.

The princess watched him and then said bitterly, 'You are wondering how I came to live here. I must tell you that it is the doing of the British. They saw how my business grew and they thought that since I was of the royal line and increasingly wealthy, I would become a focus of rebellion and a threat to their rule, so they conspired to take my wealth from me.'

'But surely the British knew that you wouldn't be a threat.'

The princess pointed at Andrew. 'You know nothing! British intelligence is full of liars and inept idiots plotting to feather their own nests. But they know that there are rebels trying to get rid of the British. Even some of the monks are prepared to act! Many Burmese are tired of seeing the riches of the country stolen from our shrines and pagodas and, more than that, the Burmese just don't want to be ruled by another nation. We want to run things our way. The British knew that I had been involved in the nationalist movement in India, so they were not going to take any chances.'

'The British have brought a lot of prosperity to Burma. Opened up business opportunities, built roads and ports. They have brought benefits to this country,' said Andrew stiffly, feeling that as an Englishman he should defend the empire builders.

'They help themselves for the benefit of Britain, not for the benefit of the Burmese,' she answered.

'How did the British rob you of your wealth?' asked Andrew, not believing that something so underhanded could have occurred.

'They denied me contracts and gave them to my competitors who did not deserve them. My goods were held up in the ports. Shipping manifests were mislaid. Customs officers took their time. Banks called in loans. It's easy to organise these things when you have the power. Gradually, bit by bit, all my things had to be sold off, just to keep this miserable roof over my head.'

'But surely you don't mean that every Britisher has wronged you? There must be some who have not been so greedy.'

'If you are referring to that nice Mr Watt you are right. He is a good man, but he is married to a Burmese woman so he has a better understanding of things. But he is the only one. They take and they take. Just recently I had to give up something I treasured to a pompous little Scot, with his silly pince-nez. It would have been less galling if I'd been robbed by a local looking for a means to buy food.'

'What did you give up?' asked Andrew.

'Perhaps "give up" is not quite correct.' The princess lifted her shoulders. 'He was very persuasive. And I needed money. Now I am deeply regretful and sad. I had promised myself that no matter what happened I would not sell the last thing I owned that I had from my brother. I feel that I was pressured and intimidated. And I am not even sure that I sold it for its true value.'

'What was it?' asked Andrew quietly.

'I parted with a kammavaca. Do you know what this is? It is a Buddhist text usually written on palm leaves, except this was not on a palm leaf. It was made especially for my brother by monks and there is a great story attached to it.' She sighed. 'It should be treated with respect.' She lifted her hand in a small sad gesture. 'Now I have sold it just to survive. Maybe you would say that I was willingly robbed, but once again I know that I was bullied by the British who always expect to get their way.'

Andrew shifted uncomfortably. He had an idea of

28

who might have bought the princess's kammavaca. He remembered Ferguson, the self-important art dealer he had met when he first came to Burma. Andrew hadn't crossed paths with the Scot since he'd been back, but he recalled that Ferguson liked to tell everyone that he was an expert on eastern art. It sounded as though the man was in Burma and still in the business of acquiring antiquities and cultural artefacts.

'That is very unfortunate. I'm sorry that you felt forced to sell something from your brother. What is the story behind the kammavaca?' asked Andrew.

'It had been made with such reverence and patience by the monks. And it was my last link with my family. My brother gave it to me just before he died and told me that the kammavaca held the secret to my family's return to power. Now it is gone and my family remains powerless so my hatred of the British is greater than ever,' she said calmly.

'I can understand you feeling like that. Perhaps you will be able to get it back one day,' said Andrew in the face of her justifiable bitterness. Suddenly he found himself adding, 'What if I could get it back for you?'

She glared at his little smile. 'Don't serve me platitudes,' she snapped.

Andrew, seeing the princess's steely expression and burning eyes, knew she was angry, not just at the British administration and the likes of Ferguson, but also at herself, for having sold something so precious. 'If you tell me more of your story, it may help my readers in England know Burma and its people a little better, and why you feel the way you do. I understand your anger, I really do. I am often ashamed by the conduct of some of my compatriots,' he finished.

'I'd like to believe you. I'd like to believe my kammavaca could be retrieved. The king placed such importance in it. But why should I trust you?' The princess stopped. 'Enough. I have said enough already.' With that she hit the little gong again and when the young Shan entered the room she told him that Andrew was leaving and directed him to escort the photographer to the front gate.

'I wanted to thank you for the introduction to the princess,' said Andrew as he walked back into Mr Watt's bookshop after his abrupt dismissal by the princess.

Mr Watt chuckled. 'I had wondered how you survived the interview. Did she give you the rounds of the kitchen about us colonials?'

'Indeed she did. I can understand why she feels that way. But I held my tongue,' said Andrew.

'Ah, wise move. Did she reveal any details about her extraordinary life?'

'Not as many as I would have liked. I caught her at a bad time. And I have to say I felt uncomfortable, in fact somewhat guilty, as she'd just been taken advantage of by a rather obnoxious Scot who'd pressured her into selling him the last remaining possession that had been her brother's. I think that it not only had sentimental value but was of some great cultural significance.'

'That is a shame. You can't be responsible for the behaviour of others whether they are British or Bolivian,' said Mr Watt. 'But I must agree with you, the British rulers are a rapacious lot out here. Take everything that's not nailed down and even then they take the nails. Difficult for the Burmese to stop it and such behaviour creates a lot of ill will.'

'The princess seems such a formidable character, but she is a forgotten woman. She lives in utter poverty!' exclaimed Andrew. 'It amazes me that she has nothing, after being so rich. I really felt that she had been cheated, so I offered to get her kammavaca back for her. I think that the person who bought it could be a man called Ferguson. I met him once when I was here before the war.'

'I know Ferguson. Greedy little man. No respect for Burmese artefacts. Well, that's not entirely true, he knows their cash value to him on the open market. I believe he has made a lot of money selling artworks and statuary in Europe and America.'

'I doubt what he's bought from her is that valuable,' said Andrew.

'But if this one was made for the king, it gives it more cachet. A certain unique provenance,' said Mr Watt. 'If you can get it back, I'm sure the princess will be grateful. Maybe she'll tell you more about her life – then you'll have a great story, believe me.'

'You've fired my enthusiasm even more. I can redeem some honour for my country by returning the kammavaca that means so much to her and find a great story as well,' said Andrew. 'I'm sure I'll be able to track Ferguson down, and on the way there will be some great tales to sell to the magazines back home.'

Mr Watt shook Andrew's hand. 'Good luck, and be careful. Away from the cities Burma can be a dangerous place these days. I will be keen to hear of your progress.'

'I'll see you when I get back, and with any luck I'll have a good reason to see the princess, too.'


Andrew walked into the British Pegu Club, a modest club by some colonial standards, and, hearing the thwack of tennis balls, wondered at the madness of some members choosing to play an energetic game in the heat of the day. He ordered a gin, eschewing the club's Pegu cocktail, and wandered out to the verandah to admire the profusion of English flowers being tended by the Indian gardener. Andrew was an infrequent visitor to the Rangoon club as he quickly tired of the all-white male members' gossip. He thought their banter about the inadequacies of the Burmese and their complaints about the laziness of the Indian and Chinese coolies and servants were demeaning.

Andrew never ceased to be shocked by the imperious attitude of the British civil servants. The British police officers often made rather incendiary and unnecessary remarks about the local people. Andrew had fought beside Indian military companies in the trenches on the Western Front so he knew what brave and reliable soldiers they were. Many of the comments he had to listen to were nonsense, but he held his tongue and kept his opinions to himself. Tipi Si's story had yet again reaffirmed his discomfort at British behaviour in Burma. Nevertheless he chatted briefly with several regular members and the club secretary, and eventually learned that Ferguson was indeed in Burma. He had recently set off on a trip north, presumably to collect more artefacts. Cheered by this information, Andrew departed the club and set about planning his own foray to the north.


Andrew felt his legs wobble and feet bounce as he stepped onto the narrow plank linking the old boat to the landing. Surrounded by goods and other passengers, he'd been the only European on the boat since its dawn departure from the busy port of Sittwe. The creek was low and the mud shone in the last light of the day. It had been an arduous journey up the Kaladan River and now the simple village of Thantara looked very welcome.

Andrew managed to get directions to a small guesthouse where he stayed the night. There he made arrangements to travel by pony cart to Mrauk-U, the place where he'd been told Ferguson was working.

Andrew had been on Ferguson's trail for weeks, travelling overland and along rivers. He had taken photographs of the countryside with its ancient temples and little villages, as well as the Burmese people. Every place he'd been to seemed to have a story to tell and Andrew knew that he would be able to sell most of them. Mrauk-U was not easily accessed but not a surprising destination for the Scot as the ancient capital was filled with the remains of temples and pagodas.

As the little pony trotted through the ruins, Andrew saw that village life continued to flourish among the crumbling stupas. Goats fed on the grasses around the hilltop pagodas, and the village itself encircled the area where a royal palace once stood. It didn't take long to learn that Ferguson had hired several locals to help him work at the Shitthaung Pagoda.


The following day just after sunrise, Andrew headed to the ridge where the sprawling pagoda was reflected in the early morning light. It was surrounded by bell-shaped stupas the size of small cottages, built to house Buddhist relics. But Andrew was dismayed to find that the great temple was very dilapidated and seemed to be deserted.

He walked through it, negotiating piles of forest debris and animal droppings, recoiling from the stench of the bat colony that had taken up residence. He groped his way into a narrow corridor as best he could and tried to find his way to the central sanctum. In a pale beam of light, a row of large carved Buddha figures sat along the inner wall and stared silently into the shadows. Andrew quickly counted twenty-eight of them.

He paused. He could hear a faint tapping sound. He turned a corner and entered a room that had more light

33

and saw that the walls and ceiling of the temple were covered in carvings. He was astounded by the intricacy and detail of these small sculptures that depicted animals, goddesses and scenes from the spirit world and from Buddha's life. Looking closely he saw that some of them had been painted. They were faded now, but Andrew could imagine how brilliant and vibrant this gallery must have been when it was first completed.

The tapping had grown louder. Turning another corner into a long stone passageway, he saw a small light at the far end and several figures moving about. He realised that this must be Ferguson and his team. He called out.

'Who's there?' demanded Ferguson.

'It's me, Hancock. Andrew Hancock,' called Andrew, waving his torch. 'We met once, years ago.'

'Good lord! What are you doing here? Wait there, and I'll come and show you the way.' Ferguson hurried down the corridor. 'This way, this way.'

As he walked into the bright sunlight, Andrew saw that age had faded Ferguson's sandy hair and he had grown more rotund, but his air of confidence remained, as did the old-fashioned pince-nez, which was still firmly planted on his nose.

'Remind me where we've met. I can't quite place you,' said Ferguson, squinting.

'I'm not surprised,' replied Andrew. 'It was before the war, on a paddle-steamer to Mandalay. I had just arrived in Burma and you were explaining that you were an authority on Burmese art and architecture.'

Ferguson sat down on a broken pillar and lit a small cheroot. 'Can't say that I remember, but never mind. Bit of an out-of-the-way place to run into you, again,' he commented as he took a puff of the small cigar.

'Amazing place. Shame it's so dilapidated,' said Andrew. 'Where's the central sanctum?'

'Oh, down there. Can you see that small alcove? Follow me.'

Andrew did as he was told and at the end of the narrow corridor he stepped into the small chamber. Even in the dim light he could make out the huge statue of the Buddha sitting cross-legged on an ornamental stone platform, gazing calmly, staring into the gloom of centuries. Andrew found it awe inspiring.

'Incredible. I see why you're so fascinated with all this. What are you planning to do?' asked Andrew as Ferguson led the way outside.

'Looking at what can be restored and what should be removed for safekeeping.'

'How fascinating,' said Andrew cheerfully. He peered around the temple. 'Well, I'm on the hunt for stories. I've been travelling all over the country and I've come across a few decent ones. The *Illustrated London News* has taken some. Anyway, I was in Sittwe and I heard you were here and I thought I might find a good story for the magazines back home. And I was told that the ruins at Mrauk-U are fascinating.' While this was all true, Andrew hoped above all that Ferguson would still have the princess's kammavaca and that he would be able to persuade the art dealer to sell it to him.

'Jolly good. What do you want from me?' Ferguson seemed eager to help.

'I've just got a few questions,' said Andrew. 'How long have you been working in Mrauk-U? Who do you work for, who are the people you sell to and what sorts of things do they buy? What do you think would be of interest to people back in England?'

Ferguson studied the younger man for a moment. 'I don't want you to think that I sell everything I come across. A lot is being transported for safekeeping. I mean, look at this place.' He waved his arms towards the row of small stupas. Many were smashed, now looking like defeated, broken bells. 'Weather, time, treasure hunters and looters. So many relics have gone.'

'What was inside those small stupas?'

'Could have been gold figurines, gems, bronzes or religious texts, just waiting there for me to show them to the world. Such a shame they've all gone. You must remember, art belongs to everyone, laddie. Many of those beautiful things should be in the British Museum, for example. Not lying around in the jungle for thieves to pilfer, or rotting away in abandoned shrines for a few local villagers to notice, if indeed they do.'

'But,' said Andrew, looking at the hundreds of ruins in front of him, 'surely there is too much here for museums. They couldn't take it all.'

'You're right, laddie. But there are a lot of collectors in Europe and especially in America who are pleased to pay for a Burmese artefact. And I'm happy to sell them. Allows me to continue my work out here.'

'Have you been in Mrauk-U long enough to excavate anything of major importance, Mr Ferguson?'

'Nothing really spectacular yet, but it's early days. Would you like to see what I've found?'

Ferguson walked over to where a large cart was piled with bulky objects covered by a blanket. Two local men were lifting a stone Buddha the size of a large boulder into the last space in the ox cart. Ferguson pulled back the blanket. Andrew could see that the cart was full of stone Buddhas.

'What will you do with these?' he asked.

'They aren't particularly exceptional pieces, so I'll put them on the open market. I send them to agents, runners. Occasionally I go over to Ceylon and Siam with items, trading with serious collectors and such.'

'I wouldn't mind a memento of Burma. It's a pity

36

these are so big. Have you got anything that doesn't need porters to carry?'

'What, gems or gold, or a small statue?'

'Goodness, no. I probably couldn't afford anything like that.'

'I have got something small that might interest you. It won't be cheap because it has an interesting history. But I'll show it to you and you can see what you think.'

Ferguson led the way to his small tent, which had a table and chair outside it. He reached in under the fly netting for his satchel and took out a small, narrow box, covered in gold engraving.

'The kammavaca in this box belonged to the last king of Burma,' he told Andrew.

Andrew couldn't believe his luck, but he knew that he would have to be very careful so Ferguson did not suspect his real reason for wanting to buy this particular artefact.

'How on earth did you come by it?' he asked innocently.

'It belonged to his half sister. She's had an eventful life and now lives quietly. Told me that this was the last thing of value that she had, but I'm sure she has a few other treasures, a few last jewels tucked away. You never know with these people. I've seen others like her. They all complain that they're down on their luck. Blame the British administration. But funnily enough they always manage to find something to sell.'

Andrew bit his tongue. 'Can you explain this piece to me? I'm certainly no expert, like you.'

'This is a particularly fine and unusual kammavaca because of the exquisite illustrations. It's a bit like the illuminated manuscripts that were produced in Europe before the advent of printing. And it's not made on palm leaf, either, as they usually are, but specially treated cloth. And that it was made for the king gives it an impressive provenance,' said Ferguson knowledgeably.

'So it's kind of a family heirloom,' said Andrew.

Ferguson unfolded the little sections and carefully handed the kammavaca to Andrew, who turned it over and studied it.

'What does it say?'

Ferguson peered at it. 'I haven't looked at it much. But usually these sorts of things are just prayers and sacred texts from the Pali canon. Not worthwhile bothering to translate them, really. I thought I had a buyer in Mandalay so I carried it with me up there, rather than leaving it in Rangoon, but the chap had gone back to England before I could contact him. Bit of good fortune for you, young man.'

'It is delightful. This is just the sort of thing I had in mind,' said Andrew. He carefully refolded the sections of the long, banner-like kammavaca and placed it in its box. 'It rather intrigues me. I'd like to take home one souvenir of Burma and this is easy to carry if it's not too expensive.'

'I couldn't let it go cheaply. It's definitely a collector's piece,' said Ferguson, getting down to business.

'But if it belonged to the former king, it's not very old, is it?' said Andrew. 'You're very knowledgeable and lead such a fascinating life, I'm sure that any article I wrote about you would be very well received in England. People outside the world of archaeology would certainly learn all about you.'

Ferguson considered this. 'You'd have to be careful what you wrote. Can't have every Johnny racing out to Burma and clearing out the tombs and temples, eh?' began Ferguson, but Andrew could see he was flattered by the idea of appearing in a publication as prestigious as the *Illustrated London News*.

They bartered back and forth and in a short while had agreed on a price for the kammavaca, on the condition that Andrew should write an article about Ferguson and his work in Burma.

Andrew extracted some English pounds from his wallet. While the price for the kammavaca was not a huge sum, it left a bit of a hole in his savings. But for Andrew it was a matter of principle. The meeting with Princess Tipi Si had affected him deeply and had brought to the surface his own embarrassment at the greedy and unscrupulous behaviour of his countrymen in Burma. If he could show the princess that not all of them behaved so badly by returning the king's kammavaca, then he would feel better. It would be his moral victory.

Andrew took some photographs of Ferguson working at the Shitthaung Pagoda and other locations in Mrauk-U, and of three red-robed monks making their way down the green hillside from their monastery to the village with their alms bowls. He then packed away his camera, settled the small teak box with the kammavaca inside his luggage, and began the arduous journey back to Rangoon to see the princess and return her family heirloom.

# 2

## Gold Coast, Queensland, 2006

NATALIE GRASPED MARK'S ARM, closed her eyes and held her breath.

'Going once . . . Going twice . . .' The auctioneer paused, holding his gavel aloft, and glanced around at the small crowd standing on the footpath.

'Last chance for what could be the best waterfront living on the hottest part of the Gold Coast.'

'Oh no, that couple are going to get it. Mark, bid again!' whispered Natalie urgently.

'We've already gone past our limit.'

'Please try another five thousand dollars, quick.' She pushed his elbow and Mark's arm shot up.

'Thank you, sir. Now, going once, twice, going three times . . . Sold!' The agent banged the hammer onto the lectern in front of him and pointed to Natalie and Mark.

'Congratulations to the young couple with the stroller! If you could just come this way, we'll sort out all the details.'

Mark and Natalie walked back through the house, now seeing it through different eyes. They were about to be its new owners.

'Scary but wonderful, isn't it?' said Natalie, already visualising the changes she wanted to make to their purchase.


That was six months ago. How excited they'd been to buy the house of their dreams. Natalie and Mark Cutler had been married for five years. But with the arrival of their children, Charlotte, who was now three, and eighteen-month-old Adam, they'd outgrown their house in Brisbane. They'd decided to move to the Gold Coast, mainly for the lifestyle it offered, but also because they'd be a bit closer, but not too close, to Natalie's mother who lived over the border in northern New South Wales now less than two hours away. Mark, who was an electrician, had mates who assured him there was plenty of work available for good tradesmen on the Gold Coast. So they'd sold their nicely renovated house in Brisbane for a better price than they'd expected and spent the following weekends looking at homes on the Gold Coast.


Being a holiday and a tourist destination, highrises dominated the skyline and hugged the beachfronts. But with a growing family, an apartment was not for them. Slowly they began to explore the suburbs away from the beach strip and discovered that they liked many of them, although a lot of the houses were way out of their price range.

One day as they drove from one house inspection to the next, Mark said, 'I don't want to move out into the hinterland. Too rural. Too isolated. Let's stay fairly close to the coast.'

Natalie looked at her fit and handsome husband, who at thirty-eight was still sports mad even though he didn't play competitive football anymore. His hair was sun bleached and he had a year-round tan. Both of them liked swimming and surfing, so finding a home close to water had been high on their wish list.

'Oh, I agree,' said Natalie. 'I want to be close to shopping. With Charlotte and Adam we need to be near a park, perhaps a play group and a doctor. All that sort of thing. But I don't want to get caught in an area that's full of holidaymakers, either, so that I can never park the car, and where there could be a lot of party noise.'

'I really don't want to be in a part of town surrounded by stuffy retirees,' said Mark. 'It would be great to have families our own age nearby so the kids have someone to play with.'

Eventually they found what they thought was the perfect place. It was a rather run-down seventies house that they knew would need a lot of work, but they loved the area, which was full of well-kept houses and mature gardens. There was a handy corner shop and a park at the end of the street. Most of all, they loved the position of the house. It sat on one of the wide canal developments so that from the back of the house the view was of a broad expanse of sparkling blue water.

'I think this place has fantastic potential,' Natalie whispered to Mark the first time they inspected it. 'The bones of the house are terrific, and how about that outlook? Can't you see us fishing off our own little wharf? We might even be able to buy a boat and tie it up at the bottom of our garden.'

'This place is really run-down,' Mark cautioned.

'I know. But we'd never be able to afford a place in

such a fabulous position if it wasn't. If we can do up a place in Brissie, we can do this one up. You're handy, and all your mates are tradies. Surely we can get things done for mates' rates, and we can paint and do a lot of the renovations ourselves!' exclaimed Natalie.

Mark smiled. 'You really want this place, don't you?'

Natalie steered him onto the deck that overlooked the patchy lawn running to the water's edge. Beside it was a swimming pool that desperately needed cleaning. 'I didn't want to seem too keen, but I know that we could fix this place up and make it a really wonderful house to live in.'

'It's big enough with five bedrooms, but there's only one bathroom and a dinky ensuite. And there's no big work area for me,' said Mark.

Natalie gave a dismissive wave. 'I can see it! I can just see how we can fix this place up.'

'I don't know. It's going to be a big job and it's not going to be cheap.' Mark looked out at the canal and the houses opposite with their fancy swimming pools and thatched Balinese-style cabanas. Many of them had boats moored to their own private landing or pontoon.

'Mark, we've got the experience. I'll draw up some of my ideas for you tonight,' said Natalie with confidence.

Mark stared at her. 'The renovations we did at our place were cosmetic. Paint, carpets, a deck, garden. This would be structural, you'd need an architect or at least a builder who knows what he's doing.'

'Let me show you. I can see it,' insisted Natalie.

Later, they talked into the night, discussing their budget and working out a rough costing of Natalie's ideas. With the knowledge that they could eventually renovate the house into something very special, they went to the auction with enthusiasm and enough money from the bank to buy their dream home.

After they'd bought the house and moved in, they spent the first few days settling, getting to know all aspects, good and bad, of their new home. It was soon apparent that the massive renovation job together with their bigger mortgage and the expenses of the move meant they had to re-evaluate their financial position.

'Finding the money for the renovations is going to be more difficult than I thought,' said Mark. 'And are you still thinking of another baby?'

'Of course I am! I adore being a mother. But, well, it isn't really the right time, is it?' Natalie said with a sigh. 'And I'm disappointed about the renovations. You're right. I don't think we can find enough time and money to do them quickly. How are we ever going to save enough to do the really big jobs, like the bathrooms and the kitchen, let alone fixing up the pool? Maybe I should go back to work.'

'I'm not sure about that. By the time we pay for daycare, babysitting and another car, I don't know that your teacher's salary is going to cover what we'll need. And we've always agreed that being at home to look after the kids while they are little is the best thing for them. I think we should stick to our plan of you having these years off and only going back to paid work when they're older and in school,' said Mark.

'I know,' said Natalie. 'Perhaps we should do as much work on the house as we can ourselves, and then when we've saved up a bit, we'll do the more expensive bits. We'll get there.'


Over the next few weekends they began to renovate the house. They ripped up the carpets and painted the walls in one of the spare rooms.

After dinner one night when the children had gone to bed, Mark poured them both a glass of wine. 'Sit down, I want to talk to you, Nat.'

'Hmm. Sounds serious. Or have we won the lottery and you haven't told me?' she asked lightly, not liking the look on her husband's face.

'Look, this renovating the house bit by bit isn't going to work, is it?'

Natalie was about to disagree with him, but in the end she quietly nodded her head. 'You're right. We're spending every weekend working on the house, but it's so hard with the kids around. They just get into everything and you have to watch them all the time. You know what Adam did with that paintbrush. I mean, it only took a couple of hours to fix up the mess he made, but it wasn't helpful. We are living in chaos. We can't have our friends around because there's nowhere nice to entertain them. At least we didn't get carried away and rip out the kitchen, but it's so awful to cook there because the stove barely works and the oven takes an age to heat up. If it weren't for the barbeque, we'd never have a meal at a reasonable hour. I don't regret taking on this place, but I wish we could speed up the renovations.'

'I've worked out a way we can fix this place up much faster than we're doing, and without you having to go back to work.'

'Really? How?' Natalie looked puzzled.

'I'm going to apply for a new job.'

'Doing what?'

'Still a sparky, of course. But away from here . . .'

'Move? Oh no! Do you want us to move? Do you want to rent this place out?'

'Calm down, Nat. No, of course not. Anyway,' he smiled at her, 'who'd rent the place in the state it's in? No, what I meant was that I'll be away, but you and the kids will stay here. I won't be away all the time. But I can make a lot more money working out at a mine site. It'll be long hours but great money. And they tell me the conditions aren't bad.'

'You mean you're going to be a fly in – fly out worker?' said Natalie quietly. 'How long would you be away for?'

'It's four weeks on, one week off. Twelve working days a fortnight.'

'That's ridiculous! Crazy.'

'I know it's not perfect for us, Nat, but it's great take-home pay, much more than what I earn now.'

'Where would you be?' asked Natalie, trying to settle her jumbled feelings and emotions. The money sounded terrific but the hours were horrendous for Mark, she would miss him and how would she manage on her own for such long stretches at a time?

'Central Queensland. There's a lot of work for good electricians: keeping machinery operating, wiring work sites and building living quarters and facilities for the workers.'

'It's such a long time away . . .' began Natalie, feeling close to tears.

'It's the only way we can save enough money to get the renovations done quickly. Just for a year or two, say. And after each shift, when I come back, I'll have seven days just to be here with you and the kids. That will give you a break. You can have lunch with your girlfriends, and I'll spend quality time with the kids.'

Natalie stared at Mark. 'You'll need time-out after working those hideous hours. It's your break, too.'

'I've talked to other people who have done it. Jason's working as a plumber over in the west. Saving up for a house. Says he's whacking nearly a grand into the bank every pay.'

'I have to think about this.' Natalie got up. She was too tired for another glass of wine and she wanted to think about the whole idea before discussing it further.

'I need to get to bed. Adam is waking so early these mornings. Let's talk about this some more before we make a decision.'

Slowly Natalie got used to the idea and the lure of the extra money seemed too good an opportunity to pass up.

But when Mark started his new job the adjustment for them all was much greater than they had imagined. The children became clingy and needy while he was away. When Mark came home he was exhausted and slept for hours at a stretch. It took at least two days for him to reset his body clock, regain his good temper and enjoy playing with them, and then it was time for him to go again.

'It's not like you've flown in from Alaska,' complained Natalie. 'I don't understand why the job has had such an impact on you.'

Mark sighed. 'I don't stay up late boozing, watching DVDs or anything like that,' he said defensively. 'Anyway, we get tested for alcohol and drugs and you can't work if they're in your system.'

'Drugs! You get drug tested?' exclaimed Natalie.

'People are driving expensive equipment, working with explosives. It's a safety thing. Jeez, I don't want to work with someone who's not all there.'

'What are you doing that makes you so tired?'

'I'm working. But it's hard physical work, even my job. There's a lot of noise, speed, shouting, whistles, machinery, trucks, trains hauling coal. It's full-on madness. And people are working round the clock, working under lights, twenty-four seven. There's constant pressure. When I have time off I stick to my room to get a bit of peace and quiet.'

'It sounds awful.'

'It's better than it used to be, I hear. The first workers on the site lived really rough. Now there are sealed roads, a rec centre with a pool and a club social room and a big dining hall with really good meals. Even landscaped gardens! It's a plush camp in the middle of nowhere.'

'What about the people you work with? Have you made friends? Hung out together after work? Are you working with the same people all the time?'

'Not really, said Mark, 'I work with different people a lot because I move around to different jobs. Everyone has different rosters, too, and they seem to come and go, quit and move on, very regularly. Most don't see it as a long-term job. Like me, they're in it for the money. Hanging out! I'm too buggered to socialise. Twelve-hour days are pretty full-on, takes its toll.'

'I'm trying to imagine it. Can you take some photos?'

'We'll see.'


In the beginning Natalie had missed Mark terribly. When he came home she changed her routine to fit in with him. Because he slept late for the first couple of days, she kept the kids home from their preschool so that he could spend time with them when he woke up. She appreciated taking time-out for herself, even if it was just for a doctor's appointment or grocery shopping in peace without the kids, or getting the car serviced. And she delighted in the four of them spending time together, going to the beach for a swim or packing a picnic lunch and finding a park with lots of things for the children to play on.

As time went by, Natalie found that she adjusted to Mark's long absences. She liked not having to prepare elaborate meals, especially when it was so hard to cook in their kitchen. Eating an egg and a piece of fruit with the children was much easier, and she found that having only herself to please could make life very simple. While Mark was away, she took over those jobs that he had usually done, including mowing the grass in the front of the house and, while it added to her workload, Natalie felt a small twinge of pride in managing everything. At night, when she was on her own and the children were asleep, she refined her plans for the renovations. The more she lived in her house, the more she loved it. She wasn't bothering to watch TV of an evening but instead listened to her iPod as she made sketches, took measurements and flipped through country-inspired decorating magazines.

The kitchen was not just going to be replaced. She wanted to enlarge it by knocking out the wall between it and the laundry. And what had been a small office at the end of the hall, opening onto the side garden, she would turn into a new laundry with a fold-down clothesline on the outside wall facing the morning sun. The fourth and fifth bedrooms, which were fairly big but dark and depressing, she planned to make into one big play area for the kids, with one of the walls to be replaced with folding plantation doors. These would open onto the sheltered and fenced front garden, which she would plant with tropical flowers, or maybe herb beds, and perhaps construct a sandpit there, as well.

She planned to throw white paint over all the dark rooms with their old stained-wood panelling, which Mark had said was only wood veneer anyway. She'd decided to go with a colour scheme of white and indigo blue with splashes of yellow. Fresh, clean, cool.

She'd get Mark to slash back some of the rampant tropical growth that shaded so much of the garden and verandah and harboured, as she'd discovered, hordes of mosquitoes. The length of scrubby grass that stretched from their fence to the edge of the canal needed work. She wished she could wave a wand and transform it into a green lawn with a white picket fence and gate flanked by cheerful white daisies. She'd add a small path to a jasmine-covered pergola, under which they would walk to reach the landing, where there would be chairs ready for fishing, and a little boat moored.

But most of her plans would have to wait. All these dreams cost money. Poor Mark. He was working so hard so they could afford it all, thought Natalie, though I'm still chipping away at the small jobs.

One night Sarah, her mother, called. 'We've sold our place! Never thought we'd find a buyer for the farm, at least not at the price we're asking.'

'Congratulations. Is Steve pleased?'

'Frankly, he's in a bit of shock. Reality sinking in. And it's a short settlement time and you can imagine how long it's going to take to clear out and pack. Do you want to come and help? Bring the kids down for the weekend?'

'Don't know how much help I'll be with those two in tow, but I'd love to come.'

Natalie hurried through the rain to the shed behind the farmhouse. It was already overflowing with piles of packing boxes. She stacked the one she was carrying on top of the others and drew a breath as she surveyed the pillars of brown cartons that held the essentials of her mother's life and which Sarah insisted she had to bring to her new home.

Natalie didn't know whether to laugh or cry. 'There's no way!' she exclaimed aloud.

Her mother and stepfather were downsizing and facing an enormous challenge in packing up a farmhouse where they'd had sheds and a double garage in which to store things. They were moving to a neat house with a tidy garden on the ridge above Lismore.

Natalie knew that her mother was pleased they were moving. Sarah had decided that the daily commute from the farm to Lismore, where she owned a fashion boutique, was getting too much.

'Fifty minutes on a good day because the road is full of potholes and it's prone to flooding if there's even a drop of rain!' Sarah often said. Steve had been finding the farm tiring ever since a little accident had thrown his back out, so Sarah was pleased she was able to persuade him it was time to move. And when that buyer turned up and agreed to their price for the place, lock, stock and barrel, well, Steve felt he couldn't refuse. He was a bit sad about leaving his family home. But he had no kids to leave it to and Sarah was confident he'd be happy once they were settled.

Natalie certainly hoped so. Her mother had married Steve just after Natalie had graduated from university with an education degree. She was thrilled that her mother had made a new life, and she liked Steve, a solid, calm, good-natured dairy farmer. Natalie and Mark enjoyed visiting the farm in the tranquil valley where they were always welcome.

Natalie knew that leaving the farm would be a huge change for Steve and hoped her mother's confidence that he'd be happy pottering about in a small suburban garden with neighbours close by and town just down the hill was not misplaced. Life in town would be dramatically different from the lush green paddocks encircled by the dramatic mountain range where the only noises were from the small creek, the call of birds and the occasional lowing of the cows. Steve, however, was the first to admit that he wouldn't miss rising from bed in the pre-dawn dark, the occasional frost underfoot in winter, to milk the sometimes uncooperative animals, and the endless cleaning of the bails. But still, he loved the simple routine of his days and the placid company of his herd.

Although Sarah worked six days a week herself, she was quick to say, with a laugh, that being married to a dairy farmer meant no holidays for either of them. She'd had little to do with the dairy herd but she helped Steve in the vegetable garden and enjoyed having friends over for long elaborate Sunday lunches that she spent hours preparing.

Natalie stared across the wet paddocks, thinking that this must be what Ireland looked like: lustrous emerald green, mist curling on the top of the ranges, a gentle drizzly rain. There was a lush softness to the Northern Rivers compared with the Gold Coast. Natalie had never travelled overseas and now, with their hefty mortgage, an overseas trip was out of reach. Natalie was grateful they had a house that she loved and which she knew they could transform into a very beautiful home, but she was sad that holidays at the farm were coming to an end.

Her musing was broken by her mother calling, 'Natalie! I need more flatpacks. Can you bring me some, please?'

Natalie shook her head. The amount of stuff her mother had brought to Steve's when they married was incredible. There were boxes, cupboards and trunks that Natalie knew had not been opened for years. Some had been packed away after Natalie's father died, others came from her grandmother's house. Sarah had kept putting off sorting them, partly because she had the luxury of storage space at Steve's farm.

'It'll be my retirement project,' she told the family when they teased her about them. But now downsizing was proving to be a headache. Natalie dragged out several more cartons and hurried back to the house.

'Mum, this is a nightmare. You'll have to have a clearing sale to get rid of it all. I mean, what's in all those old boxes?'

'I can't remember. Some of it's from your grandmother.'

'Well let's go through them. This is the time. You can't take all this to your new house. It won't fit and I don't want the job of having to sort it all out when you kick the bucket,' said Natalie cheerfully.

Sarah laughed. 'You're right. A good rainy day job. I'll make a pot of tea, you get some of the old boxes together. It's lucky that young Imogen down the road is happy looking after Charlotte and Adam.'

Three hours later, the lounge room was littered with piles of books, china plates, ornaments, LP records, clothes, packets of letters and several shoeboxes of photographs.

'I see why you put off going through all this,' said Natalie. 'Do you know why you packed all of this stuff up?'

'Not really. I was so emotional at the time, I don't recall much about it. I hope I didn't throw out anything valuable.'

'Mum, I don't think you threw out anything!' Natalie was beginning to wonder if they should have started this job.

Sarah was wallowing in nostalgia as she went through her mother's possessions. 'This triggers so many memories,' she said sighing.

'Mum, the to-go pile isn't very big. Let's try and cull a bit more,' said Natalie, fearful that all the mess was going to be repacked and stored again. 'I can't take any of it to my place. Mark would have a fit.'

'That's probably because he's a no-frills man who spends most of his time in a tent.'

'Mum! He doesn't live in a tent. Actually, the conditions in the camp sound great. Better than our place in its current state! The mining company provides excellent facilities and he's earning enough money so we can save up for the renos.'

Sarah sighed. They'd been over this before. 'I still think it's very hard on you, carrying the load of the house and the kids. Don't you miss your job? You're such a gifted teacher, darling.'

'Thanks, Mum. I love teaching, and I have every intention of going back, but I love being a mother even more. There'll be time to go back to teaching when the kids are older.'

'It sounds like Mark has a holiday when he comes home!'

'He has an exhausting job. And I want him to have quality time with the children,' said Natalie shortly. To change the direction of the conversation she picked up a small box from a pile of her grandmother's little treasures. 'What's this?'

'Oh, that sat on Mum's bookcase for years. Came from her mother, your great-granny Florence. I have no idea what it is. Anything else in there with it?'

'A bundle of old papers. Some knick-knacks. A set of thimbles,' said Natalie.

The old box intrigued her so she opened it and lifted out an ornately lacquered panel. 'What's this? Looks like a fat ruler.'

When she held it up, it opened into a series of maroon folds joined together by narrow ribs of polished bamboo. 'What on earth is it? Some sort of wall hanging?' she asked, fiddling with it, turning it over. 'There are pictures on this side and weird squiggles on the other. Is that writing? Mum, this side is covered with the most exquisite pictures. Look, that's an elephant. Do you think this is Indian?'

'Heavens, I have no idea. I don't think I've ever seen it out of the box. Do you want it? Or could we sell it?' said Sarah. She delved into another box. 'Oh, god, her old furs!'

'Get rid of them,' shrieked Natalie, holding her nose. 'Ohh, the poor creature. It's moulting.' She recoiled as her mother held up a ratty, balding fox fur. 'It's got feet! A face! Snout! Beady eyes! How could anyone wear such a thing?'

'It was very fashionable in my grandmother's time. Imagine what would happen if this made an appearance on the red carpet now,' said Sarah with a giggle.

Natalie couldn't help smiling as she held her nose. 'Mum, dump it in the rubbish or at least put it aside for the clearing sale.'

'Maybe the whole lot should go. Who on earth would buy any of this stuff?'

'Sense at last,' said Natalie as they gathered up the furs, an old beaded handbag in poor condition, some junk jewellery and several tarnished picture frames and put them in a carton.

'What about that thing?' Sarah pointed to the box and the unusual scroll. 'Do you think anyone would want that?'

Natalie hesitated. 'It's sort of interesting. With its little pictures and funny writing.' She put it to one side. 'I'll hang on to it for a bit.'

'Now who's being a pack rat?'

'How's it going, girls?' Steve came in and smiled seeing his wife and stepdaughter together. 'You two really look alike,' he said.

Natalie thought he was pleased about the move. He had been talking about a holiday, going somewhere he and Sarah could enjoy time together. He smiled broadly but then baulked at the sight of all the things spread over the floor. 'Sarah, what's all this?'

'Culling, sweetie. Don't worry. Just checking Mother or Granny didn't stash some bank notes in with this junk, so we can take it to the tip with a clear conscience,' said Sarah.

'I'm pleased to hear it. You're going to miss having two sheds, a barn and a garage to store your things in.'

'It's her new resolution, to pare back,' said Natalie. 'Streamline her lifestyle to fit in a modern house. You won't know yourselves.'

Steve didn't answer, but looked unconvinced.

'He wants to keep some vintage farm machinery,' said Sarah. 'As if we'll have any use for that.'

'It was my dad's. My grandad's before that,' began Steve.

'Natalie says we're going to make a fortune in the clearing sale,' said Sarah.

'I don't think so. If you're lucky you'll have enough to have dinner at the RSL and put twenty bucks through the pokies,' said her daughter with a smile as she put the strange little hanging back into its box and placed it to one side. 'You won't miss this in your new streamlined modern house. Minimalist living. Stylish. The new you.'

'Doesn't sound like me,' muttered Steve as he clumped out of the room in his workboots.

'He sounds stubborn like Mark, doesn't he?' said Sarah.

Natalie didn't answer. She wished her mother would stop criticising Mark. It wasn't as if Mark really wanted to spend so much time away from his family. He was doing it for them. As he'd once commented to her when he arrived home, straight off the red-eye flight, tired and still in his grubby work clothes, 'I can see why people don't last long in this job. Everyone's only in it for the money and once we've saved enough for the renovations, I'm out of there, too.'

But, most of the time, they were grateful for the extra money he was earning, despite the toll it took on family life.

It was almost dark by the time Sarah and Natalie had gone through the boxes and sorted them into piles.

'I'm proud of you, Mum. You're down to keeping just six cartons.'

'And those papers? Do you think they're of any interest?' Sarah pointed to the bundles of letters tied with ribbon and packed in plastic bags.

'Mum, I have no idea what's in them. Why don't you read them? Skim through them at night while watching the TV,' suggested Natalie. 'Now I've got to get the kids' dinner.'

Later Natalie stood on the verandah watching the cows settle down. Steve had finished cleaning the milking

56

machinery and had come indoors for the evening. It was the time that Mark called to say goodnight to Charlotte and Adam.

'What plans do you have tonight?' asked Mark. 'Surely you've finished going through that stuff. I reckon you should just dump it all.'

'We're nearly finished. Mum's culling now. What did you have for dinner?'

'Veal schnitzel, potatoes duchesse and peas, and floating islands for dessert.'

'Those caterers spoil you! I hope you're getting some hints on how to cook nice things. I'm looking forward to a special dinner when you get home.'

'It'll be special all right! How are the kids? Does Charlotte understand what's going on with the farm?'

'Kind of, but she won't really understand that we won't ever come back here until she sees Mum and Steve in their new house. She'll miss the calves. She has drawings she wants to show you.'

'Well, sounds like you're having fun.'

'Mark, this isn't fun. It's a disaster here. You can't believe the stuff Mum has, even things from my great-grandmother. And poor Steve is – I don't know – a bit ambivalent. Big wrench for him,' she added softly into the phone.

'Yes. But he should be happy he has a buyer who's taking everything. Maybe they should have thrown in all your mum's stuff as an extra! You never know there could be something valuable in there,' he said with a laugh.

'I don't think so. Most of it just has sentimental value, no-one else would be interested. You should have seen this old fox fur. Yuck! Charlotte freaked out when I showed her. It had the head with its beady eyes and little feet. Anyway, Mum's going to go through the old papers and photos later. Not that we know who half the people in them are.'

'Nat, please, just don't bring anything back with you.'

'No, I won't. Promise. Just a couple of eggcups that are old but cute, and some books that I loved as a child and I hope Charlotte and Adam will love as well, and an odd little thing I have no idea what it is, but it's old and maybe I'll hang it on a wall,' said Natalie.

'Sounds good. I'd better go. Put the kids on to say g'night. Miss you. Love you.'

'Love you, too.' Natalie went back inside and handed the phone to Charlotte. 'Daddy wants to say goodnight.'

'Natalie, come and see what you think,' called Sarah as Steve settled in front of the TV.

Natalie went into the front room, which Steve rarely used but was now piled with furniture. Adam, in his pyjamas, was climbing over the chairs and a sofa.

'Be careful, mister,' warned Natalie. 'He loves climbing, Mum. Is all this furniture going to the new house?'

'Most of it. I've been mentally furnishing rooms in the new place but those things over there I can't see working. Do you want any of it? Otherwise it's the charity shop or the tip.'

'Some of it does look old, but useful. I'm trying to get a fresh clean look in our place. Mark would hate anything that doesn't fit in. He's not a retro kind of guy.'

Adam let out a yell as a pile of cushions collapsed and he tumbled down to the floor.

'I said be careful! You're all right,' Natalie assured him as she picked up the little boy and hugged him. 'What's this under here?'

'Some old chair of Steve's. Dreadfully old-fashioned, I don't want it.'

Natalie sat in the chair cuddling Adam. 'Very comfy. Plumpy cushions. It's a wingback, too. Unusual.'

'Hideous fabric. It's got a footrest, pouf thing that goes with it,' said Sarah.

'Mum, I'll take this if you're sure Steve doesn't want it.'

'Good grief! I wouldn't allow it in the house. What are you going to do with it?'

'I just had an idea for the playroom. It's comfortable, you can put your feet up, and because it's in sections I'm going to upholster it in fabric that's different, but matches in tone, if you know what I mean. A kind of pretty patchwork chair. Stripes and flowers kind of thing,' said Natalie.

'Can you fit it in the back of your station wagon? The sooner it's out of here the happier I'll be,' said Sarah. 'At least Steve will be pleased it's gone to a loving home and not the tip.'

'He mightn't like it being mint green and lemon stripes with pink and green flowers. Or whatever.' Natalie said smiling.

A month later Natalie was at home reading a story to the two children when her mother rang.

'Hi, Mum, when's the big move happening?'

'Truck's coming next week. I'm going up to the new house this weekend to work out where things are going. Do you want to come down to Lismore and help? We could have lunch.'

'Can't, Mum. Mark is away and Charlotte has a ballet class. It's a great idea to walk through the empty house to decide where to put things. Then you just tell the removalists to put it there and Steve won't have to drag furniture around. Are you excited?'

'Yes, I think so. I just want to get settled as soon as possible. At least I'll have extra hours in the day without that damn travelling to and from the farm.'

'How's the shop going?'

'Good. I've got some gorgeous new tops in. You'd love them.'

59

'Sorry, Mum, we're on a budget. And I don't need anything. If I was still working, it'd be a different story.'

'Yes, you must have been the best-dressed primary teacher in Queensland.'

'Thanks to all your sales and generosity,' said Natalie. 'I wish you'd stock children's clothes.'

'Too hard. Now, listen, I've been going through the letters and I've found an intriguing one from my great-uncle Andrew. Your great-great-uncle.'

'I've never heard of him.'

'He was my grandmother Florence's brother.'

'You'll have to tell me about this great-great-uncle.'

'I never knew him; he died long before I was born. Granny Flo told me some stories about him. They started to come back when I read the letter and saw some photos.'

'Where did he live? Did he have any family?' asked Natalie.

'Don't think so. He travelled a lot. I've got a couple of postcards from India, and from reading the letter it seems he was also in Burma.'

'In the Second World War?' said Natalie.

'No, long before that. He was there between the wars, I'm pretty sure. I'll have to sit down and go through everything to see if there's anything else. I just skimmed them to sort them out.'

'Why was he in Burma? I mean, what kind of place was that?' asked Natalie. 'I don't even know much about it now. It's never in the news. No-one goes there. It's communist, isn't it? Like North Korea?'

'Military dictatorship. I think it's where they locked up that lovely lady in her house to stop her being the leader or something. I'll have to look it up,' said Sarah.

'Yes, the pretty one who wears flowers in her hair,' said Natalie. 'But why would someone from our family have been in Burma in the 1920s or whenever it was?'

'Might be in the letters. I'm pretty sure he was born in England.'

'That's right, Granny Florence was English, wasn't she? How'd she end up out here?'

'Now that's a story I do know. Granny Flo met my grandfather, Wally, when he was on leave in England during World War One. He fought on the Western Front. She told me that they met on Palace Pier in Brighton. He was this jaunty, cheeky Australian soldier and he swept her off her feet. He proposed and she came out to Australia on a ship to marry him. He became a soldier settler. The government gave the returned men blocks of land as a reward for fighting in the war. It was a bit of a lottery, evidently, because some of the blocks were useless, but Wally was lucky and got a good block of land on the Richmond River, up in this area, not far from where Steve's family lived, and started dairy farming. Granny said they knew nothing about farming so they struggled for a bit. Things got worse during the Depression, but they managed to make a go of it and had a family. They sold their farm and retired just before things went bad again.'

'Why? What happened? It's good dairy country out there,' said Natalie.

'Mum said that when Britain moved into the Common Market and stopped giving preference to Australian dairy products, the milk and cheese market collapsed. Steve's family was one of the few who hung on as dairy farmers. A lot of farmers went into beef cattle and much of the grazing land was turned into macadamia plantations.'

'Did Granny Flo ever go back to England?'

'I think she went back once. She talked about it and there are photos. I have no idea what relatives we have back there. I'm pretty sure that Great Uncle Andrew never married.'

'What was he doing in India and Burma?' said Natalie.

'What did he do? We know nothing about our English side.'

'There's a box of old photographs that look very Asian. Maybe that's something to do with Andrew. I'll let you know.'

Natalie wondered when her mother was going to find time to browse through the photos with her impending move and settling into a new house, so she said impetuously, 'Why don't you send them to me? I can go through them when the children are in bed.'

Sarah laughed. 'I thought you spent your long lonely nights slaving away painting, sanding and pulling up old carpet. What are you up to now?'

'I've been painting the urns to go around the pool. I'd love to knock out some old cupboards but that's too noisy while the kids are asleep. So send me those things and I'll go through them. There's nothing to watch on TV. But register them, Mum. Don't want to lose them,' cautioned Natalie.

'They have been in storage for so long I hope they're still okay. Some of the ones I looked at are pretty faded. Thanks, darling. Ring if there's anything of interest.' Sarah said, sounding relieved.


Mark put his feet up on the coffee table and watched Natalie curled in the armchair she'd brought home from the farm. He studied his wife, struck again by seeing her after several weeks' absence. She'd changed. Not physically, she was still slim, her dark brown hair a mass of tousled curls, her skin glowing without make-up, her dark lashes hiding her large brown eyes. She was chewing the curve of her bottom lip as she read. She had the natural beauty of a young girl, but now, in her thirties, she had poise and a strength that had developed only recently.

Or maybe he was noticing it because of their absences. He didn't often like to address the fact she was carrying the burden of running the house and caring for the kids while he was gone for a month. Although she was managing very well, he felt guilty for being away from his family so much.

'That's a really ugly chair,' he commented.

She looked up. 'It's very comfortable. I like it. And you won't recognise it when I've finished with it.'

'I hope it's not going to cost too much,' said Mark.

'No way. I found some fabric at a garage sale. Really gorgeous. It was a set of contrasting curtains. Upholstering the chair will give me something to do in the evenings. Can't be too hard. I can sew.'

'I'm sure you'll do a great job, Nat.'

'Hmmm,' replied Natalie, who was now deeply engrossed in an old letter her mother had sent her and didn't look up again.

Mark turned on the TV and began surfing the channels.

Eventually Natalie folded the letter and sat quietly.

Mark flicked the sound down on a cable sports channel, knowing she hated American football. When there was no reaction he glanced at her. Natalie was staring thoughtfully into space.

'What's up? Found a skeleton in the closet?' Mark asked.

'Not really.'

'Who's it from?' Mark was trying to fathom the expression on her face.

'It's from my great-grandmother's brother, Andrew. It's so . . . touching.'

'What does it say?' asked Mark.

'It's quite an extraordinary story,' replied Natalie. 'It seems that he was in Burma, working for an English publication, when he met a Burmese princess called Tipi Si. She was very poorly treated by the British and as a result, lived in terrible poverty. In a weak moment, she sold something to an art dealer called Ferguson, but she regretted doing so immediately. The item, a thing called a kammavaca, had been given to her for safekeeping by her brother, the last king of Burma. Anyway, Uncle Andrew was so moved by her problems that he told her that he would track down the dealer, and get it back.'

'So what happened?'

'He found this dealer and got the kammavaca for the princess at a low price by promising to write an article about him. Ferguson sounds pretty ordinary to me, but Andrew just sounds wonderful. Listen to this last part of the letter,' said Natalie.

*While one might not grasp the intricacies of the Buddhist faith straight away, there is no doubt that the Burmese idols, pagodas and stupas are magnificent. Perhaps it is the utter richness of this land, with its golden temples, its lush countryside; its wealth and its gentle people; that makes our men think that they have the right to casually plunder. But I know this is dreadfully wrong. Indeed, I think that in times to come, we British will be criticised for our destruction of ancient monuments, the heedless trampling of traditions and the outright stealing of precious artefacts.*

*I am intrigued by the writing on this kammavaca, a beautiful curling script, but what it says is anybody's guess. I shall ask the princess more about it when I surprise her with its return. I know it will mean a lot to her, but truly dear sister, it means a lot to me as well. In all my time here in this very special country, I have been treated with respect, friendship and generosity- and not just because I'm British! I have met some good people here, Burmese as well as colonial chaps, and I feel affection for this lovely golden land. So if I can do one right thing for this country and restore the kammavaca to the princess, maybe I'll gain merit of my own. I just feel it so much the right and proper thing to do and will give me much pleasure and peace of mind.*

*However, before I return to Rangoon, I want to visit the Shan people and then go on to visit the primitive Naga people on the Indian border. Truly this is a country of many peoples with their own customs, habits and food – all most beguiling.*

*I do miss our chats Florrie. I feel very sure that when we do meet on whatever distant shore, you and I shall pick up where we left off, in Mother's warm kitchen that rainy night before we parted company and you left to go to Australia.*

*Please give my best wishes to Wally and the children. Love from your brother,*
*Andrew*

Mark took the paper from Natalie and read the whole letter. Then he folded the pages up, with its neat, closely written lines, and looked at Natalie. 'Interesting. I wouldn't say it was a sad letter. But it's intriguing stuff. Do you think it was the start of a beautiful romance between the princess and your uncle? I suppose we'll never know. And that thing your uncle bought for her. Do you think she was pleased to get it back?'

Natalie shook her head. 'Returning it meant so much to him and yet he never gave it back to her. Isn't that strange?'

'How do you know?' asked Mark.

'Because I have it, Mark. It was in Great Granny Florence's things. Mum nearly threw it out. It's in the desk.'

'You're kidding! You brought it home from the farm?' Mark leapt up and went to the desk they shared and picked up the little teak box. 'It sounds like something unusual.'

He carefully unfolded the illustrated manuscript. He squinted at the strange curling script on the back.

'Wonder what all this is about?' said Mark.

'According to Andrew's letter, it's religious – scriptures or prayers by the sound of it.'

'How old would this be?'

'I've got no idea. The letter says it was a gift to the king, but I don't know anything about the kings of Burma or when they ruled. I could Google it.'

'What are you going to do with it now?'

'What do you mean? I guess I could hang it on the wall or display it somehow. It's special,' said Natalie thoughtfully.

'Could be worth a few dollars.'

'Mark! I wouldn't sell it. It's been in the family all this time.'

'Sitting in a shed!'

'I wonder how Great Granny Florence got it? He must have given it to her.'

'Why would Andrew have given it to his sister when he was so keen to return it to the princess?' said Mark.

'It's a bit of a puzzle that it never got back to its rightful owner. He was certainly passionate about returning it,' said Natalie, carefully folding the little kammavaca back into shape and slipping it into its narrow box.

'It looks more like the sort of thing you see in a museum or a church, well, a temple.'

'I like it. Maybe I should look at getting it framed. A family heirloom.'

'Nat, it's not your family treasure. It belonged to some princess in Burma!' Mark said with a laugh.

'True. Okay. I've had enough letter reading for tonight. My mind is overloaded.'

Mark reached for her. 'Let me distract you.'

Natalie curled into his arms. 'I do miss you. How much longer, Mark?'

'Sweetheart, it's hardly been any time. Hang in there. I'm really proud of you.'

Natalie rested her head on Mark's shoulder and closed her eyes. As she lay in his warm embrace, her thoughts drifted back to the odd curio she had found. She could feel that Mark had fallen asleep. So she slid from his arms as gently as she could, and padded quietly across the room to her desk. She took out the box and unfolded the manuscript. She bent closer to study the little illustrations. A musty smell, not unpleasant, vaguely citrusy, clung to the cloth. She stared at a picture of a little white elephant standing in a jungle. Suddenly there was a flash of light from the painted forest. Or was it from the jewelled headpiece of the elephant? Natalie shut her eyes and when she opened them she realised it was merely the desklight catching specks of gold paint.

But in that moment, she'd felt as if she had been standing in that jungle clearing.

It was such a strong sensation that she decided that she had to find out what had stopped her great-great-uncle from returning this odd artefact to its rightful owner.

# 3

MARK PULLED INTO THE driveway and before he could get Adam out of his car seat, Charlotte jumped from the car.

'There's Mummy!'

'What?' Mark scooped up Adam as Charlotte ran down the footpath towards Natalie who was coming towards them, dragging two narrow wooden doors behind her. A scarf covered her hair and her face and hands were splattered in paint.

'Be careful, Charlotte. Don't run onto the road,' called Natalie. 'How was your swimming class?'

'Daddy said I am really good! I went under the water today. What's that?' Charlotte demanded.

'You are a clever girl, aren't you? Mark, can you help me drag this lot inside?'

Natalie dropped the wood and waved to Adam as Mark came up and asked, 'What are you doing? What's all that?'

'It's the council clean-up. Everyone is putting out stuff they don't want. I found these.'

'A couple of old doors? What do you want these for?'

'You'll see. There's some more of them. Could you go and get them, please? They're only a few houses down the street.'

Mark shook his head in amazement and handed Adam to her. 'If you really want them, I'll take these two inside and go and get them.'

'Did you have a good time with Daddy at swimming, buttercup? I'm sure you impressed him. C'mon, it's lunchtime.'

There was a thud as Mark dropped the other doors outside the kitchen and came inside. 'They look like old wooden slatted pantry doors. Please don't tell me you want them for our new kitchen?'

'No, of course not. They're going outside.' Natalie handed Charlotte a cheese sandwich and tore up a piece of ham, which she gave to Adam. 'I'm going to paint them blue, and hang them on either side of the front windows so that they'll look like shutters. Maybe you could put hinges on them so that we can fold them over the window if we want to.'

Mark opened his mouth to object, but then went and looked again at the wooden doors. 'Could work, I suppose. I'd have to cut them to size. Let me think about the best way of doing it.'

'See. I thought it'd work. It'll give the house a more cottagey look. I thought we could build a little front porch and put some white wicker furniture on it. If we trimmed it with wooden fretwork we could paint it the same blue as the shutters and keep the rest white. I hate coming up

the front path and seeing the front door in a blank wall.
I want something more interesting.'

'Aren't you getting ahead of yourself? I suppose you'll
want a windowbox and a flowerbed in front as well.'

'Yes, please. But that can wait until we've finished the
renovations. I don't want my flowers trampled by tradies.
So, darling, how did you enjoy Charlotte's swimming
class?'

'Charlotte's no trouble at all. She's going to be a good
little swimmer, but keeping tabs on Adam in that play
area is chaotic. He wants to climb onto the top of everything. Trying to stop him from hurting himself is hard
work. I'm bushed,' said Mark. He dropped into the still
unrenovated wingback armchair and glanced at the pile of
photos beside it. 'Had any further thoughts about Uncle
Andrew's whatchamacallit? I'd like to know more about
it.'

'I haven't had time to look into it. The kammavaca
he called it.'

'To me, the big mystery is why Andrew didn't return
it to the princess like he said he was going to in his letter.
He sounded keen enough,' said Mark.

'I have no idea. I don't know a thing about him,' said
Natalie.

'I suppose he went back to England. You sure you
don't have any relatives back there? Your mum said her
grandmother came from Brighton.' Mark carefully picked
up Andrew's letter and skimmed through it again. 'Sounds
an interesting sort of a bloke. Was he a writer or a photographer? If those are his photos, they're pretty good.'

'Both, I guess. Maybe more a writer.'

'What's the *Illustrated London News* he talks about?'
asked Mark.

'I asked Mum about that,' said Natalie. 'She said it
was a cross between a newspaper and a magazine with

long articles, a few photographs and fancy black and white artwork.'

'I'm sure it's on the net. Be interesting to read what he wrote and that might give you a clue about where he went,' suggested Mark.

'I'll look it up when I get the chance. What are you up to now, great renovator?'

'I can take a hint. I'm stripping the old wallpaper off the third bedroom.' Mark grinned. 'Or I can help you paint the furniture. Are you sure you want to paint those old chairs bright yellow?'

'You mean the gorgeous bentwood chairs I found in that junk shop? They'll be sensational in the breakfast nook. When you're back at the mine, I'm getting out the sewing machine and making seat cushions for them.'

'What about this chair? It is pretty comfortable. But I don't like the material,' said Mark, patting the arm of the chair she'd brought back from Steve's.

'I'll get to it.'

It wasn't until Mark had flown back to the mine and Natalie had the evenings to herself, after the children were in bed, that she found time to sit at her computer. Armed with a cup of tea, she began her search. She quickly discovered that it was worth the small price she'd paid to access the archives of the grand old Victorian newspaper, and it didn't take long before she found herself getting lost in the fascinating maze of articles in the *Illustrated London News*. 'The world's first weekly illustrated newspaper,' she read aloud to herself. 'Started in 1842 and only ended in 2003 – more than one hundred and fifty years. It was no fly-by-night publication you were working for, Uncle Andrew!' After a while, she had to stop herself from browsing through unrelated, but intriguing, articles and concentrate on what she was looking for.

When she eventually came across a story written by Andrew Hancock, she felt goosebumps rise on her skin. There it was, an article about Burma, accompanied by a stunning photograph of a strange beehive-shaped building. Beside the building stood a Burmese man leading a pony laden with packing cases. Natalie could see what a terrific picture it was. It immediately caught the eye and the composition of the photo hinted at an intriguing story.

Without drawing a breath, she read the article about an excavated eleventh-century stupa found by a farmer digging in his field. The article explained how the farmer had found several valuable gold artefacts inside the stupa, which led to a stampede as other farmers and locals attacked the many mounds in the area in the hope of unearthing more treasures. When a bronze Buddha figure was uncovered, there was a frenzy in the countryside. The Burmese Archaeological Society wanted to move the relics to a pagoda in Mandalay but the villagers objected.

Andrew wrote about the ensuing furore with a sensitive understanding of the villagers' situation. He explained the role of religion in Burmese society, the people's belief in miracles and manifestations of the supernatural. He painted a fascinating picture of the observances of people who believed that their donations, prayers, pilgrimages and daily worship would ensure that prayers were not only answered but earned them merit towards the next, and presumably better, life. Eventually, Andrew reported, a compromise had been reached between the Burmese Archaeological Society and the locals and the village site became a new place of worship, bringing pilgrims and prosperity to the villagers.

Natalie liked Andrew's writing, because although it was respectful, it was also tinged with a faint, dry sense of humour.

She returned to the table of contents on the database

and found another story by Andrew called 'Saviour of Sacred Art: Looters Foiled in Lost Kingdom Artefacts'.

Heading the story was a dramatic photo of a rotund and, Natalie thought, florid-looking man dressed in billowing shorts, a matching tailored shirt with many pockets, a sola topee on his head and a ridiculous pince-nez jammed onto his nose. His expression was one of smug self-satisfaction; his pose studied nonchalance. He stood at the entrance to a temple. At his feet were some carved stone statues. Beneath the picture a caption read:

Scottish art historian Ian Ferguson has spent more than twenty years in the Far East unearthing ancient relics from temples in India, Ceylon and Burma. He believes that it is his duty to retrieve and relocate these objects to museums in the United Kingdom and other parts of the world for safekeeping before 'neglect by locals, the creeping jungle, weather and animals destroy these valuable religious curiosities'.

While the Scotsman was the focal point of the picture, the photographer had also captured a figure crouching beside the entrance to the temple. Natalie guessed he was a local man, probably hired to act as a bearer or porter. He squatted on his haunches, his bare feet visible beneath his long sarong, his head resting on one hand as he waited. The expression on his face as he watched the white man strike his pose was clearly visible in the bright sun. To Natalie it looked like disdain and dismay, or perhaps sadness, and it gave quite a different interpretation to the photo.

This must be the Scot who cheated the princess. He looks like a pompous idiot, thought Natalie.

After refilling her teacup she went back to the computer and continued searching through the archives until she found Andrew Hancock again. This time there was a photograph of him under the heading, 'Demise of a Loyal Correspondent in Far-Off Jungle'.

Natalie stared at the formal portrait of the fair-haired man in a starched high collar and tie. He had a long face, deep-set eyes and voluptuous lips. He wore a serious expression for the camera. He seemed to be staring directly at her.

'Hello, Uncle Andrew,' she said softly. Slowly she read on as the paper reported the death of its intrepid correspondent:

Mr Andrew Hancock, our highly respected correspondent, was killed by tribesmen in a remote district of Upper Burma while covering a story for this publication about the anti-British rebels in the region. Mr Hancock was an old Burma hand, a noted photographer as well as writer on Burmese and Indian affairs in the years before the War. He had returned to Burma after serving in Flanders.

Mr Hancock was born in England, and first visited India, Singapore and Burma as a young man travelling just 'with a camera, a notebook and a spirit of curiosity'. He asserted that Burma has been one of the most intriguing centres of Buddhist learning and worship for many thousands of years, and he also frequently wrote that Burma's greatest asset is the warmth of its friendly peoples. It is tragic that a country of which he was so fond should be the place of his death.

His fascinating stories and renowned photography skills were always welcomed by the readers of this publication.

'Killed!' Natalie looked around in shock, wishing Mark was there to share this news. She searched the website to see if there were anymore references to Andrew but nothing came up. She tried Googling him but she could find no more information. She glanced at her watch but realised that it was too late to ring Mark. She would have to wait to tell him about her discoveries.

Natalie opened the shoebox of photographs and studied them more closely. Uncle Andrew was a superb photographer. She looked at each photo, thinking how strange and mysterious the landscape seemed. Street scenes and expanses of river, a busy harbour and some grand old buildings seemed less exotic than the dozens of pictures of temples. She turned one over and found a neatly pencilled place name. It was quite faded but she could make out what it said: *Mrauk-U.*

'So, that explains how Uncle Andrew's thing ended up with your mother. After he was killed his effects must have been sent on to your great-grandmother, Florence, as his closest relative. Now that you've solved that mystery, Nat, what are you going to do this weekend?' Mark was matter-of-fact when Natalie phoned him to tell him what she had found out.

'I heard about a little community market out in the hinterland. Thought it might be a bit of an outing for the kids. They have pony rides and bric-a-brac and local produce.'

'Bric-a-brac, magic words for my girl. Looking for something for the house? You know I even wish I was going. Better than here. Days all blur together.'

'I wish you were here, too. Charlotte and Adam really miss you,' said Natalie.

'Yeah,' Mark said sighing. 'I suppose it'll be worth it in the end.'

'Mark, it will be wonderful when all the renos are finished. We'll have a beautiful house to raise the kids in, far better than we ever imagined. The house will be big enough; we won't have to extend it, and we'll never have to move again. We'll be sitting pretty. I know this situation with you so far away isn't ideal, but it's the best option.'

'Yeah you're right. Are you still thinking of putting a shower beside the pool?'

'Sure am. We don't really want wet people and children walking through the house. Better if they wash off and dry themselves outside.'

'Don't get too many other clever ideas or I'll be stuck out here for another year,' Mark said. 'Let me know what the market is like.'


The children loved the community market in the small village that was tucked in the fertile Gold Coast hinterland. It was unlike the large farmers' markets Natalie was used to, the ones that attracted interstate tourists. This market was designed more for the locals who came to catch up on news and gossip. There was a craft table and a few stalls selling backyard produce, others sold knick-knacks, homemade cakes and chutneys. Over in one corner was an area containing chickens, ducks, rabbits and even guinea pigs, all of which caught the children's attention. Charlotte was thrilled when she saw a docile Shetland pony plodding around a grassy area carrying youthful passengers. While Adam was not interested in riding, Charlotte loved the idea, and bubbled with anticipation when the pony's handler put her onto the back of the little Shetland.

Natalie noticed a small hall set with tables and chairs where tea and snacks were served. After Charlotte's ride she suggested that the children might like a drink and something to eat. Sitting at one of the tables, she watched as cheesecakes, homemade pies and quiches, and a selection of delicious Asian specialities emerged from the little kitchen. Natalie ordered a Sri Lankan fish curry and rice with spicy tomato and cucumber in yoghurt on the side.

It came in a takeaway container and she was pleased she wouldn't have to make dinner for herself that evening. The children tucked into sweet potato fries and little flaky pastries stuffed with minced meat and vegetables while she had a coffee and a slice of mango cheesecake.

'Worth coming just for the food,' declared Natalie. 'I think we'll take some of that fresh fruit home, too. What do you both think?'

The door at the rear of the hall had been left open and she could see that a charming garden was planted outside, filled with fresh greens, tomatoes and other plants that she didn't recognise. Behind the mulched garden beds were several fruit trees. One of the girls from the kitchen was picking ingredients for a salad.

Before they left, Charlotte wanted one more pony ride and this time Adam wanted to sit on it with her. Assured by the pony's owner that they'd be fine riding double, Natalie knew that she had five minutes to look at a stall that she hadn't had a chance to visit. It was piled with all manner of items – old chairs and pottery, coins and bits of machinery. When she looked more closely, she saw a table covered with ornaments, several paintings, antiquarian books and memorabilia. Beside the table stood a carved wooden screen. The more she looked, the more she was intrigued by the unusual pieces. She couldn't tell exactly what they were but they looked Asian. It occurred to her that the man who owned the stall might be able to tell her something about the kammavaca. Maybe she should come back here next time the market was held. The kids would like that and Mark might be able to come, too.

'Do you buy old things?' she asked the stallholder.

'Depends what they are. What do you have?'

'Oh, a souvenir from Burma that belonged to my great-great-uncle.'

'Come back and bring your piece along and I'll have look. I've got a few Thai pieces here. Brass Buddha, and that's an old native fish trap. I've got some antique silk but there's not a lot of call for pieces like that at the moment. Most people are more interested in books, coins, you know, collectables. Where are you from? Haven't seen you around before.'

'I live at the Gold Coast. Brought the kids out here for an outing.'

'You've picked a pretty spot; nice little community. Bit of a dynamo runs the market. She set up the community garden and other projects. I used to travel round the state. Sometimes I'd go down south to do the big markets. Too much trouble now. I'm just selling off what I have left in my shed. This market is on every two weeks.'

'Thanks. I'll be back.'

Natalie collected the children from the pony handler, picked up the knitted toys they'd chosen from the craft stall and gave Charlotte and Adam a homemade Anzac biscuit each for the journey home.

'It was a great morning,' she enthused to Mark that night. 'Charlotte was crazy about the pony. I'd like to take you to this market when you get home. I want to show Uncle Andrew's kammavaca to the old chap who has an antique stall.'

'What would a Sunday market stallholder, way out in the boonies, know?' said Mark. 'We should take it to a professional dealer and get a proper valuation.'

'No, I told you I'm just interested in knowing more about it.'

'But we already know a lot about its origins from your internet research. What would be really interesting would be getting that funny writing translated,' said Mark.

'Yeah, although according to Uncle Andrew's letter, it's probably just religious stuff.'

\*

Windemere Preschool was housed in a brightly painted purpose-built building with a fenced play area containing a sandpit, cubby house and climbing apparatus. It was run by Jodie Price, one of Natalie's oldest friends. Jodie had moved down from Brisbane and worked hard to set up the preschool, and she was proud of her dedicated staff and the knowledge that her establishment provided an excellent service for parents and the young children of the area. Although the facility was not particularly close to Natalie, there was no question that her children would go anywhere else, and she looked forward to the two days a week that Charlotte and Adam went there. It gave her some time to herself but also because she loved the security of knowing there was a place where Charlotte and Adam were not only cared for but were stimulated and could play with other children, learn social skills and adjust to being away from home for a short time. While every cold and sniffle seemed to be passed around among the children, the advantages of attending the centre far outweighed the disadvantages.

One sunny morning Charlotte danced off with her friend Heidi to play in the cubby house while Adam stayed close to Natalie before a staff member led him away and distracted him by playing with him. Jodie came over to speak to her friend.

'He gets a bit clingy just after Mark leaves for the mine,' said Natalie.

'He misses his dad but I thought he played well with Aaron last week,' said Jodie. 'Though it's more parallel play at their age.'

'That's right, sitting side by side, building blocks, playing trains, whatever, but ignoring each other,' said Natalie.

'Hard, isn't it, when fathers aren't around? Heidi's dad goes overseas every couple of months and it takes a week or more for her to adjust. Must be hard on you with a fly in – fly out hubby. How do you keep the kids entertained all the time?'

'This place is such a godsend, Jodie. I like taking them out. And I like some of the other mothers whose kids come here. We occasionally meet for morning coffee at child-friendly cafés. Pity you can't join us. Maybe one Saturday? I like to get away from the house and the reno mess when I can. I took the kids to the market in the hinterland on the weekend. When Mark comes home I think I'll take him back there.'

'That good, huh?' asked Jodie.

'I like being in the country, so green and lush. Charlotte loved the pony rides. The food was absolutely delicious and there was a great junk stall.'

'There're plenty of old-wares places around the coast. What are you looking for? I'm amazed at how you pick up old things and transform them for your house.'

'Thanks. I just wish we could get on with the big renos. I'm so sick of all the mess around us. I just want to throw money at it. Get a team in to bash out walls, replace almost all the kitchen and do something with the bathroom. Get it over and done with. I saw a screen at that stall and I've worked out what I can do with it. I don't think it will cost very much, so it would be great if it's still there. I also want to show the man running the stall a little knick-knack that belonged to my uncle and see if he knows what it is.'

'You mean, value it?' asked Jodie. 'What is it?'

'I don't know if he could value it. I don't expect it's worth much anyway. I really just want to know more about it. It's a sort of cloth manuscript thing that folds up in sections between painted bits of bamboo. It's covered in illustrations and old writing that we can't read. It came from Burma.'

'Wow, how cool. I studied a bit about Burma in a unit on South East Asia when I was at uni,' said Jodie.

'Really? I don't know a thing about Burma.'

'It's called Myanmar now. There was a coup and a bunch of generals took over in the 1960s. Was your uncle there then?'

'Actually, he was my great-great-uncle. Mum found a whole box of old photos he'd sent to Great Granny Florence.'

'Gosh, that's amazing. Are you going to try to find out more? What was he doing out there? Civil service, the army? The twenties, that would've still been the raj era. Very pukka,' said Jodie.

'S'pose he was what we'd call a photojournalist. His photographs are fantastic. I'm going to get some of them blown up and framed.' Natalie cast an eye over to where Adam was playing with some building blocks. 'He didn't have a lot of positive things to say about the British in Burma, though.'

'Colonial days . . . There was a book we read in the course that he would have agreed with – George Orwell's *Burmese Days*. It's about how the colonial Brits behaved, or behaved badly more like.'

'Wow, Jodie, you're a font of information! Uncle Andrew's a bit of an unfinished story. He was trying to get a kammavaca back to its rightful owner, but he died before he could.'

'Wouldn't you be better off going to an Asian art specialist?' asked Jodie.

'That's what Mark said. We'll see. Anyway, I want to go back to the markets and see if the screen is still there.'

'What are you doing with the screen? I assume you're not going to use it as a room divider or what it's actually meant for?'

Natalie laughed. 'Of course not. It's in four jointed sections and the top bit of each is all cut-out fretwork in a kind of lacy flower pattern. It looks a bit Indian or Arabian. It has teeny mirrors stuck in the centre of each wooden flower, but the rest of it is just wood. I'm going to try turning it into four white folding doors that can open onto the garden from the playroom.'

'Sounds lovely. You are clever.'


With the children asleep Natalie reached for her book, *Burmese Days*. She'd hunted it out at the local library. She studied the cover photograph that showed two languid men, presumably British, relaxing on a verandah somewhere in the tropics. One was stretched out asleep in a planters' chair, his legs draped over its extended arms, one hand clasping a newspaper, the other flung above his head, his supine pose contrasting with his stiffly waxed moustache. One shoe had fallen to the floor.

The other man, still dressed in a formal white shirt, sat reading in a rattan chair, chewing on a cigar as a turbaned, dark-skinned boy fanned him. A small table held cigarettes and matches beside two whisky glasses. A couple of chubby terriers looked as languid as their owners. The photo was credited to an A G E Newland and titled *The Long, Long Burmese Day*. It looked like a pretty privileged life, thought Natalie.


She was well into the book when Mark came home several days later.

'Listen to this, Mark,' she said, interrupting his TV program. 'This character Elizabeth is just vile.'

'Who's Elizabeth?' asked Mark, turning down the sound on his movie.

'She's an English girl who goes out to Burma to live with her relations and is courted by Flory, the so-called hero of the book. He's an English timber merchant and doesn't quite fit in with the colonial society in Burma.'

'When is it set?'

'The 1920s, about the time that Uncle Andrew went back to Burma. When you read this, you understand how Andrew must have felt. Those British were awful. But Flory is different, he sympathises with the Burmese and tries to get Elizabeth to like them, too. But this is what she thinks.'

Natalie lifted the book and read:

When he spoke of the 'natives', he spoke nearly always IN FAVOUR of them. He was forever praising Burmese customs and the Burmese character; he even went so far as to contrast them favourably with the British. It disquieted her. After all, natives were natives – interesting, no doubt, but finally only a 'subject' people, an inferior people with black faces.

'Isn't that appalling?' said Natalie.

'Yes, but that's probably the way the British thought in those days. I still hear some pretty racist comments about Asians at the mine,' said Mark.

'That's not right, either. You know, I'm really pleased Uncle Andrew was like Flory. He liked the Burmese and he thought that the British were ripping them off. I think that it's a pity he couldn't return the kammavaca to the princess to show her that there were some decent Englishmen who weren't there just to exploit the country and its people.'

'I agree. It's such a shame but that's life, I guess.'

As they drove along the country road to the market the following weekend, Natalie winced when Mark hit a pothole. 'Can't you drive more carefully?' she snapped.

'Can't do much about these potholes.' Mark glanced at her. 'Why are you so cranky this morning?'

'Am I? Sorry. I don't feel well.'

'Say, that's a nice-looking little golf course,' said Mark, changing the subject. 'Didn't know that was here. Hmm, eighteen holes, too.' Mark slowed as he drove past the undulating rich-green course shaded by trees, its neat clubhouse surrounded by cars. 'Might have to get Tony to come and have a game with me. Haven't played for ages.'

'Don't they have a golf course at the mine?'

Mark looked as though he was about to say something, but changed his mind. 'Okay, here we are. What's first?'

'Pony ride, Daddy!' squealed Charlotte.

'Right. I'll take them, Nat. Do you want a coffee and some cake first?' asked Mark.

Natalie shook her head. 'No, thanks. My tummy feels a bit wobbly. I'd like to see the man with the collectables and see if he's still got the screen I saw. If he has, can you throw it into the back of the station wagon?'

'Of course. You go and chase him up. It's not a huge market, so I'll find you.' He took the children by the hand and walked off towards the pony rides.

Natalie walked past the stalls with their homemade goodies but she couldn't work up a lot of enthusiasm for them. She headed over to where she could see the collectables spread out on tables under the shade of a tree.

'Hello there! You've come back,' the stall owner greeted her warmly.

'Yes. Oh, good, you've still got the screen I saw last time. I was hoping it would still be here. I'll pay you for it, and my husband will come and get it for me.' She glanced at the selection on the tables and the larger items standing around. 'I like that old Singer sewing machine. I have my grandmother's old one.'

84

'Do you use it?'

Natalie laughed. 'No. I use a modern sewing machine.'

'Did you bring your Burmese souvenir that you were talking about? There's someone at the markets today who might be able to help you with it.'

'Really? Here it is. Tell me what you think.' Natalie pulled the kammavaca from her handbag, took off the silk scarf it was wrapped in, opened the box and gently unfurled the scroll of painted images and writing.

'I've seen these before. Palm-leaf manuscripts. They're quite common in South Asia, India, Sri Lanka, Thailand, those places. They're still made, of course. But this one is unusual.' He fingered it carefully. 'It's made of cloth. Different. Illustrations are really beautiful. Could be worth a couple of hundred dollars, maybe. Thi might have a better idea.'

'Thi? Who's that?'

'Thi is Burmese. She's the one who runs the market though she's been in Australia for yonks. She's set up a school in a village in Burma and what we raise here at the market she sends over to keep it running.'

'That's incredible! I mean, to find a Burmese woman here.' Natalie was a bit lost for words. 'I've just been reading about Burma. In the old days. Is Thi here? I'd love to meet her.'

'She'll be running around somewhere. You won't miss her. She's wearing a T-shirt with "Free Aung San Suu Kyi" printed on it.'

Natalie found Thi in the community garden energetically picking salad greens and tomatoes while directing another volunteer to add mulch and water to the garden beds. Someone sang out from the kitchen window to say that they needed some spring onions.

Shyly Natalie approached the small Burmese woman. 'Hello, you must be Thi. I'm Natalie.'

Thi straightened up and gave Natalie a smile. She was probably in her fifties, her hair flecked with grey, her olive skin sun wrinkled, her eyes a sparkling brown. A large smile split her face. 'That's me. How can I help?'

'The man with the collectables and old wares suggested I see you. It's about something Burmese my great-great-uncle left me. I'm just beginning to learn about Burma.'

Thi reached out and touched Natalie's arm. 'I always like talking about my country.'

She pointed to the picture on her T-shirt. 'There's a lot that needs to change and many people need to help. Go and have a coffee and some cheesecake and I'll be with you soon.'

Natalie watched Thi bustle around among the patrons of the café, who mostly seemed to be locals. She was obviously well known as several people stopped her for a chat. She finally sat down opposite Natalie at the little table and looked at the iced water Natalie was drinking.

'Oh, you need something to nibble on.'

Before Natalie could protest Thi popped into the kitchen and then came and sat back down.

'Now we have a few minutes.'

'Yes, sorry to interrupt. I can't stay too long; my husband has our two children out there somewhere,' began Natalie.

'They'll find you when they want something.' Thi smiled. 'Now, why are you interested in Burma?'

Briefly Natalie told her about Uncle Andrew then she pulled the kammavaca from her bag.

Thi chewed her lip, put the glasses that hung around her neck on a chain onto her nose and examined the kammavaca closely.

'This is very beautiful. And it must be very special to

be on this cloth.' She touched it reverently. 'It is the colour of the monks' robes.'

Natalie told her what Andrew had written in his letter.

Thi nodded. 'This kammavaca is very special. It was made with reverence for King Thibaw. It has travelled far from its rightful home. But at least it is intact. So many treasures have been destroyed.' She handed it back to Natalie. 'What do you plan to do with it?'

'Keep it, of course! But I was hoping to learn more about it. Maybe have the writing translated. My husband wonders if it is valuable,' she added.

Thi was thoughtful for a moment. 'What is valuable to one might be less so to another. And something is worth what another will pay. I cannot give you a value. The writing on this side is old calligraphy, only a special scholar could translate it.'

A glass of juice and a small bowl of yoghurt and figs were put in front of Natalie.

Thi motioned her to eat and continued. 'I'm glad you know something of Burma, so few people do. Our country is suffering. It is cut off from the rest of the world by the generals. They have committed many horrors. They take the wealth of the country for themselves and let the people struggle and starve.'

'Yes, I heard about your school and how you send money from here,' said Natalie.

Thi waved a hand. 'A drop in the ocean but I have to do it secretly. The generals do not allow foreign aid or any outside help into Burma. Our country is secretive but there are people risking their lives to get the word out about what goes on there – the atrocities the army are inflicting on dissidents and anyone who even hints at being critical of the regime.'

'Do you ever go back to Burma?' asked Natalie.

'No. It would be too dangerous. There are people who

manage to get visas but it can be difficult. I always hope that things will change one day. There are good people around the world supporting Burma.'

'I'm afraid I don't know very much about all this,' confessed Natalie.

'Most people don't.'

'I have a lot to learn,' said Natalie quietly. 'I have heard about Aung San Suu Kyi but I'm not sure why she's so important.'

'In Burma she is greatly loved. We call her "The Lady" because to speak her name can bring trouble on yourself.'

'What has she done?'

Thi gently leaned over and took Natalie's hand. 'The Lady has given up her freedom for our country. Would you like me to tell you why I say that?'

Natalie nodded.

'After the Second World War, Burma was able to gain its independence from Britain and in the first elections General Aung San, who was the leader of the Burmese resistance, and his party won easily. But Burma remained a violent and divided country, and before he was able to take up government he and most of his cabinet were assassinated by members of the military. Aung San Suu Kyi was his daughter and she was only two years old.'

'That's terrible,' murmured Natalie, but Thi continued as though she had not heard her.

'Her mother was a diplomat and so Aung San Suu Kyi was educated abroad and at Oxford University. She married an Englishman and had two sons. She was leading the life of an academic's wife when her mother had a stroke so she flew back to Rangoon. At that time General Ne Win, who had been the dictator of Burma for many years, announced that he would retire. So there was an uprising among the people demanding free elections. The military brutally tried to suppress this movement so instead of flying back to Britain and her family Aung San Suu Kyi challenged the military. People were very pleased by this because they remembered how her father had stood up to the British. When her mother died there was a huge funeral and the military realised just how popular The Lady had become, so they forbade her to run into the election and put her under house arrest.'

'That's unbelievable. What happened in the election?'

'Her party, the National League for Democracy, got more than eighty per cent of the vote.'

'That's amazing. Did she form a government?'

'No, no. The generals ignored the results and kept her under house arrest.'

'But didn't someone – the world or the UN – do something about it?' asked Natalie.

'No, because although Aung San Suu Kyi won the Nobel Peace Prize, the Chinese backed the military junta. What was really cruel was that when she found out that her husband was dying, the military told her that she could leave Burma to look after him, but she knew that they would never let her back in again. She had to choose between her husband and doing the right thing for her country. She stayed in Burma and was never able to say goodbye to her husband.'

Natalie felt her tears welling up. 'That is just awful. I can't imagine having to make such a decision. She sounds an extraordinary person.'

'Yes,' said Thi. 'She is. Sometimes the military release her from house arrest but when they see how popular she still is, they re-arrest her. It is very difficult for her to speak out to the world, or to her people, but we all know the sacrifices that she is making to make Burma a free country and we all love her for it.'

'That is the bravest and saddest story,' said Natalie. 'Thank you so much for telling me.'

'I am glad that I could. The more people who know

about the plight of Burma and Aung San Suu Kyi, the more pressure there will be on the military to change. That is what I think anyway.'

'I hope you're right.'

'Hey, there you are!' called Mark, and Natalie turned and waved to him.

'Mummy, can we have ice-cream?' Charlotte ran to Natalie and stared at the bowl of food in front of her. 'What's that?' she asked.

'That's fresh figs from my garden with homemade yoghurt and local Ridge Lake honey. Would you like some, too?' asked Thi.

'No, thank you. I'd like ice-cream, please.'

'I'm sure we can find some.' Thi stood up.

'Thi, this is my husband, Mark, and my children,' said Natalie, 'Charlotte and Adam.'

'A beautiful family. Let me give you my phone number. Hope to see you again here. We like new visitors to our market.'

'All for a good cause,' said Natalie, smiling. 'It's been eye-opening. I'd like to talk some more. And the figs are delicious.'

'I like the sound of the mango cheesecake,' said Mark, sitting down.

'I'll organise that for you.' Thi excused herself.

'How amazing to meet a Burmese woman way out here,' said Natalie.

'Did she say anything about Uncle Andrew's thingy?' said Mark.

'Not a lot, except it's special. She told me a bit about what's been happening in Burma. Wait till I tell you what Thi told me.'

A young girl came over with their order and Thi came back and handed Natalie a slip of paper as well as a bag of fruit and a bunch of flowers.

'My contact details, some figs and the flowers are from my garden,' said Thi. 'Come and visit us again some time, you are always welcome.'

'What a lovely person,' Natalie said to Mark. 'I bought the screen by the way. Can you get it into the station wagon? The man at the stall thinks that I should see an expert if I want to get the kammavaca valued properly.'

'Which is what I said. What do you want to do?' asked Mark, nibbling at his cheesecake.

'Uncle Andrew has made me curious about Burma and so has Thi,' said Natalie.

'I meant about the kammavaca. You might have to get it insured. Who knows what it could be worth?' said Mark lightly.

'Hmm. We'll see. How about one more pony ride before we go home?' said Natalie cheerfully.

'Yay!' Charlotte jumped off Mark's lap and Adam clapped his little hands together.

Mark smiled at Natalie. 'Glad you're feeling better. I'll pay the bill, you take the kids over to the pony.'


Later in the week, Natalie was working in the kitchen when she heard Charlotte call out.

'Mummy, Mummy, the floor's leaking!'

'Charlotte, what are you talking about?' Natalie followed Charlotte into the main bathroom, where she saw water all over the floor. It seemed to be coming from the drain in the middle of the bathroom floor.

'What happened? Have you and Adam been playing in here?'

'No, Mummy. It was just like this.'

'What is going on? Sweetie, go outside while I clean this up. Why do these things happen when Mark is away!' When Charlotte looked worried, Natalie smiled. 'It's all right, honey, we'll get the plumber over. He'll fix it. You can use Mummy's bathroom.'

But when Jodie rang, Natalie couldn't help dumping her woes on her friend.

'The water's backing up the drain. It must be really blocked. I can't use that bathroom at all and the plumber I rang can't come for two days! Do you know a good plumber? I suppose we're lucky that we have the ensuite.'

By the time Mark rang that evening she was very upset about the whole plumbing problem.

'I know we have the ensuite, but it only has a shower and it's really difficult to wash the kids properly without a bath. Adam just squirms and I'm as wet as he is in the end.'

'I'm sorry I'm not there to help you, darling, but it's going to be fine. It's probably just a clogged drain. We're going to renovate the bathroom anyway, right?'

'Yes, but that's way down on our list. We have to be able to use it in the meantime!'

'Shouldn't be a hard thing to fix. Let me know what the plumber says. Couldn't you get Roger?'

'No, he's on some building job up on the Sunshine Coast. Jodie's given me the name of her plumber.'

'Jodie's guy will be all right. How's everything else?'

'The usual. I think Adam is coming down with something but you know what kids are like, dying one day and running around like mad things the next. There's a funny noise in the car, and I still feel crook and can't be bothered cooking so the kids got a frozen dinner tonight. And I'm behind with the bookkeeping. Other than that, everything is great,' said Natalie tartly.

'Frozen meals aren't going to do you or the kids any harm. But listen, Nat, have an early night. Get a good sleep,' said Mark calmly. 'You'll feel better in the morning, you know how you get when you're overtired.

You're doing too much around the house. Try and relax in the evenings.'

'It's the only time I have to myself,' said Natalie miserably.

'I know and I'm sorry I'm not there, sweetheart. Love you and sleep tight.'

Mark hung up leaving Natalie holding the phone. He was right; she knew she was overtired.

At the bathroom sink, after brushing her teeth, Natalie was reaching into the medicine cabinet for her face cream when she suddenly noticed her contraceptive pills. She'd gone off them when Mark had started working out at the mine. There hadn't seemed much point with him away a month at a time. She felt better for it even though she had felt under the weather lately. Then she realised that she had forgotten to bring in the washing and she didn't want to leave it outside to get damp again in the night air. Sighing, she turned around and headed to the clothesline. As the cool evening air hit her, so did a sudden thought or, rather, a sudden knowingness.

She was pregnant. She had to be. She'd lost track of time, her period must be weeks overdue. And the way she'd been feeling. Why hadn't it occurred to her before? They'd been being careful but clearly not careful enough.

She felt shaky and not sure if she was in shock or excited. It was too late to ring Mark. She went back into the house, poured herself a glass of water, took a head-ache pill and went to bed.

She lay in the dark, her hands clasped protectively over her belly. She'd do a pregnancy test tomorrow to be sure before telling Mark. While she was beginning to feel joyful, other thoughts crowded into her mind. Would the major renovations be done in time? Having a new baby in the house while building work was in progress would be a nightmare. And Mark wouldn't be around much to help, but they needed the money more than ever now. Happy as she was, the timing was terrible.

'Mark? Mark? What do you think? Are you happy?' asked Natalie after she broke the news to him the next evening.

'Yes, yes, of course. It's just that, well, the timing isn't great. How are you going to manage?'

'You mean how are *we* going to manage?' she said, laughing.

'I'll do what I can, but seriously, I have to keep working out here. I'd never make this kind of money on the Gold Coast. And we're really going to need it now. Renovations and a new baby! Maybe you could get some help in the house. I can't give up this job now.'

'I know. I don't know what to say. I just want the renos done. ASAP. The plumber's coming tomorrow.'

'I am pleased about the baby, Nat. What do you want? Boy? Girl? Have you told your mum yet? Maybe she could come over and help out.'

'Not for very long. She has her business to run. We'll have to think this through,' said Natalie.

'It might be better if we cut back on some of our ideas. We can draw up a list of essential renovations and ones that can be done later. But promise me, Nat, look after yourself. No lifting heavy things, okay? Don't do any full-on work around the house. Nothing rash. We'll be able to work this out.'

'Yeah. Don't worry. I'm not silly.' Mentally she was culling her list of things to do.

'I've got at least seven more months out here before the baby comes. If you can get some help around the home, I'll be able to work here longer, until we've saved enough to get all the essential jobs done.'

'Yeah. I just hate the idea of you being away any longer than necessary. I'll draw up my list and compare it with yours and we'll go from there.'

'Sounds like a plan. Everything is going to be okay.'


Natalie crouched down beside the plumber in the bathroom. He lifted the grate over the drain on the floor and peered down into the exposed drainpipe.

'I can see why it's clogged up. See all that? Tree roots. The drain is full of them. No wonder the water can't get away.'

'They're everywhere!' exclaimed Natalie.

'Sure are. These pipes are full of roots, probably from that tree next door, and they're going to have to be completely replaced.'

'Well, we were going to renovate the bathroom anyway.'

'This isn't cosmetic. This is a major plumbing job. All the old clay pipes are full of roots. They're going to have to be torn up and replaced with new plastic piping and a whole new cement floor is going to have to be laid before you can put down any new tiles, and a bath and shower. Not cheap.'

Natalie looked at him in horror. 'But I'm going to have a baby.'

'Congratulations, but that doesn't change anything. All these pipes have to be replaced and you're going to need a completely new bathroom. The faster we get started, the better. If I were you I'd talk to your neighbour about chopping down that tree.'

'I don't even know our neighbours. We haven't been here very long and thanks to the tree we never see them. I can't believe this.' She looked at the back of the bathroom. 'I have such big plans for the bathroom. I want a separate little pool shower, solar panels on the roof, a fabulous extra large bathroom.' She stopped. 'Do you know what a vichy shower is? It's a row of shower heads where the water sluices down on you when you're having a special massage. It made me think, why couldn't we put all the plumbing up on the roof?'

'Water doesn't run uphill.'

'How expensive would a pump be? Compared to all this underground plumbing?'

'Not that simple. Whatever you do you're looking at a big whack of money. Better talk to the neighbours, anyway. They've probably got roots in their drains, too.'

'Would you have any idea of what kind of money we'd be looking at?' she asked.

'I'll send you a quote, but costs also depend on how much money you want to spend on your shower and bath fittings.'


'How much?' Mark sounded incredulous. 'That sounds like a rip-off to me. Why don't you get another quote?'

'You're right. I'll ring around in the morning. We'll have to put more of the other renos on hold.'

'We'll work it out. I'll just have to keep working out here a bit longer. Do you think you could cope?'

'Not happy with the idea at the moment, Mark, but when the time comes, I guess we could see. We could bite the bullet, get the bathroom done, and the nursery, but the kitchen will have to wait.'

Mark groaned. 'I really wanted to get that done,' he said. 'I hate that kitchen, it has to be the worst design I've ever seen, but if you can live with it a bit longer, so can I.'

'Maybe this house wasn't the bargain we thought.' Natalie sighed.

'Location, location, location, sweetheart. If I can stick

it out here for as long as possible and we cut a few corners, it will work out.'


'Yes, Mum, it is a bit unexpected,' Natalie told Sarah a few days later.

'I'm very happy for all of you. Another baby will be wonderful. I'll do everything I can to help you. It's a shame that I can't stay with you for long when it comes, but the shop is six days a week,' replied Sarah.

'I know, Mum. Mark and I will manage. I got another quote for the bathroom and it's slightly cheaper than the first, but it's certainly not what I would call cheap. Anyway, Mark and I have talked things over. If we budget and I manage a bit longer by myself and we leave some of the renovations until later, we'll still be able to do most of what we want. But it's going to be tight.'

'Why don't you have a break from all these renovations for a couple of days and bring the kids down to Lismore to see the new house? We'd both love to see you.'

'Thanks, Mum. A break with you and Steve is a great idea and now that you're less than two hours away, the kids won't mind the drive too much. I'll come down soon.'

Natalie put the phone down with a smile. It would be lovely to get away from the plumbing problems, the disorder of their house for a couple of days and have two other people keeping an eye on Charlotte and Adam to give her a bit of a break. The time between Mark's home visits seemed to be getting longer and longer. She wished her mother was still at the farm, but she knew the new house would be very comfortable and there was a verandah and a garden for Adam to let off steam. He wasn't good around glass vases and knick-knacks on coffee tables.

At a couple of months pregnant, Natalie was feeling tired each day and the idea of reading and relaxing on her own seemed a luxury. A break away from home couldn't come fast enough.

# 4

IN THE LAZY SUNRISE hours of Sunday morning, Natalie lay curled in Mark's arms in their bed, both resting their hands on her slightly rounded belly.

'Have you thought about names yet?' Mark said nuzzling her ear.

'Kind of. If it's a boy I'd like to call him Andrew.'

'Really? After your unknown uncle?'

'He's known to me now. And I think he must have been a good guy. He had principles, you know.'

Mark smiled. 'Okay then. That's fine by me, if I get to choose a girl's name.' He kissed her tenderly, then looked up as the bedroom door opened with a bang and Adam raced over to them clutching his old blue teddy bear.

Mark swung him onto the bed. 'Hey there, mister. You love that blue bear, eh?'

'You're still my baby boy, Adam,' said Natalie, looking at his ruffled hair and happy expression. 'Even if you can get out of your cot by yourself now.'

'Do you think it's a good idea to leave the side of his cot down, especially as he can open his bedroom door?'

'If I leave it up, he tries to climb over the side and ends up falling onto the floor. I think I'll have to get a baby gate and put it across his doorway. That'll keep him in his room. I know that you're not supposed to compare girls with boys, but he's much more of a climber than Charlotte was. But it's also because he knows you're home and he can't wait to see you. We're lucky he let us sleep this late,' said Natalie.

'What about me?' A sleepy Charlotte appeared at the door. 'What's going on?' she demanded.

'Just having a cuddle. Come on up here, too, buttercup,' called Mark as Adam wriggled under the covers.


Natalie smiled as she made breakfast. 'Tickles and giggles and cuddles. What a lovely way to start the day. What are we going to do today?'

'You mentioned seeing your mother. Do you want to do it today or have you got something else planned?'

'Mum has invited us down for lunch, but I was going to drive down when you were back at work. I don't want to make you give up your time at home to drive down to Lismore.'

'Nat, it's not a problem. I enjoy seeing your mother and Steve, and I'd like to see their new place. Why don't you ring Sarah and tell her to expect us all in a couple of hours?'

\*

Steve and Sarah's new house was at the end of a quiet cul-de-sac. The homes on either side had well-established gardens and that tidy look that showed the owners were proud of their properties.

'Looks very nice and neat,' commented Mark as they pulled into the driveway.

'No cows, no paddocks, no wide open spaces. But it's smart. A big change for Steve, but I can see why Mum loves it.'

The roller door to the garage rattled open and Steve came out to greet them. The garage was full of tools, the lawnmower and many unpacked boxes that stood either side of Sarah's compact car.

'Does it all fit?' asked Mark, getting out and shaking Steve's hand. 'Bet you miss those sheds of yours.'

'Yeah. Sure do. Lucky we got rid of a lot of stuff in the clearing sale. Anyway, welcome to the new place.'

Sarah appeared and the children ran to her. 'At last. I've made muffins, and they're getting cold. Come in, come in.'

'Why are you here, Nanny?' asked Charlotte.

'This is my new house. Come and see inside.'

'But where are the cows?' Charlotte looked concerned.

'I'll let you handle that one, Mum,' said Natalie as Adam headed towards the treasure trove he could see scattered around the garage. 'How're you settling in, Steve?'

'Don't miss the early morning milking, that's for sure. But it's a different lifestyle. New phase of our lives.' He said with a shrug.

'You're too fit and young to retire,' said Mark.

'Yes, what are you going to do with yourself while Mum's at work?' asked Natalie.

'I've got some new interests! Hey, young man, get out of my drill bits.' He picked up Adam and carried him into the house as Mark and Natalie followed.

'It all looks lovely, Mum,' said Natalie. 'Nice to see some familiar things in their new surroundings.' She looked around at this strange modern and more compact house. She missed the big lawns and the paddocks and animals that had been part of Steve's farm.

'This place makes my life much simpler, I can tell you. It's much easier to keep clean, not to mention the five-minute drive to the shop! It takes the pressure off when I know that I can always get home if it's been raining and not be suddenly stranded by flooded roads. But enough about me! How are you feeling, Natalie? Had any morning sickness?' asked Sarah.

'Not really. I get a bit tired but that's kind of normal for me anyway. I think it's a permanent state for the mothers of toddlers.'

'You do too much. You should make Mark give you more of a break when he's home,' said Sarah.

'He works long hours, too. And if we want to get the renovations finished quickly, it's the most practical solution. Especially now. We don't want to be stuck too long in a half-finished house with three little ones. What a nightmare,' said Natalie. 'Anyway, Mark does help me when he's home. He takes the kids out, so I can do things in the house without sticky fingers getting in the way. He's considerate, Mum.'

Sarah shook her head. 'You two seem to have everything worked out. Sometimes I think that your marriage seems too good to be true. Don't you ever argue about anything?'

'Of course we have disagreements. But not often, we're a team. We think that what we are doing is the best for all of us in the long run, even if it doesn't feel like that at times. You and Steve get on well though, don't you?'

'We do. Steve's so placid and easygoing. I know he had second thoughts about leaving his farm, but we're trying to be sensible, too.'

'What's he doing with his spare time now?'

'He's playing the stock market with money left over from the sale of the farm. He says he's learning a lot,' said Sarah.

'You haven't thought about giving up the shop, have you, Mum?'

'Certainly not, especially as it's so much easier for me to run it now. Are you concerned that I won't be able to help very much with the new baby?'

'No, Mum. I don't expect you to drop everything for me. We've got it all worked out so that we can manage on our own. Then in a couple of years Mark can give up the FIFO job and get one on the Gold Coast. I know it'll be difficult with three kids for a while but we'll be fine,' said Natalie.

'I'm glad you've got things worked out. I'm so look-ing forward to seeing the little one when he or she is born,' said Sarah. 'But you'll certainly have your hands full.'

Lunch was set up at the glass table on the patio and looked very pretty if rather more formal than the lunches they'd had at the casual long wooden table set under trees at the farm. Charlotte looked slightly intimidated by the formality.

'What's happening out at the mine, Mark? You going to buy any shares in it?' asked Steve.

Mark shook his head. 'No way. I'm not into that sort of thing.'

'Really?' said Sarah. 'Wouldn't you rather own Aussie mining shares than work for a foreign-owned company that keeps the bulk of the profits for themselves?'

'But, Mum, those mining companies have bought the rights to extract the minerals, so don't you think they have the right to the profits?' asked Natalie.

'Well,' said Mark, 'your mother has a point. Some people would argue that those resources below the surface, in the ground, belong to all of Australia, so it would be fairer if a bigger share of that wealth went to all Australians and not just to overseas shareholders.'

'But the mining companies are taxed, aren't they?' said Natalie.

'They try to pay as little tax as possible, like most companies. And what they make out of mining is massive. Some of it goes to the states as royalties, but the states that don't have a lot of mines are missing out. People say other states should get their share, too. I mean, they are part of this country and should be part of the bonanza,' said Mark.

Before Natalie could respond, Sarah held up her hand and said, 'What I'm really concerned about is that I've heard that those mining companies destroy the environment. If the profits from mining go overseas and the environment is wrecked, what's really in it for us? For Australia?'

'The mining company I work for seems to want to do the right thing. They treat their workers well, and they look after the environment. They spend a lot of money on regeneration,' said Mark.

'Yeah, but once they rip the guts out of the land, it never comes back to its original condition,' said Steve.

'I think that some of the mining companies think that they don't have to play by the rules. They're part of the Australian community, aren't they? Really, it makes me very cross,' said Sarah as she removed their plates.

'Calm down, love,' said Steve. 'At least Mark is making hay while the sun shines, like so many others.'

'You know, a lot of the mining staff – engineers, geologists, the bigwigs – and just ordinary blokes like me, say they're really proud of what they're doing. They think that they are making a better Australia. But, yes, I agree with both you and Steve that once those minerals are gone, they're gone, and so the mining companies should be paying top dollar for the privilege of taking them.' Mark leaned back in his chair. 'This argument goes on all the time at work. I don't want to have it at home, too.' He stood up. He smiled at Charlotte and Adam. 'Nanny has ice-cream. Shall we go and help her serve it?'

Steve poured Natalie a glass of water as Sarah and Mark dished out ice-cream to the children in the kitchen. 'I tell you what, Nat, this is not the same country as the one my dad and my grandfather and me grew up in. I don't like it. Too much greed. Wind farms, gas wells, mines everywhere. I was happy knowing I could feed my family with my own hands. That there were decent people looking after farms, investing in our country by sharing it, in the good times and the bad times. We all paid our dues and some of us did better than others. And I was as good as the next fella. And if I didn't like what was going on, I had a vote and I could say my piece.' He shook his head. 'Now I ask myself, who owns Australia? Doesn't feel like I do.' He downed his beer. 'Anyway, enough with the lecture. You feeling okay with the new kiddy coming on?'

Natalie smiled at Steve and nodded. He sounded like a grumpy old man. Maybe he regretted selling the farm and giving up the secure life he'd always known, she thought. But it was too late now. She hoped he would settle into suburbia quickly.


Natalie took one final glance over her shoulder as Jodie took Charlotte and Adam out into the garden of the Windemere Preschool. Adam could be difficult when he knew that she would be leaving him but, with Charlotte beside him, the lure of the sandpit and slippery dip diverted his attention from his mother heading out the door.

*

105

'I'm in the car on my way to Woolloongabba, Mum. In Brisbane. Yes, I'm using the hands-free phone.'

'Why are you going up there? Meeting some of the girls?'

'I'm having a coffee with a girlfriend. I'm looking for some bathroom fittings, and some light fittings, too. I also want to browse through some antique shops.'

'What do you need antiques now for? Can't you wait till you finish those renovations?'

'I'm not shopping. I'm going to see if I can find a place I've been told about that specialises in Asian antiques. I'm taking Uncle Andrew's kammavaca with me.'

'Are you going to get it valued? That's a good idea, I suppose, but don't get your hopes up too high. It's such a simple little thing,' said Sarah.

'No, Mum. The more I look at it the more intriguing I find the little pictures painted on it. You're right. It probably has no great value, but it's nice to have it in the family. Uncle Andrew sounded so interesting. I want to find out more about this thing that was so important to him.'

'I agree. It makes me wonder if we had anyone else in the family who was adventurous like him. I have to say, the places he went to intrigue me. Especially Burma. I can see from his photographs why he was so captivated by the place. I don't think Brighton was quite as exotic. But that's where most of our rellies stayed, except, of course, my grandmother,' said Sarah.

'I think she must have been pretty brave to have left England for the wilds of northern New South Wales.'

'Yes, she must have been and in love. Let me know what you find out. And restrain yourself. I know what you're like in antique shops! Don't go buying some Victorian baby cradle in need of a coat of paint.'

'What a fabulous idea!' laughed Natalie. 'No, I'll be good. It's plumbing fixtures for the new bathroom I'm after. Something stylish.'

Natalie was pleased with herself when she found a two-hour parking spot in Logan Road, not far from the Gabba cricket ground. She stopped outside an antique shop. She could see that it was a wonderland of delights and temptation, crammed with tasteful and trashy collectables. Not all the pieces were genuine, some were beautifully crafted replicas rather than collectors' gems but after the antiseptic plumbing shops Natalie loved the clutter. She dragged herself away and found the store she was after – Asian Antiques and Art.

In its window a long and lethal-looking Samurai sword rested on a stand against a stark white background. The stylish restraint made the sword look dramatic. Natalie went through the front door with its gilded lettering and into a beautiful room. A faint smell of incense, soft gamelan music, a hint of mustiness, and a huge and ornate Cambodian Buddha head greeted her. The fragile silk kimonos, brass gongs, intricate lacquered and gold-embossed screens and tall Chinese porcelain jars all sent a powerful message of prestige, knowledge and money to any prospective buyer. She realised when glancing at the discreetly displayed prices that the items in this shop were extremely expensive. These were obviously museum-quality pieces.

The proprietor turned to greet Natalie. She wore a business suit with a crisp white shirt, which, in casual Queensland, gave her an instant air of authority and gravitas. Natalie was reassured that here was someone who knew about Asian art and artefacts.

'Adele Simpson? I spoke to you on the phone a few days ago. About looking at a piece I've inherited,' said Natalie.

'Ah, yes, the kammavaca. Please come and take a seat.' She waved her hand towards two black carved lacquer chairs, inset with mother of pearl, which stood in a corner of the display room.

'You have some beautiful pieces,' said Natalie. 'Do they come from all over Asia?'

'Mostly South Asia, though I do have a penchant for Japanese Imari ceramics. Now, let me see what you have.'

'I've been told that palm-leaf manuscripts are pretty common, but this one is a bit different,' said Natalie as she took out the little teak box.

'Hmm, possibly,' murmured Adele.

She was silent as Natalie carefully spread the kammavaca on the round table between them. She studied it slowly and carefully, handling it almost reverently.

Eventually she said, 'This is quality work. And you're right, the cloth does make it unusual. Obviously the cloth was once a monk's robe. So the monks who did this work paid great attention to detail as they were working on sacred cloth.'

'Can you read it? What does it say?' asked Natalie, pleased she seemed to know so much.

'That's beyond my capabilities unfortunately. But I can tell you something about what I assume it says. Traditionally a kammavaca is a collection of extracts in the Pali language from the Vinaya Pitaka, the name given to the monastic code of discipline. As you probably know, they are still very common throughout South Asia, but only in Burma are kammavacas produced as such highly ornate and decorative manuscripts.' She paused and bent closer. 'The artwork is so delicate and detailed. See, some of it is decorative but if you look closely you can see paintings that are quite figurative. This one looks like a monastery. There's a river.'

'Really? I hadn't noticed.' Natalie leaned down and saw the quite distinct outline of a building. It looked ornate. 'What are these curly bits? Is that a spire?'

'I'd say fretwork. If the building was gilded, the artist

would have added the gold leaf as he has on this Buddha image. No, I'd say that the fretwork and the lack of gilt indicates a wooden monastery. Probably teak.'

'How beautiful. Look at the trees bending over the river. Do you think it's a real place?'

'It might be, or it may be just an imagined building,' said Adele cautiously. 'It would seem logical that if a monk was the artist, he would have depicted his own monastery. Do you know anything about the history of this piece?'

Natalie took a photocopy of Andrew Hancock's letter from her handbag. 'This is a letter my great-great-uncle wrote to his sister, my great-grandmother.'

Adele read the letter and solemnly handed it back to Natalie.

'How very interesting.' She turned the kammavaca over, gently refolded it and put it back into its box, finally saying, 'If this was made specifically as a gift for King Thibaw, it gives it some value and interest over and above an ordinary kammavaca, even one as beautifully decorated as this. But I wouldn't like to speculate on its value without further research.'

'Yes. I see. I'm not planning on selling it,' said Natalie. 'But my husband was interested in a valuation for insurance purposes.'

'Yes.' Adele gave a small smile. 'I'm curious as to why this piece was never returned to the princess, as your relative seemed intent on doing?'

'I found the answer to that. It's quite sad. He was killed before he could return it and it was among his possessions, which were forwarded to his sister, my great-grandmother.'

'A fascinating story. I do know of a dealer in London who might be able to help you more than I can. I will put you in contact with him if you like. He's an expert on all

109

things Burmese and he would be interested in your kam-mavaca, especially as I think it is of museum quality. He could give you a reliable valuation.'

'Great, I will email photographs of the kammavaca and get his opinion,' said Natalie. 'Now I've started, I want to go on.'

'I'm sure you'll find him helpful. I know he has con-nections in Burma and he would be intrigued by the colourful provenance of your piece. I'm sorry I can't be of any more help myself.'

'Oh, you've been very helpful. Would you give me the details of the dealer, so that I can contact him?'

'Of course. His name is Peter Michaelson. I'll write out his email address for you.'


Mark linked his arm through Natalie's as they walked out of the doctor's rooms.

'How do you feel after seeing your ultrasound?'

'Strange to think that the funny little peanut we could see in the ultrasound is going to be a person one day. See-ing it makes it feel very real,' she said. 'I wish the kids could understand. I suppose Charlotte will soon enough, but I think Adam's a bit young.'

'I hate being away from you and the kids, especially now. I wish there was another way,' said Mark.

'I know. These conversations go round in circles. All we ever seem to do is talk about the kids and money. Do you know what the other workers at the mine are doing with their money?' asked Natalie.

'Not really, we don't talk about stuff like that. It's not like you and your friends at Jodie's preschool telling each other everything,' Mark said with a smile. 'I don't think they're doing anything very original with the money. They seem to be buying homes, paying off mortgages, planning holidays, moving to flash places on the Gold Coast and one bloke is talking about buying a place in Bali.'

Natalie sighed. She patted her curved belly. 'What Mum said the other day really made me start thinking. I worry about what we're doing to the environment. Do you really think that ripping the heart out of the land for minerals, iron, coal whatever, is a totally good thing?'

'Hey, it's paying our mortgage,' began Mark, and then stopped. 'But you're right. Perhaps we should question things. I'm like everyone else, thinking of my family, my hip pocket first. But, think of what's happening in other countries. I mean, what kind of a life would our children have if we were living in Afghanistan or Burma? I know that our country isn't perfect and there are always ways to do things better but, overall, we're pretty lucky to be living here.'

'I know. Wouldn't it be awful to live in a place like North Korea? And Thi told me some terrible things about living in Burma, but what do we really know about it? In Uncle Andrew's letters, he talked about its people and the beautiful countryside, but life there now seems hard. We do live on a bit of an island, here in Australia, isolated from those sorts of troubles, don't we?' said Natalie thoughtfully.

'And a bloody good thing, too,' said Mark cheerfully. 'Come on, let's have a coffee before we pick the kids up.'

As they walked down the sunny street to a café, Natalie was still trying to identify the disquiet she felt. She put her tendency to be reflective, protective and concerned about the future down to being pregnant. Bringing new life into the world made her consider what sort of place this child would inherit. And, strangely, Mark's mention of life in Burma also had her thinking. She was so wrapped up in her day-to-day existence, worrying about what colour to paint a chair but, even though they had the

111

expenses of the renovations hanging over their heads, she knew her children would never go hungry. What was it like for the mothers of Burma? She'd never thought about such things. And, she was sure, neither had any of their friends. They made sympathetic noises over coffee at the preschool when tragic world events broke through their daily bubble: tsunamis, cyclones, bushfires, floods. They helped with fundraisers and made donations but generally money flowed more readily if the cause was for something closer to home – a new soccer field, equipment for the school or the hospital, books for the library, things that were tangible and part of their lives.

The ongoing impact of events in far-off countries quickly faded from their consciousness. And the actual knowledge of conditions, glimpsed through news bulletins, newspapers or the occasional documentary, shocking as they might be, were sometimes difficult to comprehend. Famines, wars, political upheaval, climate-change disasters, mistreated and threatened animals – they were all part of a depressing parade that elicited momentary sympathy, or even a donation, before Natalie and her friends moved back to focusing on immediate personal issues.

'I know nothing about other countries, really,' she told Mark over their coffee. 'And I haven't really cared enough to find out.'


She continued to mull over new and complex thoughts during the next few days. After Mark had returned to the mine, she rang Thi.

'It is lovely to hear from you again, Natalie. When are you coming back to see us?' said Thi.

'Soon, I hope. Charlotte is pestering me for another pony ride and if you have any more figs I'd love to buy some,' said Natalie.

'Oh, just come out to the house then. You don't have to wait till market day; the kids can help you pick them off the tree. There are still plenty.'

'That's very kind of you.'

'Did you find out anything about your kammavaca?' asked Thi.

'A bit. I went to see a dealer in Brisbane and she's put me in touch with an expert in London.'

'I'll be interested to hear what he tells you. Are you thinking of selling it now?'

'No. I'm just curious. The more I can't find out, the more interested I become!' Natalie said with a laugh.

'Interested just in the history of your little kammavaca, or curious about the place it came from?' asked Thi.

Natalie paused. 'Funny you should say that. It crossed my mind how little I know about Burma. I never dreamed such a place would ever cross my radar. But now I feel I have a personal connection and I'm meeting people who are also connected with Burma. What do you think that means?'

'I could give you a very Buddhist answer!' Thi said laughing. 'Or simply say, life is a series of coincidences. It makes sense that you've rung me today.'

'Why is that?' asked Natalie.

'I'm arranging a get-together of a group, the Friends of Burma. Why don't you come, too?'

'Sounds interesting. What goes on?'

'Lots of things. We have a program of plans to raise awareness in the Australian community about Burma's plight. Most Aussies have no idea what's going on over there because Burma is so closed to the outside world. Apart from occasional small items in the newspaper, hardly anyone in Australia really understands what's happening there and how oppressed everyone is. Our group also tries to help the Burmese people. Now that you know what it's about, come along. Maybe you can help us.'

113

'What could I do?'

'You decide. Talk to our people, listen to their stories.' Thi's voice was enthusiastic. 'Read some of the material we have about Burma. You're already one or two steps ahead of most Australians. You have a relative who lived there! How many of your friends would even know what a Burmese kammavaca is? Then, once you know more, you can tell them about the plight of the Burmese.'

Natalie laughed. 'You're right. I can do that.'

'You must come! You'll meet some lovely people. We meet on the coast, not so far for you to drive. Just come along and meet everyone, hear some of their stories. You can't really understand Burma until you know what has happened to its people,' said Thi.


The meeting was held in a room at the rear of a large house that served as a skin clinic. There was a flat above the clinic, while this back room opened onto a garden and was for private hire. From the notices adorning the walls, it seemed to be generally used for classes for origami and bridge as well as for small community meetings and social groups. A dozen chairs had been drawn up around a table, and other chairs lined a wall. There was a kitchenette to one side. Natalie came in with Charlotte and Adam shyly clutching her hands. Their eyes lit up when they spotted a woman carrying a plate of small cakes.

Thi bustled forward, embraced Natalie and greeted the children. 'Hello, little ones. It's nice to see you again. Would you like a cold drink and a little cake, or a sandwich? A cheese stick?'

Thi gave the children a sandwich each, and introduced Natalie to the other people there. Natalie struggled to remember the unfamiliar names.

She was surprised that the Friends of Burma was such

a small group. From the way Thi had spoken, she had expected there to be more people. Tea and coffee were served straightaway and the meeting was very informal and friendly. There were a couple of older Burmese men who were very charming. The children took to them immediately, especially when they commandeered a plate of food and shared it with Charlotte and Adam. There were no other children, except for a baby being held by a young Burmese woman who explained that her other children were at school.

'It's lovely to have your children here,' Thi said.

'They would normally be at their preschool but everyone there has been sick and I didn't want them to bring home another bug. It's hard dealing with two sick children on your own,' said Natalie. 'And it's worse when you get sick, too.'

'You're on your own? That must be hard.'

'Oh, no, I didn't mean it like that. My husband has a job where he works away from home for weeks at a time.'

'It's difficult when your husband is away a lot,' agreed another woman. 'When you have children, it is a demanding job on your own.'

Natalie looked across the room and saw a familiar face. She realised that it belonged to a woman she had regularly seen walking her dog past their house. She went over and introduced herself.

'I'm Vicki Fletcher,' the blond woman responded. 'So you live in Taylor Street, too? It's trite, but true: it is a small world, and it's great to see a new face in this group.'

'Have you been coming to the Friends of Burma meetings for very long or are you new like me?'

'I've been coming for a couple of years now,' Vicki replied. 'The trouble is, the group doesn't seem to get any bigger. The Burmese are lovely people but they are not very good at selling themselves. What I'd like them to do is broaden their horizons. You wouldn't like to help, would you?'

Before Natalie could commit herself, Vicki greeted another woman entering the room.

'It's wonderful to see you here, Mi Mi!' she exclaimed. 'Natalie, I'd like you to meet Mi Mi Rao,' Vicki added.

Natalie smiled at the attractive Burmese woman who was probably in her early forties. Unlike Thi's unruly greying curls, Mi Mi had smooth jet-black hair pulled back in a tight coil at the nape of her neck. Natalie shook the woman's hand.

'Mi Mi is a doctor. She donates her time to a clinic in Sydney,' said Thi, who came over to join them. 'We have a clinic there to help migrants. It started out assisting the Burmese community in Sydney but as the number of new arrivals and refugees grew, more volunteers were needed to help guide people through the settlement process. The health of the refugees also became an issue, so Mi Mi decided to help out.'

'I fly down every two weeks, just for the day. But there is always more help needed,' said Mi Mi.

'This get-together is to finalise our plans for our information day,' said Thi. 'I agree with Vicki that we need to get the message out there about what's happening in Burma, and that it's been happening for a long time. Mi Mi, tell Natalie your story. Then she will understand what I mean.'

'It's such a long story, Thi. I'm not sure Natalie wants to hear it right now,' began the doctor.

'It's the reason I asked her along!' said Thi forthrightly.

'I'm really interested, Mi Mi. I would like to know more about Burma,' said Natalie. 'When did you come to Australia? Did you come with your family?'

'My family? No.' Mi Mi looked down, her face creased in pain. 'I haven't seen my Burmese family in a very long time. I can't go back to see them. It would be too risky because of my activism. The authorities, the military junta, might detain me and I couldn't take that chance – of being kept in Burma and not being able to see my children.'

'You mean like Aung San Suu Kyi?' asked Natalie, remembering what Thi had told her.

'Yes.'

'How old were you when you came here?'

'I was in my twenties. I'll tell you as briefly as I can how I arrived in your country, although now it is my country, too.'

Thi stood up. 'I'll leave you two for a bit. Have another coffee. I can see Vicki trying to get the committee together to talk about the information day. Don't worry about Charlotte and Adam, Natalie, it looks as though they're enjoying themselves.'

Natalie glanced at her children as they sat with a group of Burmese, and she smiled. 'Who is that man?' she asked Thi, nodding to the man in the group.

'That's Thomas. He's a lovely man who's suffered a lot and also has an amazing story to tell,' replied Thi as she moved away towards the other committee members, who were seated around the table.

'What happened to you, Mi Mi? Why did you leave Burma?' asked Natalie, who now realised that the people in this room had stories and it was important for them to share them with outsiders. So she felt no shyness in asking Mi Mi for hers.

'I left not long after the 1988 uprising. You have heard of it?' Mi Mi started.

Natalie shook her head.

'The uprising was due to one man, General Ne Win. He was the head of the junta that had ruled Burma since 1962, when the army staged a coup. Under him, Burma

117

became isolated from the rest of the world, politically and economically. Ne Win retired in 1981, but still effectively governed the country because Burma is a one-party state and he controlled the party. Then, in 1987, he made a decision that made the poor economy of the country even worse. He was a very superstitious man and he was told that nine was a lucky number, so he had all the denominations of money that weren't divisible by the number nine cancelled. The only notes that he wanted to keep were the forty-five and ninety kyat note. All others had to be destroyed. Because most people held notes of other values, their savings were destroyed. Burma was bankrupted. My parents lost all their money and my mother had to sell her jewellery to survive.'

Natalie looked at Mi Mi in disbelief.

'Have I got this right? General Ne Win destroyed people's savings and bankrupted his country because he believed that nine was a lucky number? That's insane.'

'Then students started to revolt around the University of Rangoon and the whole country grew restless, especially after a student, Phone Maw, was shot. Ordinary people, workers, housewives, people from all levels of society and even the monks began to join in the protests. In August 1988 there was a general strike and thousands marched demanding change. Aung San Suu Kyi addressed the crowds and called for democracy. Suddenly there was general euphoria throughout the country, a belief that things would get better.

'Despite its natural riches everyone in Burma, except the members of the junta, was poor. We had been ruled by a one-party regime that was worse than the Soviet government under Stalin. People had been very downtrodden and afraid to speak out. They'd felt they had to accept that this was how things were done in Burma, and just hope that one day change would come and they would be allowed to speak freely, mix with whomever they wanted, and even openly criticise the government. But the army had no intention of changing anything and during one protest march, they started to shoot the protestors. At least three thousand pro-democracy supporters were killed.'

'That's terrible,' said Natalie. 'How could the army fire on their own people?'

'Who was there to stop them?' Mi Mi asked. 'I was there. I tried to help the injured. Doctors, nurses, even medical students like me, all tried to help those who were wounded. My parents were very concerned for me, but they also wanted to stand against the government. Many people were arrested.'

She looked away and Natalie asked quietly. 'You were arrested, too?'

Mi Mi lowered her voice and spoke in an unemotional tone, as though she had told this story many times before. 'I was detained for several months with no charges brought against me. It was a difficult time, not just for me, but for everyone who was locked up without justification. Men were beaten and psychologically and physically tortured. Women were raped.' She stopped and looked at Natalie, who understood that this had happened to Mi Mi.

'What did you do? What happened?' she asked, not taking her eyes from Mi Mi's unflinching gaze.

'When I was released, I spoke to my family and told them I had to leave Rangoon. They were worried for my safety and understood. My father told me to follow what I believed.' Mi Mi's voice wavered.

'I went to Karen, which is near the Thai border. Students organised pro-democracy demonstrations and public forums about human rights and political systems. The Buddhist monks in the area made sure that our demonstrations remained peaceful. Senior monks even stayed with us at our headquarters, which was in part of a Buddhist temple compound.

'Although I was still not a qualified doctor I helped treat the sick and the wounded. The military began to reassert its authority, but the monks kept us safe until we were able to secretly leave for Thailand. Tens of thousands fled, university students, young people and intellectuals. They took different routes, but eventually they joined the rebel groups in the border area of Thailand and maintained armed opposition to the junta.

'I lived in a Thai village, but I crossed over the border at night to treat the wounded fighters. I met quite a few other students who had come from Rangoon. In fact, several of them are now here, in Australia. We were a dedicated student army but we had come straight from the classroom and had no military training. We had few weapons and, although there was support from outside, we weren't really skilled at warfare.'

'How long did you stay in the border region? Did you ever get the chance to go back and see your parents?' asked Natalie. She glanced over at her children, and thought how terrible it would be not to ever see Charlotte and Adam again. 'I can't imagine living like that.'

'It was tough fighting the military regime in the jungle. They poisoned our wells and our food, and we had a group of ex-soldiers and thugs penetrate our head-quarters. We knew we could not go back to Rangoon without being arrested or, at the very least, making trouble for our families. A few decided to take the risk and return, but the rest of us were resettled in other countries as political refugees, under the UNHCR. I went first to India then back to Thailand, helping as best I could.' She paused. 'We had some unofficial political support and financial help from people who were sympathetic. Some of us were given travel documents and money. With this help I was able to leave Thailand and come to Australia. I later heard that the Burmese army went to the border region and wiped out the villages where the student army had been based. But that student army was an important part of modern Burmese history, and I am very proud to have been in it.'

Natalie was trying to picture herself in a similar position, cut adrift, unable to see her family, unable to live in her country. She simply couldn't conceive the idea. 'How did you manage after you arrived in Australia?'

'At first the Burmese community here helped me. My Burmese medical credentials weren't recognised and I had never been able to finish my course, anyway, so I had to start again and study and pass my exams until I finally qualified as a doctor. I met my husband, whose family came originally from India, and who is also a doctor. We married and had children and now I work part-time in his practice.' She lifted her shoulders. 'I have never been back, and I have never seen any of my Burmese family again.'

Natalie stared at her. 'That's awful. It's so sad. I can't imagine not seeing my mother again. We are very close.'

'My parents made me promise that I would consider my future. They did not think that I would have a bright one if I stayed in Burma. In recent years we've made contact with each other. We've exchanged letters and I've sent them photos of their grandchildren and my husband, and I've got messages to them telling them my phone number. I'd like to send them money, but they are still being watched.

'People are afraid of a knock on the door and being taken away, never to be seen again, and for no reason. My parents are elderly, so I didn't want to distress them by causing them any trouble. They are content that I got out of Burma and they are happy that I've made a new life. But I did get a call one night. I could hardly hear the person on the other end of the line, but I realised that it was my mother. She wanted me to know that she was proud of me and that I had made the right choice. She said that she hoped she'd live long enough to see Burma a free country. She said that everyone supported The Lady but that people were still very afraid of the military and what it could do to those who campaigned for freedom.' Mi Mi smiled gently, but tears shone in the corners of her eyes.

'The Burmese people ask for support in our fight for democracy, because it is so hard for us to have freedom in our country without help.'

Natalie was very moved and glanced outside to the safe, sunny garden where Thi and Thomas were now pushing Charlotte and Adam on the swings. 'There must be lots of stories like yours. But hearing about Burma makes me feel quite helpless. The country is so far away, what can I do? It's not like raising awareness for a temporary crisis, is it? This is ongoing repression and it's so wrong. It makes me realise we are lucky to live in Australia.'

Mi Mi nodded. 'The generals do not allow any interference. There are people working behind the scenes, trying to organise international pressure for change, but it is very, very difficult.' She looked at her coffee, which had gone cold. 'I'm glad you came. You can help Burma by simply talking to your friends. Talk to the others here, too. I'm sorry that I monopolised you.'

'No, you certainly have not. I'm so pleased that you shared your story with me. I hope we see each other again,' said Natalie sincerely.

'I'm sure we will. You will come to the information day? We Burmese living in Australia just wish that our country had the same opportunities for its people as Australia has. All we can do is keep speaking from the heart, hoping that people will understand.' She stood up. 'I'd better go and talk to the other committee people. Bye for now.'

Natalie watched her carry her cup to the small kitchen.

Thi came in and pointed to the garden. 'Thomas has won a couple of hearts out there.'

'I didn't expect him to look after my kids the whole time,' said Natalie. 'It's very kind of him.'

'He loves it. He enjoys the company of your little ones. I do hope you'll be able to help us with our information day. I'll email you the details.'

'Please do that, Thi, but I'd better go now. The children will be ready for lunch. It's been a very emotional morning. Mi Mi's so brave. What a life she's led! I suppose she couldn't be more than ten years older than me,' said Natalie.

'Yes. She's one of many Burmese who have led extraordinary lives. You know, we are thankful and happy to live in Australia but it's hard to enjoy such a privileged life when you know how those back home are suffering. We all try to do our bit. So we'll see you at the information day?'

'What will happen there?'

'We want the rest of the world to understand the courageous fight that the people of Burma are quietly putting up under a cruel regime. We will talk to people and hand out brochures. We are trying to show our support for Burma and for The Lady, Aung San Suu Kyi. She will know about our work, and be grateful that we are trying to raise awareness of the plight of her country and its people. She has set an example that we all should follow.'

'Where are we meeting?'

'The main booth is at Pacific Fair shopping centre but there'll be stands at other places. I'll let you know the final details. Thank you so much for popping in. See you soon.'

The children skipped beside Natalie as she walked back to the car.

'When are we going to see Uncle Thomas again?' asked Charlotte.

'Soon. Why did you like him so much?' Natalie said smiling.

'He's funny. And he has a smiley face,' declared Charlotte.

'Yes, he has, hasn't he,' said Natalie as she lifted Adam into his car seat. She wondered what Thomas's story might be. All the Burmese people she'd met so far seemed so warm-hearted and yet having met Mi Mi, she was beginning to realise that many had suffered and they lived with the pain that they might never see their families again.


Natalie dragged the wet hand towel off her forehead and groaned as she slid her legs off the bed and onto the floor. She'd heard a crash followed by a despairing wail from Charlotte and a frustrated scream from Adam. She propelled herself from where she had been resting, and she staggered into the living room.

'What's going on here? You're supposed to be playing in your room, Charlotte. Adam, you were having a nap. What's all this?' Natalie surveyed the crayons, paint box, paper and spilled water.

'He's spoiled my painting!' cried Charlotte in dismay as she tried to grab her painting away from Adam's destructive grip.

'Meee,' wailed Adam and lunged for the paintbrush.

'Stop that,' said Natalie firmly. 'Mummy isn't well. You promised me you'd both be good and play quietly.'

'I was good, Mummy. But Adam got up and took my picture for Daddy!'

Natalie wrenched Charlotte's picture from Adam's grasp and admonished him as Charlotte broke into fresh sobs. When peace was finally restored, Natalie poured herself a glass of water and picked up the phone.

'Hi, it's me. Jodie, I'm at my wits' end with these two,' said Natalie. 'It's not their fault. They're bored and I'm feeling sick as a dog. I know it's Saturday and your day off, but could they go to your place and play with your two for an hour or so? If I don't get some sleep, I'm going to fall over. I was up half the night with Adam because he's got a tooth coming through.'

Ten minutes later Natalie opened the door and Jodie bustled in.

'You look awful, Nat. So pale. Have you seen a doctor?'

'No, Jodie, I'm just feeling a bit queasy. I never felt like this when I was pregnant with the other two. I haven't had much sleep, either. The kids are on different schedules now so I don't get that break in the day when they used to nap at the same time. And Adam is becoming so naughty. Teases and torments Charlotte like crazy.'

'You monkey,' said Jodie, as Adam gave her a beatific smile. 'C'mon, grab your things, kids, let's go. We're all going to the aquarium.'

'Yay!' cried Charlotte as Adam looked dubious.

'Can you manage them all?' asked Natalie.

'Nat, I can manage four children. Mum is with us. She'll help. See you in a couple of hours. Have a rest. I'll feed them with my lot, so you don't have to worry. See you later and take it easy, Nat.'

'You're such a good friend, Jodie,' Natalie said sighing. 'I hope I get over this nausea soon.'

'Promise me you'll rest. No fiddling with odd jobs.'

'Believe me, I'm going to crash,' said Natalie as the kids headed for the door with Jodie, who had them outside before Adam realised that Natalie wasn't going with them.

That evening, feeling refreshed after her break, the children in bed, she called Mark.

'They were pooped, Mark, I couldn't keep them up until you'd finished work, but they can't wait to tell you about their visit to the aquarium. Jodie is such a trouper.'

'Are you feeling any better?'

'Yes. But this baby is tiring me out more than my other pregnancies did.'

'You didn't have two toddlers during the other pregnancies,' said Mark logically.

Natalie didn't add that she hadn't had to manage on her own, either.

After saying goodnight to Mark, Natalie sat in what she hoped would be the new nursery and took out her notebook. She sketched where she wanted the new partition and window to be, as well as the play area. She hesitated over the colour scheme of the nursery, wondering if she should wait until she knew the sex of the baby. She and Mark had never asked about the other two, preferring to be surprised, and caring only that they were healthy. Maybe this time it would be nice to know in advance so that she could prepare the nursery accordingly.

She and Mark would definitely have to sit down and work out a schedule for the renovations on his next trip home. She was adjusting to the idea of a new baby and, despite the initial morning sickness, she was feeling warm and fuzzy about its impending arrival. They had to finish the nursery before it came and the extra expense of fixing the bathroom concerned her.

Natalie decided to ask their friend Geoff to draw up the plans as soon as possible. That would be one positive step. Why wait? she thought. She knew exactly what she wanted. They'd have to figure out if they could do the work in stages or all at once.

Feeling slighter better, Natalie headed to bed. She was getting used to having the bed all to herself, she had to admit. Spreading across it on a comfortable diagonal, listening to the radio, reading, falling asleep sometimes with the light and music on – these treats were not available to her when Mark was home.

The following evening after the kids went to bed, Natalie was tidying the clutter on her desk when her eye fell on the kammavaca box. Why not ask the expert, Peter Michaelson, whom Adele Simpson had recommended? She rescued the piece of paper Adele had given her, spread out a plain dark cloth on the kitchen table, and unrolled the kammavaca. She took a couple of photos and uploaded them to her computer. She composed an accompanying email explaining the story of her great-great-uncle Andrew and how she wished to know more about this piece, and, in passing, what its value might be, stressing that she was not trying to sell it but was simply curious. She sent off the email and packed up the kammavaca and headed off to bed.

# 5

NATALIE WAS CURLED UP on her beautifully renovated arm-chair watching TV and thinking she should do some ironing, but with Mark away it didn't seem so urgent. The phone rang and she was surprised to hear Mark's loving voice.

'I know it's late and I'm sorry I missed saying good-night to the kids, but there was a safety meeting on. I've been speaking to Brad, he's new to the mine and a bit of a mate, and he's dead keen to come back home with me for the week.'

'Oh, Mark, I don't know that we're ready to cope with visitors,' said Natalie. 'The house is so disorganised. The biggest problem is not having the big bathroom working. Your friend would have to share our ensuite!'

'It's not that bad, sweetie. Brad's used to roughing it. Before he came to Queensland he was mining out in the

Pilbara. You should hear what he's told me about work out there!'

'Didn't he like it?'

'He'll tell you. Got fed up with the mining town where he was working even though he was a FIFO. We'll get in about two tomorrow. Don't worry about dinner. We can get takeaway. Brad's pretty easygoing.'

'It'll be good to meet him. But have you told him about the mess our house is in?' asked Natalie.

'He doesn't care. He's never been to Surfers. He just wants me to show him around the Gold Coast. I promise, you'll enjoy his company. What have you been up to? How's that little bub coming along?'

'Fine, I guess. I made a doctor's appointment for this week, so you can come along.'

'That'll be something to look forward to. Everything else okay?'

She could tell that Mark was tired, so she didn't want to go into the details of what the children had been up to. That could wait until he came home.

'Yes, thanks. But god I'm tired. Your children keep me busy! I'm off to bed. The kids are so anxious to see you. They have a pile of things to show you; they're looking forward to you coming home. They miss you heaps when you go. They just get used to having you around and you're gone again. I'm sure Brad will understand how they want to spend time with you,' said Natalie.

'Of course. I miss them, too. But they'll get a kick out of Brad, he's a livewire,' said Mark.

'I'm glad you've got a friend up there and I'm looking forward to meeting him. Sleep tight, darling.'


Brad radiated energy, if somewhat frenetically. He had ginger hair, fair eyebrows and reddish-gold stubble on his sunburnt face. He bounced into the family room to join Natalie and Mark. Charlotte had already shown him to his bedroom and then had invited him to have a look at her dolls' house.

'I've checked out the accommodation for the prince and the fairy,' he laughed. 'My room is great. Really terrific place you got here. Great to be right on the water. Fantastic position. Just look at that view! I love seeing water. You can't believe the dust in the Pilbara. The red dirt is like fine powder and if it ever rains it gets as thick as glue. Stains your gear, too. You never get it out of your clothes. You seen pictures of the joint?'

'The photos Mark showed me had gardens and some nice buildings—' began Natalie but Brad interjected.

'Not that plush watering hole they call a camp where I work now! I was talking about the Pilbara!'

'Oh, right, well yes. I have seen photos of the Pilbara . . . Wasn't there Aboriginal rock art over there that got moved for the mining?'

'Yeah. Though that all happened before I got there. But, look, if you find a picture of a lizard scratched on a boulder when you're driving a bloody big excavator, you're not going to stop and move the thing. You're flat out chewing through what you can in your shift, without stopping all the time for some old art.'

Natalie changed the subject. 'Were you living in a camp out there, too?'

'I started out at the mine site but it was pretty rough, so I moved into a house in town with some other blokes. But the cost of living there was through the roof. The locals might complain about the way their town is changing, so many blokes living there or flying in and out, but they take advantage of the conditions, too. Rents are sky high. A hamburger is double what you'd pay in Broome or Perth. But a lot of the shops are closing down.'

130

'Why is that, if there's all that money sloshing around?' asked Natalie.

'A lot of people move away. People can sell their house for triple or even quadruple what they originally paid. They'll never see gains like that again. Can you blame them? Still, a lot of them moan that mining has trashed their community! You just can't please everyone!'

'Why did you decide to come to Queensland?' asked Natalie.

'You can only take that climate for so long. And I wanted a change. See what things are like this side of the country.' He shrugged. 'Money's just as good and I reckon that the conditions are better, too, at least out where Mark and I are. And I reckon I'd better do something with me money, so I'm thinking of buying a unit in one of the high-rises here. Mark is going to show me around.'

'Tomorrow. If you haven't got anything planned, Nat?' said Mark, coming from the kitchen with two fresh beers.

'I was thinking of a picnic at the beach with the kids. There's that spot with that lovely kids' pool. And you two could surf,' said Natalie quickly.

'Not me, mate! I'm no surfer dude. Don't worry, I'll check out some other things, you hang with the kids,' said Brad cheerfully.

'I'll drop you down at Main Beach and point out where we'll be. You can join us later, if you want,' offered Mark.

'Yeah, that would be great, thanks.'


Mark and Natalie held hands, watching their children run along the water's edge in the dribbling wavelets. Everywhere there seemed to be people, walking, jogging, throwing a ball for a dog or playing in the water.

131

'It's so nice and safe for the kids here. If you don't look behind us, we could be on a tropical island,' said Natalie.

'Except that the swaying coconut palms are highrise apartments,' said Mark.

'I know. And it's a shame they cast long shadows across the beaches in the afternoon but there are so many pretty places like this. I think we're lucky to live here. I love the little park at the end of our street that faces the water. When the tide's out, people let their dogs race around on the sandflats. The big kids sail model boats and even little boys can fish there. We've found all these spots where we can go for picnics. People pay to come here on holidays, and we get to enjoy it every day. Well, I do at least. And you will, too, eventually.'

'Yes. I appreciate it more every time I come home,' said Mark. 'Especially after the boring landscape near work, and the dirt and noise of the mine site. No wonder Brad wants to buy a piece of paradise here.'

'I think it must have been more of a paradise before all this development,' said Natalie. 'Years back, Brisbane people used to come down here by boat for holidays. Jodie was telling me that when her grandfather came here in the thirties there were still sandy bush tracks down to the beach. It all really started to develop in the 1950s. Honeymooners came from everywhere in the sixties and that big Japanese boom in the seventies pushed things along, too.'

'I suppose it's had its ups and downs over the years, like lots of places. When I was first working here, the Barrier Reef islands were a popular holiday spot for international tourists. But Australians still come here for holidays and lots decide that they'd like to live here permanently. It used to be the retirees and now it's people like us. We're very lucky to have the place we have on the canal. Even with the midges,' Mark said laughing.

'They're not that bad! Haven't you heard of insect

repellent? Anyway, we're putting in screens and if you'd cut back some of those overhanging trees there'd be less of a problem, I think,' said Natalie. 'I love our house. It's going to be fabulous when it's all renovated.'

Mark sighed. 'It's a hard one. The bathroom has turned into a big job, it's blown out the budget no end. And the baby's thrown a bit of a spanner in the works re the timetable. Not that you're not welcome, kiddo.' He patted Natalie's growing tummy.

'I talked to Geoff and gave him some of my scribbles,' said Natalie.

'You did! Why didn't you wait till I was home? We need to look at those pretty carefully – together,' he added.

'Mark, we've talked about it. I've told you what I was thinking and you always said it sounded fine.'

'I guess so. But you're right about needing to decide how we do it. Let's see what Geoff comes up with. He's good at his job and he won't charge us an arm and a leg.'

'That's what I'm hoping.'

Mark looked amused. 'Okay, boss. Keep me in the loop. Hiya, Brad.' Mark waved to his friend. 'Did you see anything you fancy buying? We're going over to the Ferry Road Markets for ice-cream. Want to join us?'

As the car stopped outside their house, there was a call from further up the road. Natalie looked up and saw a woman walking her dog. She gave a wave.

'Who's that?' said Mark.

'A neighbour I've just met. Vicki Fletcher.'

'I'll take the kids in if you want to chat. Adam is nearly asleep. Brad, can you give me a hand with all the stuff that needs to come inside?'

'I want to see the puppy,' said Charlotte when she spotted the spaniel straining on its leash, tail wagging.

'Hi Vicki. I knew that once we met, we'd start running into each other,' Natalie said laughing.

'Isn't it the way! I walk past your place every day, and I think I've only seen you once before. I was going to drop a note into your letterbox. About the information day.'

Charlotte bent down to greet the dog, who licked her effusively.

'This is Ipoh. He'll lick you to pieces if you let him. Here, give him a scratch behind his ears.' Vicki bent down and showed Charlotte where to rub the curls behind his droopy ears. 'He loves that.'

'You mean something about the Friends of Burma information day? You said you would email me,' said Natalie.

'Yes. I'm sorry that this is very short notice to ask you, because it's tomorrow, but it's pretty low-key. We want to have a big rally in support of Burmese democracy fairly soon, so tomorrow we want to give people information about what's happening in Burma so they'll understand what the rally is all about, and hopefully join it. We'll have booths around town. I'm on the Pacific Fair stand. Could you come and help hand out leaflets? I'd love you to come, any time. We're there most of the day.'

'Actually, my husband is home at the moment and he'll be happy to look after the kids. I'm sure I can come for a while,' said Natalie.

'You won't miss us. Look for the flags and bunting. I sewed the bunting, so it's pretty big!' Vicki said laughing. 'I'm supposed to be the media liaison person, but I also got stuck with the decorations. You have to be versatile.'

'You seem very active. Being on the committee,' said Natalie.

'Yes.' Vicki looked thoughtful. 'I'm very committed for reasons I'll tell you when we have more time. Ipoh is anxious to get going so I'll see you tomorrow. And thanks. Bye bye, Charlotte.'

'Can we have our own puppy, Mummy?' asked Charlotte as Natalie locked the car.

'One day, but not at the moment. I'm sure that we can go walking with Ipoh sometimes, darling. He seems a very nice dog.' With a partly renovated house, two littlies and another one on the way, this was definitely not the time for another complication Natalie thought.

The next day, as she prepared to go and help at the information booth, Natalie still felt a little tired from the previous night out with Mark and Brad. Mark had suggested that they go for cocktails in Cavill Avenue in the heart of Surfers Paradise and Brad had been captivated by the buzz of the tourist strip. Brad had then insisted on taking them both out for dinner at Main Beach. It was a beautiful evening sitting out under the stars eating fresh crab and prawns, even if Natalie couldn't drink anything other than sparkling water. It hadn't been a particularly late night, as Natalie didn't want to keep the babysitter up, but since they'd been saving for their renovations they hadn't been out for an evening like that for some time. She had enjoyed every minute of it and when they got home couldn't thank Brad enough.

'No worries. It's been my pleasure. After all, you guys are putting me up and showing me around. It's the least I can do.'

'I'll take you to Jupiter's Casino another night,' promised Mark.

'Yes,' said Natalie. 'You two should enjoy that, but you can leave me out. I'm not really into losing what little money we have at the gaming tables.'

'You never know. We might win,' said Brad.

Natalie said nothing, but gave both men a withering look.

'I hope your Friends of Burma won't work you too hard,' said Mark as he walked out to the car with her the next morning. 'Don't stay on your feet too long.'

'No, I won't. I'm only helping for an hour or so.'

By the time she reached the shopping mall, Natalie was wondering if a famine was looming. She could see people milling about in shops under signs advertising specials and sales in order to generate a shopping frenzy. It all seemed a bit incongruous when she was here to tell these carefree shoppers about the deprivation and repression of the Burmese people.

She soon spotted the Friends of Burma stall set up in the open-air central plaza opposite the escalator. The stand was festooned with Burmese flags, placards and posters of Aung San Suu Kyi. Thi, Mi Mi and Vicki were handing out leaflets. There was a petition for people to sign and Thi was chatting animatedly to some bystanders. A banner strung across the top of the canvas stand read: 'Help the People of Burma Achieve Democracy! Free Aung San Suu Kyi.'

Thi waved to her. 'Hello, Natalie! Glad you're here.'

'Hi, Thi. Are a lot of people stopping to sign and take pamphlets?'

'Yes. The Lady's beautiful face makes them go, "Ah, I've heard of her." And that gives us an opportunity to give them a few facts about Burma.'

'Is that enough?' asked Natalie.

'It is never enough, but by getting people interested, we are raising awareness and that's a good step. If enough people ask the Australian government to put pressure on the Burmese military regime to release The Lady from house arrest, along with all other political prisoners who are held in Burmese gaols, the junta will have to listen. Eventually. We also want people to write to the Burmese ambassador in Canberra and lobby him to tell his military government to stop the dreadful human rights abuses that continue in Burma, not just to the Burmese and to the other ethnic groups. You know this also includes the systemic rape of women by the military? They use rape as a weapon of war,' said Thi, shaking her head.

'Natalie, word of what we are doing will filter back to Burma and give moral support to those who suffer silently, to those who are unjustly arrested, and to those whose family members have been killed and tortured by a junta that imposed itself on a country against the will of the people. Our country has been in a state of suspended animation since 1962. The generals raid the country's riches for themselves, but we have never given up hope.'

Natalie struggled to absorb this passionate torrent. 'How will people in Burma know what you are trying to do?' she asked.

'People here in Australia have no idea how fortunate their lives are. People are starving in Burma, making do with very little, afraid to speak aloud, unable to meet openly with friends and discuss what they all hate and fear. But quietly, at night behind closed doors, Burmese people listen to their little radios – the Democratic Voice of Burma that comes from Norway, the BBC and Radio Australia – telling them not only what is happening outside their borders, but also what is going on in other parts of Burma. Brave people also smuggle news in from outside. There are organisations and groups and individuals helping those who have managed to escape and have become refugees.'

A man standing behind Natalie spoke up. 'My father fought in Burma more than sixty years ago. He always said they were good people. I've read about what is happening in that country now and your friend is right. We don't know how damn lucky we are. Where do I sign?'

Natalie stood quietly, handing out pamphlets as people drifted past. The curious paused and were gently drawn into discussions. Natalie listened as well, absorbing the information that her friends were relating and the depth of passion and pain felt by all Burmese.

She had planned to stay only for a short time, as she wanted to get back to Mark and the children and Brad, but she found that listening to Thi, Mi Mi and Vicki talking to the ordinary shoppers was inspiring. Their message was conveyed without hubris, on a very human level. It seemed to touch most of the people who stopped to listen and Natalie was surprised at how many of them signed the petition and took a pamphlet.

Suddenly she began feeling weak, her head began to spin and she reached behind her for a chair.

'Are you all right, Natalie?' asked Thi, looking concerned. 'You look so pale. Mi Mi!' she called as Natalie swayed and then slumped in the chair.

When Natalie opened her eyes, she found she was stretched out in the chair with her legs propped up on another, a sweater rolled up behind her head and Mi Mi staring down at her with a calm, serious face.

'What happened?' Natalie glanced around. 'Did I pass out?'

'You're fine, Natalie. Your blood pressure is probably a bit low. Here, have a sip of water.' Mi Mi handed her a bottle of water. 'Just rest for a few minutes and we'll get you home. Did you drive here?'

Natalie nodded, feeling embarrassed and rather shaky. 'Has Vicki gone? She could have driven me home. But I'll be fine.'

'Vicki had another appointment. You can't drive

home. Thomas is due here any moment so I'll take you. Where's your car?'

'Oh, that's all right. Thank you. I'll be fine in a minute. I can ring Mark.'

'No, Natalie, let Mi Mi take you. She doesn't mind,' said Thi.

'I'm fine. I feel so silly . . .'

'You're pregnant, these things happen,' said Mi Mi, glad to see the colour start to come back into Natalie's cheeks.

'This has never happened to me before.' As soon as Natalie tried to stand up she knew she still felt a bit odd. 'You're right. I can't drive.'

'That's okay, I'll drive you home. Are you up to walking to your car?' asked Mi Mi.

Natalie nodded. 'Yes, it's not too far. I'm sorry about this, Thi.'

Thomas, who had just arrived, came and patted her hand. 'You take care of yourself. We're so glad you came and helped us. Mi Mi will look after you,' he said gently.

Natalie didn't argue. She felt weak still and was glad of Mi Mi's firm hand under her elbow as they walked to the carpark.

At home and settled on her chair, Natalie glanced at her watch. 'Mark and the children must have gone out. He has a friend staying and they're probably down at the park. Would you like a coffee or a tea, Mi Mi?'

'A tea, please. You, too? I'll make it.' She bustled into the kitchen.

Natalie called out to her to tell her where the tea was kept. 'Please excuse the chaos. We're renovating.'

Sipping her tea, Natalie thanked Mi Mi again. 'This has been a bit of a shock. I've never had any problem with my previous pregnancies.'

'It's nothing to worry about, I'm sure. But mention it next time you see your doctor. I understand that your husband is away from home a lot, and you must be very busy with your two small children. Maybe you need to have a bit of time for yourself. Is that possible?'

'You're right. I don't seem to have any time at all to relax. I seem to always be on the go, organising the renovations or doing things myself. Actually, I covered the chair I'm sitting in,' said Natalie proudly.

Mi Mi looked at it. The chair was certainly different. Natalie had used contrasting swatches of fabrics, featuring flowers, stripes and tiny geometric sections to cover the arms, the ends of the arms, the wingback seat cushion, the back and front of the upright and the skirt at the base of the chair. While the patterns were different, because the colours were in the same range, the yellow, pink and green flowers, the stripes and the shapes all blended and married together perfectly making the deep, comfy chair almost a work of art.

'That's really lovely,' said Mi Mi. 'How clever of you.'

'Thank you, Mi Mi, I enjoyed doing it. You should have seen it when I rescued it from my step father's farm! But you are right about my lack of time. When I have the chance to leave the children at preschool, I use the time to shop or pay bills, or for appointments. You know the sort of thing. The last time I had a day to myself, I went to Brisbane to see an antique dealer about my kammavaca and to buy bathroom fittings.'

'You should rest occasionally. There is a place not very far from here where they teach yoga and relaxation exercises that are very useful to pregnant women. I recommend it highly and I think you will find it of great benefit, even if you can only get there for an hour or so each week.'

'Thanks, that sounds great. I haven't done yoga since we moved. You'll have to give me their address and I

140

promise to go, Mi Mi,' said Natalie, looking at her friend earnestly. 'Today was fascinating. I have so much to learn about Burma, but I noticed today, when people heard about what's going on in your country, they tended to be sympathetic, didn't they? I mean, how could they not? It's funny, Burma seems like such a faraway country, a place we'll never see, a place we have no connection with, and yet it's just as close as the places Australians do go, like Thailand and Vietnam.'

'Yes, Australians might feel they have more in common with countries like Britain and the United States, but South East Asia is so close geographically. I think that many Aussies only think of Asia as a stopover destination on the way to somewhere else, or as a cheap holiday to somewhere beautiful where they can get spoilt,' said Mi Mi.

'And the Burmese military government has made it very difficult for people to enter our country, so the tourist trade is very weak. Also, The Lady has made it known that foreign visitors legitimise the junta, so she discourages tourism. So not many people come to Burma.' She paused. 'You said that you have a kammavaca? May I see it? We had one made when my brother went into the monastery. He is still a monk; he enjoys the religious life. As I told you, the monks sheltered us when we were escaping the Burmese army. But I haven't heard from my brother in a long time.'

'My kammavaca is on top of my desk, over there,' said Natalie.

Mi Mi picked up the little box and unrolled the kammavaca, studying it carefully. Eventually she looked at Natalie and smiled. 'This is exquisite. Very unusual. What surprises me is the quality of the artwork. Burmese art tends to the religious and spiritual. It's not known for fine murals and frescoes. These little paintings are quite realistic. I feel that monastery must exist somewhere. Do you know where this came from?'

'There's a bit of a story attached to it,' said Natalie and told Mi Mi the story of her great-great-uncle Andrew, the princess and the unscrupulous art dealer.

Mi Mi listened and when Natalie had finished she looked at the kammavaca again and said, 'What a shame this has passed out of the royal family, but it's fortunate that it has been kept so carefully by your family.' She fingered the old manuscript carefully, looking at the beautiful work that had gone into making it. 'I think the script is most likely prayers.' She folded it back up and returned it to its teak box. 'Have you ever thought of contacting the royal family?'

Natalie raised her eyebrows. 'I thought they were all dead. Didn't most of them die in exile in India?'

Mi Mi shook her head. 'No, not at all. King Thibaw had children and grandchildren. The royal family was an extended one because King Thibaw had different consorts and their children had children. So there are many descendants. I actually know one of his granddaughters. She's quite a remarkable woman.'

As Mi Mi walked over to the desk to return the teak box to its place there was a clamour at the door. Mark called out as Charlotte and Adam dashed in, jumping on Natalie.

'Hi, darling, Brad's just coming. We've been out entertaining the children. Are you okay?'

'Actually, I'm feeling a bit fragile. I had a bit of a turn while I was handing out pamphlets for the Friends of Burma. Mark, this is Mi Mi, the friend I was telling you about. She drove me home in our car as I wasn't up to driving,' said Natalie. 'I am so lucky she was there.'

'That was kind of you, thanks.' Mark looked carefully at Natalie. 'You still look a little peaky, Nat. Were you standing in the sun for hours or something?'

'No, there was shade at the stand at Pacific Fair.

I don't know what came over me. I hope it was a one-off,' sighed Natalie.

'I'm sure it won't happen again,' said Mi Mi.

'Mark, I showed Mi Mi the kammavaca and she told me that she knows a granddaughter of King Thibaw. Isn't that amazing?' said Natalie.

'No kidding. But didn't the king die years ago?'

'Yes,' replied Mi Mi. 'In 1916, so his granddaughter is quite old, but she still, as you Australians say, has all her marbles. I'd better get back there and help them pack up. I'll ring for a taxi now.'

'Don't worry about that. I'll drive you back to Pac Fair,' said Mark as Brad joined them. 'Mi Mi, this is Brad, a friend from work. I'm driving Mi Mi back to Pacific Fair. Want to come for the ride? Right to go, Mi Mi?'

'Yes, take it easy, Natalie. And thanks for your help today,' said Mi Mi.

'I enjoyed myself. Thank you for looking after me and suggesting those classes.'


Natalie sat upright and stretched. It was wonderful having Mark home for a few days. After an hour sitting at the sewing machine running up curtains for the nursery, her back was aching. Natalie stood up and stretched, patting her ever-expanding belly. She made herself a cup of tea and checked her emails and was pleased to see a reply from the antique dealer in London.

*Dear Mrs Cutler*
*Thank you for your enquiry. Your kammavaca is indeed interesting and appears to be of exceptional quality. As you are probably aware these sorts of manuscripts are still being made today on palm leaf. Taking your provenance at face value and without seeing the object myself, the best*

*valuation would be between £800 and £1000, depending*
*on its condition. My gallery is prepared to make such an*
*offer to you.*
   *I look forward to hearing from you.*
*Sincerely*
*P. Michaelson*

That's good to know, thought Natalie, but sorry, Mr Michaelson, I'm not in the selling market. What I really wanted you to do was to give me more information about my kammavaca, but you didn't shed much light on it at all. Natalie glanced at the teak box on her desk. A thousand pounds would be handy, but I'd rather keep you.


That evening after she'd changed into fresh, comfortable clothes and glanced at herself in the mirror, Natalie went into the living room and said to Mark, 'This huge T-shirt and leggings don't do a lot for me. I look like a whale and some days I feel like one, too.'

   Mark looked at her fondly. 'You look pretty good to me. Don't worry about the kids. Brad and I will find something to do with them when they wake up. You relax and enjoy yourself. I just hope you'll be able to get yourself up off the floor.'

   'If I can't, I'll just have to stay there all night! Be a nice rest, away from this madhouse,' Natalie replied with a laugh.

   Natalie parked the car and went into the building where the yoga classes were held. The minute she stepped inside she saw that this centre wasn't just a studio space for classes but an oasis of Buddhist calm. There was a meditation room, a classroom, and a massage and healing room. A sign pointed upstairs to the yoga classes. Even though the centre appeared busy, no particular activity dominated. At the reception desk, where she signed in, there were flowers floating in a bowl of water. A book of the sayings of the Buddha was opened to a page which read: 'Do not dwell in the past, do not dream of the future, concentrate the mind on the present moment.'

Natalie smiled at the girl behind the desk as she paid her money. 'That's good advice.'

The girl nodded. 'Yes, live in the moment. Welcome, Natalie, your class starts upstairs in ten minutes. Take a few moments to catch your breath if you like. You can make lemongrass tea in the kitchen. Please help yourself.'

Natalie declined the tea and went slowly up the stairs, looking at the prints of colourful mandalas and tapestries illustrating stories about Buddha's life. Somewhere else in the building she could hear the sound of wind chimes and the low murmur of voices chanting in a singsong rhythm.

She loved the class. Focusing her mind totally on what she was doing with her breathing and her body, and with no other thoughts in her head, she found the exercises were refreshing and relaxing. Her class was a mixed group of men and women of varying ages, and the instructor advised her on gentle exercises suitable for pregnant women.

Afterwards, she found the kitchen and helped herself to a cup of delicate, fragrant lemongrass tea. A tall thin man, possibly in his forties, smiled at her as he also helped himself to tea, adding honey to it.

'You're new, aren't you? Although I can see you've done yoga before. Have you just moved into the area?'

'We haven't been on the Gold Coast very long. I moved here with my husband and children a few months ago. I haven't been to yoga since my last child was born. I should have been before, but I just don't seem to have the time. It feels great to do it again – it certainly makes me feel very relaxed,' said Natalie.

'Yes.' He smiled. 'Yoga is good for the mind as well as

145

the body. I guess you don't get a lot of time to yourself if you have children. How many have you got?'

'Two. With three I'm not sure when I'll have time for this luxury.'

'Enjoy it while you can,' he answered philosophically. 'I'm Moss.' He held out his hand.

'Natalie.' She noticed his ponytail, baggy pants and loose shirt and wondered whether Moss was his first name or surname. Instead she asked, 'Do you come every week?'

'I try to, but sometimes I have to teach the odd evening class. I'm a teacher.'

'I'm a teacher, too. Primary school. What do you teach?' asked Natalie.

'I'm an art historian – I teach mainly South East Asian Buddhist art, with a bit of religion and philosophy thrown in.'

'Really?' exclaimed Natalie.

'It's not as esoteric as it sounds. It may surprise you but there's a lot of interest in Buddhist studies in Australia these days. People want to know more about Buddhism.'

'It does sound like a fascinating religion,' replied Natalie.

'Strictly speaking, Buddhism is not a religion,' said Moss. 'It's really a moral code. Buddha was born into a royal family, but he left it and began to develop philosophies that would help people deal with life. He thought that because everyone suffers, the way to avoid suffering was to develop a higher consciousness. This can be done through a combination of meditation and by practising this better moral code.'

'That's a big aspiration. Does that do away with suffering?' asked Natalie.

'Eventually. After many rebirths and stages of spiritual development, enlightenment can finally be reached. This is called nirvana.'

'Is that what nirvana means? I thought it was like karma?'

'Karma is central to the idea of rebirth because each time you are reborn, it is the result of a previous action in your former life, for good or ill.'

'What goes around, comes around?'

'I suppose so,' said Moss, with a smile. 'Do you find these ideas strange?'

'No, not really. They're just different, that's all. I've not taken a lot of interest in Asian ideas before, but it's interesting that you said you taught Asian art. I've never had anything to do with Asian art, but not long ago I inherited an artefact from Burma and I've been trying to find out as much as I can about it. And then by chance I meet you, a teacher on the subject!'

Moss shrugged. 'That's how the universe works some-times. When you become interested in something, everything points in that direction. What sort of artefact have you got? Perhaps I can explain the significance of your piece.'

'That's exactly what I'd like to know!' said Natalie. 'It's a little kammavaca.'

'Palm-leaf manuscripts, fascinating things. Is it a recent one, or old?'

'Quite old, nineteenth century. I mean, not like eleventh century or anything really old. It was made for King Thibaw.'

'Really. How do you know that? Thibaw, the last king of Burma, it's such a sad story. I suppose you know all about that.'

'Yes,' replied Natalie. 'I have been doing some research. This kammavaca belonged to my great-great-uncle. It's not made from palm leaf, it's made from cloth.'

'Very intriguing. I'd love to see it.'

'Are you on email? I could send you photos,' said Natalie.

'I'd rather see the real thing. How did your great-great-uncle acquire it?'

Natalie was pleased at his enthusiasm. 'Do you have time for another cup of tea?'

They sat in a small lounge room and Natalie told Moss the story of Uncle Andrew, the princess, the unscrupulous dealer Ian Ferguson and the little kammavaca. 'I've had two antique dealers who specialise in Asian art look at it. I'm told the writing on it is probably religious texts.'

Moss nodded. 'Pali sutras. Pali is the language of Buddha's time. But the fact it's on cloth, and very likely from a venerated monk's robe, gives it special meaning. If it was made for the king, who chose to take it with him into exile, it means that he too must have thought that it had considerable significance,' said Moss thoughtfully.

'I hadn't considered that,' said Natalie slowly. 'No wonder his half sister didn't want to give it up.'

'What do you plan to do with it?'

'Keep it, now that I'm starting to piece together bits of the story. I wish I'd known Uncle Andrew. I think he must have been quite remarkable,' said Natalie.

'Yes, indeed. I've never heard of that Ferguson. If you like, I could do some research? See what I can find out. But with its provenance, maybe a museum would be glad to have it, should you want to gift it,' suggested Moss. 'And collectors of these things would probably pay quite well for it.'

'Oh, no. I don't want to sell it – even though a dealer in London did offer me a thousand pounds or so,' said Natalie.

Moss raised an eyebrow. 'Did he? But please, if you do consider selling it, get second and third opinions.' He glanced at his watch. 'I have to go. If you'd like to learn more about how those manuscripts are made, I can explain it to you. Some of them are very old, and many of them are hidden away in monasteries and caves. Some of the old ones were taken back to Europe as curios, and are tucked away in museums or in people's homes, quite forgotten.'

'That's so true. My kammavaca was stored away for eighty-odd years and nearly ended up in a clearing sale. But now I have something physical, something tangible, that makes the past come to life. I hold that little kammavaca and I know my great-great-uncle held it too,' said Natalie, starting to formulate thoughts that hadn't occurred to her before.

'Indeed. And do you also think of the monks who created it and the king it was made for?' posed Moss.

She paused before she answered the question. 'I guess they'd be disappointed that it ended up so far from home. But at least it's safe with me and appreciated. Are there any good books you could recommend to me to learn more about Buddhist art?' she added.

'There are plenty. How about you give me your email address and I'll send you some titles?'

'Yes. Thank you so much, Moss. I hope I see you again next week.'


'How was yoga, Nat?' Mark asked.

'Wonderful. So relaxing and the exercises did me a lot of good, I can feel it. The place that Mi Mi sent me to was brilliant. It has a strong Buddhist influence and it seems very popular. My class was quite large. I met a really interesting university lecturer who teaches Buddhist art.'

'Is he a hippy or a nerd? You seem to be falling over the weirdest people.'

'I know!' Natalie said laughing. 'Same as when I'm pregnant, all I seem to see are other pregnant women. Now, since I've become interested in my kammavaca and

Burma, I'm meeting people who know about both these things. It's how the universe operates, Moss says.'

'Moss? His name is Moss? His parents have got to be flower people. Does he have a brother called Rolling Stone? Or a sister called River or Flower?' Mark joked. 'Is he from the Northern Rivers?'

'Stop it, Mark. He's really nice. I wish I'd had more teachers like him instead of ones with droning voices who put you to sleep.'

'So what's the bottom line, about the kammavaca?'

'He said he'd recommend some books so I can learn more about these things,' said Natalie.

'Hi, guys.' Brad wandered into the family room with both children clinging to his legs.

'Look at us,' chirped Charlotte. 'Uncle Brad walked us right up the street with us on his legs. Everyone was looking.'

'I'm not surprised,' muttered Mark. 'It's Uncle Brad now, is it, mate?'

'Can't help it. Your kids are just great. I reckon we should all go somewhere like Sea World or Dreamworld before we have to go back to work.'

Natalie smiled. 'It's great having access to someone else's children, isn't it? Gives you the perfect excuse to go to those places that you wouldn't like to go by yourself.'

'Absolutely. How was yoga?'

'Wonderful, thanks. I was just telling Mark about a man I met there who knows about kammavacas.'

'Was that the thing I heard you talking about to that Burmese doctor?'

'Yep. It's some weird little knick-knack that Nat's family inherited.' Mark opened up the box that the kammavaca was kept in and lifted it out.

'Be gentle, it's old and delicate,' said Natalie. 'And it's quite valuable. I got an offer of a thousand pounds from an expert in England.'

'Hey, darling, you didn't tell me that. That's a big surprise.'

'What is it?' said Brad as he carefully took the kammavaca from Mark. 'I mean, it's cool, but what's it for? What's it do?' He laughed at his own ignorance.

'It's a religious artefact from Burma,' said Mark.

'From where? Just kidding, I have heard of it,' joked Brad. 'How'd you get it?'

'It belonged to Nat's great-great-uncle. It's unusual because it used to belong to the king. And now she's been offered a thousand pounds for it.'

'Wow. You going to take the money, Nat?'

'Brad, I don't want to sell it,' said Natalie firmly. 'Anyway, Moss said that I should get more than one valuation, a second or third opinion.'

'How are you going to do that? You've already asked that expert in Brissie and she didn't tell you that much.'

'Listen, guys, get into the twenty-first century. What you should do is go on the net and put it up for sale and see if you flush out someone who knows its real worth and makes you an offer you can't refuse,' said Brad.

'I'm not doing that!' said Natalie.

'That's a great idea, Brad. What have you got to lose, Nat?'

'Let me do it for you. I've put things on sale on the net before, a couple of my fishing rods. It's easy. Put up some photos of it and let's see what comes back,' said Brad.

'All right, then,' conceded Natalie. 'Just to get a second opinion.'


Mark stretched out on the sand, dozing in the sun as he dried off after his swim. The children were busy with buckets and spades, helping Brad build a sandcastle. Natalie was reading a book when she stopped, pressed her hand to her belly and reached for Mark with the other.

'It's kicking! Feel the baby! Quick!'

Sleepily, Mark rested his hand on her belly beside her hand and grinned. 'A little flutter. Like a butterfly. Only three months to go, hey Nat.'

'It felt more like a footballer to me. I'm so relieved,' said Natalie. 'It's wonderful to feel the baby moving strongly. I'm so glad you were here.'

Natalie lay back down, feeling contented. While she had Mark's attention and the children were happily occupied, she decided to explain what she'd been thinking. 'Darling, I know that you want to wait until we have enough money saved to start all the major renovations but I can't stand leaving the bathroom till then. It's really hard trying to shower both the kids in our ensuite. And this week Brad's had to use it as well. It's made me realise that we need to fix the bathroom sooner rather than later. What do you think?'

'I suppose so. We'll want to get it done before the baby arrives. I wanted to be there to help, but if you feel okay to go ahead on your own, go for it. But we need to know exactly what it's going to cost.'

Back at home, Mark read Charlotte and Adam their bedtime stories and put them to bed while Brad helped Natalie tidy up before he put his feet on the coffee table and, with a beer in his hand, began to watch television. Mark reappeared, sat down beside Brad and topped up his glass before reaching for the remote.

'There's a footy game on. Want to watch it?'

'I guess I'll go to bed and leave you guys to it,' said Natalie.

'You sure you don't want to watch the Broncos?' said Mark.

'No, but you two enjoy it. Good luck tomorrow with the apartment hunting, Brad.'

'Righto, thanks, Natalie. How'd you go with the online sale?'

'No idea! I forgot to look.'

'Have a look, could be bids coming in,' said Brad cheerfully.

Natalie sat at the desk and logged on to her computer. She was surprised to find that there were several bids for her kammavaca.

She skimmed through the first few then read the next with interest. 'Listen to this. There's a man in Connecticut in the US who's prepared to pay three thousand dollars!'

'What! I know you don't want to sell it but maybe you should consider it. That's more than that guy in England. Think he's legit?' exclaimed Mark.

'No, no, hang on, you two, play the game. You gotta be cagey, that's only his first bid. It could mean anything. Maybe he owns a museum or something,' said Brad.

'You do it, if you like. I'm too tired to wait around for someone on the other side of the world to bid again,' said Natalie. 'But I told you it's not for sale! I just want to see what it's worth.'

Natalie went to bed and left Brad at the computer with Mark leaning over his shoulder.

The children were well into their breakfast when Mark emerged from the shower and Brad wandered in from his bedroom the next morning.

'I smell coffee! I need my caffeine fix before I can function. Morning, all,' he called as he looked for a cup.

'Morning, Brad. Hope you slept well,' said Natalie.

'Crashed. Sun, the beach and a few beers will do that.' Brad poured his coffee and reached for the sugar. 'How did the bidding end up? Have you checked this morning?' he asked.

'Not yet. What did you do after I went to bed?'

'Oh, we posted a few comments. You know, just giving more info about your thingamajig. Drumming up some interest.' Brad grinned.

Natalie raced to her computer. 'I hope you guys haven't messed this up. What did you say about it?'

'Just that it belonged to the king of Burma, the stuff Uncle Andrew talked about,' said Mark.

Natalie shook her head in exasperation. But then she looked at the bids. She stopped and rechecked them and turned to Mark. 'Come and look at this!'

Mark let out a low whistle. 'Wow! Five thousand two hundred! When we left it, the top price was three thousand three hundred.'

'And it ain't over yet!' Brad said with a laugh.

'There's no point going on with this,' said Natalie, turning off the computer. 'It's not for sale.'

'C'mon, Nat. What if it gets above ten grand? That's a fair slice of the bathroom,' said Mark.

'Don't be silly. It won't reach anything like that. Come on, kids. Let's get cleaned up.' Charlotte and Adam followed her out of the room.

She didn't want to sell her kammavaca, but the offers really surprised her. It was very special to her and now it seemed other people thought it was special, too. But no-one else had a link to it as she did through Uncle Andrew. One day she would tell her children the story of their long-ago relative and the little kammavaca. She wanted them to be able to see what it was and also enjoy the illustrations as she did. She'd studied them so often they were now very familiar to her. She even had a favourite.

It was a picture of a misty jungle with a tiny temple sitting on a distant mountain peak. In a clearing in the foreground stood a small white elephant decorated with a jewelled headdress. A richly embroidered cloth hung across its back. The jewels and beading in the tiny painting must have been done with a brush of only a single strand. When Natalie recalled the image in her mind it was as if she was really standing there in the steamy sunrise in a faraway place.

# 6

THEY SEEMED TO BE everywhere, swarming like ants or bees, wherever Natalie turned. Tony, Mark's friend, a builder, had pulled in tradesmen to assess and check out the whole house for the eventual renovations. They started looking at the internal structure of the frame-work and joists, rattling around in the ceiling. Natalie felt as though she were transparent. No-one spoke to her except Tony, who listened patiently to her, nodded and then talked about what he thought needed to be done. It seemed to Natalie that her careful plans and ideas were being ignored.

The tradies certainly made their presence felt. They all had their radios going at full throttle, even after she asked them to turn them off while the children were hav-ing a nap. They camped around the pool for their breaks, pulling up her garden chairs to sit in while they ate from their cooler boxes, although one bloke asked if she'd mind heating up his lunch in her microwave. They talked loudly about football and generally intruded on her personal space.

Before they started on the bathroom Tony explained that in order to replace all the pipes, the cement floor would have to be ripped up.

'How will you do that?'

'With a jackhammer,' replied Tony. 'It will be pretty noisy. Might want to cover your things with sheets. Everything will get dusty. Jackhammering's a messy business.'

Natalie covered everything she could and tried not to think of the huge clean-up she would have to do later. Not being able to stand things any longer, she headed out for a solitary walk since Charlotte and Adam were at preschool.

Near the end of her street she was hailed by Vicki who was walking Ipoh up from the tidal sandspit.

'Got time for a coffee? I've just let Ipoh have a run. He loves the shallows. Chases all the tiddlers.'

'I'd love one. I had to get out of the house. The tradies are making me demented. They're about to start jackhammering the cement in the bathroom floor,' said Natalie.

'You've started renovating?' said Vicki as she opened her front gate and let the spaniel off his leash.

'Only the main bathroom, but we have major plans. The builder seems to think he'll be starting on it all pretty soon but, actually, we think that the budget mightn't stretch to the dream house being completed for quite a bit.'

'Get the essentials done,' advised Vicki. 'The rest can wait. How's your husband doing? I saw he had a pal with him last visit.'

'Mark's fine. Yes, Brad works with him at the mine.'

'This mining thing is paying mad money. Come on in.'

Natalie glanced around at the well-worn, but comfortable, sun-faded decor of Vicki's house. Ipoh obviously ruled the roost, settling onto an armchair, though by the look of the doggy-worn throw rugs and cushions on the sofas, anywhere he chose was his place. Vicki set mugs, a coffee pot and milk onto the kitchen bench, inviting Natalie to pull out the stool on the other side.

'Where're your kids?' asked Vicki.

'At preschool. They really enjoy it so I feel happy about them going there, especially with all the tradies at home. I'll have to book them in more often now. I can't have them around the house all the time, especially with the jackhammering. That'll be another expense, I'm afraid.'

'You have no family close by who can help?'

'No. Mum lives in Lismore. She owns a dress shop there, and she works six days a week.'

'That's a bit of a drive just to drop the kids off, I guess. What is it? About two hours? Listen, never feel guilty about saving your sanity. I don't have kids. Never wanted them, but that doesn't mean that I don't like other people's. And not having children certainly made divorcing simpler.'

'Oh, I suppose,' said Natalie, somewhat surprised by Vicki's forthright views. 'Have you been divorced a long time?'

'Years now. My husband was a manager at a tin mine in Malaysia, near Ipoh, before tin prices went into free-fall. It was a nice lifestyle. Free house, servants; social life was a bit cliquey but that's expat living for you.'

'Sounds exotic,' said Natalie. 'Did you get divorced while you were living over there? I don't mean to pry,' she added quickly.

'I don't have any secrets,' said Vicki, laughing. 'Though I was the last to know, probably because I was young and naive, my husband, who was fast becoming an alcoholic, was having it off with the wife of a local bigwig. She was a very ambitious woman who felt she'd moved up a notch or three in that little social world.'

'Oh,' said Natalie, 'So you came back to Australia?'

Vicki smiled at her as she poured the coffee. 'Not before I had a jolly good fling with a terribly nice man. What started out as revenge became a very pleasant interlude.'

'You didn't stay with him?' Natalie was a little taken aback.

'Matt wasn't the settling-down type. He was a Canadian backpacker, a bit younger than me, but we certainly had fun together. After my marriage ended I decided to travel around Asia a bit before I came home, and to make my money last longer, I roughed it. You know, public buses, slow boats and cheap hotels.'

Natalie nodded. She didn't want to sound ignorant by telling Vicki that she'd never been out of Australia.

'Anyway, I met Matt in a dinky hotel in K.L. and we just clicked, so we ended up travelling together. The travel was pretty rugged at times but I felt safe and I loved doing as I pleased. And the backblocks of South East Asia were still pretty much undiscovered, so we explored them. It was all so different and so cheap, and quite exciting at times. That's when I first went to Burma.'

'Wow! What was it like?' asked Natalie.

'Absolutely amazing. Pagodas and stupas everywhere, gold glistening in the sunlight, scenery that's just breathtakingly lovely, but it was the people that struck me the most. They were so poor. We thought that we were living on a shoestring but compared to them we were millionaires. And the fear that filled that country. It was awful. We had flown into Burma quite legally, but we were watched by the military all the time. People we met were very nervous talking to us. In the end we didn't like to ask anything but the most basic of questions because we were worried that they would get into trouble with the authorities just by being seen speaking to us. Just the same, there were some Burmese who wanted to practise their English on us and they would talk to us on buses or on those ancient trains when no-one else was watching. They would tell us how oppressive the military regime was and how they hoped that the day would come when there would be changes for the better. They asked us to tell people outside Burma what it was like.'

'Is that why you became interested in the politics of Burma?'

'Yes. I love the people and I know that by myself I can't do much to change things but if enough people are interested and work towards change, who knows? Anyway, speaking of all this, are you coming to the next meeting?'

'To organise the rally?'

'Yes. We're getting close and I think it needs a bit of a poke along with the nitty-gritty details. The philosophical and political content is there but always the practical things get forgotten. We need more participants. Not much point in having a rally if no-one comes. Got to give the press something to write about so that Australians will sit up and take notice. We're doing something for Aung San Suu Kyi. For her birthday.'

'That sounds like a good idea. I'm finding Burma a bit like an exotic jigsaw. As I learn something, another little piece of the puzzle helps to fill in a bigger picture. But I'm very happy to help. Gives me an excuse to get away from the house,' said Natalie.

Vicki topped up their coffee mugs. 'You'll find that the more you do learn, the more the country draws you in. Myanmar, as Burma's now called, has a tremendously ancient history, but it's generally ignored in favour of what happened in colonial times and in the Second World War.'

'I must say I was shocked to learn about the British role in Burma,' said Natalie. 'I always thought of the English as upstandingly correct. And yet I read how they annexed Burma as a present to Queen Victoria so that Burma became part of the British Indian Empire. I found that pretty disgusting. I've been doing a lot of research,' she explained.

'Yes. The British invaders were different from the others, like the Chinese and Siamese. They came, took their loot and went home. But the British, well, they were foreign not only in their looks, culture and heritage, but they wanted to stay and impose their ways onto a country anchored in thousands of years of its own beliefs and systems of government.'

Natalie stared at this woman in her bright Bermuda shorts, halterneck top, scarlet nails and startling coloured hair. Vicki looked like a person who spent her time trawling the shops in the recycled air of the air-conditioned malls, not someone who was impassioned about another country and worked to improve conditions there.

Vicki gave a small smile as if she'd read Natalie's thoughts. 'Yes, I'm hooked on Burma. I'm even doing a degree in Burmese studies so I can bore you at great length about the Pagan, Ava and Pegu dynasties.'

Natalie laughed. 'You are full of surprises. I feel so out of touch with all kinds of things, even local current affairs. My life is absorbed with the house, the kids . . . I just collapse at night after I've put them to bed. I talk to Mark on the phone every night, but his world seems to have shrunk, too. The mine dominates his every waking minute. When he comes home he just wants to chill out, play with the kids, not that I blame him because he works very hard. If I get a movie, he falls asleep in front of it.'

'Life goes in stages, Natalie. You're in the raising-the-kids phase. And I've seen enough to know that it's all consuming.' Vicki took a large sip of her coffee. 'I imagine that husband, family, daily life can swamp you. Just make sure you think about yourself. Occasionally you should think about who you were at sixteen. What were your dreams and ambitions then? Like most of us, probably pretty unrealistic!' Vicki said with a laugh. 'But it's useful to remember that once you were someone with perhaps a different dream. I never imagined where my life would take me.'

'To Burma, you mean?' asked Natalie. 'Do you ever go back?'

'Yes, when I get the chance or actually the money. Burma's not as cheap as other places in Asia because there's no mass-market tourism, but I still like to go, even though Aung San Suu Kyi does not encourage it. The country's still beautiful. I ostensibly go as a tourist and that's pretty safe, although the military watch you. I'm quite sure that they have searched my belongings in my hotel room, from time to time, to see if I'm carrying secret information, or some such thing. The military is paranoid, but that doesn't stop me from trying to help.'

'They search your things! That's outrageous.'

'That's Burma. It's what you have to put up with if you want to see for yourself what is happening in that country.'

'It's like another world,' said Natalie. 'It makes me realise how comfortable we are, and how little we know outside our backyards. It makes me want to help if I can. I mean, I've never felt strongly enough, spoken out, stood up for anything – or thought I could make any kind of difference.'

'Well, it seems to me you've started. By caring enough to want to know about things and come along to the rally,' said Vicki. 'Why don't you bring some friends? That's how it begins.'

'I will. I wonder who will take me up on it. I know everyone is always so busy with kids and their own lives,' Natalie said with a laugh. 'There I go again. But what you said earlier about when you were sixteen . . . It's made me think. I'd love to have some time for me. Though when that's going to happen I can't imagine, with another baby on the way . . .' She looked down at the bulge under her shirt.

'Use your mind, Natalie. Read and talk to people. That's a form of travel, you know.'

'Actually, I have a list of books that someone I met at yoga sent me. Once I've been to the library, I'll try to read at night when I'm by myself. Thanks for the coffee.' Natalie wanted to say more but was unsure what she was trying to thank Vicki for, except that she realised that the other woman had stirred something within her, something vague and ephemeral that she couldn't explain even to herself.

Natalie reached for the phone before little fingers, sticky from playdough, could get to it.

'Hello, Mi Mi. How are you?'

'I'm very well. I thought I'd ring to see how you are feeling.'

'Oh, that's nice of you. I feel fine. I think my fainting was the culmination of things. I have a checkup in a few days.'

'That's good. How is your family?'

'Mark is away, but we've started renovations on our bathroom, which is causing a lot of chaos. I have to watch Adam all the time. He's fascinated by the tradies and their tools and he tries to help them, which is a worry. I'm trying to keep away from the house as much as possible.'

'In that case, will you come to our Friends of Burma meeting? It's the last one before the rally. I do hope we get people to come. It's so important.'

'Yes. Vicki has already been speaking to me about it. I'll be there. I'm going to try and spread the word among my friends. I'm slowly coming to grips with the story of Aung San Suu Kyi. But so many people haven't heard of her.'

'They will. This is what the rally is all about. Telling people about The Lady. Our country has been locked away from the world for many years, and she is our hope to bring the light back into Burma and its people.'

'Well, let's hope she will be released from house arrest some day soon,' said Natalie, though she couldn't imagine how one woman confined to her house could bring about any kind of change at all, let alone democracy and freedom.

'What sort of a house is she in?' she asked Mi Mi suddenly. 'I'm trying to get a picture of what it must be like.'

'The family home where she lives is a big old colonial house, badly in need of repair, with large unkept gardens. It is in an area of grand homes and foreign residences, left over from the colonial days, and has a wonderful view of Lake Inya. She is permitted very few visitors and only has a maid to help her. She is allowed little communication with the outside world, no internet, and her phone is always monitored but ways have been found to keep in touch with her and tell her what is going on. The generals treat her better than many of her followers. The fact that she is confined to her house shows what high respect there still is for her late father and her role in assuming his mantle, although I think that the generals know that they could not dare hurt her without the wrath of the world coming down on them. Others are not so fortunate. People who have shown their support for her have been sentenced to long stays in Insein Prison, which is a horrific place. Many are in solitary confinement,' said Mi Mi.

'I can't imagine what it would be like for Aung San Suu Kyi to spend year after year in such isolation when you know that your country needs you. She must feel so impotent,' said Natalie, trying to visualise the lonely, imprisoned lady by the lake.

'She says her mind is not imprisoned. And she has her faith, she's a very devout Buddhist. Which reminds me, what about your kammavaca? Do you still have it? It is a very beautiful example. Have you done anything more about it?'

'Yes, there have been a few developments. I wrote to a dealer in London, trying to find out more information about it and he has come back with an offer to buy it. Then Mark's friend Brad put it on the net and offers for it have rolled in, which is quite astounding.'

'Perhaps you should get in touch with Aye Aye, the princess I was telling you about. She doesn't think of herself as a princess, but she is a royal descendant. She might know something about it. I've got her address if you'd like to write to her. No email in Burma,' she added. 'And the mail service is pretty irregular. A letter might reach her quickly or it could take three weeks or it could never get there. But perhaps you'd like to try?'

'Absolutely!' said Natalie, suddenly very excited. 'You said her English was good? Or should I have my letter translated into Burmese?'

'No, that's not necessary. Her English is excellent. Aye Aye was born in India after the family were exiled. Aye Aye's grandmother was quite ambitious. She was eighteen when she became the fourth wife of King Thibaw and she was determined that her children should be well educated. Aye Aye's mother thought the same, so Aye Aye was sent to a very good English school in Calcutta. Anyway,

Aye Aye eventually returned to Burma, so I'll give you her address.'

'Just a moment, while I get a pen.'

That evening Natalie thought of what she could write to the princess but in the end she decided to keep the letter brief by explaining how she came by the kammavaca and asking if the princess could tell her anything about it. As an afterthought, she enclosed a copy of Uncle Andrew's letter.

The following weekend, Natalie arranged to meet some of the other mothers from the preschool at a new children's play centre Jodie had told them about. It was a large barn of a place but had easy parking. When they got inside Natalie, as well as the children, were delighted to find they'd entered a captivating toyland.

The centre was built as a miniature township with a long main street with small replica buildings in which the children could play. Some had dress-up clothes, in others there were little cars, trucks and equipment to entertain them. A fire station was complete with helmets, jackets, buckets and non-working hoses. Outside stood a big red, pedal fire truck, with whistles and a bell that the little boys, in particular, liked to use. The girls loved the beauty salon where they could do each other's hair and give make-believe manicures. The cake shop, bakery, and fruit and vegetable shops were all well stocked with plastic produce and equipped with small shopping trolleys. Young, uniformed women walked the streets, keeping the children busy by helping them to operate the toys and encouraging them to share.

Throughout the centre, parents sat chatting around wrought-iron tables set under pretty arbours, next to banks of artificial flowers. Natalie was pleased to see half a dozen of her friends gathered around one of the tables. They greeted her, wanting to hear the latest update on her forthcoming baby. But when they asked what she'd been up to, Natalie surprised them by saying, 'I've been a bit swept up in helping some friends. In fact, I'm glad you're here, I'm wondering if any of you could help out as well.'

'Who, what, when?' asked Jodie. 'Of course we'll help.'

'Is someone in trouble? Sick?' asked Emma.

'You're all so nice. No, it's not quite like that,' Natalie took a deep breath. 'It's about helping a whole lot of people, and celebrating the birthday of a very important woman. I'll try and fill you in as best I can. But if you come along, you'll learn more.'

'Come along where?' asked another mother, cutting to the chase.

Natalie tried to frame her words carefully. 'It's a rally. It's sort of political, but mainly to show support for a woman who can't leave her house, who can't be with her family and who, by her quiet dignity and dedication, has earned the love and respect not just of people in her own country, but of people all around the world.'

'Is this about that woman in Burma that I heard you mention before?' said Holly.

'Aung San Suu Kyi,' said Jodie quietly.

Natalie nodded. 'This birthday party is to recognise that she has been held for another year under house arrest. She has been in and out of house arrest since 1989 so the group I've become involved with, the Friends of Burma, are holding this rally to bring her plight to the attention of Australians.'

'It sounds terrible, but what good is this birthday event going to do?' said Holly. 'Us being there isn't going to make much of an impact in Burma. I mean, I'm always happy to help people, Natalie, but this cause is a bit far from home.'

'I can understand why you'd think that. I didn't know a thing about Burma till I found my uncle's letter,' agreed Natalie. 'But now I've met some Burmese people and I'm hearing the appalling things that have happened to them and their country. The people there are very poor because the country is so isolated economically and the ruling military takes everything. They don't deserve what's happened to them. I really want to help them.'

'The generals who run Burma lead privileged lives, but everyone else lives in poverty,' said Jodie. The other women stared at her.

'Jodie studied Burma at uni,' explained Natalie.

One of the mothers looked at Natalie as she said, 'I don't think I've ever heard of this woman.'

'Oh, I have,' replied Peta, the mother of one of Charlotte's friends. 'I've heard that she's very brave and I've seen pictures of her, too. She's very beautiful, isn't she?'

'So tell us this Burmese woman's story,' said Emma.

Between them, Natalie and Jodie explained how Aung San Suu Kyi had turned her back on her privileged life in England to lead the pro-democracy movement in Burma and how her party had won the 1989 elections but had never been allowed to form government.

'The military rulers of Burma were so frightened by her popularity that they imprisoned her in her own house.'

'How horrible!' exclaimed Emma.

'It gets worse,' said Natalie and explained how Aung San Suu Kyi had had to choose between her country and her dying husband.

There was a moment of silence as the women digested this story.

'Could she speak to her husband on the phone?' asked Holly.

'Yeah, that was allowed but their phone calls were always monitored and they kept getting cut off.'

'You might have seen photos of her standing at her fence in front of her house, talking to crowds,' said Jodie. 'She's always smiling, always calm. Always has fresh flowers in her hair. The stories about her are legion. Some people are born to lead, I guess.'

'Makes our lives seem pretty lacklustre,' said Holly.

'You just wonder about that sacrifice. I think I would have gone to my dying husband,' said Emma. 'Who looked after her sons?'

'They were young adults when their father died, so I suppose they had to look after themselves. Anyway, Aung San Suu Kyi continues to fight for democracy in Burma. Later, when she formed her own political party, she was put under house arrest again, and there she remains,' said Natalie.

'She won the Nobel Peace Prize, but of course she wasn't allowed to collect it. But at least it highlighted her activities to the rest of the world,' added Jodie.

'Will anything ever change?' asked Peta.

'Well, it won't if people do nothing,' said Natalie firmly, surprising herself. 'Pressure from outside governments is one way to go. And apparently word gets back to her and other Burmese that there are people outside Burma supporting them. So, the rally is next Saturday at Sir Bruce Small Park. Tents, food, a birthday cake. There'll be a few speeches, but nothing too heavy,' said Natalie. 'Jodie, can you come?'

'Wouldn't miss it for anything.'

'I'll try to come along. If it's at the park I could bring the kids. Sounds like a good thing to do,' said Emma.


It was a bright Saturday morning, with soft breezes cooling the warmth of the sun. As Natalie pushed her double stroller along the path that weaved across the clipped green lawns, she was relieved to see other people heading in the same direction.

A large marquee, strung with bunting, had been erected in a corner of the park. Inside it was a podium that faced rows of plastic chairs and at the back of the tent were three trestle tables spread with pamphlets, a large book for people to sign petitioning the Burmese ambassador, and a huge birthday card, to be signed and sent to the Security Council of the United Nations. A large poster of a serious Aung San Suu Kyi, her trademark flowers in her hair, was hung below a banner that read: 'Democracy in Burma. Free Aung San Suu Kyi.'

Food stalls were selling Burmese food and handmade crafts to raise funds. This was staffed by women from the Burmese community who served everyone with cheerful banter and a lot of laughter. The day had the air of a picnic rather than a political rally.

Natalie spotted Jodie with her children, and soon saw Emma and Holly together with their children. The friends greeted each other and the children all started playing and chattering. When the PA system crackled to life the adults settled into the plastic chairs while the children sat on the grass beside them.

Thi stepped up to the microphone to welcome everybody on behalf of the Friends of Burma. She then spoke of Aung San Suu Kyi's courage, her resolution, her wisdom, her principles, and her kindness and humour. She hoped that the words from the next two speakers would help to illustrate the reasons the Friends of Burma were staging this rally. She emphasised how important it was to let the people of Burma know they were not alone in their struggles.

Holly leaned towards Natalie and whispered, 'Do you think that Aung San Suu Kyi will really know we're all here for her birthday?'

'Apparently,' said Natalie. 'But I don't think that all the people of Burma are as well informed, though.'

Mi Mi was the next speaker and her passionate speech called for the United Nations Security Council to launch an investigation into Burma's repressive regime and its denial of civil rights for its people. 'The very basic rights we take for granted as Australian citizens are denied to the women and men in Myanmar.' Then she told the audience her story.

The crowd listened quietly, trying to absorb the horrors of life in Burma while they sat in the sunshine and security of the park.

'That's just awful,' Jodie whispered to Natalie.

'I know,' said Natalie. 'Hearing it again makes me see a whole new level of awfulness. I don't know what I'd do if I knew I wouldn't ever see my mother again.'

After Mi Mi, Thomas took his place at the microphone and gave a hesitant smile, obviously nervous. Slowly he began to tell his story.

Like Mi Mi, Thomas had been part of the 1988 student uprising. When the pro-democracy party had been denied the right to form government, he'd used his talents as a writer to tell people what was happening in Burma, both within his country and internationally. Because he was married, he knew that his outspokenness put his family at risk, so he decided to move. Sleeping in a different safe house every night, he headed towards the border and safety in a Thai refugee camp.

But in the city his wife and her family were followed and watched. Her parents' house was searched by the military looking for him, so his wife decided that, to protect her parents, she had to leave them and follow her husband, though she had no clear idea of where he was. Thomas explained that in Burma there was a support network among the ordinary people, students, villagers and monks, which provided a cobweb of shelters for those trying to reach the refugee camps, even though those taking part in the network had little food to share and took great risks just by being involved.

After many weeks, using this network Thomas's wife managed to enter a refugee camp in Thailand. But conditions in the refugee camp were bad. There was little food and the sanitation was very poor. She became very ill and almost died. She was extremely fortunate that a doctor from Médicins Sans Frontières was able to save her life. Messages were carried between the various refugee camps and Thomas heard where she was and they were reunited. Thomas continued to write about conditions in Burma, the military junta and the problems faced by the people in the refugee camps, waiting years for some country to accept them. He started to broadcast through the Free Voice of Burma radio and, as a result, his father was arrested and tortured.

'I was telling the truth about what has happened to my country under the military regime,' said Thomas, his voice now firm and assured. 'The serious abuse of human rights committed by the armed forces, especially in ethnic-minority areas, still continues. It includes rape and torture, arbitrary executions, the indiscriminate use of landmines and the forced labour of millions of Burmese citizens. The regime is involved in a modern-day slave trade, which includes the kidnapping, buying and selling of children to be used as child soldiers.' He paused as Natalie, Holly and Jodie exchanged shocked glances.

'My country was once the rice bowl of Asia. We exported teak, jade and rubies. Now our rich resources, gas and oil, are being exploited so that the generals can become rich while the ordinary people never have enough to eat. There are few paying jobs, no health care and very limited opportunities. They remain impoverished beneath the boots of the fattened junta. We need Aung San Suu Kyi to be free, to help bring about democratic change in Burma! Please, take a leaflet with you. It will explain what action you can take to bring about change. Thank you for supporting us today.'

Thomas received an enthusiastic round of applause.

'I'll take a pamphlet but how are they ever going to boot out the military?' said Emma to Natalie.

'Peaceful persistence,' said Natalie.

There were some brief closing remarks from Thi, thanking everyone for their support, before a large birthday cake with flaring sparklers was pushed to the fore. Natalie could see Vicki trying to organise the media. Photographers from the local newspapers took pictures and a couple of cameramen filmed the cutting-of-the-cake ceremony while the crowd enthusiastically sang 'Happy Birthday'. The singing and sparklers quickly captured the children's attention, and they were soon asking for cake.

'Will this be on the news tonight?' said Emma.

'Could be,' said Natalie. 'My friend Vicki is the media organiser for the group and I saw her with a journalist interviewing Thi and Mi Mi earlier. Burma's problems need all the publicity they can get. Let's help the kids get some cake. Do you want to try some of the food?'

Natalie and her friends gathered up their things and counted heads when Natalie heard her name being called.

'Natalie! I wondered if I'd see you here,' said Moss walking towards her.

'Hi, Moss, nice to see you.'

'Which are your children?' he asked.

'Those two, Charlotte and Adam. Moss, these are my friends Jodie, Emma and Holly. Our children all go to the same preschool.' As Jodie and Moss greeted each other, Natalie added, 'Moss is in my yoga class.'

'What did you think of the rally? Not a bad rollup,' Moss said. 'Must be a few hundred people here.'

'I thought it came together well,' agreed Natalie.

'The speeches were very moving. Quite inspirational,' said Jodie. 'Are you with the Friends of Burma, too?'

Moss smiled. 'I'm a friend of Burma, and a great admirer of Aung San Suu Kyi. Especially how she combines her Buddhist philosophy with a political agenda.'

'Moss teaches Buddhism and Asian art,' explained Natalie to Jodie.

'I thought Buddhism was more pacifist, you know, not involved in politics. I always think of the three wise monkeys – hear no evil, speak no evil, see no evil,' said Jodie.

'Burmese Buddhism doesn't mean being passive, but rather calm patience without fear. It is said that's what has carried Aung San Suu Kyi through her ordeals. She demonstrates that the personal spiritual struggle can't be separated from one's political beliefs and actions,' said Moss.

'Isn't that interesting,' said Natalie. 'Moss, we've promised the kids a piece of cake. Would you join us for a coffee?'

'Yes, do,' said Jodie. 'You coming, Emma, Holly?'

'No, we've got to get back. Thanks, Nat, it's been a great morning. See you guys later,' replied Holly.

The children raced ahead towards the food stall followed by Jodie. Moss took Natalie's bag as she pushed the stroller.

'So do you still keep your finger on the pulse of what is going on in Burma?' said Natalie.

'I try to. I think Aung San Suu Kyi is an inspirational leader for many reasons. Particularly the fact she is a woman, leading by example, in a nation dominated by traditional male monasticism, not to mention a male military junta.'

'That's true,' said Natalie thoughtfully.

They found a table and the children quickly tucked into their slices of birthday cake.

'Let me treat you both to coffee,' said Moss.

'Thanks, that would be nice,' said Jodie.

Moss returned with coffee for the three of them and said to Natalie, 'Did you find any of those books I suggested?'

'Yes, a couple of them, but I haven't had much time. I'll enjoy reading them in bed at night now Mark's away again.' She smiled.

'Good on you for roping in your girlfriends today. Are they on the same path as you?' said Moss.

'What do you mean?' asked Natalie. 'I hadn't considered myself being on any path. Or do you mean my interest in Asian art objects?'

'A little of that. What I like to see is someone's mind expanding, someone being prepared to explore new things. You've become interested in a culture, a place and a people I bet your friends had never thought about till now.'

'Well, that's not entirely true, is it, Jodie? You've been interested in Burma, haven't you?'

'Only because it was in my course at uni. I have to say, you have rekindled my interest, Nat.'

'I guess when I inherited that kammavaca it set me thinking.'

'How did you go with your kammavaca? Find out any more?' asked Moss.

'Actually, my husband's friend put it up on the net and there's been a lot of interest. Not that I'm going to sell it. Mi Mi put me in touch with a descendant of the old king and I've written to her to see what she knows about it.'

'Amazing. I'd love to know what she says when you hear back,' said Moss.

*

175

But as the days went by the letter to Princess Aye Aye was pushed to the back of Natalie's mind. She was utterly drained with the dramas of the bathroom renovations, both of the children were irritable and difficult to manage, and, as she entered her final trimester, her pregnancy was tiring her. So when she opened her letterbox and discovered a blue envelope with an exotic stamp on it, her hand started to shake a little with excitement. She poured herself an orange juice, opened the letter and sat down to read the dainty handwriting.

*Dear Mrs Cutler,*
*Thank you for your letter. It was very kind of you to seek me out and tell me the story of how you came by such an important part of our family history.*

*This particular kammavaca was mentioned frequently among the family. My grandfather was very attached to it. One of my aunts was with the king on that day in Mandalay when the abbot from the monastery presented the kammavaca to him. She told me that the abbot brought the young monk who had painted the beautiful object with him to the ceremony. My mother said that the king kept the kammavaca close to him all his life but on his death it passed to his half sister. This was the person who sold it to the collector. It is good to know that your great-great-uncle kindly retrieved it for her, but so sad that he was killed before he could complete his mission.*

*To now know of the extraordinary journey it has taken and to know that it is safe moves my heart. I would dearly love to see it, since it was considered so precious by the king. But I know that this is not possible so it is good that it resides safely with you. I realise that times have moved on and the story of the kammavaca must seem like ancient history to you but, as I have learned, fate can play a powerful role in one's life. The fate of the*

*king's kammavaca is in your hands. Something tells me
there must be a reason for this.*
*Yours sincerely,*
*Aye Aye*

The signature was an almost indecipherable flourish.
Very slowly Natalie neatly refolded the letter along its
crease marks and sat absorbing what the Princess Aye
Aye had written. Natalie felt conflicted and confused.
She hadn't known what to expect in reply to her letter
but she hadn't expected to be so moved by the fact that
the exiled royal family had held her little kammavaca in
high regard.

And now she owned it by default.

She glanced at the little teak box, which she had
dusted that morning. Then she sat down at the computer
and went to the website where the kammavaca was listed.
The kammavaca was her responsibility and she wanted to
honour that by cancelling the sale.

But when she saw the latest offer she caught her
breath. It was for over nine thousand dollars. How could
it be worth that much, she wondered. Who would want to
pay nine thousand dollars for it? Clearly a personal item
of the last king of Burma was valuable, but nine thousand
dollars sounded a bit ridiculous. She swiftly hit the keys.
'Burmese artefact, 19th C kammavaca with historic provenance' disappeared from the screen.


When the banging from the bathroom began again,
Natalie took the children for a walk down to the park
at the end of the street. She thought about calling in to
see Vicki, but the kids wanted to hit the swings and the
slippery dip, and she was happy to see them expend some
pent-up energy.

After Charlotte and Adam had talked to Mark on the phone that evening, she settled them in front of a story-time DVD, took the phone to another room and told him about the letter from the princess.

'That's amazing. Hard to believe that little thing was so important to the old Burmese king. What now?' he asked.

'It's made me think about things. I really can't sell it now so I've taken it off the net. But do you know how much the latest offer was? Over nine thousand dollars!'

'No kidding! Who'd pay that much?' exclaimed Mark.

'That's what I thought. You hear stories of people paying silly prices for things, so who knows? But since Princess Aye Aye's letter arrived, the kammavaca seems even more special.'

'I'll be interested to see the letter. If you ever do sell it, you have two letters to authenticate it. Are you going to write back to the old girl?'

'Mark! Don't call her that. She's a dignified, mature woman from the former royal Burmese family.'

'You said her family was kicked out of Burma before she was even born. So what makes her so special? What did she do with her life?'

'I actually don't know,' said Natalie thoughtfully. 'Mi Mi said that she is a remarkable woman and it's clear from her letter that she is very well educated. I do know that she came back to Burma some time ago. I haven't really got a clue what her life is like.'

'Write back and ask her,' said Mark. 'If you want to know. I don't think she can tell you anything else about the kammavaca. She never even saw it, and there probably isn't anything more to tell . . . What's on the agenda for you and the gang tomorrow? How's the bathroom looking?'

'It looks like a bomb's gone off. Absolute mess! And the noise is horrendous. I can't believe they have to totally wreck the room to fix it up.'

'Yep, I know what they have to do. Glad I'm not there,' he said with a laugh.

'Thanks. Tomorrow I have a doctor's appointment and then we're joining the Little Kicks soccer club.'

'That's great. How fantastic! Adam will love hunting down a ball. Isn't Charlotte more into twirling and pretty outfits?'

'Exactly. I've been trying to get her out of princess dresses but because all the others are wearing baggy shorts and striped tops with their name and number on them, she's totally up for it. I've decided to become a soccer mum!' Natalie said laughing.

'With a big soccer ball up your jumper! How's the little one coming along?' asked Mark tenderly. 'I know how tired you get and what you've got to manage,' he added.

'Yeah, I do get tired. S'pose I'll be exhausted for the next few years. But it's okay, honey. I know what you're doing isn't ideal either. But just think of the home and the life we're building.'

'I love you, Nat.'

'I love you, too. I better go. The kids' movie is almost over, nearly time for bed.'

Natalie called Mi Mi the next day, thanked her again for putting her in touch with Princess Aye Aye and told her about the princess's letter.

'It's incredible that she knows about my kammavaca. I'm going to send her some photos when I write again.'

'She's quite a woman,' said Mi Mi. 'Burmese women are quite strong. They expect equality. They keep their own names and engage in commerce if they choose to. It seems that the royal women ran the old palace and the king as well.'

'How do you know all this?' Natalie was intrigued.

'Stories about the royal family have been handed

down and gossiped about for years, and there are still letters with tales told by those who knew them or had met them. There was a British bookseller in Rangoon who was married to a local woman who started to compile stories and anecdotes about them. But I've no idea what happened to him or his notes. Of course the king always believed that the family would be returned to power and the kingdom restored.'

Natalie nodded. She found the stories of the old royal family fascinating.

'Anyway, that's all history now. If you are interested you should stay in contact with Aye Aye. She's a prolific letter writer. She's had an amazing life and she still does wonderful things. I haven't seen her for years, but she loves to talk. She's a great charmer, a family trait, and has used her talents resourcefully.'

'What a shame I can't meet her. Yes, I'll write to her again,' said Natalie.

'I'm sure she would like that. The mail from Burma is not reliable and it's frequently read by the authorities, but hopefully her letters will get through.'

'Okay, I'll enjoy writing to her anyway,' said Natalie firmly.

'I'm so glad you haven't sold the kammavaca.'

'I never really wanted to, I mean, I rescued it from a shed where it had been sitting in a packing crate for decades, so I can't let it go to goodness knows where now. It doesn't seem right.'

'Perhaps not. It is up to you to decide,' replied Mi Mi. 'I must also thank you for your help at the rally, and for bringing your friends. It's a slow process to gradually awaken other ears and minds and hearts to our situation but with caring people we can do it.'

*

When the builders had gone for the day, and Adam and Charlotte were occupied drawing at the kitchen table, Natalie opened her emails to send some photos of the children in their new soccer gear to her mother. She was surprised to see a message from Peter Michaelson, the London art dealer.

> *I have been following the sale of your kammavaca on the net. I see you have removed it. Does this mean you have accepted an offer? As I said, I would like the opportunity to make a counter offer to any that you receive. I am willing to make a substantial increase on your last bid. As I recall the highest bid was around AU$9000. I am offering you AU$14,000 as a definite final offer. Please contact me as soon as possible.*

Natalie was shocked. Why would he leap in like that with such a high price? Surely a dealer would not be so generous unless he was sure there was an even bigger profit to be made. How strange, she thought. I'm sorry, Mr Michaelson, but the kammavaca is definitely not for sale.

'Hey, Mum, it's been ages since we spoke. Have you been busy?' asked Natalie when she rang her mother later that evening.

'Yes. Terribly.' Sarah sounded distracted and not her usual cheerful self.

'But that's a good thing, isn't it? I mean, the shop's doing well?'

'Reasonably. Are you busy Nat?'

'No, the kids are asleep already. You don't sound too good, what's up?'

'Can you chat for a minute? I've been meaning to call you, but I've been so preoccupied. How are you feeling?

181

You'd be seven months pregnant by now! I wish I could see you but it's difficult. I can't get away easily because I'm now fulltime at the shop.'

'I'm fine, Mum, but why are you slogging away every day in the shop? You need a day or so off every week. What happened to the woman you had helping you?'

'I've had to let her go. Things at home aren't too good at present. I've wanted to tell you what was happening but I didn't want to worry you.'

'Mum! What's up? Are you all right? Are you sick? Is Steve?' Natalie was now quite alarmed.

'No, nothing like that. We're fine. It's just that financially we're not very healthy at all, to tell you the truth. We've had a bit of a downturn.'

'In what way, Mum? I didn't think that you had money worries. You guys have a solid nest egg.'

'Not anymore.'

'What do you mean?'

'I told you that Steve's been dabbling on the stock market but it's been a disaster.'

'What do you mean?'

'He started to play the share market but he got caught on the downslide and he kept trying to recoup his losses. I suppose it's a classic mistake but now most of our savings are gone.' There was anger and fear in Sarah's voice.

'Oh my god. Why? Steve's never been a gambler.'

'No. He's a dairy farmer,' said Sarah bitterly.

'How serious is this, Mum? Where do you stand? We'll help you. Mark's earning good money.'

'Nat, Nat darling, I don't want you to worry. The house is paid off. We'll just have to be frugal, and live on what I make at the shop for a while. Steve is looking for some part-time work, fencing, or whatever. He feels terrible of course. We've lost our joint savings.'

Natalie couldn't believe what she was hearing. She wanted to say something about Steve but held her tongue.

'I suppose you won't be travelling any time soon then.'

'No, not even up to you at the Gold Coast because I'll have to work extra hours. We just have to pull our heads in. I feel terrible, I didn't want to worry you with the baby coming and all. I'd planned such lovely things and now I don't know if I'll be able to help you at all . . .'

'Listen, Mum, Mark and I and the kids are fine. It's you I'm worried about. Do you want me to drive down next week? I haven't seen you for ages, the kids would love to visit.'

'I have to work, sweetie. Steve feels so bad about it all. He thought he knew what he was doing. He has a friend who's been investing and he made money, and Steve thought he could do the same, but he couldn't. I mean, how could he? He had no experience playing the share market. We'll be okay. Things will work themselves out and I feel better now I've told you. It just means I can't buy you the nice things for the baby that I'd planned. And heaven knows when I can get up there to help you.'

'Mum, Mum, it's okay, we can manage. Anyway the baby's not due for two months and we'll have everything sorted by then. Well, at least the bathroom. We've got it all worked out so don't worry about us, we're okay. Just look after yourself. And Steve. But please Mum, let us help you.'

'You will do no such thing; I wouldn't dream of taking money from you. You have a young family and you might need that sort of money down the track. I want you to have the house of your dreams. Steve and I will be fine. Things haven't quite turned out as we would have liked, but we have a roof over our heads and we can pay our bills, so things aren't as bad as they could be. We'll just have to be a bit careful. I'm really grateful for your offer, darling, but I have no intention of accepting it. Things will come good, you'll see. Now tell me, what did the doctor say? Have you asked what sex the baby is?'

They talked a while longer, until Natalie heard Adam call out. 'Mum, I'll have to go. Adam's woken up.'

'Look after yourself and that baby. Give my love to Mark and the kids, and, please, don't worry about us. We're okay, truly we are.'

'I love you, Mum.'

'Love you, too.'


Sarah and Steve's finances were the first thing she raised when Mark rang the next day. He heard the worry in her voice straight away.

'What's happened?'

'Mum and Steve. Steve has lost all their savings playing the share market!'

'Shit! How did he do that? I thought they were well set up financially.'

'They were, but not now. I think Steve thought he'd improve their situation like some mate of his was doing, but now he's done the lot. Thank goodness they own the house and have an income from the shop to keep them going, but their nest egg, their security's gone. Poor Mum. She sounds very worried.'

'I'm not surprised. I know she wouldn't want to sell that house they just bought. Can she flog off the boutique?'

'Don't think she'd get all that much for it in this market. And then what would she do? You know Mum, still the glamour girl, professional working woman. I did offer to give her money but she won't have it. You don't mind, do you?'

'Of course not.'

'And Mark, I didn't tell you something else. There

was an email from that dealer, Peter Michaelson, in London. He's upped the offer quite a lot. Fourteen thousand.'

'What? Why would he do that? That's a big jump. Why wouldn't he offer, say, only one grand more? That thing could be more valuable than we think, Nat.'

'Maybe, but if we're never going to sell it, what's the difference?' said Natalie.

# 7

THEY WERE SO ENGROSSED in their little project that it took a few moments for the silence to sink in. Natalie leaned back on her heels, her gardening fork poised.

'The noise from the bathroom's stopped. Let's hope that's the end of it, at least for a while.'

'When can we have a bath again, Mummy?' asked Charlotte.

'Not till everything is back in place again, darling. There's still lots to be done in there before it gets back to normal. But I'm glad the jackhammering has finished. Okay, let's finish planting our carrots.'

The vegetable plot in the backyard had started when Natalie planted some herbs. The children had then wanted to grow something they liked eating and since carrots were one of their favourite vegetables, Natalie decided they could plant some. She showed Charlotte how to pat the earth down around the seedlings as they planted them, and managed to convince Adam not to yank the carrots up just to see how they were growing.

Natalie straightened up and rubbed her aching back. 'Let's go inside and make ourselves a milkshake.'

As she came into the house, her phone was ringing.

'Hi, Thi. How're you?'

'Natalie, put the TV on. There's something happening in Burma. The midday news reported it. There seems to be some sort of demonstration happening. It sounds terrible.'

'What? I'll turn it on now.'

But by the time Natalie turned on the TV, she only caught the tail end of the report, which mentioned a crisis in the economy in Burma due to the escalation of fuel prices. That didn't seem to be momentous, so when the newsreader moved on to the next story, she turned the TV off.

Later, while Charlotte and Adam napped, Natalie tried to clear up the dust that had spread throughout the house from the reconstruction of the bathroom. Even as she was doing it, she knew it was a pointless effort as the builders still had much more to do.

That evening, the children had finished dinner and were bathed and playing with some puzzles as they waited for Mark's phone call, so Natalie sat down and turned on the evening TV news. As soon as she realised that the headline story was about Burma, she switched to SBS, knowing that the multicultural channel would cover the story in depth. The images seemed to jump out at her. She felt so surrounded by the noise and colours on the screen that she gasped.

Hundreds of red-robed monks were massed along a street, shouting through loudhailers, waving their arms, their faces contorted in anger. Blocking their way were rows of soldiers in steel helmets holding large shields in front of their bodies, on which they banged their truncheons. People hung from balconies and windows and stood on top of the old wooden buildings that lined the street.

Natalie watched the blurry, shaking footage. She could see a stream of Burmese people, young and old, men and women, coming into the street, linking arms or holding hands to form a ring around the massed monks. They all seemed to be singing. There was no mistaking their intent to form a living barrier between the revered monks and the ominous green military at the far end of the street. A few young men dashed into the space between the two groups, hurling stones in the direction of the impassive soldiers.

Whoever was holding the camera was in the thick of the action, racing beside the crowd, trying to grab a few breathless comments, which were translated in subtitles at the bottom of Natalie's TV screen: 'There is no democracy in Burma.' 'Where are the rights of the Burmese people?'

Natalie heard the phone but ignored it. She knew it would be Mark to talk to the children and Charlotte ran to answer it but Natalie was swept up by the scenes from the streets of Rangoon. Suddenly she glimpsed a breathtaking shot of a huge golden pagoda in the background. Then she could see an old bus disgorging even more monks into the demonstration, some carrying flags and loudhailers.

Many of the bystanders bowed and clasped their hands together in reverence as the monks strode purposefully past them, while others cheered and clapped. A small boy fell to his knees and touched his forehead onto the ground. As the surging crowd jostled him, someone quickly helped him to his feet.

Suddenly there was the sound of shots. Natalie realised

the protestors were now facing soldiers armed with rifles, shields and truncheons. Puffs of smoke began to blossom from the guns.

'Oh, god, they're shooting real bullets!' she exclaimed aloud.

The children, talking to Mark, took no notice of their mother's comments.

Then, through the crowd, from the distance where the camera operator stood, she saw a wild surge. The crowd was breaking up, fleeing from gunfire and tear gas. People were running, some bent double, others covering their mouths as they fled down the streets in panic. There were people falling over and then being hurriedly dragged away by other demonstrators. All the time the unmistakable sound of gunfire continued in the background. The camera jerked wildly, as the person holding it also ran.

'They're shooting the monks!' cried Natalie, tears beginning to stream down her face. She could not believe the horrific scenes she was watching. The frightened faces of women, men and young people, the defiant expression of monks, some with bloodied shaved heads, still waving their flags in protest, flashed like a collage over the screen. A picture of a stream of blood running across the cobblestones towards a monk's solitary sandal ended the shaky footage.

The TV presenter summed up what little was known of the events they'd just shown.

These pictures of this violent demonstration have been smuggled out of Burma and at this stage we have few other details of what has happened in Rangoon today. It is known that unrest has been building for several weeks, ever since the junta suddenly removed fuel subsidies. Fuel prices have doubled and food prices have also jumped, creating great hardships for the people of Burma who are

189

already living at a subsistence level. For the first time in many years, unrest has brought the people onto the streets in a show of civil disobedience. For the monks to break their vows by engaging in politics and calling for reform is an indication of the deep resentment felt by the people in this repressed and poor country.

Natalie didn't move; tears slid down her face. The story about Burma had taken only a few minutes of air time but to Natalie it seemed like an age, and the pain and anguish she felt about the shocking scenes had frozen her to the spot. She continued to stare at the TV screen even though the program had moved on to another story. She could still hear the cries of the crowd and the sound of gunshots as the military fired on their own people, including the monks, the spiritual leaders of the country.

'Mummy, what's wrong?' Charlotte tugged at her arm. 'Daddy wants to talk now.'

'Give me the phone then, please, sweetie,' said Natalie, brushing her cheeks, not wanting the children to see how upset she was. And not wanting to explain to them what she'd just seen.

'Hey, Nat, are you okay? Charlotte said you're crying.' Mark sounded concerned.

'I just saw the most shocking thing on TV. See if you can catch it on the late news. There's been a major demonstration in Rangoon. The monks, hundreds of them, took to the streets and thousands of ordinary people joined them, trying to protect them, and then the soldiers started firing at them. They're monks, holy men, pacifists! Can you believe it?'

'Slow down, Nat. You really are worked up. From what you've told me this is a very troubled country. There's a lot of unrest.'

'How can people just stand by and watch helpless unarmed people mown down because they want basic rights – like food! They were mostly monks, Mark! It's tragic.'

'I understand you're upset, but remember, Nat, you are already doing something for Burma. It does sound terrible though. I'll catch it on the late news. Now, tell me about Charlotte's ballet concert. She sounds pretty excited about it.'

Later when the children were in bed, Natalie automatically began cleaning up the kitchen. But she felt distracted and still disturbed. She glanced outside at the lights glittering on the calm water of the canal. In the brightly lit houses opposite she could see people moving around, a TV screen flickering; she could hear the faint sound of music as families settled into their evening at home, safe and comfortable.

Her phone rang and she was surprised to hear Vicki's voice.

'Hi, Natalie, I'm at your front door. I didn't want to alarm you or wake the children. Did you see the news? I'm so upset. Can I come in?'

'Of course. I'm so glad you're here,' Natalie said in a rush of sudden relief.

Natalie put the kettle on as Vicki pulled out a kitchen chair.

'It's shocking, just dreadful.'

'Vicki, I burst into tears, I couldn't believe innocent people could be shot in cold blood like that, and the monks! Even I understand the extent to which they're held in such esteem and reverence by the Burmese people. How could the soldiers do that?'

'The generals have made the military into machines. But even so, I am really surprised that they took action against the monks.'

'Surely there has to be some retribution. Now that the international community has seen what went on,' said Natalie.

'I doubt it. The generals never take any notice of what the outside world thinks. They're a law unto themselves. Things must be very bad for people to come out onto the streets to protest. They are so afraid of the military junta and they know that if they protest, they risk their own lives and those of their families. That's how the regime gets back at you – they punish your family,' said Vicki. 'I've been trying to reach friends there, but the whole country seems to be blacked out. I couldn't get through to anyone on the phone.'

'Those pictures on the TV were like a terrible movie,' said Natalie. 'So many young people seem to be involved, even though they only had stones and sticks. Do you think the protests will make any difference?'

'I don't know. There's been protests for some time, all over the country, as people object to the way the economy is run. But when you see situations like this it's so depressing. I guess it means that people like us have to work even harder to tell people about the plight of Burma. But it's not easy.'

Natalie nodded. 'I'm thinking about my kid's safely tucked up in there, and this little baby on the way, and how lucky we are. What would it be like struggling to feed your family, worrying about a knock on the door in the middle of the night and having your husband or mother taken away?' Natalie sighed. 'I wish I could do more . . .'

She poured their tea, then said, 'Vicki, it's just struck me. Maybe I could send the kammavaca back to Burma. To Princess Aye Aye. It belonged to her family. Uncle Andrew felt that returning it was the right thing to do, because it should not have been taken in the first place, and I think that King Thibaw's kammavaca is part of Burmese culture. It belongs to that country and I think I should make sure that it goes back to its rightful owners.' She gave Vicki a worried, querying look.

Vicki nodded slowly. 'Perhaps you're right. I'm sure its return would mean a lot. The princess would never ask you for it, but, really, to you it's just a curio with a connection to a relative you never knew, an exotic family footnote. To her it has more relevance. It was cherished by her grandfather and it's a link to her family's powerful past. Returning it would be a very selfless act on your part.'

'Seeing for myself those shattering pictures on TV has made me want to help the Burmese in a more tangible way than just turning up at rallies. This is one way I can do it.'

'What will Mark say? You could do a lot with the money that dealer in London offered,' said Vicki.

'Can you put a price on the suffering and sacrifice of those people? It's not just Aung San Suu Kyi and her pro-democracy followers, it's all the Burmese people,' exclaimed Natalie vehemently. 'I see that now. Maybe sending the kammavaca back is symbolic, but I want to do it. Otherwise I'll feel so helpless. I know there are people here in Australia who are suffering but in Burma it's everyone! The whole country is being repressed!'

'You are so right.' Vicki raised her tea mug.

'I'll write to Aye Aye tonight.'

'I'm so glad I came by,' said Vicki. 'I was devastated. Well, I still am, but it's nice to know I'm not alone. I'll talk to Mi Mi and Thi tomorrow, but I just had to talk to someone straight away. Thanks, Natalie.'

'No, I should thank you. You've helped me crystallise my thoughts. The kammavaca has sent me on a bit of a trip. Now I understand so much more not just about Burma, but funnily enough, about myself as well. I'm seeing what's really important in life.' Natalie grasped for words as she tried to articulate these new thoughts occurring to her.

'How are you going to get the kammavaca to Aye Aye? I wouldn't risk posting it,' said Vicki.

'No, you're right. Don't you go back there sometimes? When are you going back to Burma? Could you return it?' asked Natalie.

'I hadn't planned on going to Burma any time soon,' said Vicki. 'But I will be going, of course, and as soon as I am, I'll let you know and I'll make sure that your precious gift gets into the hands of the princess.'

'Thank you for that. That's settled then,' said Natalie. She put down her cup, went over to her desk and returned with the little teak box. 'I guess that my gesture won't change the political landscape in Burma, but I feel that I'm completing a journey that started more than eighty years ago. This kammavaca rightfully belongs in Burma, not on the top of my desk.'

After Vicki left, Natalie sat down and wrote a letter to Princess Aye Aye, trying to formulate the words to express her decision to return the kammavaca.

*The sight of those monks, surrounded by unarmed citizens trying to protect them, touched me deeply. I'm learning about the desire of the Burmese people to have the freedom we all take for granted in Australia. The repression and poverty they suffer makes me very aware of the importance of the basic human rights denied to the Burmese. I wish I could do more to help. I have been working with like-minded people trying to raise awareness of the plight of Burma. But this is not enough, and now I would like to do something more.*

*I have been thinking a lot about my great-great-uncle, Andrew Hancock, who was determined to return your grandfather's kammavaca to Princess Tipi Si. He died while trying to fulfil his promise to her. Now I realise that my family has just been the caretaker of your kamma-vaca, which was wrongly taken in the first place, and that its importance to you is far greater than any attachment I might have. Therefore I have decided to send the kammavaca back to you for safekeeping. I have a friend who makes irregular trips to Burma and she has agreed that the next time she travels to your country she will bring the kammavaca with her and see that it reaches you. I hope this small gesture will complete the circle that links our forebears, and in a small way show you that the Burmese people are not alone.*

The following morning, after she posted the letter, she felt her heart lift.

When Natalie told Mark that evening what she had done he seemed surprised.

'Are you sure? You seemed so attached to it. The family connection and so on. You sure you're thinking straight and it's not some pregnancy whim? A rush of blood to the head?'

'No. I feel really good about it. Those scenes on TV were horrific, you saw them. I know in the scheme of things returning the kammavaca's a small gesture, but it just feels right,' said Natalie.

'It's a nice gesture and a very generous one, giving away all that money. Are you going to let that dealer in London know? How're the kids today? Charlotte still excited about the ballet concert?'

'"Concert" makes it sound pretty grand. The girls are dancing a little story about Bambi being lost in the forest. I think it's the costumes they're most excited about. I'll take lots of photos for you.'

*

195

The end-of-term ballet concert was a great success although Adam didn't find it very entertaining, and Natalie had quite a job distracting him while the older children performed onstage. Jodie's daughter was also in the concert and Natalie and Jodie sat next to each other to watch the performance.

'Aren't the girls cute? They just love dressing up. It's as though they were born to perform,' said Jodie. 'How are things with you? You look tired.'

'Situation normal. I stayed up a bit late last night writing a letter to Burma, I was so horrified by the news there. And then this morning I tripped over one of Adam's toys and fell into the washing basket. Lucky it was a soft landing, but I just felt like staying in the basket and going back to sleep. Once I'm horizontal, my eyes close.'

'Yes, that footage from Burma was shocking. It made me sit up and take notice. Listen, Nat, you're not overdoing things, are you?' Jodie put her arm around her friend and gave her a little squeeze. 'You don't have to make sure everything is perfect. There's a limit to what you can do when your house is being renovated. Leave as much of the housework as you can. When the kids are resting, have a nap or read a magazine.'

'The house is so chaotic with the builders, and with Mark away I guess I overcompensate,' said Natalie. 'But you're right. After all the excitement of this morning, I think we'll head home and hopefully we'll all have a good nap.'

That evening when Natalie spoke to Mark she thought he sounded tired, too.

'Is there something wrong? You sound very down,' said Natalie.

'Just a bit overworked. These hours can be a killer. I think that we both need a holiday, though who knows when we'll be able to do that!'

'When this place is finished, living here will be a holiday!' said Natalie, trying to make Mark feel happier.

'I'm trying to get there, sweetheart. You know that.'

'Mark, I wasn't criticising you,' said Natalie quickly. 'Just trying to look on the bright side, when all these renos are eventually finished.'

They changed the subject and after she'd hung up, Natalie decided against sorting out the washing piled in the basket and to forgo a TV program she had planned to watch, and went straight to bed. She read only two pages of her book before she fell asleep.


The luminous face of the bedside clock glowed in the dark, showing 2.40 a.m. Natalie turned over and was suddenly aware of a warm dampness beneath her. She groaned. Had she wet the bed? Thank goodness she was sleeping alone. She slid from the bed but when she felt how wet her nightdress was, her heart sank. Something wasn't right. Hurriedly she turned on the bedside light and gasped as she saw a watery stain and realised what it was.

'Oh no!' Instinctively she wrapped her arms across her belly, cradling her baby, and sat on the edge of the bed. She grabbed the phone and called Mark. The phone rang out and went to voicemail. She tried again but he still didn't answer. She lay back down again, wondering what to do. She called Jodie.

'Sorry, Jodie, it's me. I can't get onto Mark. I think I have to get to hospital. My waters have broken . . .'

'Oh, shit, Nat! Call 000, then don't do anything. I'll get dressed and come over and stay with the kids. Don't worry about them. Stay calm.'

Natalie drew deep breaths as she shakily dialled the emergency number and repeated her name and address. The operator was cool and efficient.

'Just lie quietly. Have you had any contractions?'

Natalie was about to say that she hadn't when she felt a sudden tweaking tremor ripple across her abdomen.

'Yes,' she whispered. 'Just now.'

'How far along is your pregnancy?' the operator asked.

'Not quite thirty weeks. It's too soon.'

'If we send an ambulance for you, will you be able to let the paramedics in?'

'I'll unlock the front door and leave the light on. Please ask them to be quiet. I have children sleeping.'

'Is someone available to look after them?'

'Yes, she's on her way.'

'An ambulance has been dispatched. Please stay off the phone in case they need to contact you.'

Natalie carefully lifted herself from the bed and, as calmly as she could, went to open the front door. Returning to her bed, she willed the baby to settle down, but the quivers were becoming stronger contractions. Natalie held herself gently, singing and whispering to her baby.

'Stay there, stay there. Hold on, sweetheart. It's too early. Too early. You're not ready for the world. Please, please, God, hold this baby back.'

The phone by the bed rang and Natalie grabbed it.

'Natalie, this is Sandy Fleming, I'm a paramedic. I'm in the ambulance and we're on our way. Won't be long. Can you tell me where you are in the house? Are there lights on? How old are the other children?'

'They're little, three and four. I've unlocked the front door and I have a girlfriend coming . . . Please hurry, I'm having contractions, I don't want to have this baby. It's too soon. Please hurry.'

'We're only five minutes away. It'll be all right. Listen to me, even babies at thirty weeks are strong little critters. Don't worry. Keep calm and we'll be there to help very, very soon.'

The young woman's voice was soothing and professional. Natalie wished Mark was there. How could she cope without his reassuring presence? She knew that the children would be fine with Jodie.

She waited, closing her eyes, gripping her belly and trying to block out what was happening by taking slow, deep breaths. She heard the door open and Jodie was in the room.

'I don't suppose you've got a bag ready for hospital? Where are your night things? Dressing gown? Nighties?' She pulled open the drawers as Natalie gave her instructions. 'Anything else you want?'

'Phone charger. Toothbrush. I don't know.' Tears rolled down her face.

'No matter. I'll get that gear over to you if you need it. Could just be a false alarm and you'll be home for breakfast.'

Natalie shook her head. 'I have a horrible feeling about this . . .'

'There's the ambulance out the front, I'll let them in.' Jodie hurried to the door.

But the paramedics, a man and a woman, were already through the door, both carrying a mass of equipment in backpacks, as well as an oxygen cylinder and a collapsible stretcher.

'She's through there,' said Jodie.

The young woman gave Natalie a warm smile. 'Hello, I'm Sandy. This is John. And you're Natalie?'

'Yes.' In a rush Natalie started to blurt out what had happened. As she talked, Sandy quickly took her pulse while John erected the stretcher.

'So you're thirty weeks along are you, Natalie? Any spotting or bleeding before this? Cramps? Have you recently fallen or strained yourself? We need to get you to hospital and then we'll have you into the obstetric ward in no time. Just turn around and slide over onto the stretcher. Pop your bottom on here. There we go. Lie down. Relax.'

The paramedics gave Natalie a calm and steady stream of simple instructions. While they moved swiftly, talking reassuringly, Sandy kept her fingers on Natalie's pulse, maintaining eye contact and a friendly smile.

'We'll make this a quick trip, eh?' Sandy said to John.

'Yep, no worries, mate.'

In moments they were heading for the front door with an ashen-faced Natalie under a sheet.

'She's going to be fine and so is her baby,' Sandy said to Jodie. 'You okay to hold the fort? Let's go.'

Jodie nodded as the paramedics slammed the ambulance doors shut and were off in a matter of seconds.

In the back of the ambulance, Natalie started to hyperventilate and Sandy, sitting beside her, placed an oxygen mask over her face. When Natalie pulled up her legs, Sandy asked, 'Strong contractions? Take deep breaths.'

Natalie shook her head but she saw Sandy give John a concerned look. She didn't register the siren's wail. All she saw were the streetlights and an occasional flash of neon. Suddenly she gripped Sandy's wrist.

'It's coming! Stop, stop, the ambulance. My baby's coming.'

Sandy spoke calmly. 'All right, Natalie, I'm here. If there's a problem, we'll pull over, but we're nearly at the hospital now, so we'll try and get there. Help me, now. Pull up your legs and hold on here to the sides of the bed.'

Natalie didn't notice John accelerating or feel the ambulance swinging around corners.

'I need you to help me, Natalie. Just breathe through the contractions. Try not to push just yet.'

Natalie shook her head. 'No, no. I don't want it to come. It's too early!' she cried, grasping her belly.

'Natalie, your baby is coming. There's no stopping

it now. We'll get you to hospital as quickly as we can so your baby can be looked after. Everyone is waiting for you there. It's going to be fine, okay? On three, give me a big push, breathe and push,' commanded Sandy firmly.

The next minutes were a blur as Natalie felt her baby expelled in a watery rush from her body. As she struggled to lean forward over the restraining straps of the bed, she began crying.

'Is it all right, is it all right?'

Despite the fast-moving vehicle, Sandy had the baby, a tiny bundle, laid in her lap. 'Natalie, it's a little boy. Bit on the skinny side, a bit out of breath. Couldn't wait, eh, mister?' she chatted calmly to the baby, as she quickly worked on the tiny, pale blue infant, massaging his chest with two fingers, wrapping him in a warm blanket then slipping a small oxygen mask onto his face. 'Come on, little fella, big breath.'

Natalie lay back, great sobs racking her body.

Sandy seemed to be talking to herself. 'One two three, that's my little man. Come on, one more.' She used a little suction device to get rid of the mucus from his mouth.

Natalie saw the Accident and Emergency sign as they screamed into the driveway of the hospital and turned to Sandy. 'Is he breathing?' she asked in panic.

In reply Natalie heard a faint squeak of a whimper, then a gulp as a tinge of pink crept into the baby's face.

Sandy laid the warmly wrapped infant next to Natalie in the crook of her arm. 'Have you got a name for him?'

Natalie closed her eyes. 'Andrew.'

'Nat, the kids are fine, wolfing down breakfast. How's the little bloke? And how're you? Have you talked to Mark yet?' asked Jodie over the phone.

'Mark's on his way. It's all a bit of a blur. I've been

201

given some medication, so I'm a bit woozy. The baby is in a humidicrib in the intensive care nursery. He's got breathing problems. God, Jodie, he's so tiny, so fragile, smaller than Charlotte's doll. He weighs less than one and a half kilos . . .' She started to cry.

'Nat, he's going to be fine. What did Mark say?'

'He freaked out a bit. We'll know more about the baby when I see the specialist. I'm supposed to sleep. You sure the kids are all right? I can't thank you enough. What about your kids? And what about the preschool?'

'All under control. Mum's over at my place. She'll get them organised, and I'll take your two to preschool with me. Don't worry about us, we'll be fine.'

'My mother's closing the shop as soon as she can and coming up. She's so upset of course. I didn't want to worry her but I had to tell her what was happening. She says that's what mothers are put on the planet for – to worry,' said Natalie, choking up.

'Nat, little Andrew is going to be all right. Get some rest. Let us know when you want me to bring the kids in to see you. Charlotte's fine, very calm, very grownup. Adam is a bit confused, but once he gets to preschool and sees his friends, he'll be okay.'

'Thanks, Jodie. You're such a good friend. I don't know what to do. I'm so worried,' said Natalie tearfully.

'Sleep,' said Jodie firmly. 'Get it while you can.'


When Natalie opened her eyes, she saw her mother and Steve sitting by her bed, their faces concerned.

'Hello, darling, how're you feeling?' Sarah leaned close and gave her daughter a kiss.

'I'm okay. Did you see him?'

'They let us have a peek. He's tiny but perfect. It will be all right, darling girl.'

'I'm pretty confident about him,' added Steve, trying to smile.

'Hi, Steve. Thank you for the flowers,' said Natalie, seeing the vase on the table at the foot of her bed.

'We spoke to the nurse in charge of the neonatal intensive care unit, and she told us that they're taking the best care of him, sweetie. The main thing is for you to get some rest,' said Sarah.

'I know, Mum, but I'm so worried about him. It just came out of the blue.'

'You're doing too much with Mark away all the time,' said her mother but Steve gave her a swift nudge.

'No, Mum, it's not that. It has nothing to do with Mark being away. The doctor isn't really sure why it happened. I had a fall yesterday, but it wasn't much of one.'

Sarah didn't look convinced. 'Thank goodness Jodie was able to drop everything and get over to your place to look after Charlotte and Adam,' she said.

'Yes. She's such a great friend. Mark will be able to take over when he gets home.'

'Do you know how long you'll be here?' said Steve.

'I'm not sure. Not very long, I suppose. It's Andrew who will be kept in. I just hope that Mark gets here soon. I really need him.'

Sarah hugged her daughter. 'Love you, darling girl. It's going to be okay.'

'Let us know if there's anything we can do. I'm happy to pop up any time,' offered Steve.

'Thanks so much for coming. I know it's not easy. It was good to see you both,' said Natalie, as she started to cry again.

An hour later, Mark finally arrived and rushed into her room, unshaven, pale faced and red eyed. She reached out to him and he sat on the bed beside her, wrapping her in his arms, and they wept together.

'I'm so, so sorry you had to go through this without me,' he kept repeating. 'How is our little guy?' Mark was trying to look brave and cheerful, but Natalie saw the fear in his eyes.

'They say he'll be okay, Mark. But he's not out of the woods yet. He has problems with his breathing. It's so hard to see him like that in the humidicrib. I just want to hold him.' Natalie began to dissolve into tears again.

'I know, I know. Let's just take it day by day, sweet-heart. Minute by minute. How are Charlotte and Adam? God, Jodie's amazing.'

Natalie nodded. 'Yes, she said she'll have them at her place tonight and you can pick them up in the morning. She's organised to keep them busy, doing their usual thing at the preschool.'

'I can pick them up and bring them in here, introduce them to Andrew.'

'I don't think they allow children down where Andrew is, but they might be able to see him through the window. I want to see them. But maybe they shouldn't see Andrew. I mean, what if he —' She buried her face in his chest. 'I couldn't bear it . . . Explaining it to them . . .'

Mark held her close, making soothing sounds as though unable to frame words or articulate how his heart was breaking for her, for them both. Finally he managed to say, 'He's going to be fine, darling. Our little boy will pull through. I know he will.'

Natalie blew her nose and asked in a quiet voice, 'Should we name him? Have a little naming ceremony for Andrew? Just in case? If something happens I don't want him to just . . . disappear. Like he wasn't here.'

'Oh, Nat.' Mark looked at her brave, tear-stained face. 'Don't think that. Just think about the lovely nam-ing party we're going to have in a few months. What's his middle name? Have you thought about that? Did Uncle

Andrew have a middle name?' asked Mark, trying to distract her.

'I can't remember. I really love calling him Andrew and keeping Uncle Andrew's spirit alive. I dream that he'll grow up to be talented and decent like great-great-uncle Andrew was. Do you think that's corny?'

'No, Nat, it's not corny. Uncle Andrew means a lot to you,' said Mark gently.

Natalie nodded. 'I was thinking maybe Steven for a middle name. Adam's named for your father and Steve doesn't have any kids. Mum would like that.'

'That's a nice idea, he'll be chuffed.'

'How long have you got off?' asked Natalie hesitantly.

'As long as we need. I'll take all the holiday time I'm owed and then I'll ask for leave without pay if I have to. It'll be fine. When will you come home?'

'They don't keep mothers in hospital very long these days, so I'll probably come home and then come back to the hospital every day to express my milk and be with Andrew. I so want to hold him and feed him myself. What if we don't bond? And what about Charlotte and Adam?'

'Nat, you and this baby will be especially close after all this. Don't worry. We just have to think about the day he comes home.' He thought for a moment before he added, 'He's going to need a lot of care. I wonder how we're going to manage.' Then, more definitely, 'But I'll be able to take care of Charlotte and Adam. You'll be home a lot of the time, too.'

'I just want him home. It's scary. He looks so fragile, so breakable,' whispered Natalie. A baby down the hall let out a lusty cry. 'I hate hearing those healthy babies. I know it sounds mean, but it's so unfair,' she said bitterly. 'I hope those mothers realise how lucky they are.' Mark reached for her again and held her close.

*

Natalie lost track of time in the next twenty-four hours. Minutes and hours were dictated by the bright lights of the intensive care nursery, the hospital routine, and the time she sat by the humidicrib that held her tiny son.

She was able to put her hand through a small opening and stroke him with her finger. She hated seeing the tubes surrounding him and the drip inserted into his translucent skin. She prayed that he knew she was there, loving him as much as if he were in her arms.

Nurses bustled, charts were flicked through, notes made, cheerful banter exchanged in the hall, but Natalie remained hunched, her eyes glued to her baby, willing him to grow stronger. She drank an occasional milky tea with a soggy biscuit in the saucer and avoided the maternity ward as much as possible. Thankfully, her room was at the far end of the hallway, but to get to it she couldn't avoid passing those other happy rooms where mothers were bonding, feeding, bathing and showing off their healthy new babies.

As she walked down the corridor Natalie kept her eyes lowered and in the solitude of her room she pushed her door shut and banged her fist against the wall.

'It's not fair, not fair,' she sobbed.

She could tell that the doctors were still concerned for Andrew. Although he wasn't worsening, he wasn't improving either. She watched his pale little body struggling for every breath and, leaning close, she whispered encouragement to him. She couldn't bear to be far from him.

Charlotte and Adam's visit didn't turn out as Natalie had hoped. Neither of them understood why their mother was in the hospital, or where the baby was? The hour they spent there was hectic and tiring, and turned tearful when Mark announced that they had to go back home without their mother.

The next day Andrew's condition grew far worse.

Natalie was gently told that Andrew was being taken for an X-ray, and she panicked.

'Can't I go too, please? I want to stay with my baby!'

The nurses tried to calm her down and she was taken back to her room. She rang Mark and sobbed that Andrew was getting worse.

'I'll be there as soon as I can. I'll call Jodie and see if she can have the children,' he said.


Mark sat by Natalie's bed, holding her hand, waiting to hear the results of the X-ray, or any news at all.

'The waiting is the worst,' she whispered. 'Please thank Jodie for me. How are you managing?'

Mark gave a small smile. 'They're getting a bit tired of eggs so tonight I was going to throw a pizza on. With vegetables,' he added, knowing Natalie tried to give the children fruit and vegetables every day.

'There's a lasagne in the freezer. I think you should go home now and pick the kids up. I want them to stick to their routine,' said Natalie. 'I'll be okay.'

'Are you sure?' Mark glanced at his watch. 'Call me if there's any news. Try not to worry. I know this is hard.' He kissed her and as he opened the door Dr Rasheed, Andrew's paediatrician, entered.

'How is he?' Natalie asked before they had even greeted each other.

'He's back in the nursery,' said Dr Rasheed.

Before Dr Rasheed could go on, Mark asked, 'What did the X-ray show?'

'Is he going to be all right?' added Natalie.

The doctor held up his hand. 'Please, let me explain. As you know, your son has some breathing problems due to his immature lungs, but now there is an added complication . . .'

There was an intake of breath from Mark and Natalie.

'The lobe of his left lung has collapsed. This will mean he'll have to have assisted ventilation, which will have to be initiated by the neonatologist.'

'Oh, no!' said Natalie.

'He'll require specialised treatment, so we're moving him to the Mater Children's Hospital in Brisbane,' said Dr Rasheed.

'Oh, god,' said Mark.

'Can I go with him?' asked Natalie urgently.

'The retrieval van is ready to leave for the Mater hospital. You need to sign this permission slip. Mrs Cutler, you are still post partum and we're a little concerned about your blood pressure so you need at least another night here for observation. As soon as your milk comes in you will be able to express and feed him.'

'I suppose that I'll have to travel up to the hospital each day.'

'Natalie! How's that going to work?' said Mark.

'I can drive,' said Natalie. 'That way I can see the children morning and night. You'll manage through the day.' She turned to the doctor. 'What are they going to do up there that they can't do here? It's a good sign, isn't it? That he's going there? To be fixed?' she said.

The doctor looked serious as he said, 'Your baby will be in the best possible hands at the Mater. It's a long, slow process to get his lung inflated and working properly.'

'All that matters is that he pulls through this okay,' said Mark. 'How long will it take?'

'Quite a few weeks, a couple of months, perhaps. I can't make any promises and we have to assume that all will go well and there won't be any further complications.'

'I see,' said Mark. He turned away frowning.

'But Andrew will be okay?' asked Natalie, searching

the doctor's calm face for any clues, anything he might be hiding from them.

'There are always risks with premature babies, Mrs Cutler. Continue to think positively. This procedure has been done successfully many times before. Andrew will be in very experienced hands. I have to go, if you'll excuse me, but be assured, everything possible is being done for your son.'

The door closed and Natalie and Mark turned to one another.

'My poor little boy,' said Natalie, tears filling her eyes.

'Natalie, how are we going to manage this? You're not serious about driving up and back morning and night every day? It's over an hour each way, and you've just given birth. I should drive you, and I want to see him too, but Adam and Charlotte . . . what will we do with them?'

'Mark I have to go. I have to feed him. You'll have to stay with Adam and Charlotte,' said Natalie shortly and firmly. 'There's no other way. Mum is in no position to help fulltime, she has to keep the shop going. Andrew will be a seven-days-a-week job, and where do we get that sort of longtime childcare for Charlotte and Adam?'

'Nat, there's also my work. I can take leave, but I can't stay away indefinitely. I know,' he held up his hand quickly, 'our family comes first, of course it does.'

'It mightn't be long, Mark. I just pray for the day we can bring Andrew home.'

'This is going to be difficult for us.'

'Yes, but nothing is as important as this baby,' declared Natalie.

'Of course,' said Mark, attempting to look optimistic. But Natalie knew that he was really concerned about how they would juggle their lives with Andrew in hospital in Brisbane for weeks.

When Natalie spoke to Jodie she hoped that sharing her concerns might make them seem less difficult. 'I just want to focus on the baby right now. Sometimes I have these dreams he's never coming home, that we're going to lose him.' Natalie struggled to control her tears.

'Oh Nat, that's so stressful for you,' said Jodie. 'How is Mark coping? If he is like my husband, doing the domestics, getting meals and caring for two kids won't be easy. What if you traded and he went up a day or so a week and took your milk so you could stay home? Not that it's restful! Maybe I could talk to some of the mothers here and see if someone could drive you up, even one day a week. Give you a break from the driving. Maybe someone could take your milk up so that you could spend the day with your kids and Mark, but I suppose you would want to see Andrew every day.'

'Yes, I do, but those ideas sound wonderful, Jodie. Mark said that Vicki offered to help, too. And, god bless them, so have Mi Mi and Thi. They're such lovely people, and I've known them for such a short time. I know how little time you have, running the preschool, but you have been wonderful. I don't know what we would have done without you. I'm worried, too, that Mark won't get to spend much time with Andrew.'

'I wouldn't fret about that,' said Jodie gently. 'He'll bond with him later, don't worry. Your relationship with Andrew is the most important thing now and I think you need to be with the baby for your own peace of mind.'

'I know. I'm trying to tell myself that Andrew is in limbo land, that he isn't aware of what's going on, like he's still tucked up in the womb.'

'That's a good idea,' said Jodie. 'He'll catch up, never fear.'

*

When Natalie left the hospital the next day, she felt drained. With the other two children, coming home had been joyful. Mark had carried the flowers and presents and she had carried a beautiful baby in her arms. But this time there was nothing to celebrate. Even the flowers from her mother and Steve had died and her arms were empty.

Nevertheless, Charlotte and Adam were thrilled to have their mother home, and expected life to get back to normal. Strangely, when Charlotte asked Natalie about the baby, she did not seem at all put out to hear that he was not coming home yet. She was absorbed in her own world of princesses and ballerinas. But as soon as Natalie headed out the door to drive to Brisbane for the first time, Charlotte burst into tears.

Natalie realised that she needed to explain to Charlotte about her new brother or this would happen each time she left for Brisbane. 'I'll be home tonight, darling. I'm going up to Brisbane to see your new little brother. He's very tiny and he won't be allowed to come home until he's bigger. Daddy's here to look after you and we can make cupcakes for dessert,' cajoled Natalie. But Charlotte would not be consoled and as Natalie drove away leaving Mark to sort things out she felt very guilty.

The day didn't improve when she got a frantic text message from Mark that Adam wouldn't go down for his nap because he couldn't find his security rug.

*I've ripped this house apart*, Mark texted.

Natalie gave him a list of places to look but she could sense his frustration when he wrote back, *I've looked everywhere. He won't go to sleep, won't stop crying and calling for his blanky.*

*Just cuddle him and hope he settles down*, she sent back. *The specialist is with Andrew now.*

*Call me when you can.*

211

When she arrived home Natalie could hear Adam crying even before she opened the door.

'Mummy,' squealed Charlotte in delight as soon as she saw her. Adam immediately gulped back his tears.

'How's Andrew?'

'They say he's doing as well as can be expected, whatever that means.' Natalie's face crumpled and she collapsed onto the sofa as the children scrambled into her lap.

'He's going to be fine, Nat. You look exhausted, do you want a cup of tea?'

Natalie nodded. 'Did you find Adam's little blanket?'

'No. It's been a nightmare. Can't you get a duplicate and hide it? I don't want to go through this drama again,' Mark said, hurriedly scooping the dirty dishes into the dishwasher.

'I'll look.' Natalie got up and went into Charlotte's bedroom and emerged a few minutes later with the blue blanket. Adam rushed to grab it from her.

'Where was it?' demanded Mark.

'In Charlotte's chest of drawers.'

'I looked there!'

'In the back.'

'How did it get in the back?'

'He sometimes stuffs his toys there.'

The rest of the evening passed with the distraction of dealing with dinner and settling the two children.

'There's a movie on that you might like,' said Mark as they sat quietly in the lounge room. Natalie looked pale and drawn. This should have been the joyous time of being home with their newborn son, doting on him, discussing who he looked like, and holding him close. Natalie wrapped her arms around herself feeling empty and sad.

She shook her head. 'You can watch it. Or a game, I don't care.'

'I'm going to have a beer,' said Mark.

'I'll have another cup of tea. I'm suddenly so tired,' said Natalie. 'I think I'll have an early night.'

Before she went to bed she sat at the computer to check her emails.

Long-distance friends were being supportive on her Facebook page and there were lovely email messages from Mi Mi and Thi, who said Thomas had offered to come round and help in her garden, if she needed it. It was nice to know that she was not alone and that her friends were concerned for her and baby Andrew.

The next day Jodie called in on her way home from work, glad to find Natalie at home.

'How're things? You look tired. Mark, too.'

'We aren't sleeping well,' said Natalie.

'I can imagine. It's a lot of stress,' agreed Jodie.

'But thank you for all your help,' said Natalie quickly. 'Want a coffee?'

'I just popped in and I don't want to put you to any trouble. How does Mark like being a full-time at-home dad?'

'He's coping okay,' said Natalie, smiling. 'It's hard for all of us right now.'

'I just wanted to bring you a little present. I saw these and thought they were so cute.'

She handed Natalie a small parcel wrapped in blue tissue with a card. Natalie opened the card and read what Jodie had written: 'Hi, Andrew, and welcome! We're looking forward to meeting you and playing together.' It was signed Jodie, and her children had written their names in crayon. Natalie's eyes filled with tears as she unwrapped a pair of tiny blue sneakers with stars on their toes.

'Oh, Jodie. They're adorable. They'll swim on him

213

for a long time yet, even though they're so little. It's his first present! It's not like when I had the other two. It's almost as though people are too afraid to give me anything in case . . . I know that sounds crazy and I suppose that I can sort of understand it, but it makes me think that they see him as a non-person, just waiting to see what'll happen. You are so, so sweet. You don't know what this means to me,' said Natalie, reaching out to hug her friend.

'I think I do,' said Jodie.


Two days later, with her breasts feeling taut and leaking painfully, Natalie drove back to the hospital and went to the unit where Andrew was being monitored. He was still in a humidicrib and hooked up to a drip. He was dressed and wrapped in a cotton blanket. His colour was good and, although his breathing was raspy, it didn't seem as laboured as it had been, nor did he struggle so much with each intake of breath.

'How are you my darling little boy?' She put her hand through the opening and gently caressed him with her fingers.

A nurse came over to Natalie. 'I'm Karen, I'm in charge of Andrew today.' She smiled. 'Would you like to hold him for a minute?'

'Yes, yes,' breathed Natalie.

Tenderly Andrew was lifted from the humidicrib and placed in Natalie's arms for the first time. She stroked his cheek, marvelling at his perfect little features and hands, although initially the lightness and smallness of him shocked her. Then he wiggled, seeming to make himself comfortable, and opened his eyes and looked straight at her. In that moment Natalie felt overwhelming love for her son. Bonding with him was not ever going to be a problem now.

'My brave boy. What a trip you've had. It's going to

be fine.' She looked at the nurse. 'My milk is leaking. I'd love to be able to feed him.'

'He's not strong enough to suck yet. But we'll get you to express your milk and he can have it by tube. Maybe, when he's stronger, you can try breastfeeding. Let's see how he goes. The doctors are pleased with his progress,' she said.

For Natalie, holding her son in her arms, nothing else mattered but this moment.

Days passed, and Mark and Natalie had the hospital routine down pat. Mark managed Charlotte and Adam during the day. Natalie knew that he didn't keep the house in the same clean state as she did, but she didn't criticise the mess. Some evenings Mark liked to go up to the Mater after Natalie had arrived home. He told Natalie how much he loved his little son and enjoyed holding him, even if just for a few minutes.

Natalie had been going to the Mater hospital for more than two weeks and was taking a morning tea break in the cafeteria. From her bag she pulled out the mail that she'd grabbed from the letterbox and started to go through it. Putting the bills to one side, she eagerly opened the blue envelope from Burma addressed to her in Princess Aye Aye's elegant handwriting.

*Dear Mrs Cutler,*
*I thank you for your generous and beautiful letter. Thank you for your heartfelt expression of sympathy for the tragic and sad news of the death and hurt inflicted on our people. It is prudent I do not say more in this letter.*

*As you know, the kammavaca was given to my great-aunt, the Princess Tipi Si, for safekeeping and the family has always been dismayed that her circumstances forced*

*her to sell it, although I cannot blame her for that. I am*
*not sure exactly why this particular kammavaca was of*
*such great significance to King Thibaw, but it has always*
*been known in my family that it was important. So I am*
*very pleased by your very generous and kind promise to*
*fulfil the wish of your great-great-uncle and see its safe*
*return to my family. It shows me that you have the same*
*high principles as Andrew Hancock.*

*Times are not easy in our country, but we all hold the*
*hope that life will one day gives us the freedoms for which*
*we pray at the feet of the Great One.*

*I send you my deepest thanks and look forward to the*
*day when King Thibaw's kammavaca returns to Burma.*
*Thank you for your kindness.*

*With metta and heartfelt thanks,*
*Aye Aye, former princess of Burma*

'Oh, Uncle Andrew, I do hope you're proud of me,' whispered Natalie.

She folded the letter and, feeling calmer and stronger than she had since the birth of Andrew, she finished her tea and returned to the vigil at her baby's side.

# 8

MARK WAS SETTLING INTO a routine. The novelty of being at home with the children all the time had worn off and things had become easier. Each morning Natalie kissed them all goodbye after breakfast and headed out the door to drive to Brisbane in Mark's old work ute. She was home in the early evening to help Mark cope with late-afternoon tiredness, tantrums over toys and the juggling act of getting the dinner ready, bathtime and bed.

Mark, working in the kitchen, had revised his ideas about its renovation as he saw the more practical aspects of functioning in a space with small children. He realised that cooking utensils needed to be in easy reach, while childproof food storage was important and child-safe cupboards were paramount. He still took Charlotte and Adam to their favourite play centre, although infrequently, as he was now watching every dollar. Natalie's friends there had taken him under their collective wing and occasionally asked him for his opinion on whatever specific child-rearing issue was being discussed. Often Mark was the one asked to help with a problem stroller or to lift a child down from the top of the slippery dip when they changed their mind about going down the slide. He listened and sometimes joined in the women's discussions about local issues, sport and politics. He was pleased when they gave him hints for meals and snacks or recommended suitable children's books and DVDs.

Being part of this group was a far cry from the one-dimensional working world at the mine where conversation was pretty much work-related. Even at mealtimes, Mark had found that not many of his co-workers wanted to sit and chat at length or in depth about other subjects. The easy warmth of Natalie's friends made him feel both welcome and supported.


'Has the doctor given you any idea how much longer before we can bring Andrew home?' Mark asked Natalie one night. 'I told human resources today I was going to need more time off.'

'I think a few more weeks. He's gaining weight slowly. I tried breastfeeding him again today but he's still not strong enough to suck properly, so they'll continue tube feeding. The staff said it was going to be a slow process. But he's hanging in there. There are little improvements every day,' said Natalie. 'I know it's hard, but what can we do?'

'I haven't seen him for a couple of days. I'd like to go up sometime today and see his doctors as well,' said Mark. 'Vicki offered to help out if we needed her. Maybe she could watch the kids after preschool and you and I could go up together. Or if you want a day off, I can take your milk up.'

'No, I'll come with you. I like to feed him myself. So if it's okay with Vicki to mind the kids, we could go up to see Andrew together.'

Later that day at the hospital, the medical staff told them both that, although Andrew was improving, he was still struggling with some breathing problems. When the doctors left, Natalie and Mark sat quietly, Andrew resting in Mark's arms. Natalie gently stroked his tiny head. 'When I hold Andrew now he seems more of a real person. I just feel overwhelmed with love for him. And not just him, Nat, but for you, Charlotte and Adam, too,' said Mark as Andrew wriggled and gave a little cry.

Mark was quiet on the way home. Natalie knew that he was concerned that Andrew's recovery was still a long haul. They were both worried about keeping their family functioning, the costs of preschool and other activities were mounting, not to mention the petrol to drive the ute up and down to Brisbane every day. They knew that Mark had to get back to work because their savings were running out fast.


One morning Mark was watching Adam and Charlotte at the playground. A small boy tried to push in front of Adam at the slippery dip and Adam objected. During the ensuing scuffle Mark's phone rang.

'Hello—Calm down, Adam, it's your turn next. Charlotte, hold your skirt up, otherwise you're going to trip up the steps. Sorry, who is this? Oh, right, yes.' Watching Charlotte in her long skirt Mark wished he'd insisted on her wearing something more practical to play in. He was only partly listening to the voice of a woman from the mine's human resources unit.

'I'm sorry, I'm with my children. Could you run that past me again?' As he listened, the colour drained from his face. 'But you can't do that. I have a family to support. My son is very ill in hospital,' he started to explain. He could not believe what this woman was telling him. Then he stopped speaking and slowly rubbed his eyes. 'I see. Yes. I understand, but it all seems very unfair to me.'

'Daddy, Daddy, look at me!' Charlotte squealed as she slid down the slide.

But Mark found it hard to smile and appear enthusiastic as he absorbed this latest blow. The mine management had undertaken some redundancies and his position was one of those that had gone. He no longer had a job.

He didn't break the news to Natalie for several days, praying that he would find work quickly. But without a date for Andrew's release from hospital and no immediate offers of work, he had to tell her.

When the children were asleep, Mark asked Natalie to sit down and said, 'Nat, we have to talk about where we're going from here. How we're going to manage.' He looked distracted and concerned.

'Andrew is doing okay. At least now we know he will be coming home, even if not exactly when,' said Natalie.

'I know, it's wonderful. But, darling, it's not going to be that easy.'

'I know it's been hard for you,' began Natalie. 'But once he's home, I'll manage the three of them when you go back to the mine. I know I will.'

'Natalie, I haven't got a job to go back to,' blurted out Mark.

Natalie looked at him incredulously. 'What do you mean?'

'The mine let me go. They did a round of redundancies and my job was one of them.'

'That is so unfair! How could they do that with everything we're going through?'

'I know, Nat, but that's business, I guess. No place for sentiment. They just do what is best for the company and the investors. It had nothing to do with my being off work. It was just a coincidence.'

'Mark, what are we going to do? What about a redundancy payout? Will you get anything?'

Mark shook his head. 'I don't think so. I wasn't there very long. Not a full year. And I've used up my holiday pay.'

Natalie was struggling with this news. 'Well, maybe losing the mining job's a blessing. You can get a job here, locally. Not as much money but it will be great to have you based here again,' she said, sounding almost relieved. 'Especially when we bring little Andrew home.'

'Nat, I've been asking around, and the building industry on the coast is quite depressed at present. There don't seem to be any jobs going.'

'What about your mates? Tony and the others?' she asked in alarm.

'I've been asking. Things are tight. My mates all say that if anything comes up, they'll keep me in mind,' he added. 'I'll start looking further afield.'

'Are there any mining jobs going?' she asked, feeling slightly desperate.

'I'm looking, but there doesn't seem to be anything right now. I guess with the downturn here, more tradies are applying to go out west. And, anyway, what can I promise companies when I don't know how long it will be before I can start?'

Natalie's mind was whirling. She was trying to think laterally, trying to stem her rising panic. 'Mark, you're such a good electrician, you've never had trouble getting work before.'

'I know, but it seems that times are tougher than they've been and it might take a while to get a job. Even a FIFO one. But what do we do in the meantime? We've used up our immediate savings and the mortgage won't wait.'

'Then we have to use the savings we've put aside for the major renovations. I know that I had my heart set on doing them, but I understand that we can't.'

'You're sure? I know how much you want to fix this place up.'

'We can't do it without an income, so we'll just have to bite the bullet till you get work.'

Natalie was surprised by how easy the decision was but she knew it was only a short-term solution to their problems. She remained deeply concerned about their financial and future prospects and she knew Mark was, too.

After weeks of travelling up to Brisbane each day, Natalie finally conceded that she needed a day to herself and Mark went to Brisbane to visit Andrew on his own. She sent Charlotte and Adam to preschool as usual although she didn't know how much longer they would be able to afford it. Natalie decided to make the most of having the time to drive into the hinterland to see Thi. When she arrived, Thomas was in Thi's front garden planting some herbs.

'Natalie! What a nice surprise! I've come to see Thi and now she's got me gardening. Her husband is away at present so I'm happy to lend a hand. Come in. She didn't tell me she was expecting you.'

'She doesn't know. I just decided to go for a drive while the kids are in preschool. I need a bit of a break.'

'Yes, I have heard that it's been very difficult for you,' said Thomas. 'How is your little Andrew? Let us go and make some English tea. Thi has made some biscuits. She'll be back shortly.'

'She's certainly a multitalented cook. Do you know how the markets are going?' said Natalie.

'Very well, Thi tells me,' said Thomas laughing. 'This weather, good rain, lots of sunshine, has been good for the gardeners. I'm sure she'll make you take home some fresh vegetables and fruit, and of course some flowers. How is your husband?'

'He's good but it's been an adjustment looking after the house and the children. I've been spending every day at the hospital in Brisbane. But today he's sitting with Andrew, so while I have a couple of hours to myself I decided to drive out here. We hope the baby will be coming home in a few weeks.'

'That's wonderful news!' exclaimed Thi, coming into the kitchen and giving Natalie a hug. 'You look tired, but it's wonderful to see you.'

'Yes, I feel tired, but I thought a trip to the lovely countryside out here, and to see you, would be good for me. Bit spur of the moment, I hope you don't mind.'

'Of course not! Bring the children next time.'

'I will. They would enjoy it. Thi, it seems ages since I've seen you. Before the Saffron Revolution.'

'Such a terrible thing. You saw footage of it on TV? I spoke to Mi Mi yesterday. There are some awful stories coming out. The monks, as well as the ordinary people, have lost their rights under military rule. The military can arrest and kill anyone at any time. There is no law in our country. They arrested the monks and people for praying for the wellbeing of others.' Thi shook her head. 'Some of the monasteries are still surrounded by soldiers so that the monks can't go out and demonstrate, but neither can they go on their morning rounds with their alms bowls asking for food.'

'I saw some photos in the paper of some of the monks marching with their bowls upside down. What does that mean?' asked Natalie.

'The monks hold the moral and spiritual authority in Burma, even though the country is ruled by the military, so the junta has always tried to establish its credibility and legitimacy by acknowledging the monks' religious position. By holding their bowls upside down, the monks were symbolically rejecting alms from the military, and excommunicating the soldiers from the spirituality that is the core of Burmese life,' explained Thi.

'So the monks were trying to make the point without confrontation?' said Natalie.

'Except, of course, with the junta that is impossible,' said Thomas sadly. 'These demonstrations will have ramifications for a long time to come.'

'They said on the news that people were protesting because fuel prices went up very sharply,' said Natalie.

'Oh, the craziness of the generals. They have no idea how to run Burma's economy except to benefit themselves. Do you know that they stole land from poor farmers in order to start building a new capital city called Naypyidaw? Burma doesn't need a new expensive capital in the middle of nowhere,' added Thi.

'Perhaps this Saffron Revolution has lit a small fire in the hearts of people outside Burma,' said Thomas.

'I was really shocked and upset at what I saw on TV, and now, from what you say, what I saw was only a small part of the protests,' said Natalie. 'In fact, I was so moved I wanted to help in some way. Mi Mi told me that she knows Princess Aye Aye, King Thibaw's granddaughter, and so I decided to return my kammavaca to her. I think that it should be back in Burma with its rightful owners, so, I'm completing Uncle Andrew's original mission and that feels important, too.'

Thi put down her cup and reached out to cover Natalie's hand with hers. 'That is a very special gesture. It will mean a lot to people in Burma when they hear about it.'

While they talked some more, Natalie felt herself relaxing for the first time in many weeks.

'When you bring the baby home, can we help?' asked Thi. 'I am happy to do what I can and I'm sure that Thomas is too.'

Thomas smiled and nodded in agreement.

'Thanks, you're both kind, but Mark will be there. It's going to be a bit scary, having Andrew home without the backup of the medical expertise he's had in the hospital.'

'You'll manage just fine. But if you want help, you just call,' said Thi.

'Thank you,' stammered Natalie, close to tears. She wished she could share the burden of Mark's desperate search for work, but she held her tongue. 'It's just been lovely to have a break like this.'

When Mark got home from the hospital later that afternoon, he eyed the fresh vegetables, leftover biscuits, jam and spicy pickles Thi had sent home with Natalie. 'That's a lovely lot of food, Nat. Thi is very generous, but I hope she doesn't think we need charity.'

'Don't be silly. Thi is just a generous person. She gives stuff to everyone. I didn't say anything about you being made redundant. You really should go to her community market again. Thi would love to see the kids, and Charlotte would like another pony ride,' said Natalie lightly. She could tell from his comment about charity that Mark was deeply worried.

Later, sitting at her computer to send her mother an update on Andrew's progress, Natalie saw an email from Peter

Michaelson, the antiques trader in London. Perplexed, she opened the email.

*I am wondering if you are still holding the kammavaca you asked me about? If you have not yet sold it, I am still interested in acquiring it. I have a serious collector who would be willing to offer you AU$40,000 for your arte-fact. Could you please let me know if you will sell it to me at this price?*

Natalie stared at the message in shock then burst out laughing and called out to Mark, 'You're not going to believe this.'

Mark didn't show much reaction when Natalie read him the offer but instead looked at her seriously and said, 'That's a lot of money, Natalie.'

'Yes, someone really wants it!'

'What are you going to do?' asked Mark evenly.

'I told you. I'm sending it back to Princess Aye Aye. I'm going to email Michaelson and tell him I'm sorry, but it's being returned to its rightful owner.'

'But, Natalie, we need that money!' exploded Mark. 'That offer could save us.'

'Mark, I've already written to Aye Aye and told her that I'm returning the kammavaca, and I'm not going back on my word. I owe it to Uncle Andrew. He wanted to do the right thing, and so do I,' she said stubbornly.

'I agree, and it was a nice gesture when the thing was only worth a third of this offer and I had a job! But we need that money now! Our circumstances have changed. We have to keep a roof over our heads, put food on the table and be responsible for three children!'

'Mark! Yes, we need money, but we also need a long-term solution. Selling the kammavaca is a drastic step that we may not even need to take. Sure, we didn't see things unfolding like this but you won't be out of work forever. We have to bite the bullet and hope —'

'That's the point, Nat. I don't know how long it's going to take for me to get a job again. Everyone is doing it tough, there's been a downturn and companies are cagey. We're not just talking about putting the renovations on hold. We're using up all our money.'

'I understand that. But we'd be in the same boat with or without the kammavaca. You were okay about returning it to the princess when it was worth a lot less.'

Mark answered through gritted teeth. 'Exactly. Now we know it's worth a helluva lot more, and selling it can *help us* now we're in financial trouble.'

'I'm not going back on my word,' repeated Natalie stubbornly. 'I promised the princess that I would return it. It should never have been taken in the first place. Keeping it is wrong and so is selling it.'

'If it goes back to Burma, who's to know, and what's to stop her from getting forty grand for it?'

'Aye Aye wouldn't sell it! It means something special to her. It's about giving, Mark, about karma!' retorted Natalie.

'Nat, sit down, and let's talk this through sensibly.' Mark led her to the sofa.

'Don't treat me like a child.'

'I'm not, I'm just trying to get you to see the sense of this. Perhaps that thing did come to you for a reason. And this is it. We need the money we can get by selling it. Don't you think Uncle Andrew would have liked to help you and see some good come of his kammavaca? Help his namesake?'

Natalie was annoyed at Mark's calm and reasonable voice. 'It was not *his* kammavaca. He only got it so he could return it to Princess Tipi Si. There's a very big principle involved and I'm not selling out my principle. I saw people dying for their belief in doing the right thing!'

'Yes, I saw that TV coverage, too.'

'It was *real*. Why should I compromise my beliefs and principles now, just weeks after realising what the right thing to do is? I won't go back on my word. It's what Uncle Andrew wanted, I know it. I've been given the chance to complete his journey. That's the reason I found the kammavaca. We could have just as easily got rid of it in the clearing sale.'

'But you didn't. It's here, and it gives us a chance to get over a rough patch,' insisted Mark.

'Mark, don't you see? I can't go back on my promise,' said Natalie quietly. 'We have a baby called Andrew because I admire my uncle and what he was trying to do. How can we teach our children about principles and standing up for what is right if I can't lead by example?'

'The old princess didn't look after her family's precious kammavaca! She sold it *because she needed the money*! What's the difference for us?' demanded Mark.

'She regretted it straight away, Mark. I don't want to be like that. We can't get it back once it's sold. I'm happy to sell anything of mine that's worth selling if we need to but not the kammavaca.'

Natalie stood up and walked from the room. She heard the front door close as she stood in the half-finished bathroom, the cold light of the unshaded light globe illuminating the unfinished walls and untiled floor.

Natalie was more than upset. She was hurt and angry, and frightened about the severity of their financial situation, which scared her as much as it did Mark. But the fact that he couldn't see, or wouldn't agree, with her point of view was like a huge boulder landing on their relationship. She knew they were both stressed and tired since Andrew's premature birth, each out of their comfort zone, but the severity and intensity of her feelings and the stalemate she'd come up against with Mark was,

228

she hated to admit, making her wonder just how well they knew each other.

This was the first big test of their marriage. Her mother had always said that if things fall down, it's almost always over money.

Natalie had never thought of herself or Mark as being money hungry. She and Mark had sometimes giggled over the ostentatious vulgarities of style on the Gold Coast. The pampered women wearing too much jewellery and make-up, owning too big a home, too many cars and enormous boats, while ageing men in white linen pants and artificial tans escorted partners who were either too young for them or who'd had too much cosmetic surgery.

But she and Mark had found a different lifestyle. When they'd moved into their house they'd met neighbours like Vicki and other young couples who were also struggling to raise families and make ends meet. They were making sacrifices to establish homes and build family lives that were more authentic than the shiny tourist exterior of this strip of prized Queensland coast. Perhaps she and Mark were being too ambitious. Had they taken on too much when they'd bought this house?

Confused by all that had happened to them, she went to bed and fell into a troubled sleep. When she woke up she was surprised to find it was already 7 a.m. She could hear Mark giving the children their breakfast. Her breasts felt hard and she knew she had to express some milk.

By the time she was ready to leave for the hospital, the children were playing outside and Mark was cleaning the kitchen.

'Thanks for doing that. You're a good father. I'm heading off now. Do you need me to do anything?' she asked quietly.

'No, dinner's taken care of. You have Andrew's breakfast?'

Natalie gave him a small smile. 'Yes. Take-away.'

'I'll see you later, then.'

'I'm sorry about last night, Mark. But I haven't changed my mind.'

'Nat, I can't believe we can't agree on something this important.'

'Me either.' Natalie walked outside and got in the ute.


At the hospital, she found Andrew very alert and when he gave her a smile, her spirits lifted.

'I'm sure you mean that, my lovely boy, and it's not just tummy gas.' She smiled back at him.

After she'd fed him and he'd gone to sleep, she went outside the hospital into the sunshine with a bottle of water and rang her mother at the shop.

'That's wonderful, he's gaining even more weight,' exclaimed Sarah. 'He'll be home before you know it. What's the plan then? Is Mark going straight back to work? How long can he be on leave?'

'Mum, I have to tell you, the mine has made a lot of people redundant, and Mark was one of them. He's out of a job.'

'What?' exclaimed Sarah. 'Darling, that's terrible. Didn't they know about Andrew? That's outrageous. Can't he go back to his old job? He must know every builder on the Gold Coast. Why didn't you tell me?'

Natalie hesitated. Why had she delayed telling her mother about Mark when usually her mother was the first person she called in any crisis? 'I'm not sure,' she said slowly. 'Maybe because it's scary and upsetting, and I didn't want to worry you.'

'Mark will get another job, darling!'

'He's been searching, but things aren't looking good.'

'Nat, how bad is it? I mean, I can't believe Mark can't get a job. It won't be long, I'm sure.'

'I hope so. It's just that we're going to have to live on our renovation savings.'

'There'll be plenty of time for renos, Natalie, don't worry.'

'Yes. Unless . . . no, forget it.'

'Unless what?' asked Sarah, sensing something was amiss.

'Mark wants me to sell the kammavaca.'

'For heaven's sake! It's not worth that much is it? It won't keep you going long. I thought you wanted to keep it.'

'I've had an offer of forty thousand dollars, which would be a huge help now. Mark wants to sell it because he doesn't know how long it will be before he sees another pay cheque and I want to return it to Burma. It's caused a bit of a rift between us.'

'Good grief!' exclaimed her mother. 'Forty thousand. To think we nearly threw it out. Who wants to pay that?'

'A dealer in London. He said he had a buyer. But Mum, I've already made up my mind that I'm going to send it back to the family it came from in Burma. I've already offered it to the person concerned and she's really pleased, so I can't go back on my word, can I?' said Natalie.

'Natalie, are you sure? I mean, no-one would blame you for changing your mind. Seeing you have very different circumstances now,' added Sarah quickly.

'Mum, I can't go back on my word! I've learned a lot about Burma and I know that this is the right thing to do. I can't sell something that doesn't really belong to me. Uncle Andrew was trying to return it to this family when he was killed. He never got to return it to the rightful owner!'

'I see,' said Sarah quietly. 'And that's why you named the baby Andrew.'

'Yes. But Mark and I have had a huge fight over the kammavaca.'

'I'm not surprised and I can see your point of view,' said Sarah. 'But surely your family should come before some strangers in Burma? How do you know she won't sell it once they get it?'

'I don't know, though I'd be very surprised. But even if she does, it's her decision,' said Natalie adamantly.

Sarah didn't sound convinced. 'Nat, are you sure that you're not just emotionally exhausted by all that you've been through? Are you sure that you're making the right decision? That sort of money would come in awfully handy for you both right now. And how are you going to manage? I just wish I could give you some money, but after Steve's misadventure with the shares, I'm not in a financial position to help at all. Have you thought about returning to work?'

'Mum, how can I possibly go back to work with a sick, premature baby in hospital? It would be completely impractical. I would have to express my milk every morning, get Mark to drive it up to Brisbane, with the other two in the ute, more than an hour each way, because he couldn't leave them by themselves. Anyway, even if I was mad enough to try to return to work, I wouldn't really be able to concentrate knowing that I had abandoned my baby. It's out of the question.'

'I didn't mean to upset you, Nat. I was just looking at options.'

'It's all right, Mum. We'll manage somehow. As you say, I'm sure Mark will land a job soon.'

'The main thing is little Andrew has pulled through,' said Sarah. 'When will you bring him home?'

'I'm not exactly sure. It will be good to have him at home, but it's going to be a challenge,' said Natalie. 'I'm a bit scared about it. He's still so tiny, and I've got two others who aren't very old either.'

'I know, but there's a lot of pressure on Mark, too.'

'Me too, Mum! We're using up our savings so we can't do the renos and we're living in chaos. We won't be able to afford preschool so the kids will be home twenty-four seven with a fragile new baby, and I'll have a grumpy husband getting depressed and feeling a failure,' said Natalie.

'And you have a solution but you don't like it,' said her mother.

'Mum, it's a temporary solution. When that money's gone, what then? You said yourself, Mark could land a job at any moment, we just have to hang in there. I can't go back on my word, I just can't.' Natalie felt close to tears. Surely her mother could understand her wish to do the right thing.

'But what if it takes much longer than you think for Mark to find work? You don't want to lose that house!'

'I hope it's not going to come to that, Mum. I'm just going day by day at the moment.'

'Why don't you take a Sunday off and trade with Mark on the hospital run and come and visit us?' suggested Sarah, changing the subject. 'I think you need a bit of space.'

'I'll think about it,' answered Natalie.

Life staggered on at home with uncomfortable silences, neither Natalie nor Mark mentioning the offer from Michaelson. Mark had contacted everyone he knew and complained to Natalie about his bad luck with timing as there seemed to be no openings. He spent a lot of time on the phone chasing up people in the local building industry as well as companies using electrical contractors. As soon as Natalie arrived home, he'd head out the door to drop off a resume, or meet with someone who might know about a job.

Natalie didn't say anything but she knew he was becoming increasingly frustrated by his inability to find work. She knew that he felt diminished by his lack of success.

Three weeks later Andrew was discharged from hospital.

Natalie and Mark felt a mix of elation and apprehension about caring for their tiny son. He was still barely the weight of a newborn, although he was thriving and gaining weight each week.

Charlotte was delighted to have her little baby brother home at last and introduced him to some of her favourite toys, promising him that he could play with them whenever he wanted. 'If you ask nicely,' she added.

Adam seemed uninterested initially, but whenever he heard Andrew cry, he would run to a parent to let them know at once that his little brother wanted them. Both Mark and Natalie were surprised by the children's calm acceptance of this new family member.

Natalie was told to feed Andrew every three hours and she was relieved when an early childhood nurse came every few days to check on his progress, weight and oxygen levels, and to answer any questions she might have. It was comforting for her to be able to talk to an understanding specialist about her fears, especially her anxiety at night.

'I sleep so lightly, because I'm listening for any little snuffle or breathing problem,' said Natalie. 'I feel so responsible for him. Before there were professionals looking after him, so there would always be help on hand if something happened. Now, there's just me.'

'Your feelings are perfectly normal. But you do need to get your rest. Perhaps you could have a nap in the daytime between feeds and let your husband look after the baby and the other children.'

'Yes, he's at home right now,' said Natalie.

It was tricky to find a time when the house was quiet

and Natalie could rest without being disturbed. But Vicki came to the rescue and offered to have Charlotte and Adam at her place in the afternoon after their naps for a couple of days a week, while Mark looked after Andrew and Natalie slept. The children loved playing with Ipoh and sometimes Thomas or Thi stopped by during their visit. Whether Vicki had asked them or whether their good Burmese friends had volunteered to help, Natalie didn't ask. She was grateful that the children were happy and enjoyed being at Vicki's, and she could get some welcome sleep.

The routine and atmosphere in the house changed considerably when Brad arrived unexpectedly at the door.

'Hi, Brad! This is a surprise. What are you doing here?' asked Natalie. 'Mark is out for a little while. Does he know you're coming?' She ushered him inside, surprised at how pleased she was to see the ever-optimistic and cheerful Brad.

'No, he doesn't. But no worries, I won't impose on you. Could I leave my bags here till I get a car organised?'

'You're not staying with us? That's a pity. Are you staying in the unit you bought?'

'Nope. It's rented. I'm going to a motel. You must have your hands full with the new bub. I'm only passing through for a few days. Taking a break, having a swim, anything that's away from holes in the ground and dust.'

'Would you like a coffee?'

'That'd be great. I'll just get my stuff.'

Natalie started to make coffee and then stuck her head outside where the children were playing in the garden.

'Charlotte, Adam! We have a visitor!'

The children shrieked with delight and flung themselves at Brad as he struggled through the door with two large bags.

'How come you've got so much stuff?' asked Natalie. 'I've left the mine.'

'Did they make you redundant, too?' asked Natalie.

'No way. I got in first and quit.' He tickled Charlotte, making her squeal, while Adam tried to climb onto his back.

'Why did you do that, if you don't mind my asking?'

'They were pretty rotten about Mark, I thought. I know that other people were made redundant, but what they did to Mark was wrong, I reckon. Everyone hits a rough patch in life at some stage and I always figure if you give them a hand, be a bit understanding, especially if you're a boss, then you'll get it back ten times over. They didn't do the right thing by Mark,' he said simply, 'so I left them.'

'The right thing,' she echoed. 'I hope you tell Mark that. It's really decent of you, Brad, but can you manage now that you have a mortgage?'

'I'm not worried, something will turn up. I'm not married and I haven't got kids. Things are much tougher for Mark.' Brad gave a shrug and a grin. 'Change is as good as a holiday, I reckon.'

'Don't think Mark agrees. He hasn't been able to find work here on the coast at all. But it will mean a lot to him that you walked away from the mine because of the way he was treated.'

'Nat, don't worry. Sparkies will always be in demand but the work goes in cycles. Just have to hang in there.'

Natalie was tempted to tell Brad just how bad their situation was, but decided she'd let Mark choose what to share with his friend. 'Would you like to take a peek at our new addition? Andrew's come home.'

'Lead the way!' Brad followed Natalie into the bedroom where Andrew was sleeping in a bassinet beside their bed.

'Wow, he's a little guy. Like a doll,' whispered Brad, sounding awestruck. 'Cutie, though.'

Natalie nodded as they tiptoed out of the bedroom. 'It's still a bit scary. We sort of wish that we could have brought all the hospital equipment and staff home with us. We got so used to seeing him all hooked up to machinery in the humidicrib.'

'What do you think of your new little brother, Charlotte?' Brad asked as she pounced on him.

'He sleeps a lot and he cries like a little mouse.'

'What've you been up to? Still dancing?'

'Can we put on a show?' asked Charlotte excitedly. 'I will dance the princess,' she announced as she headed into the lounge room.

As they were applauding and the princess was taking her bows, Mark came in and did a double take to see Natalie sitting on the lounge and Brad holding Adam.

'You missed my show, Daddy!'

'I'll catch the second act, honey. Brad, good to see you, mate. What are you doing here? How long are you around?'

Natalie excused herself, gathering up the children to leave Brad and Mark together to catch up.


Mark was the most animated he'd been in weeks. Brad's presence and his stand against Mark's treatment cheered them both up. But things were still strained as Natalie continued to stand her ground over the sale of the kammavaca, even when Mark told her that he could not see how they could manage the mortgage repayments much longer. If they couldn't talk the bank into a new arrangement, they could lose the house.

With Brad there to keep Mark company, Natalie decided to go to yoga classes again to help calm her mind.

She felt she needed it, even if only one day a week, and worked out that they could afford it if they tweaked the household budget. Mark and Brad assured her that they would have no trouble looking after the three children. So Natalie fed Andrew and headed off to class.

The quiet commands of the instructor and the gentle, relaxed breathing of the class during meditation calmed Natalie. She was glad that she'd made the effort to come, and after the class she had a mug of chai with Moss.

'It's good to see you. I heard that you were on quite a trip with your surprise package,' said Moss as he passed her the honey.

'You mean Andrew coming early? Yes, it was a big surprise. A big scare, actually, but thank god he's doing okay. It's wonderful what they can do for premmie babies these days, so he'll catch up.' Natalie declined the honey for her tea and blinked back a tear.

Moss reached over and put his hand on her arm. 'That's one thing about being a Buddhist, you learn to simply accept. One accepts the gifts one is given and, for you, Andrew is a special gift.'

Natalie nodded. 'I realise that. I'm trying to accept what each day brings.'

'I'm sure he's on the road to wellness and you have to let him start his journey,' said Moss. 'How are things with you? I expect you haven't had much time for yourself. What happened with your kammavaca? Do you still have it?'

'Yes. Though it's caused a bit of controversy in our household,' she said lightly, trying to make it seem less than the contentious issue it was. 'We've had an insane offer from the London dealer I think I told you about and Mark wants me to sell it.'

'I thought you'd decided not to sell,' said Moss.

'I still don't want to. It didn't matter whether we sold

it or not when it was only worth a few thousand. But forty thousand dollars suddenly puts a different light on things, especially for my husband.'

Moss's eyebrows shot up. 'Why did the price rise?'

'I don't know. Michaelson said he had a serious collector keen to buy it.'

'That is substantial money,' said Moss. 'Did he say whether it was a private collector or an institution?'

Natalie shook her head. 'No idea. He just said a collector. Anyway, it's not for sale and I'm not keeping it either. I saw the scenes of the monks demonstrating in the Saffron Revolution on TV and the army firing on them. I was really shocked, and I wanted to do something for Burma, besides just handing out pamphlets. My friend Mi Mi told me that she knew a granddaughter of King Thibaw. So I wrote to her in Burma and said I'd send the kammavaca back to her.'

'That is a big decision and one I admire. I imagine the recipient was pleased, too.'

'She was, very much so. It seems the family had been told by King Thibaw to keep the kammavaca safe always. But, well, things happen, times change,' said Natalie.

'Are you questioning your decision now?'

'Not at all,' said Natalie firmly.

'Then that's your answer,' said Moss. 'Did this dealer tell you anything about the kammavaca?'

'No. A dealer in Brisbane suggested that Michaelson could get it translated for me, but I never followed that up. I was told that the writing was probably sacred texts.'

'Whatever is written in the manuscript, it is probably the object itself that would appeal to a dealer. Its age, condition and, especially in this instance, its provenance. There's certainly a fascinating story attached to this piece.'

'Yes, Princess Aye Aye has confirmed that Tipi Si was cheated.'

'Yes, Ferguson had a reputation for shady dealings.'

Natalie reacted with surprise. 'Ferguson, the art dealer? How do you know about him? Was he famous?'

'You told me about him when you first explained the story. So I thought I'd see what I could find out about him.'

'I'd forgotten I'd told you.'

Moss smiled. 'Hardly surprising after all you've been through. Well, I did a little research. Ferguson is variously described as a colourful chap or an interesting fellow. I think we would call him a bit of a self-promoter. Your uncle did a feature on him in the *Illustrated London News*.'

'Yes,' said Natalie. 'I found that article, too.'

'It seems that Ferguson became a bit of legend with all of his grand gestures of donations to museums and so forth, although not every deal panned out for him. Just the same, he must have made a very tidy sum for himself, because he acquired a Victorian pile in the Scottish highlands.'

'A castle?'

'Complete with kilt, pipes and crest. An avid collector, he also collected a family history with all the trappings, including a title.'

'You have done some homework! He doesn't sound like a very nice person at all. I think it was smart of Uncle Andrew to do a deal with him and buy the kammavaca back.'

'Yes. But I suspect Ferguson came to regret that transaction.' Moss straightened up. 'I would very much like to see the object of all this intrigue.'

'I'd love you to see it, too. And to meet Mark. Why don't you come over on Saturday afternoon?'

'Wonderful. I accept. Are you going to take the kammavaca back to Burma?'

'No way. I couldn't afford to. And I've never travelled outside Australia. But I have a friend who sometimes goes to Burma and she said she'd return it for me.'

'If that doesn't work out and you need another courier, I'd be happy to help,' said Moss. 'Remember that,' he added and smiled at Natalie.

'That's really nice of you, Moss. Thank you,' said Natalie.


'So tell me again, who's this guy from your yoga class?' asked Mark on Saturday when Natalie reminded him Moss was coming around.

'Moss is a uni lecturer in Buddhist art history. He's travelled a lot around Asia and he's interested in Burma. He's really knowledgeable and . . . sensitive. He's interested in the kammavaca and I thought it might be nice for you to meet him.'

'Doesn't sound like someone I'd have much in common with,' said Mark. Nevertheless he put on a clean T-shirt and asked if there was anything Natalie wanted him to do.

'No, it's okay. Moss seems pretty easygoing.'

When Mark opened the door he was greeted by a tall, slim man with loose shoulder-length hair and round tinted glasses reminiscent of John Lennon's. 'Hi, I'm Moss. Pleased to meet you.'

'Come on in,' said Mark.

Natalie came out from the kitchen. 'Hi, Moss. As it's a nice day I thought we'd sit outside. You remember my two big kids, Charlotte and Adam?'

'Yes, from the rally. I brought you a book.' Moss handed Natalie a small package.

'Thank you.'

'Coffee or tea?' asked Mark.

'Tea will be fine, if you're making it, or just water,'

said Moss, sitting down as Adam dragged his wooden train over to show him.

'Natalie said you're a teacher? You know about these kammavaca things then?' said Mark.

'Not a lot. But I'd like to see this one as it has such an interesting history.'

'Yeah. Did Nat tell you she's knocked back an offer of forty grand for it?' Mark shook his head in bewilderment. 'Beats me that it's worth so much.'

'Well, I guess some collector thinks it is,' said Moss.

'We could do with that money right now, but Nat's determined to send it back to Burma,' said Mark. 'I wish I could change her mind.'

'Yes, I can imagine how you feel. But one has to respect her principles. Perhaps she is hoping a solution will present itself. You sometimes have to just trust in the universe, don't you?' said Moss.

'I'd better get the tea,' said Mark.

Natalie came out with the teak box containing the kammavaca and watched Moss carefully open it and delicately unfold the manuscript.

'Wow.' He spread it on the table. 'This is beautiful. Look at the artwork.' He peered at it closely. 'Do you have a magnifying glass?'

'Yes. I'll get it.'

Using the magnifying glass, Moss peered closely at each illustration. 'I wonder if there might be some detail that might tell us more.'

'Like a clue?' asked Mark, returning with the tea. 'Can you read that stuff?'

'Not this old script,' said Moss. 'But the pictures are so beautiful and so realistic. Look at that monastery. From the setting and the figures of the monks, it must be a real place, don't you think? Look at that gorgeously ornate elephant. The whole feel of it is wonderful.'

242

'So is it worth forty thousand dollars, do you think?' asked Mark lightly.

Moss straightened up. 'This kammavaca was made for the king and he took it into exile with him, so it must have meant a lot to him.'

At that moment Charlotte tumbled off her tricycle and started crying. 'I'll go,' said Mark, sprinting down the garden.

'Thanks, Natalie but I must be going. I can see that you and your husband have your hands full,' said Moss. 'You have a difficult choice on your hands. Please let me know if I can help, whatever you decide. But it would certainly be unwise to post it.'

'I will definitely consider your offer, just in case Vicki can't take it. And thank you for the book.'

'Goodbye, Mark,' Moss called out to Mark, who was helping Charlotte untangle herself from the tricycle.

Later Brad came around to see them both and picked up the book Moss had brought Natalie and glanced at the title. 'This book on Buddhism looks pretty heavy to me,' he said.

Natalie took the book from him. 'It's beyond me, too. But my friend's intention was kind and that's what friends do,' she commented.


The following morning as she was settling Andrew down for a sleep, Natalie's phone rang.

'Hello, Natalie, it's Mi Mi. I was wondering if you'd like to come out for a coffee so I can meet your beautiful boy. How is he settling in at home?'

'He's great. I still get a bit wobbly at times. I keep checking him and worrying if he makes an unusual sound. But he's feeding and sleeping well, and starting to be aware of his surroundings. He sleeps through anything. I guess he got used to the noise and activity around him in the hospital.'

'That's good news. I'm going to Pacific Fair later this morning, are you free?'

'Yes, Mark and his mate have taken the children to the park, so there's just Andrew and me. I'd love to get out for a bit. Shall we meet at that coffee shop on the mezzanine level?'


Natalie cradled Andrew in a sling close to her chest as she strolled past the shops at the shopping centre. When she turned into the little café, she saw Mi Mi straight away. Mi Mi rose and waved.

'Let me have a peek.' She pulled the sling back and gently stroked Andrew's head. 'He's doing well,' she said softly. 'What a trip it's been for you both. You know, when he's eighteen and a football star, no-one will believe that he was a premmie baby.'

'I hope you're right, Mi Mi. I saw such terrible things in the NICU. Babies you knew weren't going to make it, others so small that even if they did survive you wonder if they're going to have some handicap in life. I swung between such intense emotions. Sometimes, just after Andrew was born, the nurses used to send me back to my room to get some sleep. I think they got sick of me glued to Andrew's humidicrib. But when I went back to the ward and saw all those big healthy babies, I got so upset, I'd start pacing around my room. And then I had to travel up to Brisbane every day . . . that car trip was like leaving the normal world and flying to some weird planet where I had this other life, this other child.'

Natalie stopped and looked down at Andrew, shocked that she was suddenly letting out her feelings. She hadn't even really told Mark what she had felt during all those weeks.

Mi Mi was calm. She ordered their coffees and asked,

'Did you blame yourself, too? That's a normal response. Whether you fell over the washing basket or not, Andrew still could have come prematurely. Even if you'd spent weeks flat on your back in bed, things could've still gone wrong. The main thing is you got through it and so did Andrew, and you'll both continue to grow into a place where this can all be put into perspective and eventually packed away.'

'Mi Mi, I wish things were that simple. Andrew is doing well, but his birth and his long time in hospital have given us problems that we didn't foresee, so we're having a bit of a rough time. Mark's been made redundant.'

'That's awful! And so unfeeling given Andrew's condition. I suppose they would call it business, but it's a lot more than that for your family, isn't it? Are there prospects on the horizon for your husband?'

Natalie shook her head. 'Not at the moment. I'm sure things will come good but in the meantime we've used up most of our savings and he's saying we might have to sell the house. And it's all my fault . . .' Natalie stopped, brushed away a tear and sipped her coffee. 'Sorry, I shouldn't be dumping all this on you.'

'This isn't your fault, how can that be?'

'Well, losing his job wasn't my fault, but if I sold that kammavaca, I could bail us out. I've had an offer from a dealer in London of forty thousand dollars, but I've promised to return it to Princess Aye Aye and I really, really want it to go back to her. She's already written to me saying how pleased she is that it's coming back.' Natalie looked at Mi Mi with stricken eyes. 'It's what Uncle Andrew wanted, too.'

'Natalie! What a terrible situation. How dreadful for you. But of course you must sell it. I know that you have already made the commitment and your intentions were good and pure, but Aye Aye would never expect you to sacrifice your home for the sake of returning the kammavaca.'

'But I promised. I know she was so thrilled that it was coming back. There's something very special about that kammavaca. I can't go back on my word,' said Natalie.

Mi Mi reached out and took Natalie's hand. 'Special, yes, but that can mean different things to different people. Think of how that little artefact has brought you into the circle of friends connected to our country. How you have learned about our history and how you have helped us make more Australians aware of Burma's plight. This may all be part of what you know as karma. The kammavaca's journey might not be complete yet. The offer of the money is a way of helping you because you generously offered to return the kammavaca to King Thibaw's family. But no-one, especially Aye Aye, would expect you to sacrifice your home and cause problems for your family by this kindness. Take the money that has been offered. The kammavaca has passed through your hands for a reason that might never be known. Aye Aye would feel the gesture tainted if it cost you so much. Please, I know everyone would feel the same. You must look after your family. I will write to Aye Aye and explain everything to her. She will hold nothing against you for changing your mind. She will understand that the main thing is that your heart and intentions remain true.'

Natalie saw her tears falling on Andrew's cheek. She gently wiped them away and sniffed as she reached for a tissue. 'Thank you, Mi Mi.'

'Let's order another coffee. I just had a feeling that I wanted to see you today. I'm so glad I did. Now, can I have a cuddle of the young man, please?'

*

Mark listened quietly as Natalie told him that, after talking to Mi Mi, she was reassessing the situation.

'She told me that Aye Aye would be devastated if she knew that I had lost my home or put my family in desperate circumstances because of the kammavaca. That what I was doing is morally correct, but it is not the time right now. She said that the kammavaça is still on its journey,' added Natalie forlornly.

Mark nodded. 'I know how much returning it means to you, Nat. And I really admire you for wanting to do that. But Mi Mi is right. We do have to think about our family.'

'I didn't want to seem selfish. It doesn't seem right wanting money to decorate the house and things like that when now I know how tough it is for families in places like Burma. And now that Andrew is safe and growing I want him to be proud of his namesake. I want to finish what my uncle started.'

Mark took her hand. 'Nat, you are the most generous person I know. You are not frivolous. I'm very proud of you. In fact, I'm in awe of how you got involved and learned about Burma and are trying to help. I really would like to see the kammavaca go back to where it belongs. But maybe it's come our way at this time to help us. You know, we're not down to the wire just yet. We have a couple of weeks till the next mortgage is due and bills can wait until the end of the month, then we are in trouble. Let's compromise.'

'What do you mean?'

'Let's hang on up to the last possible moment. Tell Mi Mi to hold off writing to Aye Aye until we are up against the wall. If I don't get a job or a sniff of prospects by then, we will have to sell it. But if I get a job, it can go back to Burma. What do you think?'

Natalie stared at him, her eyes filling with tears. 'I love you, Mark.'

'I don't understand all this karma stuff,' he said gently, 'but I understand that sometimes in life you have to be prepared to do the right thing simply because it is right, with no thought of personal gain. I respect your ideals and I love you, Nat, and whatever I say or do, you know it's for you and our kids.'

'I hope our children turn out to be like you, Mark. You're a good person.' Natalie drew a deep breath. 'Okay, then. A moratorium. I feel so much better. If it has to be sold, then we both agree that's what has to be done. That we are together on this means a lot. Thank you, Mark.' She kissed him and held him tightly, feeling reunited with the man she'd fallen in love with.

Andrew's first big outing was a trip to Lismore with his parents, Adam and Charlotte to visit Sarah and Steve. He was alert and curious, seemingly aware he was in new surroundings. Steve carried him around the garden, chatting quietly to him. Mark pushed the children on the swing Steve had hung from a tree for them.

Natalie looked out the window into the garden and smiled. 'Steve is being very sweet. Does he still miss the farm?'

'Oh, he talks about the farm from time to time. He's feeling at a bit of a loose end. And I know he feels bad about losing all that money. But we're hanging in there. The shop is doing all right, at least.' Sarah turned to her daughter and asked gently, 'What's happening with you and Mark? The job? The money?'

'We've come to an understanding. We're waiting till the last possible moment and then, if we have to, we'll sell the kammavaca.'

'Oh. I'm sorry. I know you wanted to return it to Burma. But it's the sensible thing to do. I'm glad you two have agreed.'

'It's been a joint decision. Mark said if something comes along then we won't have to sell it. But I feel okay about it. I made the offer to return it with the best motives in my heart, but Mi Mi told me there was no way Aye Aye would accept the kammavaca at such a personal cost. So we'll just have to trust that whatever happens, it was meant to be,' said Natalie.

'I'm glad to see you're being so philosophical about it,' said Sarah, trying to hide her slight surprise.


A couple of days later, Jodie dropped around to see Natalie and the baby. 'I won't stay long. I have to get my two from their music lesson. I won't beat around the bush. I know things are very tight for you guys right now and I want to make it clear to you that you can leave Charlotte and Adam in preschool as long as you want. I know you have money worries at the moment and as far as I'm concerned you don't have to stump up the fees. You can't be at home without a break with three littlies. You'd go nuts. And preschool is good for their development. And we're friends, for goodness sake, you can pay me back later, when you can.'

'Jodie, thanks. That's a wonderful offer. You are a good friend, but it's okay. Really it is.' Natalie held up her hand as Jodie went to protest. 'We're fine, really we are.' She gave a broad smile. 'Mark got a job.'

'Nat! That's wonderful. I'm so happy for you,' said Jodie, hugging her.

'Yes, his mate Brad came around a couple of hours ago. He's been offered a new job in Western Australia and he's managed to wrangle one for Mark as well, with more money than he was getting at his old job. The commute is going to be intense, but we'll survive.'

'Western Australia! The other side of the country!'

exclaimed Jodie but quickly added, 'Well, it's a job even if he's a FIFO worker. Hard for you though.'

'At the moment, I couldn't care less. I'm just happy Mark has a job that pays well and we'll be able to start saving again. But believe me, this job came along just in the nick of time.'

'Funny how things can work out,' said Jodie. 'What do they say? Trust in the universe?' She laughed.

'Something like that,' Natalie said smiling.

# 9

**Eighteen months later**

'LOOK AT HIM GO!' Mark burst out laughing as they watched Andrew's little legs race across the grass, his favourite ball tucked under his arm.

'He's so fast. So much energy. Can you believe it?' said Natalie.

'He might be a bit on the small side but there's nothing wrong with his spirit. Anyway, the doctor says he'll grow. He certainly eats enough,' said Mark.

'When you're away,' said Natalie, 'we sometimes eat quite simply.'

'Mmm. Baked beans on toast doesn't do it for me,' said Mark. 'They feed us like horses out west. I'm a bit over well-done red meat. But I'm not whingeing,' he quickly added.

He'd been working with Brad out in the Pilbara for

a year and a half. The commute from Brisbane to Perth was tedious but, as he said to Natalie, he was asleep the minute he buckled himself into his plane seat.

'The last leg is the worst. It's a small plane that flies into the mining site. Pretty uncomfortable,' he'd said. Although conditions were rougher out west, the pay was thirty per cent more than he'd been earning in Queensland, so he didn't complain.

Despite the pay rise they had been very frugal and had managed to recoup their savings, and even finish the bathroom, which was a huge relief. They were holding off on the other major renovations for the time being, until they were sure of their finances. They never wanted to be caught short again. Nevertheless, Natalie had finalised her plans and chosen all the fittings and accessories. Everything was awaiting a start date so that their dream home could become a reality.

The kammavaca was still in its box on her desk and was rarely touched. Natalie was waiting for Vicki to go to Burma and return it to Princess Aye Aye. When this would be Natalie was not quite sure because Vicki's life had taken a very different turn after she'd met and fallen in love with Finn, a happy and good-natured Dane who travelled to far-flung locations in Australia in order to help businesses improve their communications infrastructure. Although he was five years Vicki's junior, they'd clicked romantically and Vicki had decided to travel with him. Currently they were based in tropical Port Douglas. Vicki kept in touch with Natalie, emailing her photos of stunning sunsets and waving palm trees. The pictures usually featured the sturdy Finn in a tight T-shirt. Vicki was so happy in North Queensland that she had even sent for her dog, Ipoh.

*

Life was busy for Natalie with three small children and Mark travelling back and forth to Western Australia every three weeks. Charlotte had started school, and there were swimming and music lessons after school. Adam still enjoyed preschool and Natalie thought that she would shortly send Andrew, too, for one day a week. While Charlotte was at school Natalie spent a lot of time at the park with the boys, working off their excess energy.

On the weekends Natalie liked to take them all to Thi's market, where Charlotte had graduated from the Shetland pony to a slightly larger one. The carrots they grew in their back garden were now saved to feed her special friend.

Natalie occasionally saw Thomas at the markets, and Mi Mi sometimes dropped in to her place for coffee. She still liked to meet her friends from the preschool mothers' group and was a regular at the Friends of Burma meetings. The one thing Natalie had trouble fitting into her busy life was yoga. She didn't go as often as she would have liked, so she hadn't seen Moss in a long time, although she did manage to return his book on Buddhism, unread. She had tried to read it, but it had been incomprehensible.

'Nat,' Mark asked on the telephone one night, 'when I come home this weekend, Brad plans to come back, too. I invited him to stay for a few days, is that all right with you?'

Natalie hesitated. It was her birthday and she would have liked to have Mark to herself. But he always enjoyed Brad's company when they had a break together, and, as he had helped get Mark his job in the Pilbara, she felt grateful to him. 'I guess so.'

'He's thinking of selling his unit. He's keen on the idea of buying a place in Perth, or even Bali.'

'If he does, maybe we can go to see him there one day,' said Natalie. 'A family holiday – that's something we haven't done for a while. I miss Steve and Mum's farm.

253

I spoke to Mum today and she said a bundle of his shares have suddenly started to improve. She told him to sell them and put the profits into a high-yield account. Much safer. Shop seems to be doing all right. It must be a relief for them. Just like us.'

'Do you think they will ever take off on that trip around Australia that they talk about?' asked Mark.

'Eventually. It's more Steve's idea than Mum's. Anyway, I don't think he's as bored like he was since he's been helping out on a friend's property. Says he gets all the fun and none of the responsibility!'

'Okay, Nat, don't make any plans for Saturday night, will you? I'm taking you to dinner for your birthday,' said Mark.

'How lovely! I thought you might have forgotten.'

'As if. Don't forget to book that babysitter. See you soon and talk tomorrow.'


Brad was, as usual, full of cheeky smiles and bonhomie. Mark was pleased to be home and didn't seem nearly as exhausted as he usually did when he arrived back after a long shift. On Natalie's birthday they all spent time with the children, then Brad and Mark disappeared on an errand. Natalie suspected that they were going to the pub for a drink while she prepared for the night out. She had that luxury because she'd asked the babysitter, Brooke, to come early. Brooke had originally been recommended by Jodie and Natalie had used her several times before, so she was not at all concerned about leaving the children with her.

'Where are we going?' she asked Mark when he got back. 'Why do I have to dress up?'

'We're starting off at the casino, there's a cocktail do on. Brad got us invitations and he's waiting for us there. I just have to make a quick stop on the way.'

Natalie wrinkled her nose. 'I'm not sure about the casino. You know it's not my thing. Mark, I don't want anything fancy, just a romantic evening with my husband where I can finish my meal and we can talk without being interrupted by a child!'

Mark chuckled. 'That might happen, too. Just go with the flow, okay?'

As they left the house, Natalie kept running through the detailed instructions she'd left with Brooke, hoping she hadn't forgotten anything.

'Nat! Relax, this is a night off!' said Mark. 'Anyway, Brooke is always reliable, just trust her to do her usual good job. The kids will be fine.'

He drove through the glittering, busy strip of Surfers Paradise towards Southport, and then turned into a side street towards the beach.

'Why are we driving down here?'

'I'm just doing Brad a favour. Have to pick someone up for him.'

'Bit of an inconvenience, isn't it?' said Natalie. 'On our one night out.'

'He has a friend living down this way and I said we'd bring him along to the casino.'

'Can't he drive himself?' said Natalie, thinking that her birthday treat was getting out of hand. 'This is a pretty posh area. Look at these highrises.'

'These older places are very spacious. I think I'd rather be in one of these than some of the buildings going up now.'

'I'll wait here,' said Natalie.

'No, come up, you might get to peek inside, apparently it's quite something. The car will be fine.'

They walked through a marble, mirrored foyer full of tropical plants and large, bright modern art, and entered a teak-lined lift.

Natalie caught a glimpse of herself and Mark in its tinted mirror and couldn't help smiling. 'I didn't recognise us. We look so glamorous. We almost look as if we live here!'

They got out on the twelfth floor and walked along the plush, carpeted hallway. Mark pushed the buzzer at the end apartment.

'I bet they have a fantastic view,' whispered Natalie.

Mark glanced at his watch as they waited for a few moments before the door was answered.

A teenage girl opened the door and smiled at Mark. 'Come in, we've been expecting you.' She shot Natalie a look and ushered them inside.

Natalie hung back, but Mark propelled her forward.

Suddenly they were in a large living room which lead out to an enormous balcony, crammed with people and alive with music.

'Mark, we shouldn't be here. They're having a party,' said Natalie, immediately feeling embarrassed.

Then she saw Brad coming towards them and her mouth fell open.

'Yes, a party for you!'

Mark kissed her as people began coming in from the balcony, laughing and calling out, 'Surprise!'

Familiar faces appeared before Natalie as she tried to take it all in. 'For me? Everyone's here. I can't believe it!'

Mi Mi came towards them, a handsome Indian with greying temples beside her. 'Happy birthday!' She gave Natalie a hug. 'Mark, I don't think you've met my husband Nanda. I hope you are surprised, Natalie. Mark has been planning this for weeks.'

Natalie was still in shock. 'Is this your new apartment? I had no idea when you said you were buying a new one that it would be this grand. And I didn't even recognise your Serena when she opened the door.'

'I'm not surprised,' replied Mi Mi. 'She does look grownup when she wears all that make-up. And our son Shanti is over there, practising being a waiter.'

'How kind of you to do all this.' Natalie turned to Mark. 'I can't believe it. And Mi Mi, so much for you to do.'

'Mark and Brad should take the credit. They have put a lot of hard work and effort into making this party a surprise for you. We have only supplied the venue.'

'Nearly everyone is here except Vicki,' said Mark. 'She's still in Port Douglas with her toy boy.'

'Mark! Finn's only five years younger and they adore each other. I think it's lovely,' admonished Natalie. 'But I'm sorry she's not here. There's Thi and her husband. And Thomas. And Jodie, Holly . . . And my mother is here! And Steve . . .'

Natalie was overwhelmed by the party, and by the presence of so many friends. She was thrilled that her mother and Steve had driven up for the night. The setting was fabulous for a party. Standing on the balcony, looking across the Nerang River to the lights of Surfers Paradise, she leaned against Mark.

'I can't believe you've done this. How lovely of Mi Mi. I had no idea her new place was so beautiful. Mi Mi is so down-to-earth. After her hard life she deserves something like this. She is so generous. It's unfair that she doesn't feel it's safe enough for her to go back to Burma. She would love to see her parents.'

'I guess Burma is still an unpredictable place.' Mark looked concerned for a moment but quickly said, 'Never mind, let's talk about that later. Come on, it's time to see the cake Thi's made for you.'

Thi was dressed in a silk longyi and lace top, her wild curls drawn to one side with a tortoiseshell comb and a fresh flower. Her husband, a towering Australian called Mick, was dressed in a dark plaid longyi and a stiffly formal white mandarin-collared shirt with woven frog-loop buttons. He looked completely at home in the Burmese outfit, as though he had worn it many times before.

'I made you Burmese savouries and finger food, and of course mohinga soup, but your birthday cake had to be an Aussie one. Pavlova!' declared Thi, revealing a high, crisp meringue piled with slices of mango, kiwifruit, strawberries and whipped cream dotted with passionfruit.

'That looks absolutely delicious.' Natalie said, smiling at Mark. He knew how much she liked pavlova and she guessed he'd suggested it to Thi.

Later in the evening, when all the guests had finished Thi's delicious food, everyone gathered around and sang 'Happy Birthday' while Natalie blew out the candles and cut the pavlova. She kissed Mark.

'Thank you, darling. This has been the most wonderful evening. I can't believe that you went to all this trouble.'

'We're not done yet,' he said. 'Thi has something she'd like to say.' Mark stepped to one side as Thi joined them. Everyone listened as she spoke to Natalie.

'Natalie, we are all very happy to share your birthday and bring together two parts of your life – your family and your old friends, and your new family: your Burmese friends,' said Thi with a smile. 'We have all watched you grow, as a mother, wife and friend. My community is very grateful for your interest and commitment to our country of Burma. We appreciate your genuine interest in our homeland and to show support for all that has happened, not just to those of us here, but to those we left behind. While we await the day our inspirational Aung San Suu Kyi and other fighters for democracy will be released, we know that you, too, will continue to work towards a free Burma. Your interest, we know, has been sparked by the kammavaca you inherited and which you have promised will be returned one day to its rightful owner.'

Thi paused and Natalie looked at the warm, smiling faces around her. She was lucky, she thought, to count these extraordinary people as her friends.

'Your husband has a very special gift for you and it comes also with our metta,' continued Thi, 'our loving kindness and good wishes.'

Mark placed his arm around Natalie's waist and looked at her face.

'Natalie, I love you very much. You are the best wife and mother in the world. I leave you for weeks at a time to run the household by yourself and you are great at it. We have three very little children, whom you mainly look after by yourself, but you are always patient and loving. We live in a house that needs a lot of major renovations, which we can't quite afford, but you don't complain. Well, you did a bit about the bathroom! And you were prepared to compromise your very strongly held principles by selling something that meant a great deal to you, to help your family out of a tight spot. I think you are just about perfect and I can't believe how lucky I am to have you. So, please open this card.'

Mark had an enormous smile on his face. Natalie could also see that Brad was grinning broadly. On the card Mark had written, *Happy Birthday. We love you, Mark, Charlotte, Adam and Andrew.* On the other side he'd added a note: 'Your gift is a trip to Burma. And with the help of your friends, you will meet Princess Aye Aye and return to her the you-know-what! Travel safely and we will hold the fort.'

Natalie blinked. 'I don't understand. What does this note mean?'

Mark hugged her. 'Exactly what it says. It's all arranged, except your passport. You have to do that yourself, but everything else is organised. Flights, accommodation and the travel agent will arrange the visa.'

'But, Mark, going to Burma on my own?'

'It will be safe for you. We've arranged for people to look after you. You'll be in good hands, never fear,' said Thi.

'I don't know what to say . . .' began Natalie. 'It's like a dream . . . Mark, are you sure about this? The children?'

'All taken care of. Listen, we can discuss the details but you're definitely going.'

Brad lifted his glass. 'Here's to Natalie! On her way to Burma! Happy birthday!'

Sarah and Steve came up and hugged her.

'Are you surprised?' asked Steve.

'I'm shocked. You knew about this?'

'Of course, Mark told us all about it. We're all in on it,' said Sarah.

'Mum, I don't feel I can leave the children. And Mark. Will he manage? And also how can we afford this? I mean, it's a lovely idea . . .'

'Listen, I've been convinced by Thi and Mi Mi. Even your friend Vicki rang me,' said Sarah. 'They think it's important for you to find Aye Aye and give her back the kammavaca. You've wanted to return it for ages. I've been persuaded it's safe enough to go to Burma as a tourist, seeing the sights. As Mark said, you're raising a beautiful family, you're a great wife, and you have a husband willing to do this for you. You might never have a chance like this again.'

Mark handed Natalie a glass of champagne. 'Don't worry. It's all going to be fine. Start getting used to the idea.'

'I guess it was a surprise, huh?' said Brad wandering over with a drink in his hand. 'Mark's been worried you'd twig to his plan.'

'Are you joking? I would have never imagined in my wildest fantasies he was planning this!' Natalie said with a laugh. 'How can we afford it?'

'It's not going to cost very much and all your Burmese friends have taken care of the accommodation inside

Burma. They insisted. Mind you, it's not five star, but you'll see the real Burma,' said Mark. He looked suddenly concerned. 'You do want to do this, don't you?'

'Oh, Mark, I'll miss the children and you. But I'm suddenly feeling excited,' said Natalie. 'What about you? I feel mean that I'm going and leaving you behind. Will you be all right juggling the kids?'

'I'd love to come with you, but someone has to stay and look after those three little monsters. I've got plenty of holiday leave I can take and you can't say I haven't got the experience. For sure, dead set, all agreed,' he added quickly. 'Jodie has offered backup if I need it. Not to mention all these Burmese aunties. What a crew.' He shook his head. 'I just hope you're not disillusioned when you get to Burma and find not everyone is as nice as these people.'

'I'll learn one way or another, won't I?' said Natalie with a broad smile, and they both laughed.

'It's nice to see you laugh like that,' said Sarah. 'Of course, I'm going to worry myself sick till you come back.'

'No, you're not, Sarah,' cautioned Steve. 'Natalie will be just fine. She can look after herself.'

'Let's not worry about those things tonight,' said Mark and he took Natalie's hand.

Later, as some guests left and others helped to clear away plates, food and glasses, Natalie and Mark leaned against the balcony as a breeze lifted the ends of Natalie's hair. They stared at the twinkling lights of the skyscrapers reflected in the river.

'This is a birthday I'll never forget. I can't believe you did this.' She looked at him. 'Why did you do it? Because of Andrew? The kammavaca?'

'Both. I feel you deserve it. When we bought the house, life seemed so straightforward. Then suddenly I'm gone for weeks and you had to do everything on your own. And then you had to deal with poor little Andrew, and me getting made redundant, and we then had the hassle over the kammavaca.'

'Mark, none of what happened was your fault. Anyway, we share the load. That's what a marriage is about.'

'I just wanted to do something special for you. I wasn't sure that it was going to work because you haven't even been outside Australia and Burma does seem a bit of a challenge. Funny thing is that when I told Brad my idea, I thought he'd say I was nuts, but he didn't. He said you were resilient and curious and strong, and you've never had the chance to see what's over the other side of the fence and that you should. So I stopped worrying.'

'Did he? I have to say I'm already getting used to the idea of going to Burma,' said Natalie. 'I feel I have a bunch of people looking out for me. In the morning I might feel different, but that doesn't matter because you've done something wild and wonderful, and I love you for it.'


Natalie opened her eyes to the bright morning light. Had she been dreaming? No, there was the card propped up by her bed. Before she could reach for it, she heard Andrew whimper sleepily so she slid from bed and went to get him up before he woke everyone else.

Later, after making pancakes for breakfast, Natalie took her cup of tea and rang Vicki.

'Sorry I couldn't be there. Were you surprised?' asked her friend.

'Vicki, I'm still in shock. I feel a bit nervous in the cold light of day. I so wish you were coming with me. Someone who knows the ropes.'

'Of course I'd like to be with you, but Finn is working on a project at the moment, and I'm working on him. Anyway, I think it is important for you to make your own journey. You'll be looked after, and because you're just travelling to see the tourist sites you pose no threat to the authorities, so you'll be safe. I have a friend in Rangoon, Consolina Gambrio, everyone calls her Connie, and I've told her you're coming and she said that she'd love you to stay with her and her husband. They'll give you whatever help you need. They know everybody.'

'That's really kind of you,' said Natalie. 'Tell me about Connie. Is she Italian?'

'She is. You'll like her. She is very charming and knowledgeable about Burma. She's lived there for about ten years and is married to a famous Burmese painter, U Win Thant. They run an art studio and gallery.'

'What does he paint? When I think of Burmese art I think of religious, Buddhist art,' said Natalie.

'He's a modern artist. There's huge interest in modern art in Burma. The British introduced western styles during colonial times and some local artists still like to paint contemporary art. Its importance is growing, thanks largely to Connie and Win. If you like, I'll run through some dos and don'ts and the logistics of entering Burma with you later, though I think Mark is on top of that. I'm afraid there are no banks or credit card facilities so you can only take in cash, in pristine US dollars, and the amount is very limited. Has Mi Mi talked to you about finding Aye Aye?'

'Not yet. We'll go over the details next week. Vicki, I was wondering whether I should offer to look up her family? I know that Mi Mi worries about them.'

'That's a difficult one. I'm sure she would love that, but she probably doesn't want to ask you to go to the trouble of tracking them down. And she's frightened of getting them into trouble. A foreign visitor taking an interest in them might not be a good thing. By the way, how are you going to carry the kammavaca? I don't think you should put it in your luggage. Better you keep it with you at all times.'

'Yes, I thought about that. Do you think it might get taken off me by customs or someone?'

'I don't think that customs will be looking for a Burmese artefact coming into the country. But I suggest that you don't take any jewellery with you. The authorities keep a close check on what you bring in, and they'll check it again when you leave, just to make sure that you haven't sold it or given it away. Now, it's going to be very hot and humid. I don't have to tell you to dress modestly. No shorts or bare arms. The Burmese are conservative people.'

'Of course!' The trip was becoming more real. 'I still can't believe I'm going.'

'You'll love Rangoon and there're some nice places to see around Mandalay, too. The bus ride from Rangoon is a bugger of a trip and the train takes forever, so I'm glad Mark has organised a flight. It's barely an hour by air. If I think of anything else I'll let you know and if you think of questions, just shout.'


Although she practised yoga at home, Natalie liked going to classes. With Mark at home, Natalie was determined it was time to get to a class. As she settled into her first pose at the centre, her eyes closed, concentrating on her breathing, she felt relaxed and pleased that she had come. When she changed position, she was aware of movement beside her. She opened her eyes and saw Moss sitting next to her, his eyes closed, his long limbs folded into the lotus position.

They didn't speak until the class was finished.

'It's good to see you again, it's been a while. Have you got time for tea?' asked Moss. 'How are things with you?'

'Amazing,' replied Natalie as she poured herself a cup of lemongrass tea. 'I've had the best birthday of my life.'

'I'm pleased to hear it.' Moss smiled.

'In fact, Mark tried to reach you. He said he left a message here. He wanted to invite you to my surprise party.'

'That was nice of him, but I've been running a course in Adelaide and travelling for research, so I haven't been around. So were you surprised?'

'Was I ever! It was a total shock and so many of my family and friends were there. And you'll never guess what Mark gave me as a gift,' bubbled Natalie. Then she proceeded to tell him about her trip to Burma.

'That's certainly a surprise present all right. Is this trip part of the proceeds from the sale of the kammavaca? Did your husband persuade you to sell it?'

'Oh no, we didn't sell it in the end, so I'm going to take it with me to return it to Princess Aye Aye. Isn't that wonderful?'

'How about that! I hope she doesn't live in the Irrawaddy Delta region. Travel there has been limited since Cyclone Nargis.'

'I'm going to Rangoon and Mandalay.'

'Where does your mysterious princess live?'

'Somewhere near Mandalay. I'm so excited I can't believe I'm going.'

'It's certainly an important undertaking. Do you have a friend going with you?'

'I'm staying with a friend of a friend. Everyone has been so kind. I feel very nervous but, except for meeting the princess, I'm just a tourist going to the tourist spots.'

'You must feel a little sad at parting with that kammavaca,' said Moss.

'Not at all. I'm pleased that its journey will be complete.'

'When are you leaving?' Moss asked.

'Soon. Mark's sprung it on me but he's been incredibly organised. Things have worked out well. And you? Are you back here on the Gold Coast for good?'

'I've got plans for more travel. I'm taking several students on a study trip mainly to Bodhgaya in India. I look forward to hearing all about your adventures. I feel it will change you, Natalie. Spiritually, I mean.'

'I don't know about that, though I've never been exposed to another culture before, so everything will be different for me.'

Moss gave a little nod. 'I'm sure your appreciation of Buddhist art and history will be enriched in Burma. I hope you make many good friends, although it is difficult for local people to mix with foreigners. The military doesn't like it. I will be intrigued to hear what happens with your kammavaca. Take care and travel safe.'

'You, too, Moss.'


Natalie surveyed her clothes spread on the bed then sorted them again and repacked for the third time. Mark stood in the doorway watching her.

'Take half of that out. Travel light! You don't know where you'll end up and you have to be able to carry your own gear. Mi Mi said just to take one pair of walking shoes and a comfortable pair of sandals.'

'I feel so odd. I've never travelled overseas before and now my first trip is so adventurous. Not somewhere like New Zealand or the US. I'm going to Burma! I wish you were coming with me, Mark.'

'No way. I don't think you would fully enjoy yourself if I didn't stay here to look after the kids. This is your trip, Nat, you started this whole journey.'

'No, great-great-uncle Andrew did. I'm going to worry so much about the kids, and you . . .'

Mark walked over and wrapped his arms around her. 'The children are going to be fine. They'll have more people watching over them than the crown jewels. Vicki said that you can't use a mobile to ring home. There's no international coverage. When you phone home on a landline, you're to give us your number and we'll call you right back. Evidently it's cheaper and easier to do that because calling from Burma isn't always reliable.'

'I'll keep my watch on your time so I can look at it and know what you're all doing,' said Natalie, her voice muffled as he held her.

'I think that could become very confusing,' said her husband with a smile.

Before Natalie left, Mi Mi dropped in and handed her a small package.

'I've heard from Princess Aye Aye and she is looking forward to you coming. It is also very, very kind of you to offer to try and find my parents. Please, if it is too difficult, don't worry about it, but just in case you manage to make contact, could you give them this? It's just photos. I know they'd love to see them.'

'Of course, Mi Mi. I'll try my best.'

'And I know you're limited in the amount of money you can take in to Burma but, if you're not at your maximum limit, could you take this in, too, and give it to them, please?' Mi Mi handed Natalie some crisp US dollars. 'It's only two hundred dollars, but I worry about their health and if they have enough food, especially after this awful, horrible cyclone. Nargis was the worst natural disaster to ever hit our country. You know the tidal wave washed away entire villages, cattle, houses, people. It must have been terrifying. I've heard that sometime before the cyclone struck, my parents were considering leaving Rangoon to be closer to my brother in his monastery in the delta.'

Natalie was horrified. She had no idea that Mi Mi's parents were no longer safe in Rangoon out of the path of the cyclone.

The whole world had been appalled, not just by the destruction caused by Cyclone Nargis, but by the dreadful response of the generals. Natalie had read in detail that when the cyclone had hit the delta in May nearly three million Burmese had been affected by it, and more than one hundred thousand people had been killed. Initially the generals had done nothing to help the victims, and they had refused all international relief. The French and the US had sent naval supply ships, but the paranoid junta had refused to let them land, fearing that they were the vanguard of an invasion. Even international organisations like the Red Cross were not given immediate access to the stricken area as the junta made it almost impossible for relief experts to obtain visas to enter the country. The international community was outraged. Nearly two weeks later, after a lot of pressure, especially from Burma's neighbours, the generals realised that a few bags of rice and some tarps were not going to be an adequate solution to the catastrophe and agreed to allow in international aid.

'I'm sure everyone is fine,' said Natalie, trying to sound more optimistic than she felt. 'Is there anything you want me to bring back? I'll take photos of course.' She wondered how she would ever be able to find Mi Mi's aged parents, or even confirm whether or not they had moved to the delta region. It seemed such a long shot.

'A picture would be lovely. But just to know that they are all right, that's the most important thing.' Mi Mi hugged Natalie, who felt overwhelmed at the fragility she sensed in her friend who always presented such a professional and capable front to the world.


Natalie was not looking forward to saying goodbye to Charlotte and Adam, and had debated with Mark about bringing them to the airport. She finally decided to leave

Andrew with a babysitter and let the others come so that they understood she was going on a plane and hadn't just disappeared.

Adam was beside himself with excitement when he saw the huge planes. It wasn't until the final moment, as Natalie was about to walk through security, when she leaned down and wrapped her arms around Charlotte to say goodbye that the little girl took in the full import of the occasion and tears began to run down her face.

'Don't go, Mummy! Take me, too,' she wailed.

'Darling, I won't be long. Daddy will look after you, just like I do when Daddy goes away to work. Please be a big girl and look after Adam and Daddy and especially baby Andrew for me.'

Charlotte straightened her shoulders, sniffing slightly. 'All right, Mummy.'

Mark was holding Adam and she put her arms around them both. 'I'll bring you all back a lovely present.'

'Planes, look at the aeroplanes!' Adam pointed.

Mark kissed her. 'Off you go. It's an adventure, so enjoy it!'

Charlotte clutched Mark's hand and gave a small wave. 'Bye bye, Mummy.'

Natalie picked up her handbag and slung it over her shoulder. Inside it, she had carefully packed the kamma-vaca, wrapping it up in a silk scarf. 'Be good for Daddy. I'll be back soon. Talk soon. I love you.' She threw Mark a panicked look.

'We love you! Enjoy yourself! And don't worry!' he called.

By the time the plane was airborne, drinks had been served and she was irrevocably on her way, Natalie began to relax and a tingle of anticipation replaced her anxiety at leaving the children.

She spent the night in Singapore at a very comfortable

hotel. Natalie talked to Mark and the children briefly on the phone. She was relieved that everything was running normally at home and the children seemed to be settled, although Charlotte got a little teary when the time came to say goodbye. Mark took the phone from her and was upbeat.

'All good. I have a lot of projects planned. Jodie gave me the recipe for playdough. Truly, Nat, relax. You're going into a new world. Take it all in and don't worry about trying to contact us when you can't. Kids have no concept of time, so they're going to be fine. I'll keep them happy and occupied.'

'All right. I love you. When you put the kids to bed, tell them Mummy loves them.'

The plane landed in Rangoon early morning. Natalie walked across the tarmac to the low, utilitarian terminal, watched by four men in military uniforms standing at the entrance. Inside, the terminal was empty save for some wooden benches, a deserted counter and several immigration officials seated behind their desks. She moved forward and a woman took her passport, glanced at her photo and flicked through the empty pages.

'Why you come to Myanmar?' asked the unsmiling young woman.

Natalie was prepared for this question and replied, 'I've always wanted to see the temples at Bagan.'

The girl stared at her for a moment then, as she stamped Natalie's passport, said, 'Very beautiful place.' She signalled to the next person in the queue and Natalie quickly followed the other passengers to the baggage carousel.

More young and bored-looking soldiers watched the new arrivals pick up their luggage. There were a couple of rusty, old-fashioned luggage trolleys and, behind the glass exit wall, Natalie could see a gaggle of enthusiastic young men whom she presumed were porters. She pulled her small suitcase behind her, holding on tightly to her handbag, which she'd slung across her chest, and followed the other passengers over to the customs area. She hoped that her handbag would not be searched as she really had no idea how she would explain the kammavaca. Luckily, the customs officer only asked her to declare her money, which she did. When he had carefully counted it, he wrote something down, gave the money back and pointed to the exit. Breathing a sigh of relief, Natalie walked through.

On the other side of the exit Natalie was confronted by a crush of people, but immediately in front of her appeared a striking-looking woman, tall with dark hair and dressed in a colourful silk shirt over black linen pants.

'*Mingalaba*, welcome. I'm Connie. How was the trip? This way, let me take your bag.' Her accent still held traces of her northern Italian roots.

'Thanks, it's fine, lead on,' said Natalie, glad that Connie was in front of her and opening up a passage through the press of people, all of whom seemed friendly as they smiled and touted for business.

'The car is down here.' Connie pointed further along the crowded pavement to where a man was standing by an old car. 'This is Ko Wai Yan, and this is his taxi. Don't worry, it goes quite well. The doors won't fall off or anything like that,' said Connie as Natalie looked at the car doubtfully. It was old and battered and had 'Sunny Super Saloon' written on its side. It wasn't a model of car she recognised and it looked very old.

'Thank you for meeting me,' began Natalie as she settled onto the sagging back seat, wondering if the seats had any springs and what might be missing from the engine.

'No problems. We have an arrangement with Ko Wai Yan and when we need a driver, we call him. If you need to be driven anywhere, he'll be around. So, here you are.' She smiled at Natalie.

'I can't believe I'm here,' said Natalie. 'It's so hot!'

'Turn on the air conditioning,' said Connie as she leaned over and wound down the rattling window. Natalie laughed. The air rushing in was steamy.

They had left the unpaved parking lot of the airport and were now driving along a crowded road where people, bicycles, cars and pedal trishaws all jostled for space. The men and women wore longyis, some women had flowers in their hair, others had bamboo hats; children were tied to their mothers in cotton slings; toddlers perched on bicycles in front of their parents. There was a clutter of stalls and food stands along the roadside. While Natalie thought she knew what to expect, seeing Burmese street life in reality was like leaping to a different planet.

'We'll do a Cook's tour through the city so you can get a bit of a sense of the place, and then we'll go to the studio where I live,' said Connie. 'If you're up for it we can go to lunch, and then to the markets.'

'I'm up for it all,' exclaimed Natalie, feeling exhilarated. 'It's lovely of you to look after me like this. It doesn't feel so strange. But I don't want to hold you up or anything.'

'Not at all, we enjoy showing off our little part of Yangon and Win, my husband, is very happy to have someone to stay who's visiting Burma for the first time.'

As the 'Sunny Super Saloon' shuddered through the city, Connie pointed out areas of interest, and Natalie was shocked but enthralled by the colonial buildings that lined the broad avenues. Although they must once have been grand, now they were dilapidated and stained with city fumes and lichen. Many had broken windows, and sat behind iron railings in tangled gardens of unkempt shrubbery and overgrown trees.

'These buildings must have been magnificent, once. Why aren't they used now?' asked Natalie.

'Because the government decided to move the capital from Rangoon, which is now called Yangon, to Naypyidaw, over three hundred kilometres away, and the government, the military and public service all went there with it. The foreign embassies refused to budge.'

'Yes. My friend back in Australia told me about that. It sounds crazy. I don't suppose the country can afford it, either. Oh, can we stop? I'd love to take a photo of this whole block,' said Natalie as she glimpsed some ornate buildings that looked sad in their neglect.

'Not a good idea. The military can be very touchy about people taking photos,' said Connie. 'Try and snap one from the car. That building's the one where Aung San Suu Kyi's father and his cabinet were assassinated.'

They drove on further and Natalie saw a beautiful lake surrounded by large residences and English trees. She thought it looked very British. Further along the wide street Connie pointed out the leafy entrance to the University of Yangon.

'It's a good university, but it struggles.'

'What's down there? Where the road is blocked off?' asked Natalie.

'That's the part of University Avenue where Aung San Suu Kyi is under house arrest. No-one is allowed to go there.'

'Oh, I see.' Natalie found it hard to believe that she had come so close to the house of the pro-democracy leader. She felt privileged but saddened that she could get no closer.

In their meandering drive across the city Natalie began to glimpse the haunted shadows of old Rangoon, rubbing against the toughness of modern Yangon.

When, unexpectedly, a huge glittering golden dome rose up from the hurly-burly of streets, Natalie gasped. 'It's huge!'

'It certainly is. It's the Shwedagon Pagoda and it's one of the most important pagodas in all of South East Asia.

We'll take you there so that you can look at it properly. The Sule Pagoda is beautiful, too,' said Connie, leaning forward to give the driver an instruction.

Natalie was trying to absorb everything. The old buses belching fumes, the shophouses, the horsedrawn wooden carts, the swirl of people and congestion one minute and then, as the old taxi turned beneath a leafy archway, a quiet road, which, despite having no footpaths, had the elegance of a European street.

They drove into a more affluent neighbourhood made up of larger homes whose architecture was totally unfamiliar to Natalie, but she thought it attractive.

'This is Golden Valley. Our place is down here,' said Connie as the car bumped down a rutted laneway. 'The Australian Ambassador's residence is not far away.'

Dogs and children playing by the roadside scattered as the taxi approached. It slowed down outside a high iron fence and turned through the open gates, passed a sign that welcomed them to Peacock Studio.

The house was similar to its neighbours, though it seemed to have a larger garden. From what Natalie could see, the two-storey house was made of stone, and had large windows framed by shutters. A narrow verandah ran along the length of the house and its columns gave Natalie the impression of an Asian version of a Southern American plantation home.

The driver pulled up at the rear of the house next to an old car. There were two small buildings in the yard and several bicycles were parked under the large trees. Washing was strung out along a line and there was a clutter of empty paint pots and stacked boards all spilling from a small studio. An outdoor fire was smouldering in front of a small cottage and two old chairs sat under its awning. Natalie could also see that the house had an informal outdoor eating area near the kitchen.

Connie led the way inside as Ko Wai Yan carried Natalie's bag. Natalie was surprised to enter an enormous room. It had high ceilings complete with old, slowly moving fans. There was an iron spiral staircase in one corner and at the other end of the room broad polished wooden stairs led to another floor that, Natalie realised later, overlooked the gallery at the front. Leading off the spacious room were numerous bedrooms. When Natalie had been in the house longer, she discovered that upstairs, at the rear of the house, was a long sitting room and a small study, both of which had views over the garden.

The house was decorated with a mixture of colourful Italian fabrics, silk cushions, old Chinese screens, sculptured Buddha figures and Burmese lacquerware, while the walls were covered in dozens of brilliantly hued canvases of very contemporary paintings. It was an eclectic, comfortable fusion of cultures, art and business.

'How beautiful. This is the last thing I imagined I'd find on my arrival in Rangoon. Yangon,' she corrected herself. 'I still say Burma, too, like my Burmese friends at home instead of Myanmar.'

'Many people still say Burma. Myanmar is the written, literary name of the country, while "Bama" is the spoken name, adapted by the British to Burma,' said Connie. 'Natalie, please consider this your home while you are here. We'll talk about your travelling to Mandalay later. But settle in for a few days and we'll introduce you to our local lifestyle. If you're up for it, Win wanted to take you to lunch at his favourite restaurant. Come and meet him, he's probably finished his class now.'

'Who is he teaching?' asked Natalie as she followed Connie to the front gallery.

'Up-and-coming Burmese artists. He likes to nurture them and give them a bit of polish and guidance. When he thinks they are good enough, we organise a show of their work in the hope that they might sell a few paintings.'

'Do many people here buy art? Or is it just foreigners?' asked Natalie.

'There's not a big foreign market here, and few tourists carry enough money. We sometimes send pictures out to Bangkok and India. And some of the expats and diplomats are keen. Actually, one of the senior generals fancies himself as a collector. Trouble is he always wants a very preferential price, so we never display the good pieces when we know he's coming. Damned if we're giving those away! Win, here's Natalie!'

Connie's husband came to meet them from the front gallery. Still holding a paintbrush, he lifted his hands in a gesture of mingalabar, or greeting. His shirt over his longyi was spattered with coloured paint. 'Welcome, welcome, how was your journey?' He was a tall, handsome Burmese and his cultured accent sounded faintly English.

'Very good. Having a stopover in Singapore made it easy . . . Oh, wow!' Natalie stopped. The gallery walls were hung with works that were a riot of colours, patterns and abstract shapes. Canvases were stacked on the floor along one wall; in another area easels had been set up and there were several artists working.

'It is a feast for the eyes, isn't it?' said Win. 'Something to be digested slowly. Speaking of food, Connie, have you asked our visitor if she would like to come to The Garden?'

Connie laughed. 'Win might be Burmese but his stomach is international. Have you tried much Burmese cooking, Natalie? Perhaps you would prefer something more familiar? We have some quite good places that serve European food.'

'I love what I've tried of Burmese food.'

'Good. Then we shall take you for a little lunch.

I hope you are not too tired?' Win began but Connie took his arm.

'Let's not overwhelm Natalie. You go and clean up, Win.'

Natalie smiled at her hosts, so attractive and hospitable. 'I'd love to look around your gallery for a bit.'

Connie and Win left Natalie to walk quietly around the gallery and absorb the work on display. The artists smiled shyly at her, nodded politely and went about their work. Natalie was swept away by the vibrancy and creativity she saw. She stopped in front of several paintings stacked against a wall. One particularly intrigued her: a sepia and brown textured mass that could have been either an ocean or perhaps a sea of people. Standing out from the background was a slash of pink, which possibly represented a figure.

One of the artists, a woman, stood beside Natalie.

'You like this picture?'

'Yes, I do. I'm trying to understand it. Is this one of yours?'

'Oh, no, this is by a famous artist. It is sad story.'

'I would like to hear it, if you want to tell me.'

'Yes,' said the woman softly. 'I would like. The artist family come from the Irrawaddy delta and had very bad time in Cyclone Nargis. So he paint this picture about the cyclone and he win a prize. So he take the money to help his people but when he come to a village everybody all drowned. But then he see one little boy, looking for his mother, father. He was wearing a pink shirt. So the artist come back and put this pink on the picture. It means for hope and future,' she explained.

'That's beautiful,' said Natalie. 'Can you show me your work?'

The young girl showed Natalie her dramatic canvases. They were interpretations of Buddhist figures built up with thick layers of paint and gold leaf and looking as though many hands might have touched the figures and worn away some of the gold leaf.

'First I make statues with clay and then I make paintings of them on canvas,' said the artist. 'Other time I make paintings like Myanmar old art. What you see on the walls of pagodas and stupas.'

'I haven't seen those yet. This is my first day here,' said Natalie.

'Oh. I hope you like my country,' she said with a smile.

'I think I will like it very much,' said Natalie, smiling in reply.


Win insisted on ordering many different dishes for their lunch, so Natalie could taste the flavours of Yangon.

'Connie likes the Shan food from the hills, but you must try these,' he insisted as small bowls and platters of appetising soup, curries, rice, noodles and salads appeared.

They were seated in the front garden of a spacious colonial-style Burmese home, which was screened from the road by large trees. Lanterns hung from the trees and Natalie imagined that at night it must be a romantic setting. When she went inside to use the restroom, she saw that the interior of the house had been converted into several separate dining areas.

'This is lovely, Win. Thank you, Connie, I'm lost for words. This isn't what I expected at all!'

'This mightn't be the official capital anymore but Yangon is a great city, especially for tourists and the well heeled. But there's still an awful lot of hardship in this country after Cyclone Nargis,' said Connie.

'Yes, I've heard. Actually, before I leave for Mandalay

I want to try to find the family of a dear friend of mine back home. She's worried because her parents have moved out of Rangoon and she hasn't been able to find out where they are. She's been an activist and she fears that if she comes back to Burma to look for them, there will be reprisals,' said Natalie.

'I've heard that story many, many times,' said Connie. 'Do you have any clues?'

'I have their last known address in Rangoon, but they may have moved to the delta. My friend has not heard about them since the cyclone.'

'Win, do we know anyone who could help Natalie?'

'Yes, I think we might. What about Khin Myo Thein? He was helping distribute food to Kunchangon. We were hit badly here in Yangon, but not so badly as the villages further south.'

'It was amazing what the people of Burma, both rich and poor, donated or collected for the victims,' said Connie.

'I'm sure we'll be able to make enquiries for you,' said Win.

'But that is not the only reason for your visit here,' prompted Connie.

'No, apart from wanting to see Burma, there is another reason. Did Vicki fill you in?'

'She was quite discreet. We don't know what it is you have to take to Mandalay or for whom, but we are happy to help,' said Connie.

Briefly Natalie summarised the saga of her kamma-vaca. 'This is quite an emotional trip for me,' she finished. 'I so want it to work out. I have to arrange travel to a place called Maymyo. Is that near Mandalay?'

'It's now called Pyin Oo Lwin and it's about an hour outside Mandalay,' said Win.

'Natalie, we don't want to let you travel by yourself,' said Connie. 'We've contacted a friend who can help you.'

'That's very kind of you. I know I haven't even been here twenty-four hours, but this is not the scary place I'd imagined. I'm sure I'll be fine, I don't want to impose.'

Connie lowered her voice. 'Natalie, you need someone to go with you who speaks the language and will make sure that you don't inadvertently do something that could land you in trouble. You are a tourist so it is normal for you to hire a guide. Myanmar can be a difficult place for the inexperienced.'

'Burmese are usually very respectful and friendly. It is the uneducated soldiers and those working for the government who can cause trouble,' said Win gently. 'The government has people everywhere, watching, and it is very, very easy to displease them, even for no apparent reason. And this could happen if you are making contact with someone connected to the old royal family.'

'The person who will be of most help to you is an old friend,' said Connie. 'He trains teachers in specialist courses and even teaches the tour guides. You will be in very good hands.'

'Having a guide would be wonderful,' said Natalie.

'Yes, it would be a great pity not to take advantage of U Phyu Myint. He will open your eyes to the many riches Myanmar has to offer, and he will also keep you safe.'

'I hope I'm not causing you any trouble, Win,' said Natalie, concerned.

'No, no. We deal with foreigners a lot and because I am married to Connie there's no problem about having a foreign guest in our house. But it is not so easy for other people and in other places.'

'Now you're scaring me,' said Natalie, trying to smile.

'Nonsense, you're not doing anything illegal. This isn't an open country like yours, so it is always wise to be a little cautious. But you'll be fine,' said Connie.

Win left Connie and Natalie at the central market,

and Natalie was impressed by the colonial entrance and the multitude of cobblestone lanes under the huge roof, all crammed with shops and stalls.

'I could spend a week in here!' Natalie exclaimed, looking at the jewellery, handicrafts, fabrics, household wares and displays of food.

'This is a big attraction for visitors and it's still the main market for the city. It was called Scott's Markets after the British public servant who built it in the twenties but who's now mainly remembered because he introduced football to Burma,' laughed Connie. 'The name then changed to Bogyoke Aung San Markets after General Aung San. Bogyoke means general. Maybe you can find a gift for your children in here.'

The time in the markets passed very quickly. Natalie was fascinated by the busy Asian bazaar. It was so different from the shops at home, noisier, so much hustle and bustle. Food was piled in baskets or spread on raised platforms and mats. Women sat with their children and gossiped. They gave her frank, friendly and interested stares as she walked past. Natalie smiled back and asked Connie what the yellow paste was that the women had smeared on their faces.

'Thanakha. It's a paste made from a lovely smelling tree bark. It keeps your skin soft and works as a sunscreen and mosquito repellent. You can buy little sticks of thanakha, which you grind with a stone mortar and pestle. But you can buy it ready-made, too.'

A woman held out a sample of the paste for Natalie to try. 'It smells lovely. I could buy some to take home.'

She didn't see much in the way of children's toys or clothes, but Natalie knew Charlotte and Adam would love the cheap sandals she found. They were plastic and decorated with cartoon pictures. When their wearer walked, the sandals squeaked and lights flashed.

'You might regret buying those,' Connie said laughing. 'What say we go back home and have a rest and then we'll take you to the Shwedagon Pagoda at sunset? It's very special.'

'That would be wonderful,' said Natalie.


At sunset they joined the stream of people – local families, monks, business people and the elderly, as well as some other foreigners – all heading to the most famous landmark in the country. There devotees would say prayers, ask for favours, give thanks and sometimes just meditate in the peaceful surrounds. It was expected that all Burmese Buddhists should worship at least once in their life at the Shwedagon.

The sun was low in the sky as they approached, its rays setting alight the golden dome with its jewelled hti atop the pagoda. The hti was a beacon that glittered over the city.

Connie explained to Natalie that there were four different entrances at each of the cardinal points of the compass but the southern entrance was the most popular. Natalie saw that the complex of stupas, pavilions, statues, temples and shrines was spread over a very large area. The flight of steps they climbed from the street was worn by the feet of centuries of worshippers, and guarded on each side by statues of mystical chinthe.

They entered the cool shadows of a covered walkway where wandering sellers and some stallholders offered them candles, flowers, packets of gold leaf, food, books and pamphlets, miniature paper umbrellas, religious objects and souvenirs. Smiling children held up strings of fragrant flowers, and nuns dressed in pink robes with shaved heads gently asked for alms. Occasionally a woman sat calmly nursing a baby at her breast, while older children played nearby, ignoring the requests of beggars for charity, and some pilgrims just rested quietly.

Win explained to Natalie that all visitors must remove their shoes, and when she did, she found the marble cool beneath her feet. As she stepped onto the great main court of the pagoda, she caught her breath. The display of colour, the ornate and intricate carvings, the inlaid mosaic columns and shrines, and the huge towering golden domes were awe inspiring. She was stunned by the blaze of bejewelled gold and white buildings and statues. People walked about with reverence, knelt or sat to pray, made offerings or poured water over colourful statues and shrines. Yet it was all surprisingly clean and quiet: a calm, spacious area surrounded by an unplanned clutter of shrines, edifices and pavilions.

Lights were everywhere. Floodlights, candles and coloured neon lights blazed in patterns inside shrines, some even flashing like halos above the heads of Buddha figures. Everything looked freshly painted, if garishly so.

'I'm on sensory overload,' said Natalie. 'I have so many questions I don't know where to start. See those shrines over there? What are those posts? And why are people praying and pouring water?'

'Those posts are known as planetary posts,' said Win. 'Myanmar Buddhists must know the day of the week on which they were born. Then they know which shrine to go to for observances and devotions. A lot of people ask the advice of an astrologer before coming here so they know how many candles to light, or how many paper umbrellas to put with their offerings and prayers. There are eight shrines for the days of the week. Wednesday has the extra shrine because it's divided into morning and afternoon. At each shrine devotees offer flowers and prayer flags and sometimes food, and then pour water on the head of a Buddha or their birth day animal. They pray or make a request. Can you see, at the base of that post is a guardian angel? And underneath is a statue of its birth day animal?'

'I was born on a Wednesday morning, which animal am I?' asked Natalie.

'The elephant,' said Connie. 'If you were born in the morning your elephant would have tusks, but if you were born in the afternoon your elephant wouldn't.'

'I like elephants,' said Natalie, thinking of the picture of the white elephant on the kammavaca.

'And,' added Win, 'your planet would be Mercury.'

'It's just breathtaking,' said Natalie, looking around her. 'Despite the lavishness of all the gold, it's not like a church. It seems comfortable and respected but everybody uses it, and it feels very peaceful. I love the way people of all ages and even children are involved. It seems very informal, but everyone knows what they're doing. It seems so much a part of everyday life. How old is this pagoda?'

'There is supposed to have been a stupa on this site for around two thousand six hundred years, according to myths, but there's no evidence of any actual building until much later. This pagoda assumed its present size and shape in the late eighteenth century,' replied Win. 'A long time ago, the story goes, two Burmese brothers, who were merchants, went to India and gave the Buddha some gifts. In return the Buddha plucked hairs from his head and gave them to the brothers, who then became his first Burmese converts. These hairs became sacred relics and the Shwedagon was supposedly built to house them. There have been ongoing donations, gilding, new buildings and renovations at this place for years.'

'I don't think the history or precise age of the pagoda matters to worshippers. They just accept that in the time of Buddha the relics of his hair were enshrined here,'

284

added Connie. 'That small tale in the life of the Buddha certainly captured the Burmese imagination.'

'The details of the story are a bit vague but the sanctity of the Shwedagon is enough for the people to revere this place,' said Win. 'Even the generals come here to demonstrate what good Buddhists they are.'

Win pointed to a family praying at a shrine, their offering of food and flowers before them. 'These people are so poor and yet they try to donate whatever they can, even gold, in order to become rich in their next lives.'

Connie lowered her voice even though they weren't close to anyone. 'They say that General Ne Win helped himself to a big diamond and some of the generals stole jewels and other valuables when the Shwedagon was repaired in the 1970s.'

'That's shocking,' exclaimed Natalie. 'Who looks after the pagodas and the temples? The monks?'

'The military controls every pagoda and temple. The generals even put their own photos in the pagodas. They use the people's religion to support their rule,' said Win, shaking his head. 'That is why the Saffron Revolution was so important. It showed the generals that the monks do not always support their actions.'

'I can't believe they'd steal from such an important place. Are there valuable relics in other temples and pagodas?' asked Natalie.

'There are thousands of sacred sites with Buddha's relics, real or replicas, all over Burma,' said Win. 'And they are all held in reverence.'

'U Phyu Myint will tell you all about it as you travel,' said Connie.

'He has a hard name to remember.'

'U is the respectful honorific, like mister,' explained Connie. 'Burmese don't have formal family names. If you like you can just call him Mr P.'

285

They paused as they turned a corner and an avenue of shrines spread out before them.

'It's incredible. Is it all right for me to take some photos? This will be impossible to describe to Mark,' said Natalie.

'This is the prettiest time to be here,' said Connie, nodding. 'There's a place where you can sometimes see the sunset rays hit the huge diamond on top of the hti, which sits at the very top of the dome. The diamond is seventy-six carats and the hti is also encrusted in rubies, emeralds and diamonds. The generals didn't get those,' she added in a very quiet whisper.

As they turned to leave, the deep sweet tones of a giant bell being struck by a devotee throbbed behind them.

'That's the Great Bell, which was donated to the temple by a Burmese king about three hundred years ago. Ringing the bell is said to spread merit. The British tried to carry it away, but it fell into the river,' said Win. 'A monk eventually came up with a solution to raise it. He tied cables to it and floated it up with the tide. Thousands of Burmese pulled it out, throwing flowers over it, singing and dancing as they dragged it back to the Shwedagon.'

'Look, the moon is rising over the dome. That's auspicious,' said Connie, smiling at Natalie. 'Let's walk a bit more. But you need more than a day to see the Shwedagon, so I hope you can come back.'


Natalie was at a loss to describe all she'd seen to Mark once they made phone contact that evening. After the children had regaled her with their stories, Natalie tried hard to explain to Mark all that she'd seen and done that day.

'Mark, I just can't believe how amazing, stunning, fascinating it is here! I'm trying to remember to take pictures when I'm not picking my jaw up off the floor.

Win and Connie are so generous and lovely. I so want to explore this city, you can't believe the stunning old colonial buildings, all empty and falling down! What you could do with them . . .'

'Slow down . . . It sounds pretty incredible. Is your thing still safe?'

'Yes, yes. Never out of my sight. I'm really overwhelmed with so many things to plan and do. You sure everything is all right with you? Give Mum my love, won't you. '

'Nat! We love you and everything is fine —'

The line suddenly went dead and Natalie slowly replaced the receiver.

She told Connie what had happened. Connie shrugged and suggested that she try to ring again in a few minutes.

'Phones are so unreliable in Burma, I'm afraid.'

'No, it's fine. I spoke to them all, everything is good. I just wanted them to know I'd arrived safely and everything is so exciting and comfortable, thanks to you both.'

'Our pleasure. After that big lunch, I've organised some soup for dinner, a simple mohinga. You must be very tired, so perhaps we'll have an early night. Tomorrow will also be busy, I'm sure.'

As Natalie lay in bed, with images spinning in her head like a technicolour movie, she tried to plan the next day, but she was sound asleep before she'd decided what else she wanted to do and see in this enchanting city.

# 10

NATALIE AND CONNIE SAT in the early morning sunshine at the rear of the house, sipping Connie's Italian coffee. Draped across a nearby cushion was a beautiful shawl. Intrigued by its softness and earthy colours, Natalie asked, 'What is that gorgeous shawl made from?'

'Would you believe that it's made from the lotus plant? Feel it. Keeps you warm in the winter and cool in the summer.'

Natalie gently ran her hands over the textured cloth.

'The fibres are taken from inside the lotus stems. They are as fine as a spider's web. It takes a lot of them just to make one thread. It's woven by the people who live on Inle Lake,' said Connie. 'Such a beautiful place to visit.'

'I'd love to see them making this fabric. It's exquisite. Are the shawls very expensive?' asked Natalie.

'Very,' replied Connie. 'It takes so long to make them and because tourists carry so little money, it is difficult for them to find customers.'

Connie assured Natalie that Win's old friend was trustworthy and reliable. 'He hopes that, one day, the world will want to come to Burma to appreciate its culture,' Connie said. 'Mr P also works with archaeological groups, helping to preserve important sites.'

They had just finished their coffee when U Phyu Myint arrived. Natalie guessed that he was about fifty. He was slim and had warm brown eyes, a shy smile and a respectful demeanour. He was dressed in a longyi and crisp short-sleeved shirt and carried a small leather folder. He looked professional yet friendly. Connie greeted him warmly and introduced him to Natalie, who was relieved to find that although Mr P spoke softly, his English was good.

'I'll leave you two to get to know each other,' said Connie.

'Do you like the modern art my friend Win champions, Natalie?' Mr P asked after he had shaken her hand.

'Some of the paintings in the gallery are terrific. Very interesting.'

Mr P nodded. 'Yes, but to me they are like a foreign language. I have been schooled in traditional Buddhist art and I spend most of my time in the world of temples, murals, Buddhist imagery and architecture. I hope I can show some of these things to you.'

Natalie returned Mr P's smile. 'I hope so, too. I've been told about the amazing temples and Burmese art. I know that it takes a lifetime of study to understand it, but if you could help me to just get a basic sense, that would be wonderful. I feel very privileged that you're looking after me,' said Natalie enthusiastically.

'That is excellent. We want people who have a genuine interest in our culture, like you, to come here and see it for themselves,' said Mr P.

'I certainly want to see all that I can, but I need to do other things as well. I have some other priorities, too.'

'Perhaps we can walk to the tea shop down the road and talk. Have you been to a Burmese tea shop yet? It will be an experience.'

'No. I'd love to do that.'

Not far from Connie and Win's house, Natalie and Mr P turned onto the main road. Along it stood a row of shops and a tea shop. Natalie could see people sitting outside on tiny, brightly coloured plastic stools. Mr P ushered her inside and they sat at a small wooden table.

'I think that this will be more comfortable for you,' he said.

The room wasn't crowded, but the atmosphere was steamy from the boiling urns and the air was heavy with the fragrance of tea. A young boy put two small bowls in front of them and then stood, holding a large teapot.

'He wants to know if you would like green or black tea,' explained Mr P as the boy waited.

'Black, please, with milk, like that.' Natalie pointed to the glasses of thick, milky tea being sipped at the next table.

'I'll order laphet to eat. It's a very traditional snack. This is known as tea shop sitting,' said Mr P as Natalie looked around. 'Everyone likes to come and to talk about, well, everything, like football and politics. But there are often spies in the tea shops, so it wouldn't be wise to be too critical in public.'

'I understand,' said Natalie. Two women sat at another table and she could see an older woman preparing food at the rear of the tiny shop. 'Have you known Connie and Win a long time?'

'Many years now. Win is a very good artist. He has studied abroad and perhaps he and Connie would be more comfortable living in Italy, but he is helping Burmese artists by providing them with opportunities they wouldn't have otherwise. He and Connie are good people. Now, you said that you had certain priorities. Can you tell me where you would like to go?'

'I want to locate a friend's family. They used to live here, in Yangon, and I also want to go to a place called Pyin Oo Lwin because I have arranged to meet someone there.'

'Pyin Oo Lwin is an interesting place, an old British hill station. Where are you meeting your friend?'

'I don't know exactly where. We've written letters, so I have her address. She's not young, but I am really looking forward to meeting her.' Natalie lowered her voice to add, 'She is a descendant of King Thibaw. She's his granddaughter. Do you think the military would be watching her?'

'No, I don't think so,' said Mr P. 'There is no royal family anymore and if, as you say, she is old, she would pose no threat.' He stopped talking when their tea was put in front of them. When the young boy walked away, Mr P continued. 'Please, try the laphet. It's made of pick-led tea leaves, nuts, ginger, beans, garlic and a little spice and salt. Very tasty.'

Natalie spooned some of the mixture into the palm of her hand, and, using her fingers, nibbled at it. 'Unusual flavour, tangy. My husband would like some of this with beer!'

'Yes, it is very good with beer,' agreed Mr P. 'You can buy the pickled leaves in the market. Maybe you can take some home to him.'

'Australian customs won't let you bring food into the country,' said Natalie. 'But I'll tell Mark, my husband, about it anyway.'

'Can you tell me the name of the person you want to visit in Pyin Oo Lwin?' asked Mr. P.

'I have been writing to Princess Aye Aye. Now I'm here I would very much like to meet her.'

'I have heard about her. I believe she's quite a personality!' he said smiling. 'So I'll look forward to taking you to meet her. Do you like your tea?'

'It's sweet! It's half condensed milk, but it somehow works with the smoky taste of the tea.' She took another sip. 'Connie told me that you also help to preserve and restore archaeological sites.'

'Yes. There are many places in my country that are falling into disrepair and we need expertise to restore them. I am not happy that some of the restoration work has been done by the military. It's no business for soldiers. Their work is very poor and often it results in even greater destruction, but they want the publicity. They also use the opportunity to steal valuable antiquities.'

'Yes, Connie told me about that when we went to the Shwedagon Pagoda.'

Mr P dropped his voice to a whisper. 'We have lost so much of our culture to invaders, looters, the British, and now our own government steals it. No-one has treated this country's heritage as badly as this current regime. Of course, not all the British were insensitive. I believe that you had a relative who was here,' he said diplomatically.

'Yes. My great-great-uncle was in Burma before the two World Wars. I know that he didn't approve of the British taking what they pleased,' said Natalie.

'Then he must have been a good man,' Mr P said in a quiet voice. 'Now we come to the matter of locating your friend's family. What can you tell me about them?'

Natalie explained that the last time her friend Mi Mi had heard anything about her parents, they had been planning to go to the delta region. That was just before Cyclone Nargis. Since then Mi Mi had heard nothing.

'This could be very difficult. Many families were

292

separated when that terrible disaster occurred. So many people were killed or displaced, and it has not been easy to trace all the victims. It's very sad. If you give me their last known address, I'll make some enquiries. I shall ask one of my students to see what he can find out.'

'I don't want to put you out,' said Natalie.

'We can only do our best. Now I think we should discuss the places that I think you will find really interesting, starting with Bagan.'

After they had finished their tea, Mr P walked Natalie back to Connie's place.

'I'll come and see you tomorrow, to let you know if I have found out anything about your friend's parents,' he said as he shook her hand in parting.

As Natalie walked into the house, Connie called out to her, 'You're just in time. I'm taking some paintings over to one of the hotels. A few of the hotels put them on display and sometimes tourists buy them. Would you like to come with me?'

Ko Wai Yan was waiting for them with his taxi. When they got in Connie told him that she needed to call in to a nearby shopping complex.

'I have to pick up some art supplies,' she told Natalie. 'You could look around, if you like. I won't be long.'

The centre was modest, with a small food market as well as clothing, jewellery, home products and electrical stores. All the goods were inexpensive and the majority of the merchandise seemed to have come from China. Natalie browsed for a few minutes before picking up a sturdy plastic shopping basket similar to one she remembered her grandmother having, years before.

'It's made from recycled plastic,' said Connie as she rejoined her. 'The plastic is sent to Thailand, and it comes back like that. It's pretty stiff. If you want to carry things, you'd be better off with a monk's bag. They're made of soft cloth and worn on your shoulder or across your body, and they carry a lot. I love mine,' said Connie. 'Now there's something you should buy, a little cheap radio. Then you can pick up the overseas news while you travel.'

'What a good idea! I'll get it,' said Natalie. She had already discovered that the local TV coverage was in Burmese and foreign programs were limited.

After they had delivered the bulk of the paintings to one of the more modern Yangon hotels, Connie explained that she had one painting she had to deliver to the British Embassy. 'It won't take long. The Strand Hotel is next door to the Australian Embassy, half a block down there. Go and have a look round the hotel. It's a lovely old lady. You could order us both a coffee, if you like.'

'What a great idea.'

While Connie dashed into the embassy, Natalie walked down to the elegant white building with its grand colonnade facing the waterfront. The doorman in traditional Burmese dress gave her a warm smile and opened the door to the lobby. As soon as she saw it, Natalie could imagine great-great-uncle Andrew sitting in a rattan chair beneath the slowly turning ceiling fans. A broad, majestic staircase curved upwards to a huge mezzanine floor. The formal dining room and bar were closed, but a large airy restaurant to her left looked inviting, so she went and sat down.

With its starched linen napkins and heavy silver cutlery, Natalie imagined that the place had changed little from colonial days. A pretty waitress in a uniform of longyi with matching top handed her a menu, which featured mainly European dishes, but Natalie only wanted coffee for herself and Connie. While she waited, she gazed outside through the tall windows of the restaurant. She could see passersby, and hear the muffled whoosh and jangle of cars, bicycles, trishaws, trucks and buses as they jostled their way along the Strand. However, the room was a quiet oasis, and when a Burmese man came in and sat down with his English newspaper, the rustle of its pages echoed in the stately room.

'That's all my business done for the day,' said Connie when she sat down opposite Natalie. 'Coffee on its way? Excellent. So tell me, how was Mr P? He can seem quite formal and proper, but he's very warm and extremely knowledgeable about everything.'

'He seems very nice. He's asking one of his students to check out Mi Mi's parents' last address.'

'If they've gone to the delta, finding them could be very difficult. But you will have tried, and you can't do more than that,' said Connie.

'Connie, what's the best way to pay for Mr P's expenses?' asked Natalie. 'I know that he's a friend of yours, but I don't want to do the wrong thing.'

Connie brushed this question aside. 'Natalie, don't concern yourself with that. While you're here with us, you are our guest.' As Natalie started to protest, she continued, 'It's payback. Vicki has been a very good friend to us over the years, so we are pleased to be able to return the favour to a friend of hers. We are delighted to do it.'

'Thank you,' Natalie replied.


When Mr P returned to the Peacock Studio the following day, he brought news of Mi Mi's parents.

'My student found a neighbour of your friend's parents,' he told Natalie, Connie and Win. 'He says they were going to the delta but their son, who is a monk down there, persuaded them not to go. So before Cyclone Nargis devastated much of the south of this country, they had already moved north, to a village near Sagaing, which is over the river from Mandalay, to stay with relations there.'

'That's wonderful,' said Connie. 'That's far away from the cyclone, so they should be safe.'

'I wonder why they left Yangon,' said Natalie.

'Perhaps they will tell us when we find them. It's a very convenient location for us, being so close to Mandalay,' said Mr P. 'We will go first to Bagan and spend a couple of days there and then on to Mandalay. Sagaing is less than an hour away from Mandalay, although in the opposite direction from Pyin Oo Lwin.'

'That's convenient,' said Connie.

'Are we going by train or plane to Bagan?' asked Natalie.

'It is far better to fly. Internal flights are quite good, but the train is not at all reliable. It takes at least sixteen hours, sometimes even longer. I'll get your plane ticket to Mandalay changed. Mr P and I can organise your accommodation. Leave that to me,' said Win.

'What about your accommodation, Mr P?' asked Natalie.

Mr P smiled. 'There is no need to worry about me. I know all the cheapest and best places to stay.'

'I don't know how to thank you all,' said Natalie.

'There are a lot of good people outside Burma who have helped us, so this is one way we can repay what's been done for us,' said Win.

Natalie could hear a phone ringing in the next room.

Connie went to answer it and returned, saying with a smile, 'It's for you, Natalie. I think it's your family.'

Natalie's face lit up and she hurried off to speak to them.

'I can't believe I'm going to Bagan,' Natalie excitedly filled Mark in on her plans after she'd talked to the children.

'Sounds fantastic. Just so long as you are sure they know what they're doing. Be careful, Nat. I'd be unable to help you from here if you got into trouble.'

'I won't. Mark, even though I'm having the best time, I still really miss you and the kids.'

'Honey, they're fine. See, they didn't cling to the phone. They just said their bit, and now they're off playing,' said Mark.

'Okay. I love you.'

'I love you, too.'

Natalie returned to the others and said, 'I think I need to take something back to explain Burmese culture to Mark. I can take photos, but I can't remember all the things you're telling me. Is there a bookshop we could go to where I could buy a nice coffee table book?'

'Not really,' said Win. 'Burmese people respect and love books, but there's no major publishing industry in Myanmar and because of the heavy censorship, very few books are imported, so books are expensive. Yet literacy and education are big dreams for most families, so there is a large trade in secondhand books, newspapers and magazines.'

'There is a very famous street in Yangon, where a lot of secondhand books and magazines are sold,' said Connie.

'Would you like me to take you there?' asked Mr P. 'Perhaps you will be able to find something suitable and it's an interesting place to browse.'

'Yes, please, I would. Is it far?'

'It's just a few blocks from the Strand Hotel. We can go there now if you wish.'

'You might find a rare treasure. Some of the stall holders keep back special things, so ask to see everything. Have fun,' said Connie.

As they travelled through the streets in a trishaw, Natalie enjoyed the comfortable speed and the warm air on her face as the driver's wiry legs pushed firmly down on the pedals.

'I will take you to one particular shop. My friend who owns it sometimes works for me as a tour guide. It was started in the old days by his great-grandfather and he has all manner of books. Lots of full boxes upstairs, too. I am sure that he will find you what you want,' said Mr P.

Their driver pedalled steadily along the waterfront and Natalie felt pleased when she recognised where they were. She was beginning to feel quite familiar with this part of the city. Suddenly it occurred to her that the traffic didn't seem very noisy.

'Everyone at home told me that Asian traffic is always really loud,' she said to Mr P. 'But here no-one blows their horn at all, and there don't seem to be any scooters.'

'Both were banned some years ago. The Number One general was offended by someone who passed his car on a scooter and pointed a finger at him, like a gun. So scooters were banned,' said Mr P.

'What happened to the general?' asked Natalie.

'He resigned after the student uprising in 1988, but he had influence behind the scenes for quite some time. Then, about six years ago, he was put under house arrest for trying to plot a coup.' Mr P paused before he added, 'He was still under house arrest when he died but the junta didn't make any announcement about it. It was all kept quiet.'

'The general must have been hated.'

'Yes, but there are others just as bad. There are many intrigues among the military. Many just want more power for themselves, and for their friends and relatives,' said Mr P.

They passed rows of neglected colonial buildings and the Strand Hotel, and then turned into a narrow street flanked by tall buildings. Sheets of blue plastic formed awnings over stacks of old books. Dog-eared magazines were hung along the walls or spread on the ground.

At the entrance of the street, Mr P asked the driver to

stop. 'The shop is halfway down this street. We can walk and you can look at the stalls on the way,' he suggested.

Natalie looked at the displays of printed material and watched what people were buying. There were a lot of school textbooks that looked very old and out of date. Half the items were written in English, the rest in Burmese. Some sellers tried to persuade her to buy their merchandise, but Natalie shook her head. They walked further along the narrow street, past a vendor frying dough balls that were then drained and sprinkled with sugar. Natalie was tempted to try one, but Mr P walked purposefully on till he stopped outside a doorway. It was the entrance to a narrow building, wedged between identical sisters. Its metal door grille had been pulled to one side and stacked with stands of postcards, magazines and posters, which all flapped at the front of the shop.

Mr P called out to the proprietor.

As soon as Natalie stepped inside, she fell in love with the shop's unmistakable smell of old books. There was more than a tinge of mustiness from some old leather covers perspiring in the humid air. Despite the appearance of disorder, and Natalie's feeling that some of the overflowing shelves hadn't been touched in decades, she guessed that the owner knew every title in his shop and where it was located.

The proprietor was older than Mr P. He had Burmese features but Natalie could see that his small beard was of greying ginger. He greeted Mr P warmly.

'Natalie, this is U Zyaw Hin Watt. He is the owner. His great-grandfather opened this bookshop before the First World War,' said Mr P.

'Watt is actually a Scottish name,' said U Watt. 'My great-grandfather was a Scot who married a Burmese woman. Please, address me as U Watt. Are you looking for anything special? I can send for some tea?'

'I don't think I have ever seen so many old books. I would like to buy a present.'

'Maybe some books about Bagan and Mandalay?' suggested Mr P.

'What do you do, Natalie?' asked U Watt.

'I'm a teacher, but a stay-at-home mother at the moment. I've become interested in Burma since I found out that my great-great-uncle was here in the 1920s. I'm sort of retracing his footsteps,' said Natalie. 'He wrote some stories about his travels all over Burma, and he was a terrific photographer, too.'

'I suppose that was an interesting time, before the wars. My great-grandfather used to collect stories about the people who lived here in about the same period, both British and Burmese, but they were never published. I have them somewhere in the rear of the shop.'

'You told me once that your family knew some of the old royal family,' said Mr P to the bookseller. Natalie was immediately interested.

'Yes. When she lived in Yangon, the king's half sister, Princess Tipi Si, was one of my great-grandfather's customers. She used to send her Shan attendant in here to collect the books she'd ordered. According to my great-grandfather's stories, there was some dismay when Tipi Si was forced to sell all her valuables,' said U Watt.

Natalie thought for a moment and then decided not to mention her Uncle Andrew's connection with the princess. Instead she asked, 'What happened to Princess Tipi Si?'

'When she became very old, she was cared for in a nunnery,' he answered. 'I believe she was buried in Mandalay.'

'I've seen the nuns in their pink robes with their alms bowls,' said Natalie. 'Are they important, like the monks?'

U Watt and Mr P exchanged a smile. 'A long time ago, it's said that there was equality between the Buddhist nuns and monks, but when the Mongols attacked Pagan, which is now called Bagan, about seven hundred years ago, there was political unrest and this caused the dissolution of the power of the nuns who were no longer ordained. In the nineteenth century, under King Mindon, respect for the nuns was revived, especially in the area of Sagaing, but their power remained limited and so nuns still don't have equal status with the monks according to the sangha,' said Mr P.

'The sangha is the community of monks who make all the monastic decisions,' explained U Watt.

'But now there are some very active senior nuns who travel outside Burma to Buddhist conventions and they are working towards regaining their authority and equality,' said U Watt.

Natalie turned to Mr P. 'Sagaing. Isn't that where we're going?'

He nodded and said to U Watt, 'Natalie is trying to find the parents of a friend in Australia.'

'I wish you luck in finding them. Where else are you visiting?' he asked.

'We will go first to Bagan, then on to Mandalay. Natalie also wants to meet someone in Pyin Oo Lwin,' replied Mr P.

'A lovely town. There are so many places to visit in our country. It may not always be easy for tourists to get about, but most places are worth the effort.'

'Yes, there is such a lot to see. I'm so excited to be here.'

'Please, take this with you.' U Watt rose and took down a book from a shelf. There were three golden images on the cover. 'The Shwedagon Pagoda you probably recognise, and these are the Mahamuni Temple and the Golden Rock. They are the three most popular sacred sites in Burma.'

'How kind of you, but please let me pay for it,' said Natalie, for while she appreciated U Watt's gesture, she knew that she could easily afford the book. Mr P immediately understood what Natalie was doing and he told her the price of the book. She gave the money to U Watt and thanked him.

Connie had taken their late lunch out into the shady back garden. She called Win from the studio where Natalie could hear the chatter of his pupils wafting from the airy space.

'Ah, frittata and salad. Today we eat western style,' Win said as he sat down and poured himself a glass of lime juice from a large blue glass jug.

'Which you will smother in chilli sauce,' said Connie. 'Pass me your plate, please, Natalie.'

Natalie lifted the heavy blue glass plate and Connie served her a slice of the frittata. 'These plates are amazing,' she said. 'Did one of your artists make them?'

'We wish! No, the artisan who made this glass works in a special factory. May Lin's talking about retirement now, so I collect her pieces when I can,' said Connie. 'They are special, aren't they?'

'You should take Natalie to the glass factory,' said Win.

'Yes, she should see that,' said Connie. 'We could fit in a visit this afternoon, if you're up to it. But if you'd rather rest, that's fine by me.'

'I don't want to miss out on anything while I'm here, although don't go to any trouble,' said Natalie.

Win's eyes twinkled. 'Trust me, you must go, and Connie will enjoy taking you.'

'It's not far from here. It's right in the middle of Yangon,' said Connie.

Natalie couldn't imagine what a Burmese glass factory located in the middle of the city would look like.

After lunch, Ko Wai Yan drove them slowly past some shops and large homes on an old tree-lined street.

'He's looking for the right lane. It's easy to miss. There, turn there,' said Connie and they turned beside a high stone fence. They bumped along the overgrown, seldom-used lane until they came to a metal gate that had been propped open. A grassy track led into what looked like a neglected paddock. Large stands of bamboo and high trees blocked the taxi's progress and Ko Wai Yan stopped.

'On foot from here, so you'll need some of this.' Connie handed Natalie some mosquito repellent. 'We have to walk through those trees and there are clouds of mosquitoes under them.'

She wasn't wrong. The mosquitoes hung in swarms under the trees as they picked their way along a muddy path in what seemed to Natalie to be a small jungle. She saw orchids hanging in glass pots from some of the trees while tinkling glass chimes dangled from others. Connie drew Natalie's attention to a number of large mounds that were covered in rotting leaves. She bent down and brushed away some of the debris to reveal piles of coloured glass more than a metre high.

'Are these discarded bits? They don't look broken,' said Natalie as she picked through the pieces, finding small vases, glasses, plates, bowls and other ornaments.

'It's her stockpile,' said Connie, sounding amused. 'May Lin only takes special orders now, pieces for hotels or people who are prepared to pay her prices. When she needs something else to sell, she looks for it out here.'

'But will all these sell?' exclaimed Natalie. 'There is so much of it and they are such beautiful pieces.'

'Eventually. Come and see where the work is done.'

As they walked, Natalie started to feel as though she'd gone down Alice's rabbit hole. In front of her was a sort of carport made entirely of glass. Even the roof tiles were made of thick translucent squares of dark green glass. The uprights supporting the roof were covered with shards of different glass pieces arranged into a colourful mosaic. Inside the small glass palace, where the grass was growing quite high, a car was parked.

'What is that? I mean, it's an old car, but . . .' Words failed her.

'It's a 1935 Austin. May Lin's father adored it. Shame it's been left to deteriorate.'

Around the yard were mudbrick and rotting bamboo shacks, rusting kilns and stacks of well-weathered wood. Natalie could see that the paraphernalia associated with glass blowing – old iron pipes and moulds and clay samples – looked as though they hadn't been touched in decades.

The undergrowth thinned and they came to a garden, surrounded by a large open-sided building filled with tables and beautiful carved and lacquered Chinese furniture. The high shelves and glass cabinets could have graced the most formal of wealthy homes but the lovely antiques stood on a pounded mud floor, and every surface of the beautiful furniture had been covered in pieces of glass. To one side there was a small, open brick fireplace where a blackened kettle steamed and tea things were set on a shaky side table. Hanging incongruously from the ceiling tinkled several chandeliers, their glass catching the light as they moved in the slight breeze.

A young woman stood at a table wrapping up glasses in newspaper while another sat beside her, writing in a ledger. Through the trees Natalie could see two skinny dogs loping ahead of a slim, smiling woman, possibly in her sixties, who lifted an arm in greeting.

'Natalie, this is May Lin. Her father started the Rangoon Glass Factory and she and her brother have carried it on,' said Connie.

May Lin spoke beautiful English and offered to take Natalie on a tour around the workshops. She explained how they made their glass from special sand which came from a mountain near the Chinese border and that they made their own colours and glazes too. Natalie tried to absorb the information about their traditional glass-making methods but she couldn't stop staring.

She could see that someone had created a glass garden amid the jungle undergrowth at the rear of one of the workshops. Psychedelic mushrooms, animals and flowers in Dali-esque shapes sprouted around trees and undergrowth. There was also a complete gingerbread cottage, big enough for a child to play inside, made of coloured glass.

'What a wonderland for children,' she said, thinking how Charlotte would love all this. Quickly she took a photograph.

As May Lin moved ahead of them, Connie whispered to Natalie, 'Neither May Lin nor her brother married, so there are no children to carry on this business.'

'That's sad. What will happen to this place? What will they do?'

'They'll live very well when they retire. They are wait-ing, like everyone else, for the day The Lady is released and takes up her role as leader and change begins in Yangon. May Lin and her brother can see the day when investors will come and build hotels and banks and other business build-ings. This quaint place is actually four acres of land, hidden in the middle of the city. It will be worth a lot of money.'

Natalie gazed around, thinking how sad that this whimsical family factory would disappear beneath the cement feet of a modern structure because there was no-one to carry on its traditions. 'I'd love to buy something.'

She chose three little glass ornaments: a blue rabbit for Adam, a tiny green bud vase for Charlotte and for Andrew a red elephant.

Back at the Peacock Studio, Win gave her some bubblewrap for her glass gifts. 'I think you should leave these here until you are ready to go home, in case they get broken. I knew you would enjoy the glass factory,' he said. 'It's eccentric and charming, like so much of Burma is.'

'One more thing, a souvenir for you.' Connie handed her the lotus-stem shawl.

'I couldn't possibly take this,' began Natalie.

'It will be useful in the hills, it can get cool up there. When you wear it at home, think of us.'

'Thank you. I will,' said Natalie.


When they set out together for Bagan the next day, Natalie appreciated how well Mr P had organised everything, how he'd arranged a taxi to take them both to the airport and advised her to bring a book to read while they waited for their plane. He kept charge of her documents, tickets, travel papers and passport, and said he would pay any fees as they were needed. As soon as they arrived at Yangon airport for the flight to Bagan, he whisked her bag away to check it in, arranged their aircraft seats, and brought her a bottle of water and some moist tissues to wipe her face and hands. He sat near her and didn't interrupt her reading until the flight was ready to board. On the plane he sat several seats behind her. Mr P had arranged for her to have a window seat, but Natalie was disappointed because it was cloudy and she couldn't see very much.

Mr P had suggested that he pay for whatever they needed each day – food, fares and fees – in the local currency and every few days he'd work out what they'd spent in US dollars and Natalie could reimburse him. There was no official foreign exchange, though a black market operated in larger cities, so it seemed to Natalie that Mr P's system was far simpler for her.

After the plane had landed in Bagan and they had dis-embarked, Mr P told her, 'Bagan is usually very dry, but now there is still quite a lot of water lying around. Your shoes will get muddy.'

'I can wash them. It's a shame I couldn't see much while we were flying except some paddyfields and a few villages in the breaks in the clouds.'

'Then Bagan will be more of a surprise!' he said with a smile. 'There is no modern city here, just hotels. People come from all over the world to see the wonders of this place.'

From the plane they walked across the wet tarmac to a bright modern terminal with an ornate gold-painted roof. Inside, monks sat patiently and families with excited children waited for their flight. Mr P collected their luggage and then they walked towards the exit, looking for their driver.

For the first time Mr P looked ruffled, even annoyed. He asked Natalie to wait with their bags for a moment while he went to talk to a man holding up a sign with Natalie's name on it.

When he returned he said to Natalie, 'That isn't a driver I know. Something has happened to the man I usually use. But it'll be all right. Let's go.' He swung his backpack onto his shoulder, and took Natalie's bag and wheeled it to the elderly car, where the driver held open the boot. As Mr P placed the bags in the boot, the driver reached for Natalie's shoulder bag to do the same, but she shook her head and climbed into the back seat.

The road was slippery with a slick of orange mud but Natalie was glued to the window of the taxi as the bright green acacia trees and patches of raw red earth slid past. Suddenly, on either side of the road appeared domes of mossy stone and ancient red-brick stupas.

'That's called a bu stupa,' said Mr P, pointing to one

of them. 'Bu means gourd, and that stupa's shaped rather like one.'

Natalie nodded, looking at an old building surrounded by tiered terraces. In the distance she could see huge complexes of temples whose spires rose like fairytale castles; closer to the road were well-preserved, simple, one-roomed stupas.

They drove on and passed a goatherd following his bouncing charges as they reared up to eat leaves from high branches of trees by the roadside, as well as the occasional man on a bicycle, and a family in a horse-drawn cart decorated with flowers. They passed several small villages and Mr P told her that people used to live among all the stupas and monuments, but now that the region had been recognised as an important archaeological area by UNESCO, they had been moved away into new villages.

'So, we will stay in new Pagan and visit some of the best temples in old Bagan. There are thousands of them, so we will only have time to visit a few,' said Mr P.

Natalie thought the landscape was amazing, a bit like she imagined outback Australia would look, with massive termite mounds scattered across its dry plains, except these mounds were temples. 'How long has it been like this?' she asked.

'Myths say that Bagan started in the second century. It became the capital of Burma in the eleventh century and that's when over ten thousand monuments, stupas for religious relics, temples and monasteries, were built. Some of them were built from simple clay, others were very elaborate with great carvings and artwork,' explained Mr P.

'It's amazing.'

'Everyone who comes here should see the Ananda Temple, but I have found that people like different monuments for different reasons. Perhaps it is the artwork, or the architecture, maybe it's the religious significance or the carvings and the Buddha images, or for the views they offer. There is something for everyone.'

'I'm so glad you suggested coming here,' said Natalie, shaking her head in wonder.

Mr P had booked Natalie into a low-rise, older-style hotel set in attractive gardens that faced the Irrawaddy River.

'I will stay in the town in a guesthouse,' said Mr P. 'In one hour I will come back here and we can begin our tour of Bagan.'

Their driver, keen to make a good impression, tried to take Natalie's suitcase into the hotel but he was shooed away by the hotel staff. Mr P had told Natalie that there was no tipping in Burma but it seemed that in the tourist hotels it was not an unknown custom and it seemed that their driver had tried to earn one.

Her room had two hard single beds, a small bathroom (do not drink the water, Natalie reminded herself), a wardrobe and a small set of drawers. She carefully unpacked her few belongings and then went to explore the hotel. She wandered to the dining area and sat on the verandah that overlooked the wide expanse of the Irrawaddy River. Barges, low in the water, were ferrying teak logs.

There were several other tourists at the hotel. Most of them seemed to be middle-aged Europeans. She continued to watch the river traffic until Mr P arrived, this time in a small, gaily painted horse-drawn carriage with a smiling driver.

'I thought you might enjoy this. We can take this carriage off the road and go to some places few visitors go,' explained Mr P.

'This is wonderful,' said Natalie as the driver helped her up into the carriage. His teeth were stained reddish brown from chewing betel nut, his hair was slicked down with a pungent oil and he wore a longyi and a dusty shirt. His thongs were ingeniously cut from a rubber tyre.

He introduced himself as Kyaw Kyaw.

'Now we travel old style to long-ago Bagan,' announced Mr P.

The horse clipped smartly along the unpaved road, a small plastic Buddha swinging merrily from the canvas roof of the cart. Natalie waved to the smiling children as they passed through villages and into the countryside of rice paddies, where water buffalo wallowed. Women, walking from the village wells, balanced tin jugs of water on their heads while carrying urns of water on their hips with poise and barefoot grace. In the stillness, monks walked slowly back to their monastery, carrying their alms bowls. The blue smoke of wood fires curled into the air and the smell of snacks cooking over charcoal at roadside stalls was tantalising.

Wherever Natalie looked she felt a sense of time having passed this place by. She took a photo of a lichen-covered, crumbling stone wall of a brick stupa, its base overgrown save for a narrow path made by grazing goats. In the distance were thousands of ancient stone temples, their domes a reminder of an extravagant frenzy of building as the countless edifices spread from the banks of the meandering Irrawaddy River and across the plain.

'It must look amazing from the air,' she said to Mr P. 'It's like a lost world. Where did everyone go?'

'Growth in Bagan started to slow when the capital moved away in the fourteenth century, but it remained a sacred city. It is true that the bats and owls and goats and cows moved in, but perhaps they were less destructive than the earthquakes and the more recent poor attempts at restoration. Here we are in the twelfth century,' Mr P announced as the small horse trotted along the track and the magnificent spread of the Ananda Temple rose before them.

\*

When she got back to the hotel, Natalie wrote down in her little notebook her experiences of that day, taking time to describe her impressions of what she had seen.

*I felt I really did rush back in time. So little has changed here. Village life continues in its simplicity, and the people seem connected to these ancient monuments, but you can't help wondering about the people who built these magnificent religious buildings. Were they just simple folk living in humble houses, eking out their living much as they do today, or rich donors hoping for merit?*

*Some temples have stalls inside their covered walkways or courtyards. Some have artists outside them, busy working on their sand paintings, copying versions of the old murals and wall paintings in the temples. They use a local technique and paint in brilliant acrylics on canvases covered with a thick sandy surface. Their pictures flutter across the grass to dry like illuminated leaves.*

*Inside the temples it is serene. Women pray and bring offerings while the men gild the patient faces of the giant Buddha figures. (Mr P told me that women aren't allowed onto the higher platforms!) Some figures are so covered in gold leaf they have lost all detail and are huge solid gold lumps.*

*You walk through narrow passages like dungeons where stone archways give a glimpse of the sunny world outside. All is dim. But it's very calming. Winding underground, Mr P had a torch to show me the outlines and faded colours of murals and the jatakas, the illustrated stories of Buddhist folklore. Every surface is carved. You could stand and study a small area of stone for an hour and still miss tiny details. But one showed scars from where some Germans cut out murals, which are now in storage in Hamburg.*

*I climbed a narrow dark tower where the stone steps are so worn that they dip in the middle, and stepped* outside. *It is beyond words seeing, spread across the 200 square kilometres plain all the buildings, small and large, scattered and without a plan but somehow one coherent giant jigsaw puzzle. And slowly curling beside this amazing spectacle is the immense Irrawaddy River. Secluded monasteries and old pagodas are dotted along the tall cliffs that tower over the opposite side of the river. It's a breathtaking sight as they stand, seemingly ageless, glowing in the sun. Apart from the occasional bicycle, and the very occasional car, there is no sign of modern life.*

*In some dark, quiet, ancient vaults people pray, chanting their prayers, while in other vast temples it seems bats and birds and small creatures are the only worshippers. Despite the slow scraping of centuries, you can still witness the work of those long-ago artisans, the gash of a tool, the perfection of ornamentation painted over 800 years ago. You wish the architects and artisans who created these buildings could return and see their lonely handiwork still surviving.*

*Swooping pigeons broke the stillness. I didn't like to chatter. If I asked a question, it was answered softly, but generally Mr P and I wandered in silence. Occasionally he pointed to something I might have missed. We saw half buried Buddha statues. There is so much detail, from the deep underground to the dainty depictions of Buddha's life, to the enormous sky-reaching tiers of temples. Trying to visualise the old city with its palaces and pagodas amid these ruins is sometimes easy, but sometimes blurred.*

*Weaving between the walls, where lichen, grass and cactus grow, and mud sticks to your feet, there are echoes of the pounding of processions. It is easy to imagine how kings, queens, slaves, pious monks and village people once inhabited this unique landscape.*

*On the way back, the sun was setting and people were*

312

*returning home to prepare for the evening. I could hear
the gongs ringing from a monastery. There were village
boys shouting as they played soccer on a patch of grass
next to where a small stupa had squatted for centuries. My
head is still bursting. Everything is so immense, moving
and powerful it's really hard to absorb it all.*

*My final memory of today was so different. On the
way home, Kway Kway started to sing Queen's 'Who
Wants to Live Forever' in Burmese!*

Later that evening, Natalie went down to the lobby to
send Mark a short email.

She pushed the send button and nodded to the hotel
desk manager. He was almost sure, he assured her, that her
email would get through. 'Today is good,' he explained.
Natalie didn't ask why this was so because another tourist
was waiting to use the old computer in the hope of also
making contact with the modern world outside this living
museum in which they'd found themselves.

In the hotel's restaurant Natalie ordered a local beer
and went to watch the glimmer of lights on the river. She
could tell that the other guests who were returning from
exploring Bagan were drowning in all that they'd seen,
just as she was. They nodded and smiled politely to her
but did not seem anxious for social chit chat. Anyway,
thought Natalie, the day had been too overwhelming for
trivia.

She decided to return to her room to read for a while
and went to her drawer to retrieve her book. Immediately
she saw that her carefully folded clothes were not as neatly
arranged as she had left them. It was not the way she had
unpacked. Hurriedly she looked around and saw that her
small suitcase had been moved. Someone had definitely
gone through her things. Nothing seemed to have been
taken, but she felt disturbed. It was quite creepy.

313

She debated with herself about asking if she could move to another room. She wished she was having dinner with Mr P so she could ask him what to do, but tonight she would be having dinner by herself in the hotel. Suddenly the faintly lit gardens looked sinister and not as romantic as she had first thought. So she took the torch from beside her bed, thoughtfully provided by the hotel for the regular blackouts, and slipped it into her pocket.

As she walked quickly along the garden path that wound from her room to the hotel lobby, she patted her shoulder bag, feeling the hard shape of the kammavaca at the bottom as usual. She was shocked that someone had checked her room. Perhaps this happened to all foreigners. Everyone told her how there were people always watching you. She'd ask Mr P what he thought had happened when she saw him in the morning.

As she walked past the front desk, she heard several tourists talking in fractured English to the staff, asking about local restaurants. The staff explained that there were several small eating places up the road within easy walking distance. Natalie decided she didn't want to eat by herself in the hotel, so she asked the girl at the desk if she should go there too, and the girl smiled and nodded. 'They are going to good place. Very simple, nice food.'

When the foreign tourists set off, Natalie trailed behind them.

Outside the hotel the rutted road was ill lit; a few pale lights hung from power poles sagging with spaghetti nests of looped cables. It was still early evening, and there was a lot of activity on the street. Along the roadside were braziers and small fires, illuminating cheerful Burmese faces in their glow. Whole families were eating at these roadside stalls and the smells were delicious.

At one eatery the tourists ahead of her stopped to ask what was being cooked and took a photo. Bicycles without lights glided past her. When she looked into the houses she could see that their rooms were lit by a single dim bulb. Candles were burning at shrines and at a small temple a seated Buddha statue was illuminated by a string of Christmas lights.

The small party eventually arrived at a large eating house, where loud disco music roared and a bulky old TV screen was showing music clips of Burmese singers covering American hits from earlier decades. The noisy music was obviously an attraction for the Burmese, but Natalie didn't enjoy it. She was relieved when the tourists she'd been following stopped and decided to go into a smaller restaurant decked out in a lot of fluorescent pink but with no loud music. Natalie hesitated, then, as the others sat down, she brushed aside the coloured plastic strips hanging in the doorway and went inside.

A woman and her daughter, who looked to be about twelve, were running the place. The young girl smiled shyly at Natalie, who smiled in return and said, 'Just me. One person, please,' as she held up one finger.

The girl glanced at her mother, who was passing around plastic menus with coloured pictures of the dishes to the other newcomers.

One of the tourists looked up and waved to Natalie. 'Oh, hello there. Would you like to come and join us?'

'Yes, do,' echoed his wife.

'Thank you. I'm Natalie.' She shook their hands and sat down as they exchanged names.

'You are Australian?' asked the man, who introduced himself as Claudio.

'Yes. You guessed.'

'Where do you think we are from? This is Paulo, his wife Mariana and my wife Erika.'

'Maybe South America but I'm not sure,' said Natalie.

'Brazil,' said Claudio.

They were a friendly lot, though Claudio spoke the best English. They all ordered their dinner from the pictures on the menu, as well as some beer and lemonade, and then they talked about Bagan. All agreed that it was the most extraordinary place and far too big to see in a short period of time. They discussed where they had been already in Myanmar and where else they intended going. Natalie explained that she had only been to Yangon, but was going on to Mandalay and then to Pyin Oo Lwin.

'Do you feel safe travelling around Myanmar?' she asked them.

'We do. Of course, the military presence is never far away, even though it might be out of sight,' said Claudio. 'But because we are tourists I don't think that there will be any problems. And you? You are on holidays?'

'Yes, mainly, although there are a couple of people I want to look up. I left my husband and children at home,' said Natalie.

'So you are travelling alone in this country? That is a brave thing to do. Do you miss your husband and your little ones?'

Suddenly Natalie realised that she did. Especially Mark. She'd had the most wonderful day, but tonight she was at a table with two married couples who could share their experiences with each other, and she felt quite alone. She wished that Mark had been able to come as well, so that they could enjoy the wonders of Burma together. But the feeling passed and she joined in the laughter as myriad appetising dishes appeared on the table.

Natalie was impressed to learn that Claudio and Paulo were doctors who frequently travelled to third world countries to work. 'We have been working in northern Thailand, in the refugee camps, but when we finished our wives met us and we travelled to Burma. We are going to Sri Lanka as well.'

When the meal was over, Natalie reached for her wallet, but Claudio stilled her hand.

'Please, be our guest. The meal, it is so inexpensive, and your company has been delightful.'

'Thank you very much. It was delicious. I'll have to try and remember some of the dishes.'

Natalie was glad of the Brazilians' charming company as they walked back to the hotel.

'I'm sure we shall see you again, Natalie. That's how it happens. When you are visiting the popular places, you run into the same people. Sleep well.'

Claudio gave her a warm hug and kissed her on both cheeks, as did the others, so different from the Burmese protocol of respect that meant not touching people unless they were close friends or family.

Natalie had enjoyed her time with the Brazilians and she felt more of a seasoned traveller as she made her way back through the hotel garden to her room. She was glad that there was a light on above her door to ensure she'd found the right room, which looked as she'd left it. Remembering Claudio's comment about tourists being safe, she decided all would be okay, although she would talk to Mr P in the morning.

She settled into bed. The ceiling fan whirred above her and the elderly air conditioner in the room next to hers rattled. She turned on her radio and found the BBC World Service.

She must have fallen asleep. The radio was still on but the air conditioner next door had stopped. She could hear soft voices, possibly some of the staff finishing up for the night. Then she remembered that her shoulder bag was still hanging from the back of the door and she decided that she wanted it closer, so she reached for the light but it didn't go on, and she realised there was a blackout. She groped for the little torch and got up but as she reached the door, the knob began to turn. She stood frozen for a second, then she hurriedly checked that the safety chain was locked. Was someone trying to get into her room? She checked that the window was also locked. Sure that the room was secure, she put the shoulder bag under her pillow. She listened for a while, before slowly drifting asleep.


Mr P was waiting for her as she came into the lobby to check out the next morning.

'Did you have a nice meal last night?'

'Actually, I went down the street to a local place with two Brazilian couples. It was very nice. I was glad to get out of the hotel.' She lowered her voice. 'I was a bit unnerved. While we were out yesterday, I think someone went through my things in my room. When I went to my drawer my clothes had been disturbed.'

He nodded sympathetically. 'I'm afraid this happens. See the man in the corner over there?'

Natalie turned around to see a rather plump Burmese man dressed in a longyi and shirt like most of the local men.

'Military. We'll probably see him or someone like him when we get to Mandalay. What is the expression? Justifying his existence? Don't worry. They are not interested in you unless you have a pile of money, guns, drugs or stolen artefacts,' said Mr P quietly.

'Artefacts?' asked Natalie, sounding worried.

'There is still a busy trade in illegal Burmese antiques. Despite the government saying it has cracked down, it goes on.'

Natalie felt herself go cold. Did the military know about her kammavaca? No, that was silly. She wasn't trying to take it out of the country. Quite the reverse. She did wonder, however, what Mr P would say if she told him that not only had her room definitely been searched yesterday, but that later on someone may have been trying to break in to it. Now thinking about it in the light of day, she wasn't sure, however, it might be safer to tell Mr P why she was visiting the former royal princess, Aye Aye.

# 11

NATALIE LIKED THE EARLY morning start to each new day's journey with Mr P. She looked forward to the day's adventures. Life at home would be pretty dull and predictable after this! They set off for Mandalay, still with the driver who had met them at the airport, who was introduced to her as Soe Soe.

In the middle of nowhere, where two large highways intersected, they slowed at an impromptu market. In both directions dozens of people had spread out great mounds of freshly picked flowers. Roses, carnations, daisies, chrysanthemums, orchids and tropical blooms Natalie couldn't identify were laid on the ground. Buyers heaped huge bunches of them onto their bicycles and carts and into vans to drive to their stalls in nearby towns. Mr P told her that people would buy the flowers to take home and place on their household shrine. All Buddhist households had an altar with freshly cut flowers.

'They've all been here since dawn. This is a convenient place, halfway between the market gardens and the buyers,' said Mr P.

A little further on, he suggested they make a stop at a large and famous monastery. They arrived as several hundred monks were queuing patiently for their main meal of the day. Ladles of rice and vegetables were heaped into the monks' bowls from giant cooking vats in the courtyard. The monks then filed into the main dining hall where they sat cross-legged at their low tables. The senior monks sat in silence by windows, while the other monks sat along tables in order of seniority. At the tables furthest away from the stern gaze of the senior monks, the young novices giggled and chattered over their food. Local people were also welcomed in the hall, and they prayed towards the Buddha figure as they waited for the monks to begin their meal before they ate, as well.

Natalie thought that it was interesting but she also felt it was a bit invasive watching the monks eating their meal, so she was pleased when Mr P took her out quietly and showed her the grounds of the monastery. There Natalie felt calm. She was still rattled by what had happened in Bagan. Mr P must have sensed that she was distracted, so he suggested that they sit for a few moments in the sun in the garden and share some fruit he had bought earlier in the morning.

Natalie slowly peeled a banana and said, 'Last night, someone might have tried to break into my room.' She took a bite of her banana and told him what had happened.

'Sometimes the authorities can be overzealous but there could be a simple explanation,' he said calmly. 'Perhaps it was just someone getting their room confused with yours in the dark.'

'I'd like to think so. But sometimes I feel like I am being watched.'

'That is a common feeling in this country.'

'I know, and you're probably right, but I'm concerned because I am taking something to Aye Aye, and I don't want anything to happen to it. It's nothing dangerous or illegal. In fact, I'd like to show you.' She took off her shoulder bag.

'You do not have to do that. It is not my business,' said Mr P.

'I think you might find it interesting. It once belonged to King Thibaw.' She unwrapped the silk scarf from around the box, opened it, took out the kammavaca and handed it to him. Mr P wiped his hands on his handkerchief, carefully unfolded the kammavaca and studied both sides of it intently.

'This is very beautiful. Unusual. I'm sure she will be very glad to receive it.' He looked at it a while longer then, seeing the driver approach, he quickly slipped it back into its box and handed it to Natalie.

Natalie put it back in her shoulder bag. 'You said you'd heard she was a colourful personality. How do you know her?'

'I have never actually met her, but she has done some very interesting things, so she is quite well known in Myanmar.' He nodded to Soe Soe. 'The driver is here, shall we continue on to Mandalay? And then we shall see what we can discover about your friend's parents.'

As they stood up Natalie smiled. 'I feel so much better for having told you what happened in Bagan. I wouldn't want anything to happen to this kammavaca.'

'Rest assured, I do not think it is something that the authorities would be interested in. Perhaps outside Burma others might be fascinated but kammavacas are common here!'

They drove into Mandalay in the late afternoon, passing boxy new apartment blocks, office buildings and hotels.

'It's not as attractive as Yangon,' said Natalie.

'No, and it's not very old, either. It was the last capital of the Burmese kingdom and then only for a short time.'

'Is the royal palace still here? I'd like to see it,' said Natalie.

'It was bombed in World War Two and very little was left. Mandalay was neglected for many years and became run-down, and then a fire razed parts of the downtown area. However, when the road to China was repaired, Mandalay started to boom and in the 1990s a replica of the palace was built. The sad thing is while they were rebuilding this palace the military were busy pulling down the quaint Kengtung Palace, a very important part of Shan history. And then they built an ugly concrete box of a military hotel in its place. The Shan people have never forgiven them.'

'That's terrible,' said Natalie. 'Mandalay seems to be a bustling business centre.'

'Chinese money,' said Mr P. 'Mandalay is not so far from the Chinese border, so the city is regarded as something of a Chinese satellite. About fifteen years ago the Myanmar government allowed businesses to explain away undeclared profits by simply paying a special tax. Everyone was happy. The government got money it wouldn't normally have had and the businesses kept their illegal earnings. A lot of them invested their wealth here in Mandalay, hence all the new buildings.'

A large old truck laden with huge bamboo baskets and wooden crates rumbled past them.

'It's carrying produce to China and the Chinese send back their manufactured goods.' He lowered his voice. 'But there is a lot of illegal money behind the growth of the city, from heroin, rubies and jade.'

'There's the replica palace,' exclaimed Natalie as they drove past the low walls of the fort-like palace, which were reflected in its placid moat. 'So I suppose this is what it looked like when King Thibaw lived here with his queens and concubines,' she said looking at the walls and buildings surrounded by lawns.

'And there's Mandalay Hill,' said Mr P. 'We can climb to the top for the sunset. There are a few flights of steps, but the ascent is gentle. There are pagodas and monasteries all the way up the hill.'

'How do people who can't manage the steps get to the top?' asked Natalie.

'There is a lift,' he said.

'That's good,' said Natalie.

'It is broken,' said Mr P.

'Oh. I see. So we'll walk.'

'Yes.'

They both laughed.

'But there are many seats for rest stops. It is considered meritorious to climb to the top,' said Mr P.

'Then I'll do it!'

'First we shall go to your hotel. This is a modern-style place. I will go to my friend's house, where I'm staying the night, and come back for you in half an hour, okay? I will make enquiries about your friend's parents in the morning.'

Natalie thought that apart from the white stone elephants guarding the front entrance and the abundance of red and gold Burmese puppets and traditional lacquered furniture, her hotel was so modern and soulless it could have fitted in quite well on the Gold Coast. The lounge bar was named the Kipling.

She dropped her bag in her clean but charmless room, which could have been anywhere in the world. But when she opened the curtains she found she was looking up at Mandalay Hill. It was dotted with golden-roofed pagodas and red-tiled monasteries, and at its peak was spread the Sutaungpyei Pagoda, the wish-fulfilling pagoda as Mr P called it. At the base of the hill were the walls of the former royal city. She felt that she was definitely in a mix of old Burma and modern Myanmar.

Natalie and Mr P took their time trudging slowly up the canopied broad terraced steps of the hill, jammed with soothsayers, palm readers, and even tattoo artists. This place was the most crowded location she'd seen in her time in Myanmar, with lots of pilgrims and tourists. Mr P told her that as well as being a place to meditate, Mandalay Hill was a favourite spot for lovers to meet. There were lots of stalls, selling everything from food and drinks to the paraphernalia pilgrims required for their devotions. Stone seats were conveniently placed for rest stops, but since the steps were wide, shallow and gradual, Natalie didn't feel out of breath. When they finally reached the upper terrace, a panoramic view of the city spread below them.

Gazing down, Natalie could see the palace and its moat, together with its temples and pagodas. Mr P pointed to one pagoda, which was surrounded by hundreds of miniature white pagodas.

'Those shrines hold stone inscriptions of the entire Pali canon. It is known as the world's biggest book. That,' he said, pointing to the shimmering coils in the distance, 'is the mighty Irrawaddy River. Over there, behind those hills, is Sagaing.'

'Mandalay is such a dusty, dry place.'

'Trees were cut down for fuel to make bricks to build the pagodas,' said Mr P.

'I have to say, the city doesn't live up to the romance of its name,' said Natalie.

They watched as the rose-gold sun began to sink behind the western hills, and then slowly made their way back down the terraces, dodging entreaties to buy food, make donations, or purchase fragrant strands of white flowers.

Mandalay Hill was now very crowded with people watching the sunset. Natalie took her water bottle from her bag and, as she tilted her head to sip the tepid liquid, she felt her bag being tugged. Her squeal shocked the small assailant as well as Mr P, who tried to stop the boy from darting off through the crowd. Natalie clutched her bag, relieved to feel the solid shape of the kammavaca in the bottom.

'Who was that?' gasped Natalie. 'A pickpocket?'

'Bad boys, shave their heads, buy robes and pretend to be novice monks asking for donations from tourists who don't know any better.' He sounded apologetic.

'He didn't beg or ask for anything . . . He just wanted my bag. Never mind, he didn't get it,' she said, trying to sound unperturbed although her knees were shaking. 'Well. What are the plans? When do we see the palace?' she asked.

'It is best if we see the palace early in the morning, before we leave,' said Mr P. 'But if you like, we could stroll along the moat now.'

The moat is obviously popular at this time of day, thought Natalie, as they joined others meandering along the broad thoroughfare that ran beside the water.

'I'm looking forward to seeing the palace, even if it is only a replica, so I can try and imagine how it was when King Thibaw was given the kammavaca,' said Natalie to Mr P. It's so strange to finally be here. I wonder if Uncle Andrew saw the real palace, she thought to herself.

They stopped at a café and Mr P ordered local beers and salted snacks, a palata, which was a fried flat bread sprinkled with sugar and beans, some Chinese dumplings and spicy samosas. The two sat and watched the traffic sweep past as people headed to their homes. When they'd finished their beer, Mr P hailed their driver, who'd been waiting for them.

After Mr P left her at the hotel lobby, Natalie glanced at her watch and realised that the children would already be in bed asleep. She decided that she'd call home in the morning. There were a few people milling around now, so she headed to the Kipling Bar to have a drink before dinner and an early night.

There was no-one at the long bar so she went into the smaller lounge. A young waiter swiftly handed her a menu and asked her what she'd like to drink. Natalie gave him her order and leaned back in her chair, marvelling at the fact that she was in Mandalay. She tried to remember the words to the famous poem. The waiter reappeared with her drink and she signed for it.

'Do you like Mandalay?' the waiter asked politely.

'I don't know yet. I've only been up Mandalay Hill and walked around the moat. Tomorrow I'm seeing the palace but then I'm going to Sagaing.'

'Oh, there is so much more to see here than Sagaing! You should see the U Bein Bridge, longest teak bridge in the world. Very good for photographs,' said the waiter.

'Everything in Myanmar is good for photos,' said Natalie. She helped herself to some spicy peanuts and took a sip of her drink. Feeling like a sophisticated world traveller, she swivelled her chair around to see who else was in the lounge. There was a European couple and a man reading an English newspaper.

When the man lowered the paper and Natalie saw he was Burmese. He glanced at her and raised his paper again.

Natalie froze. It seemed that she'd seen him before. Or had she? Did he remind her of someone she'd met? Why was he familiar?

Then it hit her. Suddenly she was sure that it was

the same man whom she'd seen in the Strand Hotel, the morning she'd had coffee with Connie. She put her glass back down. Was she imagining things? Surely it was just a coincidence.

More people were coming into the bar, but Natalie quickly finished her drink.

The waiter paused by her chair and asked, 'Another drink, madam?'

Natalie shook her head. 'No, thank you.'

He picked up her glass and then placed a business card on the table. 'I can recommend this place in Mandalay. Very good quality.'

Natalie picked up the black and gold card and read 'The Golden Buddha. Tribal Antiques & Rare Artefacts.'

'I'm not planning on shopping, but thank you,' she said to the waiter before slipping the card into her bag and hurrying out. She sensed the waiter turning towards the man with the newspaper but she didn't look back to find out.

As she crossed the foyer, a smiling girl in a silk longyi asked if she was having dinner in the dining room, but Natalie shook her head and pushed the button for the lift.

In her room she opened her suitcase, which she hadn't unpacked. Nothing in it had been disturbed. She took out her clothes for the next day and sat on the edge of the bed.

What was going on? She wanted to talk to Mark, but that was pointless as there was nothing he could do and he would only worry. She wished she could contact Mr P, but had no idea how. Then it occurred to her that she could call Connie. She took out her notebook, found Connie's number and asked the hotel operator to connect her.

Connie sounded pleased to hear from her and asked her all about her trip. Her friendly voice made Natalie feel more relaxed. She told Connie about what she'd seen, and how amazing Bagan had been.

'So we're off to Sagaing tomorrow to try and locate

Mi Mi's parents. Then on to Pyin Oo Lwin to visit Aye Aye. And, I have to say, I'll be relieved when that's over.'

'Natalie, is everything all right? You sound a bit odd. You aren't overdoing it? You don't have to climb through every temple! You're fine with Mr P, aren't you?'

'Of course I am. Connie, I'm just a bit unnerved,' confessed Natalie. 'A few things have happened. I feel I'm being watched, followed. Mr P says it happens a lot and not to worry, but it's creepy.'

Connie didn't answer as quickly as Natalie expected. Then she said slowly, 'Look, you are perfectly safe, you won't be harmed or arrested or anything. But perhaps there is interest in the fact you are going to see someone connected with the old royal family.'

'How would anyone know that?'

'Conversations are overheard. People talk. A pretty young foreign woman on her own is noticed. It's probably just curiosity. The other day, someone in the gallery asked Win if you'd seen your friends.'

'Who was asking that?' asked Natalie in surprise.

'Win had no idea. People here love to gossip.'

'I hate the idea of people knowing my every move. I just think there's something more to this kammavaca than I know. Ever since I've had it, people have wanted to buy it. I know it's got a remarkable provenance, but maybe there's more to it, which has made people so interested.'

'Maybe the old princess will be able to tell you something, if there's anything to tell.'

'Perhaps. Anyway, I'll feel better when I've handed it over. It's stressful holding on to it!'

'Natalie, as you know, there are people watching everywhere. It's hard to explain to those from outside Myanmar, but I don't think you have anything in particular to worry about. Think of how you'll be able to tell your friends back at home all about your adventures!'

329

'I'm going to call Mark in the morning, but I won't mention this to him.'

'Of course not!'

'Thanks, Connie. I feel better being able to talk to you.'

'I'm glad I could reassure you. And good luck tomorrow. I hope you find your friend's parents without too much trouble. Take lots of photos. Natalie, you're gaining much merit here in Burma doing all these good deeds!'

'I'm not too worried about my next life. This one is wonderful enough, thanks!'

'That's another thing this country does for you, puts your priorities into perspective. Take care, Natalie, and call any time you want to.'

Natalie did feel better the next morning after a solid night's sleep in the anonymity of her hotel room and an English-style breakfast at the busy hotel buffet. She rang Mark, gaining comfort from his voice, and talked briefly to Charlotte, Adam and Andrew. Mark assured her that although everything on the home front was great, they couldn't wait for her to get back.

'But you enjoy yourself, Nat.'

After the call, she met Mr P and Soe Soe at the bottom of the hotel steps.

'It's a lovely time to visit the palace, too early for many tourists. We'll just see the highlights, then we can get to Sagaing around lunchtime. I think I've located your friend's parents, or at least the relative they joined in Sagaing,' announced Mr P.

'That's marvellous,' exclaimed Natalie. 'Was it difficult?'

'I would like to say that it was, but it turned out to be very easy. I took the name of their relative, which I learned from my student in Yangon, to the post office and they were able to tell me that he was in Sagaing. If your friend's parents are still living with him, you will be able to meet them.'

The driver took them to the palace and they walked from the car, crossed the moat and entered the grounds. Mr P explained that King Mindon had been advised by astrologers to move the centre of his kingdom here because it was auspicious. So he dismantled the royal palace at Amarapura and, using elephants, relocated it to the foot of Mandalay Hill. Thirty years later the British moved in to it without a shot being fired.

'Because the palace was rebuilt in the 1990s it looks pristine,' said Mr P. 'It is a very good replica, but it has no character, no heart, because no-one has ever lived here. And they didn't replace the original buildings with carved teak, but used modern materials, and only a small part of the original palace has been rebuilt.'

Through the eastern gate, Natalie could see three towers. Mr P suggested that they climb the spiral watchtower because it would give them a view across the palace grounds to the city and river.

'When this was the original palace, it must have been like a city in its own right,' said Natalie.

'Indeed it was.'

As they wound up the spiral stairs Mr P said, 'Apparently the king had this tower built so that the guards could watch from here to see that no-one else visited his concubines!'

Looking down at the neat green squares of lawn between the low red-roofed buildings, Natalie had the sense that the place was incomplete, an unfinished institution. But despite the empty rooms and pavilions, she could imagine the splendour that would have been created by King Mindon's original palace and how busy it would have been when later King Thibaw, Queen Supayalat and their family and entourage all lived there.

'This place needs a cast of many to bring it to life – pretty women, hardworking village people, artisans and craftsmen, gardeners. I can imagine the grave-faced old ministers walking barefoot to meet with the king over there,' said Mr P.

'What is that building with such an elaborate spire?' asked Natalie. 'I can count seven tiers.'

'That is the Hall of Audience, the Centre of the Universe. It contains the Lion Throne, the most important of the king's eight thrones. It was built like that because the more tiers, the more important the space is beneath.'

Now, save for wax and wood mannequins posing as the king and queen, the pavilions were empty. Natalie walked slowly around the buildings, trying to like the carvings, the mosaic pillars of glass and gilt, but she couldn't shake the knowledge that it was mostly fake. She thought about the elaborate furniture, the rich carpets, the jewelled spittoons and other accessories that would have graced the original palace: the Queen's Lily Throne, the Glass Palace and the official buildings like the Treasury and Royal Mint were all set amid splashing fountains in manicured courtyards under canopies of white and gold umbrellas. It must have been a dazzling wonderland of extravagance and folly, duty and religion, myth and worldliness from a time now passed.

They crossed the bridge, leaving the replica walled palace behind them, and joined Soe Soe who headed into the neat grid of streets that crisscrossed the city with mathematical precision.

'The city is all organised into small business areas, isn't it,' said Natalie. 'Makes it easy for customers to compare things when they shop!'

They passed rows of shops featuring rubies and other gemstones, then came to a street of bronze and stone Buddha statues. Turning into another street they came across a row of antique shops. Suddenly Natalie remembered the card she'd been given in the hotel, took it from her wallet and passed it to Mr P.

'Do you know this shop?'

Mr P read it aloud and Soe Soe made a comment Natalie couldn't understand.

'Where did you get this card?'

'The waiter in the bar at the hotel handed it to me. But I think it came from a man who was sitting near me. Why, do you know the shop?'

Mr P asked Soe Soe a question and there was a short exchange. Mr P handed her back the card. 'The driver says it is a well-known shop. But no good to shop there.'

'Overpriced?' asked Natalie. 'No wonder they're touting for business in a tourist hotel.'

'The shop has a dubious reputation. They sell replicas to the unwary but they also pass off good pieces as fakes.'

'Why would they do that?'

'They are stolen artefacts, taken from temples and monasteries, but if they are sold as fakes then they are easy to get out of the country,' replied Mr P. 'There are many agents working in Burma to supply western collectors who will pay large sums for them.'

'That's a shame. It means that Burma is still losing its heritage. It makes me even gladder about what I'm doing.'

Mr P pointed out the window. 'Down there is the street of marble carvers. Do you want to have a look?' he asked.

'It sounds interesting, but I'm anxious to get to Sagaing now,' said Natalie.

Soe Soe slowed so that Natalie could take photos from the car of the marble carvers, busy at work outside their shops as they carved, rubbed and polished massive white statues to a gleaming satin finish.

As they turned into another street, they passed a luxurious mansion. Through the tall iron fence Natalie was stunned to see a row of garages, their doors open to reveal a lot of very expensive cars.

'Wow, who lives there?'

The driver and Mr P exchanged a glance.

'Very rich man,' said Soe Soe.

Natalie was a bit surprised to hear Soe Soe speak English, but realised that as he was involved with the tourist trade he would probably need to.

'I'd say so, looking at those cars. What's he do?' she asked.

'He's a businessman. It helps to have friends and relatives in high official places. Contracts and deals go through with no problem. This man obviously has the right sort of friends. I don't think he would have trouble finding money, like ordinary people do, for important ceremonies and making supplications at the pagodas,' said Mr P.

'Shinbyu and ear piercing. Very important to do,' chipped in Soe Soe.

'What's that?' asked Natalie.

'All Burmese families send their sons to be novice monks before they turn twenty. It is called shinbyu. Families have to save for this important ceremony. Before girls come of age, they have their ears pierced in a very elaborate ritual. Families must save for this, too.'

Natalie sat back in the car as they drove past golden pagodas and simple rural villages, thinking that little had probably changed for a hundred years or more. She dozed off and awoke to find that they were now travelling across a long bridge, high over the Irrawaddy River.

Mr P turned and smiled at her. 'We are coming into Sagaing. They have a hill, like Mandalay, and another walkway to the top and the Soon U Ponya Shin Pagoda.'

'It must have a stunning view. How beautiful!' exclaimed Natalie as she saw that the lush hillside rising above the curving sweep of the river was sprinkled with hundreds of white and shining nunneries, monasteries and golden pagoda spires.

'This is an important centre of Burmese spiritual life. See, further up the hillside, there are caves where once holy men came to meditate. Some of the caves have the remains of frescoes and images in them,' said Mr P. 'As soon as we arrive in Sagaing, we shall go to the market-place and ask directions to the house of your friend's relative.'

'I wonder why they moved here from Yangon,' said Natalie. 'Perhaps they are very devout.'

They stopped in the centre of the main street and Soe Soe hurried away to get directions while Mr P bought some fruit and flowers.

'Perhaps you could take this as a small gift?'

'How thoughtful, of course, what a good idea.'

Instinctively, Natalie looked around, wondering if they were being watched. But the sleepiness of Sagaing was pervasive and the whole area, perhaps because it was a religious place, seemed to be in a state of repose and reflection. Even the leaves of tamarind trees appeared to droop not from the heat but from piety. From the folds and hollows of the hills drifted voices in prayer and the throb of a monastery bell.

Soe Soe returned, looking pleased, and nodded to indicate that he had been given directions to the home of Mi Mi's relatives.

The car wound a short way up the hillside, then pulled over as they came upon several simple, raised whitewashed wooden houses with woven bamboo shutters to keep out the heat. Washing fluttered in the yards and dogs sunned themselves. All seemed quiet, almost deserted.

Mr P went ahead, calling out, and disappeared behind the courtyard cooking area of one of the houses. Soon he came back with an elderly man.

'This man is your friend's uncle. I have explained to him why we are here and he will go and fetch your friend's parents so that you can meet them.'

335

The elderly man hurried away and returned a few minutes later with an old Burmese couple. Mr P explained to them in Burmese who Natalie was and why she wanted to meet them.

Mr P made the introductions. 'This is Daw Thet Wai and U Tun Oo. They would like you to come inside. It's more private.'

Natalie took off her shoes and stepped into the humble house. There was very little furniture, but the couple ushered her to join them on cushions in front of a low table that held a bowl containing betel nut and a lacquer box.

Mr P sat beside Natalie to translate. The old couple couldn't stop smiling and staring at Natalie. Then they thanked her profusely for the fruit and flowers.

Natalie reached into her bag and took out the envelope with the photographs of Mi Mi, Nanda and their two teenagers, which she handed to Mi Mi's mother. Daw Thet Wai took out the photographs and laid them in a line on the table.

The faces of her beloved daughter, her fine husband and their two happy children laughed up at her. Slowly she began to speak softly, addressing each of the pictures, tenderly and lightly touching each photograph as if caressing its subject's skin.

Mr P said quietly to Natalie, 'She is telling them she loves them and that she is so happy to see them and how beautiful they are, just as she knew they would be. She says that now she has put them in her heart so that she can speak to them each day. They will be with her and know all she is doing and how she feels.'

Tears sprang to Natalie's eyes.

Neatly and carefully Mi Mi's mother put the photos in a pile on the table, and smiled contentedly at Natalie.

Now Tun Oo, Mi Mi's father, straightened up, opened the lacquer box and took out two faded pictures.

He slid the pictures across the table to Natalie. She immediately recognised the laughing young girl as Mi Mi. The second photo was of Mi Mi and a young monk, his head shaved, proudly wearing his robes. Natalie guessed that this was Mi Mi's brother.

'We are very proud of our daughter,' Tun Oo told Mr P, who translated his words for Natalie. 'She studied to be a doctor and helped her brother and the others. We are happy to know that she has a good life in Australia.'

'Mr P, can you please tell them that Mi Mi wrote to them several times after Cyclone Nargis, and was very concerned when she did not hear back from them. She thought that they had gone into the delta region and she was very worried about their safety.'

'I see. Letters do not always reach their destination in Myanmar,' explained Tun Oo through Mr P. 'We did not go to the delta. I was a schoolteacher, but when I became too old to teach and had to retire, I lost my house because it, like my job, belonged to the government. So we could not afford to live in Yangon any longer. The rents are too high and we had not much in savings. I thought that we could move south to be near our son but because he is a monk, he was not in a position to help us. Luckily for us, my brother Sung Oo wanted to share his house with us. His wife died some years ago and he thought that our company would be good for him and he was pleased to help. So here we are.'

Natalie looked around the simple house, realising just how poor these people were. Even though Tun Oo was an educated man, a teacher, she realised that they were now existing at a subsistence level because there was no state assistance for elderly people and the children were expected to look after their elderly relatives, but Tun Oo and Thet Wai's children were not in a position to do this. Natalie knew that they had never told Mi Mi about their poverty. They must have known that their daughter had done well in Australia, but were obviously too proud to tell her the truth about their situation.

'Please tell them that Mi Mi speaks to her children about their grandparents all the time and hopes that someday they can come and visit.' She reached into her bag and took out the envelope that Mi Mi had given her. Then she quickly reached for her own money, took out three hundred dollars and added it to Mi Mi's envelope. I don't need to buy many presents to take home. Helping Mi Mi's parents is the best present I can give, she thought.

She passed them the money. When Tun Oo and Thet Wai saw how much Natalie was giving them, their faces became wreathed in smiles, and they thanked her humbly and profusely.

'They are thanking you for your kind gift. This money will help them for some time,' said Mr P. 'They wish to thank their daughter for her kindness.'

Natalie nodded, thinking how inadequate it was, but pleased that she had found out the true state of things so that she could tell Mi Mi.

Mi Mi's father spoke again. 'Perhaps one day our grandchildren can visit, but it is not yet that time. We have to wait, just as The Lady has to wait.'

'You are very patient. How do you live here? What do you do?' asked Natalie, trying to take it all in so that she could tell Mi Mi.

'We are simple people,' replied Thet Wai. 'We grow our food and trade for what we need. We support Sister Tin Tin Pe, who is the abbess of a nunnery here. There are many nunneries in Sagaing, but Daw Tin Tin Pe is very strong.'

Mr P asked Tun Oo some questions and then, looking rather impressed, said to Natalie, 'These are good people indeed. They assist the work of this senior nun by giving whatever they can in money or food. Sister Tin Tin Pe is a reformist nun who is trying to restore the equality of nuns with the monks.'

'Is this what you and U Watt were explaining to me in the bookshop?'

'That's right. Most of the nuns of Burma want to become fully ordained religious leaders again, and Mi Mi's parents are supporting one of the most active nuns in the country.'

'Mi Mi will be very proud and pleased about her parents' efforts,' said Natalie.

Mr P translated and the couple smiled and nodded.

'Their hearts are very generous,' said Mr P. 'They are asking how long you will be staying in Sagaing. They would like to show you around. They suggest that you might like to stay at their friend's nunnery rather than return to Mandalay tonight. Would you like to do that? It would be quite an experience for you.'

'I would be very happy to spend some time with them,' said Natalie. 'And whatever you say I'll go along with. But there will not be any problems for them being seen with a foreigner, will there? If it's not too much trouble for the nuns, I'd love to stay in a nunnery. It will be something to tell everyone about back at home,' she said.

'Travellers often stay at the monasteries and nunneries in Sagaing. It is a place for meditation and retreats. Mi Mi's parents will be fine. They are simply a devout couple showing us around.'

'Great! This place has such a special feeling. And I'd like to spend some time with Mi Mi's parents.'

'I'll take lots of photographs of you all together,' said Mr P.

'Where will you stay, Mr P?'

'I'll stay at a monastery nearby. Our driver can stay there, too.'

They all wandered along the leafy narrow streets that

wound up the hill from Thet Wai and Tun Oo's home. Sung Oo, Mi Mi's uncle, also joined them for the tour of Sagaing. There were many large and famous pagodas to visit, but what made Natalie happiest was seeing the places that were the favourites of Mi Mi's relatives.

Inside one cool quiet pagoda, Mr P and Mi Mi's parents knelt quietly to pray while Natalie walked through a corridor, admiring the carvings and fading frescoes of scenes from Buddha's life. In an alcove before a figure of Lord Buddha that glowed from the limpid gold pressed into his cold stone skin, a mother and child knelt to pray. The woman was young and the little girl perhaps Adam's age. Together they lifted up loops of small white flowers and held them towards the silent figure in the shrine. It was a devout but simple gesture, and Natalie thought again about the uncomplicated devotion of these gentle Buddhist worshippers. People quietly observed their duties, oblivious to passing strangers.

They went to a small village where Natalie watched some silversmiths working, beating out silver pieces with the traditional tools they had used for years. Natalie bought a small silver vase from them to take home to Mi Mi. She packed it carefully in her shoulder bag and hoped that it would mean something special to her friend because it came from the place where her parents now lived.

They stopped in a tea shop. The woman and her daughters who ran it sat knitting handbags to sell to tourists. Mr P explained that a lot of visitors came to Sagaing at the end of the rainy season for the robe-offering ceremony but for most of the year, Sagaing was simply a place for peaceful worship.

The view from the top of the hill at sunset was breathtaking, but Natalie was glad when she was finally taken to the nunnery where she would spend the night. She felt exhausted from all the sightseeing. They seemed to have

340

walked for many kilometres. She marvelled at the stamina of Mi Mi's elderly relatives.

The nunnery was a simple, new building made of brick and cement, softened by a roofline decorated with traditional wooden carvings.

Natalie was introduced to Sister Tin Tin Pe and was pleased to find that the nun spoke good English. The abbess was an impressive woman with a direct gaze, a firm, calm voice and a formidable air of authority.

'The nuns will look after your needs. There is meditation at 4 a.m. and food at 6 a.m.'

'Thank you,' said Natalie. 'I'm finding Sagaing such an interesting place. My friends tell me that you are trying to improve the status of Buddhist nuns here in Myanmar.'

'Yes, that is my life's work, my calling.'

'So this place must be very special to you,' said Natalie politely.

'This nunnery is my nerve centre, my headquarters, you might say.' Sister Tin Tin Pe smiled briefly. 'But I also need to travel and lecture in order to raise funds.'

'I suppose you need funds for your work and to keep this nunnery going?' said Natalie.

'All Buddhist institutions need financial support, but most particularly nunneries. The lack of donations is a problem for most of them. Nuns are often forced to live at the most basic level.'

'That's surprising in a country as devout as Myanmar,' replied Natalie.

'It has a lot to do with the lack of status of nuns. They are seen as having little religious power, so naturally people give their support to those who have more.'

'Then why do women become nuns? What do they do?'

'Any woman can become a nun. Sometimes women join a nunnery only for a short time, but most women stay on. They might be widows, or women who have never married. It varies. The nuns see themselves as the keepers of Buddhist virtues, and propagators of Buddhism. They learn the rituals of Buddhism and have detailed knowledge of ceremonies, so they complement the role of monks. Nuns make sure that everything runs to plan.'

'So they have an important role to play then in the spiritual life of this country.'

'That is true but it is also true that their role is not fully appreciated. Only last week, while I was absent, the nuns from here helped perform rites at a funeral. They recited protective verses and then walked with the family to the burial ground, while the monks rode there in a car. Yet the monks were given generous donations for their part in the ceremony and the nuns were given very little.'

'That doesn't seem fair,' said Natalie. She thought to herself that things might have been different had Sister Tin Tin Pe been around.

'Are all nunneries like this one?' Natalie couldn't believe that she had the chance to stay in a place like this. The experience was quite beyond anything she could have conceived of doing.

'No, they can be quite different. Some might be composed of a cluster of small houses, each housing only a handful of women and essentially independent from the others. The houses are usually donated by the families of the nuns. Other nunneries are like this one. There are fifty-four nuns here and it is run as one large house. Other nuns are attached to monasteries and there they might run the kitchens and the monastery finances. Nuns frequently make good administrators.'

'I can understand why you need to raise funds to keep this place going.'

'Yes. I raise money for other things as well. For example, we are building a shelter in Nepal for young girls at risk. Poor and uneducated village girls are sold by their families or even kidnapped, and forced into prostitution. HIV/AIDS and abortions further ruin their lives. We do what we can for these poor girls. But although this social work is important, my primary objective is to empower nuns to achieve religious equality. At the moment, the best the nuns can hope for is to be born a man in another life or to earn merit through their sons becoming novices.'

'And how can you make these changes happen? I can't imagine men willingly giving up their privileges to help Buddhist nuns become fully ordained.'

Sister Tin Tin Pe gave a big smile. 'You are right. Nuns are seen as subservient, handmaids, but that can be changed. Sometimes one has to seize the moment, and invoke past history.' She shrugged. 'In the meantime we continue working to reinforce the Buddhist way of life to the Burmese people. I hope you will be comfortable. It means a lot to Thet Wai and Tun Oo that you brought them a message from their daughter. It was a kind act on your part.'

'I just want my friend to know that her parents are well and happy,' said Natalie, at the same time thinking what strong leadership there was in Burma from women like Aung San Suu Kyi and Sister Tin Tin Pe.

Two young nuns, with shaved heads and wearing pale pink robes, shyly curious of their visitor, led Natalie to the small, sparsely furnished room where she would be sleeping, and then showed her the spartan bathing facilities. Later, after evening prayers, Natalie was taken into the communal dining hall to eat on her own as the nuns didn't eat after midday. She was served a simple but wholesome meal consisting of about five small dishes. Natalie could identify a vegetable curry and a spicy omelette, but she had no idea what the other dishes were. Nevertheless they all tasted delicious. Afterwards, she carried her plate to the sink and washed it. Before leaving the dining hall, she bowed to the Buddha figure. She then walked through the garden in the soft night air to her curtainless room and hard bed, where she slept like a log.

Dawn had already broken when Natalie woke. She could hear soft chanting and realised that she'd missed meditation and prayers, so she hurried to the bathroom and splashed herself with refreshingly cold water and quickly dressed. She returned to her room to find the two young nuns sitting on the bed holding a bowl of warm food for her. They indicated she was to eat, so Natalie dipped her spoon into the spicy vermicelli noodles topped with dried shrimp. The nuns watched, smiling and nodding, until Natalie was finished, and then they took her dish and quietly slipped away.

Natalie picked up her bag and went to the courtyard of the nunnery where Sister Tin Tin Pe was speaking to Mr P.

'Did you sleep well?' he asked.

'Unbelievably well. I think all the walking we did yesterday wore me out.'

'Everyone says they sleep well at a religious house. Perhaps it is the calm atmosphere and many blessings,' he said with a smile.

Natalie turned to Sister Tin Tin Pe. 'I hope your work continues well,' she said. Reaching into her purse, she took out some US dollars and gave them to the nun. 'Thank you for your hospitality and thank you for answering all my questions.'

'Mingalabar. Blessings for the rest of your journey and the path you are following.'

Mr P took her bag and said, 'We must go and say goodbye to your friends. And then we will drive to Pyin Oo Lwin.'

*

344

In her mind Natalie filed away the image of Mi Mi's parents standing close together, both wearing their longyi and formal tops, smiling and waving as the car drove away. She hoped Mi Mi would be pleased with the many photographs she had taken of them. Perhaps, thought Natalie, one day Mi Mi might be able to come and visit her parents. But quite a lot would have to change before that was possible.

Natalie swapped seats with Mr P and sat in the front, with her camera poised. She realised that she would be able to take much better photos from the front of the car where she could see the view ahead.

Mr P laughed and said that people would think that she was the guide and he was her tourist. Natalie was pleased that their relationship had developed to the point where they could joke with each other.

'Well,' she replied, 'I hope you're not a difficult one.'

They drove back through Mandalay towards Pyin Oo Lwin and Natalie noticed a turn-off.

'Where does that go?' she asked.

'A place called Mogok,' said Mr P.

Soe Soe, sitting beside her, shook his head. 'No good. Cannot go.'

Mr P explained. 'Mogok's where all the ruby mines are. It's a very bad road and dangerous. The military controls most of the mines and they don't allow visitors.'

'Very famous for beautiful ruby and sapphire,' added Soe Soe. 'But terrible for people.'

'It is known that the junta makes both adults and children work there as slave labour,' said Mr P quietly. 'When the rubies are in hard-to-get-at places, they send children down the crevices to mine by hand. If poor villagers find a ruby and use it as a means to try to escape over the border to buy a new life, and they're caught, they are put into one of the labour camps. All the money from

345

the sale of the rubies goes to the military. The ordinary people get nothing.'

The road began to climb up towards Pyin Oo Lwin. On the way, Mr P pointed out a teak forest. Further on, they passed a small village of thatched bamboo huts where the wood smoke from the village fires curled lazily skyward. Natalie could see bamboo pens containing pigs and goats. Then the road levelled out with paddyfields growing on one side of it.

As the car swung around a corner they were confronted with a laden wooden-wheeled ox cart on the side of the road. A man stood beside it, examining one of its wheels. He hailed them.

Soe Soe did not slow, but Natalie said, 'I think he needs help. Maybe the wheel is broken.'

Mr P spoke swiftly to Soe Soe who pulled over and reversed back along the road.

'I will see what the matter is,' Mr P told Natalie. He got out of the car and walked back to the cart.

Natalie reached for her camera. 'I must take a photo. That cart looks as though it's a hundred years old!'

'Miss, please wait,' said Soe Soe.

But Natalie got out of the car and began to take photos of the yoked ox.

Mr P called to her to get back into the car but, before she could do that, two scruffy-looking soldiers walked out from behind the cart where they had obviously been hiding. One was carrying a rifle.

Feeling very frightened, Natalie quickly got back into the car. She dropped her camera into her bag.

Mr P began talking rapidly to the soldiers and the three of them started to walk towards the car. One of the soldiers rapped on the lid of the boot. Soe Soe released its latch and the men began rifling through its contents.

Natalie stuck her head out of the car window and,

trying to sound stronger than she felt, called out, 'Mr P, what is going on? Who are these men? Why are we stopped?'

'They are soldiers. They want to know where we are going. They say they are looking for contraband,' said Mr P. 'Please stay calm.'

'What exactly are they looking for?' Natalie got out of the car.

'I do not know if they understand English, Natalie.'

Natalie took the hint and didn't say anything more.

The men poked about in the boot and then took out Mr P's backpack and Natalie's suitcase, opened them up and began rifling through their belongings.

'This is outrageous, they are personal belongings,' hissed Natalie under her breath. The sight of her clothes, her underwear and a sandal being dropped on the road-side felt like a personal violation. 'I don't believe this is happening.' But as one of the soldiers walked to the front of the car she started to panic. 'Now what?'

'They want to see your papers.' Mr P walked over to her and gently rested his hand on Natalie's arm to reassure her.

Soe Soe continued to sit stoically behind the wheel, staring straight ahead. The soldier opened the passenger door and grabbed Natalie's handbag. He barked an order at Soe Soe, who slowly got out of the car. One soldier tipped the contents of Natalie's bag onto the ground and the other one bent down and picked up her wallet. Mr P tightened his grip on her arm as she instinctively went to lunge towards her personal effects. A soldier opened her passport, looked at it and then dropped it onto the ground. He took the remaining US dollars Natalie had in her wallet.

But when he picked up her camera and radio, she shouted out, 'Leave that camera!'

The soldier looked at her in surprise. He lifted the

camera and pointed it at her, pretending to take a photo. Smiling, he shoved it into his pocket. The other soldier began to speak urgently to him.

Natalie stared down at her little cosmetics bag, a bottle of water, wet tissues, a book, a notebook and the small silver vase, all scattered beside the road. Then it hit her. The kammavaca wasn't there. She looked at Mr P, who was still gripping her arm.

Soe Soe lit a cigarette and leaned against the car, waiting patiently for the ordeal to be over.

One of the soldiers spoke to Mr P in a very aggressive manner, but Mr P shrugged and lifted his arms, to give the impression he was confused as to why the soldiers expected them to be carrying anything of value.

Then one of the soldiers picked up the silver vase and pushed it into his pocket, then both retreated down the road.

A car swung around the corner, they got into it and the vehicle sped away. As it did so, one of the soldiers leaned out of the car window and snapped Natalie's photo.

She burst into tears. 'The photos for Mi Mi . . . Oh no,' she sobbed. 'We'll have to go back. I can't go home without pictures for Mi Mi.'

Natalie began picking up her things from the side of the road and putting them in her handbag. Mr P and Soe Soe went to the rear of the car and began collecting the scattered clothes.

'Mr P, where's the kammavaca?' Natalie began frantically looking about on the floor of the car, but it wasn't there.

Mr P and Soe Soe put the bags back into the boot, Mr P returned to the back seat and Natalie sat next to Soe Soe again. Before he started the engine, the driver gave Natalie a small smile and from the pocket of his shirt, where he kept his cigarettes, he handed her a small object. It took a moment for Natalie to register what it was.

'Mr P! Look! It's the memory card out of my camera! Soe Soe, you saved my photos! Thank you, thank you so much,' she gasped.

Mr P began to smile. 'Clever. And quick thinking.'

Then Soe Soe reached under the dashboard of the car where there was normally a radio and pulled out the kammavaca, still safely rolled up in Natalie's silk scarf.

Natalie was speechless, but then she managed to ask Mr P, 'How did he know to hide this?'

Mr P asked the driver the same question. Soe Soe answered in Burmese. 'He says he heard us talking about the gift you had for the old princess,' Mr P told Natalie.

'I don't remember saying anything about the kammavaca while we were in the car. In fact I'm sure that I didn't. Maybe I did say something before I knew that he understood English. Oh, I don't know. Honestly, I'm becoming paranoid. Forget what I just said. Thank you very much, Soe Soe, for saving my pictures and the princess's kammavaca. I am going to be very pleased when I meet the princess and I can finally give her the manuscript.'

'It is also just as well that I have the rest of your money tucked away in a very safe place,' added Mr P. He opened his shirt a little to reveal an old-fashioned money belt.

'You two have been my wonderful guardian angels,' said Natalie, her voice full of gratitude.

'Please try to forget this bad episode,' said Mr P. 'Those men were not real soldiers, just a couple of – what do you call them? – cowboys. Bad men trying to make a quick profit. It sometimes happens, so we know to be prepared. If you like, Natalie, you can use my camera for the remainder of your holiday.'

Natalie leaned back and closed her eyes. The last half an hour seemed like a very bad dream. One moment she had been feeling totally at peace and relaxed in Sagaing, happy at finding Mi Mi's parents and serene after her night at the nunnery, and then she was in the middle of a nightmare scenario. But at least no-one had been hurt and she really hadn't lost anything that could not be replaced. And she certainly had another exciting story to relate when she got back home.

At a roadside truck stop, where large lorries laden with Chinese goods were pulled over, they stopped for refreshments and a sweet fried doughnut. Mr P patted Natalie's shoulder as she sipped her coffee.

'Please, do not let this make you feel badly towards my country. Theft happens everywhere.'

Natalie gave a small smile. 'Of course. It could have been worse. You know, most of the people I have met in Burma have been lovely, so that thought will outweigh what just happened.'

They got back into the car and drove on. The scenery changed and, seemingly on cue, a misty shower of rain swept in, completing what Natalie imagined a British hill station would look like. Sweeping dark fir trees and solid oaks shaded flowering bulbs that burst through patches of thick green grass. They passed a roadside stall selling strawberries. Another advertised local coffee.

Then came the houses. Here, in the middle of Burma, stood stately, sprawling British brick houses, complete with chimneypots, turrets and mock Tudor trim set behind elaborate gates and sweeping driveways. It wasn't till Soe Soe slowed the car to give Natalie a better look that she saw that the gardens were overgrown, the entrance gates rusty and the grand houses dilapidated. When a horse-drawn carriage clipped smartly past them with its red and white trim and leather seats, Natalie was convinced that the next sight would be dandies in dress coats and ladies in crinolines. It was certainly cool enough and she was glad that the thieves had overlooked her lotus shawl.

'Can we go in and look at one of these places?' she asked.

'I know one that might interest you,' said Mr P.

The car slowed and turned where a buffalo wallowed in an overgrown drain on the roadside and grass thrust through the fancy loops of an iron fence. A sign picked out in peeling paint on a gate-post pillar read: Candacraig 1904.

The car wheels crunched on the untidy gravel drive and Natalie could see that while some effort had been made to tidy the formal front garden with its silent stained fountain and overgrown arbour, the once-grand hotel screamed neglect. Natalie got out of the car and gazed at the building. It seemed so English, and she felt an over-whelming sadness at its decline.

'This must have been a marvellous hotel in its heyday. How romantic. And it could still be wonderful. I would love to fix this place up!'

She walked to the front entrance and into the hotel. The dining area and entertaining space, possibly a bar or a library, were devoid of furniture. A little girl sat playing with a kitten on the floor. A grand teak staircase swept up to the next floor.

Natalie's footsteps echoed as she wandered around admiring the beautiful carving while noticing that the walls were seeping a mildew acne in festering patches. Paler marks on them showed where paintings had once hung. All that remained was the head of a forlorn stag that had seen better days, which stared bleakly at its empty surrounds.

The doors of the rooms were open, showing that they were all empty of furniture, and from the balcony she could see the remains of a tennis court, a swimming pool and a cracked cricket pitch. What looked to have once been a conservatory now had broken panes of glass and small birds nested inside it.

But, despite the dilapidation, there hovered remnants of gay times gone by. In Natalie's imagination laughter drifted from the swimming pool, as well as the sound of the firm thunk of tennis balls, and the clink of teacups amid the drifting scent of roses and hyacinths.

'I can just imagine what this must have been like,' she said to Mr P with a sigh.

'This place is famous because of Paul Theroux, the travel writer. He stayed here and mentioned it in his book *The Great Railway Bazaar*. He came back again not long ago to see the family who had run the hotel for many, many years. It is now owned by the government. Maybe it will open again one day.'

'I hope Paul Theroux doesn't come back any time soon. I'm sure he would be sad,' said Natalie.

They drove into the township, complete with an old-fashioned clock tower and a neat row of shops and eateries. Mr P pointed out a huge area of beautiful gardens, with beds full of glorious flowers.

'This is such a surprise!' exclaimed Natalie. 'This place doesn't look like Burma. It seems quite foreign!'

Mr P chuckled. 'Yes, not a monk or a pagoda in sight.'

In the centre of Pyin Oo Lwin the streets were jammed with loaded trucks, tankers and wagons.

'They are all using the new road into China,' explained Mr P.

They drove away from the town's centre to where the dark wave of hills rolled towards the west in shrouded mist. Through dripping pines Natalie glimpsed a group of buildings that she could not quite make out.

'What is that, Mr P? It looks like a posh housing estate or maybe a rich corporate enclave. Do you have places like that in Burma?'

Mr P asked Soe Soe to turn into a road leading towards the complex of buildings Natalie had spotted.

A sentry's gatehouse stood at the entrance, but the whole place look deserted.

'What are these building? It doesn't look finished. How extraordinary. This place must have cost millions and millions to construct,' said Natalie, peering at the glass-fronted contemporary buildings. 'How can it just be left here?'

'I've heard about this,' said Mr P, craning his neck forward, trying to get a better look at the buildings. 'It's called Yatanarpon Cyber City and I believe it covers four thousand hectares. Two Chinese companies started building it a couple of years ago, to train information technology and communications students, but they seem to have come to a stop.'

'There's no-one around. Why don't we drive in and have a look?' said Natalie.

'I think we've had enough trouble for one day. Let's go and check in to our hotel and freshen up and see if we can call Princess Aye Aye to let her know that you've arrived.'

Their hotel, like many they'd passed in Pyin Oo Lwin, was eccentrically quaint. It was called The Welcome and Natalie was delighted when she saw that the clipped grass gardens were studded with massive old eucalyptus trees. 'Well, that makes me feel welcome.'

The main building had wisteria climbing over the portico and the lavender petals from a jacaranda tree melted into the lawn. A smiling man came out to help them.

Natalie stepped into the lobby, which looked as though it had not been redecorated for years, though it was spotlessly clean. In it was a circle of heavy wooden armchairs with antimacassars, some small tables topped with lace doilies, old-fashioned ashtray stands and, above the open fireplace, a banner with 'Welcome' painted on it. At the small reception desk two smiling women waited.

353

Beyond the lobby, Natalie could see a glassed-in dining room where the tables were set with small glass vinegar jugs, sauce bottles in crocheted dresses, silver-topped salt and pepper shakers and cut-glass sugar bowls. It was all very proper but modest.

Natalie followed the hotel attendant up the gleaming polished wooden staircase to the first floor. The hallway featured dark wooden panelling and a worn carpet. Her bedroom was very old-fashioned, probably decorated circa 1930. She smiled and thanked the attendant as he put her bag at the foot of the bed.

When Natalie pulled the elderly net curtain to one side, she looked down into the back garden and the remnants of a tennis court with its tattered netting, cracked surface and sagging mesh fence.

The small bathroom was also old but the water gurgling from the large brass tap was hot. Natalie washed her face, changed her top, took off her creased slacks and put on a long skirt, knotting her shirt at her waist. She smoothed her hair, put on some fresh lipstick and, on an impulse, took a fresh rose from the vase on the dressing table and tucked it in her hair before she went downstairs carrying her shoulder bag.

Mr P smiled when he saw her. 'I have found the phone number for the princess. We can call from the desk here. I think she would prefer some notice rather than our simply arriving on her doorstep.'

'I'm feeling nervous. I can't believe I'm finally here.'

The girl at the desk made the call then handed Natalie the Bakelite telephone receiver.

'Hello, hello, Princess Aye Aye? This is Natalie Cutler.' Natalie turned to Mr P, her eyes shining as she listened to the voice at the other end of the line. She had reached her destination.

# 12

THEY DROVE THROUGH AN area dotted with large bunga-
lows that were once the holiday homes of the wealthy
British when they ruled Burma. Princess Aye Aye had
invited Natalie and Mr P to share Devonshire tea with
her. Her directions to her lodgings had been precise.
The Empire Hotel was well away from the main road,
as though not wanting to promote its presence. Indeed if
they hadn't been looking out for it, they could have easily
passed its entrance, which was tucked between tall trees.
The driveway wound up to a side entrance. The front of
the hotel looked across a valley with views to the distant
hills. The windows were shuttered and the place had the
air of being closed for the season.

As they walked into the lobby, Natalie noticed that
one of the main rooms was filled with furniture sleeping

beneath dust covers. But there was a vase of fresh flowers on the reception desk and when they rang the brass bell a man appeared. Perhaps, thought Natalie, he is the Burmese equivalent of the trusty old retainer. He was courteous and asked them to take a seat while he rang through to inform Princess Aye Aye that her guests had arrived. He then led them along a corridor and through double glass doors beautifully etched with art deco birds and flowers and the words 'Private Dining Room'.

It was a small room. In the centre was a round table, immaculately set with a generous damask table cloth, silver and china. When they were seated, the attendant spread starched napkins on their laps with a flourish. Natalie's cup had the words 'The Empire Hotel, Burma' embossed on the rim.

'Very old-style British,' commented Mr P.

'Nevertheless, we do try to keep abreast of current events. And you must be Mrs Cutler.' A woman who could only be Aye Aye sailed towards them, smiling, her hand outstretched to greet them.

She was dressed in a pale green longyi of fine wool and an embroidered silk blouse. A fine shawl, draped as a scarf, hung around her neck. Her hair was coiled high on her head and secured by a delicate pin. Her skin was a creamy olive, surprisingly unlined. Her dark brown eyes seemed to take them both in and pass immediate judgment, which seemed to be favourable.

'I am so pleased you could come. This is a wonderful occasion.' Her voice was warm and musical.

Both Natalie and Mr P rose from the table and Natalie said, 'Please, call me Natalie. This is U Phyu Myint, my friend.'

Mr P gestured mingalabar and murmured that it was an honour and pleasure to meet the princess Aye Aye.

'I am simply Aye Aye. You will take tea with me? The

356

traditional Devonshire tea is a specialty here. Tell me, Natalie, how do you like the local food?'

'I enjoy it very much, although some dishes are very spicy. But they're all delicious.'

A silver teapot, cream jug and sugar bowl were placed on the table as well as perfect, mouth-watering warm scones and what was obviously homemade strawberry jam. They ate the scones and Aye Aye asked Natalie about her friend Mi Mi. 'I first met her years ago when she was working in a refugee camp in Thailand,' she told Natalie.

'She's very well and hoping so much that one day she will be able to visit Myanmar,' Natalie replied.

'Yes,' replied Aye Aye. 'Perhaps one day. Now where have you been in my country?'

Natalie told her and was particularly enthusiastic about her visit to Bagan.

'And what about you, Aye Aye? Do you live all the time in Myanmar or do you travel?' asked Natalie.

'Oh, I spent a lot of time in Thailand. I was always entranced by the stories of my royal predecessors' interest in white elephants. My grandfather and great grandfather both had white elephants when they lived in Mandalay and I have become interested in them, too.'

'You mean they're real?' exclaimed Natalie.

Aye Aye leaned back and smiled. 'They certainly are. Have you ever seen one?' she asked Mr P, who shook his head.

'I thought they were mythical,' said Natalie.

'No, they exist. Actually, they aren't pure white, more pale pink. They're a strain of albino. Because they are so rare, they are revered and people believe they are powerful and magical and are related to auspicious predictions.'

'Natalie, Aye Aye is famous for her love of elephants and she has worked to protect them for years,' said Mr P.

Aye Aye smiled. 'I lived for many years in Thailand

actually where I started a sanctuary to protect elephants. It became quite large, and included several white elephants. Now I work to protect the elephants in Myanmar. They are being threatened by so many dangers. Poachers hunt them and their habitat is being destroyed. I know my grandfather dressed his white elephants with sprays of diamonds on their heads and jewel-encrusted ornaments, and even let them drink from a golden trough, yet they were kept chained in the palace compound. Once you see elephants in their own environment, free to go to the river and bathe, you can't bear to see them mistreated in captivity. You become very attached to them. I was working with my elephants in Thailand when I met my husband.'

'Was he working with elephants, too?' asked Natalie. She could see that Aye Aye was enjoying relating her story, and Natalie wanted to hear more about her life.

'He was an English botanist who realised that we were losing plants and animals from tropical rainforests very rapidly. Rare plants often disappear even before they are documented. I try to carry on his work here in Myanmar, to have wildlife sanctuaries established to conserve the natural resources. But it is difficult to continue this work as the policies of the military government are unpredictable and they do not see the value of rare plants and animals compared with the money other natural resources like oil, gas, minerals and timber bring.'

'You still work? Do you look for new plants?' asked Natalie.

'Yes. I have a small team from the university and some visiting international institutions like the Smithsonian who work with us. My ultimate dream is to have a proper botanical conservatory like Kew Gardens, where all of Myanmar's specimens can be housed. One of the reasons I enjoy it here in Pyin Oo Lwin is the climate. There are wonderful gardens established here by the British and which the local government have turned into a showcase for Burmese plant biodiversity and a place for Burmese people to come and appreciate their national plant heritage.'

'So when you are in Myanmar, you live here?' asked Natalie.

'That's right. I always enjoy the change of climate.'

Natalie studied the elegant woman, who seemed to be in her late seventies, but who still exuded enthusiasm for what she was doing. 'It's wonderful work Aye Aye.'

Aye Aye nodded in acknowledgment of the compliment.

With the tea and scones finished, Mr P rose and excused himself. 'I know you two have much to talk about. I shall walk back into town – it's not far and I shall enjoy the air – but Soe Soe will wait for you, Natalie. It has been an honour to meet you,' he said to Aye Aye.

After Mr P quietly left the room, the attendant removed the afternoon tea cups and plates.

Natalie shook her head. 'I never imagined that we'd be sitting down to scones and tea.'

'Perhaps you would like to move out onto the terrace? It is pleasant out there and the view is spectacular,' said Aye Aye.

They crossed the room and opened the door that led to the main dining room. It had a vaulted, moulded ceiling and an elaborate bar reminiscent of an English pub, as well as a dance floor.

'What is that?' asked Natalie, peering through the gloom at what looked like a polished length of glass ringed by Grecian columns. As they walked closer Natalie exclaimed, 'It's a swimming pool! In the middle of the dining room floor? It looks fabulous.'

'Indeed. And look above. See how cleverly the roof opens up!'

They skirted the art deco pool and went out onto a stone terrace. Aye Aye selected a low lounge and settled herself gracefully at one end before she took out a long slim cheroot and lit it.

Natalie looked at her bag. 'I feel there should be a little ceremony when I give you this.'

Aye Aye nodded. 'Yes, we Burmese like ceremonies.'

Natalie took her bag off her shoulder and suddenly held it tightly to her chest. Through it she could feel every item she'd carried; her wallet, notebook, a small toiletries bag, the camera Mr P had lent her and the kammavaca, a solid shape securely tucked at the very bottom.

'I'm a bit nervous about taking it out. I've been so afraid of losing it or having it stolen. It's been close to me for so long. It's such a responsibility. I really can't believe that this is the big moment.' Natalie slowly reached into her bag and pulled out the box wrapped in her silk scarf. She looked at it and shook her head. 'Do you know, Aye Aye, that this little thing was among a lot of junk in my mother's shed? It could so easily have been thrown out.'

Aye Aye didn't take her eyes from Natalie's face as Natalie held the kammavaca in both hands.

Slowly Natalie continued. 'But the minute I really looked at it, I felt as though I was transported, as if I was in the grounds of that beautiful old monastery with the white elephant. It was a place totally strange and unknown to me, but I felt so drawn to it. That must seem odd to you. And then I learned about its connection with my uncle and its association with your family. I knew that I had to finish what he had started and see that the kammavaca was returned. Of course, never in my wildest dreams did I expect to be the one to complete the journey. To be here . . .' She stopped, suddenly at a loss.

Aye Aye nodded. 'The kammavaca could have been returned to me in other ways, but it is right that it comes from your hands to mine. I hoped that you could fulfill your offer to return the kammavaca to me, but I would not have blamed you if you had changed your mind. And when I knew you were on your way, I prayed that your journey would be a safe one. So here you are.' Suddenly there was no mistaking the excitement and joy in her face.

Natalie held the kammavaca out to her and their hands touched as they both briefly held the small box. Natalie released her grip and sat back in her chair to watch Aye Aye's face as she began to unwrap the silk scarf. At first Aye Aye simply smoothed her hands over the little polished wood box. Natalie tried to imagine the thoughts running through her mind. She understood her deliberation and hesitation in opening it. Aye Aye was savouring each moment.

'I wonder about the people who held and revered this small object before it reached me? People long gone, but now your gift has closed the circle,' said Aye Aye. Slowly she slid the box open, took out the kammavaca, unrolled it and studied each section. Natalie had no idea how much time elapsed as she watched Aye Aye carefully examining the treated cloth and delicate binding, absorbing all the illustrations. She turned it over several times and looked intently at the old script.

'I cannot read this. As I suppose it was meant to be. But the paintings, they are beautiful. A labour of love. I'm sure there is a meaning in each of these.' She put her glasses on and peered at the little pictures Natalie knew by heart.

'I'm very fond of the white elephant,' said Natalie.

'A symbol of peace, prosperity, good fortune. You're right. It is lovely.' Aye Aye returned to studying each of the sections of the kammavaca. 'It seems to have an almost feminine appeal, don't you think?' Slowly she refolded the kammavaca, placed it on the table and looked at Natalie. 'Thank you,' she said softly.

Natalie felt tears spring to her eyes, and struggled to

keep her feelings in check. 'I never imagined when I found the kammavaca it would lead to such a strange journey. I know your grandfather thought that the kammavaca was very important, so it's good that it's come back into his family.'

'This kammavaca has certainly been a legend. King Thibaw always kept it with him. Some contend that is because it was the last gift he received before he was deposed, but I am inclined to believe another rumour that I heard from some of my relatives. It is said that the monks who gave Thibaw the kammavaca incorporated a message in it.'

Natalie stared at the princess. 'What sort of message?' she asked.

'The monks sometimes had knowledge that they would pass on, but the messages were written in such a way that they needed to be deciphered by scholars. Sometimes these messages might be prophecies or special instructions, or sometimes they might be about more tangible things, such as where certain relics had been hidden or where treasure or riches could be found. These secret messages vary a lot.'

'That's incredible. I thought about trying to get the writing on the kammavaca deciphered, but everyone told me that they were most likely religious texts,' said Natalie.

'That may well be right, but the rumours that circulated in my family make me think that there might be more here than just the usual religious texts. Thibaw made it clear that on his death, the kammavaca should go to his half sister Tipi Si because she was a strong woman. He seemed to think it was important for the women of my family to protect it and keep it safe.'

'Then why didn't he give it to Queen Supayalat? She seemed to be strong, too.'

'Perhaps he thought she was too strong. She was a

very brutal and cruel woman and had made many enemies. Tipi Si was far better liked, so he decided to bequeath it to her. Such a pity she was forced to sell it. I believe she regretted that action for the rest of her life,' said Aye Aye.

'Is there any way that you can find out if anything important is written in the kammavaca?' asked Natalie.

Aye Aye looked at the steep hills surrounding the old hotel. 'There is only one way to find out. And that is to take the kammavaca to the old monastery. I am as curious as you!'

'Where is the monastery?' asked Natalie.

She was unprepared for Aye Aye's answer. 'It's not far from Mandalay, close to the Irrawaddy River. I recognised it at once from the paintings here in the kammavaca. I went there first as a child, on a steamer up the river, and I have been there on my travels around Myanmar several times since.' She paused briefly before looking intently at Natalie. 'I think it is only right that you accompany me.'

Natalie didn't hesitate. 'I'm sure Uncle Andrew would want me to go back to where it all began.'


After Natalie left Aye Aye, she met Soe Soe, who had been waiting patiently for her.

As they drove back to her hotel, Soe Soe asked if she had enjoyed her time with Aye Aye.

'It was wonderful,' Natalie replied. 'She knows the monastery where the kammavaca come from. She wants you to drive us there so she can find out what's written in it.'


Mr P surprised her when he met her later that night at her hotel for dinner by arriving in jeans and a neat T-shirt.

'There are quite a few nice places to eat in Pyin Oo Lwin. Do you have a preference?' he asked.

'I'll leave it to you.'

'Then we'll have traditional Shan noodles, vegetables and pickles in rice wine, soup and rice. Followed by fresh local strawberries,' said Mr P.

Soe Soe drove them into town and left them at the restaurant Mr P had chosen. It featured a lot of timber decoration and Natalie thought that it could be mistaken for a small hunting lodge. As they settled at the table, Natalie told Mr P about Aye Aye's reaction to the kammavaca, and the fact that she had recognised the old monastery where it had been made.

'She wants to take the kammavaca back and try to get the script translated. She thinks that there may be something important hidden among the sacred texts. She wants me to go with her. Can Soe Soe take us?'

'Of course. I will wait here unless you'd like me to accompany you,' said Mr P politely after he ordered them glasses of the local damson wine.

'I wouldn't go without you! Aren't you curious, too?' exclaimed Natalie incredulously. She smiled.

He returned her smile. 'I would indeed like to know the fate of the little object you have protected and carried about with us. It's been quite an honour to be part of this.'

'I couldn't have done all this or had such a wonderful time without your help,' said Natalie, suddenly feeling teary as she realised that their time together was coming to an end. Mr P's gentle manners, warm heart and calm demeanour had been her rock. She felt they had an empathy that had grown through their shared experiences. 'You really opened my eyes to what Myanmar is all about, and I want you to know how much I value your patience and knowledge. And friendship.'

He nodded modestly. 'Initially, when Win and Connie

asked me if I would travel with you, I thought you were just a friend and a tourist. Then I learned that you wanted to find your friend's family and I thought you had a kind spirit. But when I learned about this kammavaca and your wish to return it, after so many years, to come here alone, well, that is . . . very meritorious,' he finished.

'You mean I was very naive?' said Natalie with a quizzical expression.

'But you wanted to learn. You were interested and enjoyed the places and things we saw. You are respectful and open to knowing how we Burmese think and do things. To understand the people of Myanmar you have to know our history and what people here are suffering while they wait for change to come. Not all visitors are like you,' he added. 'You are a friend to us now.'

Natalie nodded. 'It's strange but I feel so strongly about this place. Everyone I've met has been so warm and kind, apart from a couple of exceptions. And isn't Aye Aye amazing,' said Natalie, her eyes shining.

'Yes. Princess Aye Aye is inspirational. We have some wonderful women in our country. One day maybe people will look up to you in your country.' He lifted his glass of wine in a toast.

'Oh, I don't know about that,' said Natalie, nevertheless feeling flattered and pleased by his words.

They clinked glasses.


Soe Soe seemed agitated, as though unsure of the best way to get to the old monastery. They seemed to have been travelling for hours. Aye Aye and Natalie sat in the back of the car. It bumped along a sandy track. Feathery stands of bamboo bent lithely in a gentle breeze. They created a pale green light, which was sometimes darkened by a solid grove of trees. To one side they could see the shining coppery surface of the Irrawaddy River. The softness of the track's surface made it difficult for Soe Soe to drive further. Mr P spoke to him and he stopped the car.

Mr P turned to the women in the back seat. 'We are on a side track. It will be quicker to walk, although Soe Soe can drive the long way around to the river landing if you prefer.'

'Walking's all right with me,' said Aye Aye.

Mr P opened the car door for her.

They were not isolated on the track. As the car reversed away, they heard the jangle of a cowbell and the crow of a rooster. Ahead of them a wooden cart with a huge dripping cask on top was being drawn by a plodding ox and driven by a young boy.

'He's delivering water to a village,' said Mr P.

The boy, filled with importance before the strangers, hit the ox with a bamboo pole and it broke into a lumbering trot.

They came to a small village where leaning fences surrounded some small thatched buildings. An old man was bent beneath the weight of a bamboo pole which held buckets at both ends. A woman winnowed rice, throwing up the grain from a large flat basket so that the wind could blow away the lighter husks. Each small dwelling had chickens, a goat or a pig in its yard. A young woman was cooking in a wok over an open fire. Washing was draped in the sun and children played in the dust.

The strangers, strolling along the village lane, were given curious glances. Natalie was fascinated by this panorama of rural life seemingly unchanged for decades. She smiled at a young mother sitting in the shade with two small children.

Mr P called out to the young woman, who lifted the toddler onto her hip, held the shy child by the hand and came over to the fence.

'How old are her children?' asked Natalie.

Mr P and Aye Aye exchanged a few words with the girl. Natalie saw she must be barely twenty.

'They are two and four years,' said Mr P as he pulled his backpack off his shoulder and rummaged in a side pocket.

'I have children almost the same age,' said Natalie, suddenly overwhelmed with longing for Charlotte, Adam and Andrew.

Mr P found a packet of sweets and gave some of them to the children.

'The mother says she is twenty-two. She thinks you are very beautiful,' Aye Aye told Natalie. 'She will have more children. She probably didn't have much education but hopefully it will be different for her little ones, but since they don't have running water or even a decent well in the village, a proper school out here seems a remote possibility. But it is places like this where our country needs to make changes if there is to be any progress.'

'She has such a sweet face,' said Natalie.

The toddler, cheeks full of the chewy sweet from Mr P, reached out to Natalie. Natalie leaned over the low fence as his smiling mother handed the chubby boy, dressed only in cotton pants, to her. Natalie closed her eyes, smelling his sweet hair, feeling the softness of baby skin.

'Do you want a photo?' Mr P asked.

Natalie nodded. 'Yes, please. Of all of us.'

After they had waved goodbye and continued through the village to the path that led to the monastery, Natalie asked Aye Aye, 'Do you think that young mother would know who you were? Your family?'

Aye Aye shook her head. 'No. That was old Burma. I am not important now. But I'm sure she knows who The Lady is.'

Natalie noticed that as they walked, Aye Aye continually looked around, even occasionally glancing upwards into the trees. Suddenly she stopped and pointed into a thicket. Natalie saw what she had spotted: flashes of white between the green lushness.

'Come and see these . . . such lovely gingers.' They followed Aye Aye and Natalie recognised the flower she'd seen in the markets, or as offerings at pagodas and in vases in restaurants and shops. The cascade of delicate miniature orchid-like white blooms contained explosions of golden stamens.

'This was my husband's favourite flower,' said Aye Aye. She showed Natalie the jewelled pin she wore in her hair.

'It's the same,' said Natalie, seeing the white and gold clusters of drooping blooms recreated in glittering gemstones.

Aye Aye plucked sprays of the ginger blooms and put them into Natalie's hair. 'These often grow near monasteries,' said Aye Aye.

Soon the spire of the monastery appeared and the path widened into a clearing. At the sight of the monastery, Natalie caught her breath. While it was not the magnificent, glittering gold of the Shwedagon, or the stylised symmetry of the ancient Ananda Temple, Natalie thought this monastery was one of the loveliest places she'd seen in Myanmar. Not only that, but she had looked at the little kammavaca so often and knew it so well that she had little trouble recognising the monastery.

Its intricately carved and weathered teak had a soft warmth. The moss-covered tiles on the roof, and the columns of faded gilt and vermilion spoke of venerable age but there was no ostentation. Here, for years, the lives of the monks had been played out in simple rituals upholding the traditions and beliefs of the Buddha, and this practice would continue.

A flight of stone steps flanked by elephants carved in stone led to the main building.

'They're like the ones on the kammavaca,' said Natalie.

'They guard each of the four entrances to the monastery,' said Aye Aye. 'As a little girl I loved them.'

They all paused to admire the monastery buildings. A novice monk appeared with a broom that was twice his height and began brushing and smoothing the white sand at the base of the steps. Mr P stepped forward and asked if it would be possible for them to speak with the abbot.

'He says the abbot is sleeping off his meal,' said Mr P. 'But we can speak with him when he is awake.'

As they walked, they continued to admire the monastery and its mythical carved figures, the elephants and strange bird-like creatures upon whose backs the monastery buildings rested. Several sleepy dogs lay in the shade beneath the buildings.

'It's deserted,' said Natalie.

'It is not a well-known monastery,' said Mr P.

'It's always been a quiet place,' said Aye Aye. 'We used to stay in one of the rest houses.'

They walked to the rear of the monastery where a village woman was cooking small pancakes in hot oil on a wok over a wood fire. An iron pot of Burmese tea was steeping over the coals beside it.

'Natalie, one of your favourites, I believe,' said Mr P.

'I love these pancakes, with just a sprinkle of pickle and sometimes dried shrimp,' she said.

Mr P squatted on his heels, and Natalie and Aye Aye sat on low stools as mugs of tea were passed around.

Natalie was munching her third small pancake when a young monk emerged from the monastery and told Aye Aye that the abbot was ready to receive them.

'We should all pay our respects,' said Mr P. 'Then it is up to Aye Aye to ask about the kammavaca.'

The wooden floorboards were worn silky smooth. Natalie sat with the others as the abbot and the senior monks chanted their prayers. She glanced to where the wooden pillars, as solid as tree trunks, soared into the dimness above. The musky incense, the flickering candles and the scent of flowers at the base of the Buddha shrine were calming. Aye Aye had handed the kammavaca to the abbot and it sat on the floor in front of him as he continued his prayers.

Natalie felt at peace. Whatever was to come now was nothing to do with her. Her role in this strange pageant was finished. She was comfortable as if she were in familiar surroundings.

When the abbot finished praying and gathered his robes and rose, gesturing them all to follow, Natalie walked with Aye Aye along the carved wooden corridor followed by Mr P.

They moved into a small space cluttered with two very old chests and a dusty glass-doored cabinet with shallow shelves stacked with palm-leaf manuscripts. On the walls were several hangings and paintings that seemed to Natalie to be very old. A thick red mattress and cushions were stacked around a woven floor mat, which clearly served as a table.

The abbot spread the kammavaca before him and spoke to Aye Aye, pointing to illustrations and then the script. He called for a young monk to fetch something for him. When the young monk returned, he placed a bulky parcel wrapped in an old musty carpet in front of the abbot. When the abbot unwrapped it, Natalie caught her breath. Folded neatly inside was a length of deep rusty-red cloth. Natalie guessed that this was probably the same material that had been used to make the pages of the kammavaca.

After intense conversation between Aye Aye and the abbot, Aye Aye bowed. They watched the young monk rewrap the material. The abbot rose and, carrying the kammavaca, his robe folded over his arm, left the room.

Aye Aye turned to Natalie. 'He says it will take some time to find the meaning of the kammavaca. He will see us again in the morning.'

'So we're staying here?'

'Yes. The men will sleep in the guesthouse; we can sleep here in the monastery. The village women or the young monks will bring food for us.'

Later the atmosphere was subdued, voices lowered as two women from the village brought them supper, which they ate by the cooking fire.

'You'll be fine sleeping in the monastery,' Aye Aye assured Natalie. 'The village women will loan you two longyis, one for bathing and one for sleeping.'

'Thank you,' said Natalie. 'I'm not at all concerned. I slept in a nunnery the night before last.'

The sun had set but a gold and pewter light still shone across the surface of the river as Aye Aye led Natalie down to the river's edge to wash. Natalie copied Aye Aye and tied the longyi over her breasts like a sarong as she dipped into the river water. Aye Aye handed her a creamy smear of soap that smelled of thanaka and Natalie washed her face and dunked her head in the refreshing water. She put on the dry longyi and returned to their little room in the monastery where she hung the wet longyi to dry on a window sill. As the sky darkened and the stars appeared, she lay on the thin padded mat on the rush matting floor. Her rolled neck pillow was surprisingly comfortable and her lotus shawl gave her enough warmth. She looked at her watch and saw that it was barely 8 p.m.

She whispered softly to Aye Aye, who lay only a few feet away, 'I hope the abbot can tell you what is in the kammavaca and that it's good news.'

'I've been thinking about my grandfather, his wives

and daughters, the concubines he was fond of and his half sisters, and wondering if this is what was supposed to happen. I suppose you can't blame Tipi Si for selling it.'

'But she was very regretful after she'd sold it to Ferguson. Her regret had such a strong impact on Uncle Andrew. He made such an effort to retrieve it for her,' mused Natalie.

'Yes, that is true, but it's a long time ago now. We may have some answers in the morning,' sighed Aye Aye. Then she added, 'Do you think they are watching us, curious, but glad we're here?'

'Who do you mean?' asked Natalie.

'Tipi Si, the king, your uncle?' said Aye Aye quietly.

Natalie nodded in agreement, rolled onto her side and stared through the tall open window at the night sky framed by the old carved woodwork shutters before she spoke. 'I'd like to think so. In this land where people are so devoted to spirits, the afterlife, past lives, the next life and all manner of beliefs, I feel that it is quite possible.'

'I hope you will be comfortable not sleeping in a bed,' said Aye Aye.

'Even though it's early, I'm ready to sleep. And I'm sure we'll be up early,' said Natalie. 'Good night, Aye Aye.'

'Thank you again, Natalie. We wouldn't be here without you.'

Natalie smiled and rolled over again. The spray of ginger flowers they'd picked near the monastery lay beside her on the floor, glimmering white in the moonlight. The flowers still looked fresh, and their delicate ginger perfume soothed her into a gentle sleep.


It was cool in the dawn light. A mist shivered as it rose from the river and dissolved in trees at the water's edge. Natalie could hear the faint creak of teak floorboards beneath the bare feet of the monks as they prepared for their daily meditation. In the distance she heard the sound of a motor launch.

Aye Aye was already up and she smiled as Natalie opened her eyes. 'You slept well,' she said.

'I did. Amazingly so. It's so quiet and peaceful here.'

'If you don't want to go to the river again to wash, there is water that has been drawn from the well outside that you can use. It's in an area that's separate from the monks.'

'I think that will do me,' said Natalie.

She quickly splashed her face with the cool water and dressed before she and Aye Aye walked over to the kitchen where Mr P and Soe Soe joined them.

'I wonder if the abbot was burning the midnight oil,' said Natalie as she watched another two young women from the nearby village bring in their breakfast.

They ate their noodles and Mr P said, 'The monks will be going out on their alms round soon.'

'It's barely 6 a.m.,' said Natalie. 'Will the abbot go too?'

'No, he is too elderly. The younger monks will take care of him,' said Mr P.

They watched the monks file out of the monastery and walk slowly towards the village.

'There's a small town, with just a few shops, nearby. Soe Soe tells me that there is a petrol station further on, so they'll go there, too,' said Mr P. 'Would you like to walk to the river while we wait for the abbot? It will be very pretty at this time of the day.'

As they walked towards the river, Natalie could see the rest house where Mr P and Soe Soe had spent the night. It was a very simple building: a space divided into two rooms, with a small bamboo verandah on one side. From its rear a thin plume of smoke from a cooking fire curled upwards and a path wound towards the edge of the river. As they drew level with the little building, Natalie noticed a movement, and a man stepped from one of the rooms, hands clasped beneath his chin in greeting.

'Moss,' Natalie gasped.

Mr P and Aye Aye looked sharply at Natalie.

'You know this person?' whispered Mr P as Moss, dressed in a shirt and longyi, his hair tied back in a pony-tail, walked calmly towards them.

'Yes, this is a friend of mine from my yoga class back home. What are you doing here, Moss?'

'It's a bit of a long story, Nat.' He bowed to Aye Aye. 'You must be Princess Aye Aye.' He turned to Mr P. 'I understand you have been shepherding Natalie safely on her quest to bring the kammavaca to Aye Aye.'

Mr P gave a slight bow, and in his unfailingly polite way, said, 'We have travelled successfully together, although it has not been without its small hindrances.'

'I'm pleased that it has been successful. You've given the kammavaca to Aye Aye, have you, Nat?'

'Yes she has, but I don't know what your interest is. I think you owe us an explanation,' said Aye Aye briskly.

'Of course. I'm very happy to explain why I'm here,' said Moss.

'Well, I'm listening,' said Natalie, still stunned.

'Let's go and sit on the verandah and I'll explain.'

They removed their shoes and sat together in a semi-circle on a bamboo mat on the floor.

'You know, Moss, I think that something strange is going on,' said Natalie indignantly. 'I'm pretty sure I've been followed and also I'm pretty sure that at least twice, maybe more, there have been deliberate attempts to steal the kammavaca. And now you turn up. What's going on?'

Aye Aye looked alarmed. 'I hope you weren't in danger bringing this to me,' she said.

Moss turned to Natalie. 'You're right. Something has

been going on, but fortunately I had someone looking out for you.'

'You did? Who?' asked Natalie.

Moss pointed towards Soe Soe, who was sitting quietly in the shade of a tree looking on from a distance.

'When you told me that you were going to Myanmar, I thought, like your other friends in Australia, that it can be difficult for someone travelling on their own in a country where law and order is problematic. I'm sorry now I didn't tell you. I didn't want to frighten you or put you off travelling to Burma. I had no idea that all of this would happen. I thought it would be a good idea to have someone reliable discreetly keep an eye on things. So I managed to contact the owner of a tour office in Yangon, who is a friend of mine, and he made some enquiries about your movements.'

'Did he go to Win and Connie's gallery and ask questions about me?' asked Natalie.

'Probably. Anyway, once he knew where you were going he assigned his most reliable driver.'

'So that's why my usual driver was changed,' said Mr P.

'Yes,' replied Moss. 'Soe Soe quickly realised that you were carrying something important, and he watched you very carefully to make sure that you were safe.'

'You organised Soe Soe to look after me?' Natalie was trying to absorb all this. She felt conflicted. On one hand, Moss had overstepped his bounds. But on the other, it was just as well he had.

'Soe Soe was just meant to be in the background but he took action when things began to get out of hand. He told me how your room had been searched, and he also told me that he interrupted someone trying to get into your room that night in Bagan.'

'Someone was trying to get in! I thought so,' said Natalie. 'Good on Soe Soe for stopping it.'

'Soe Soe also told me that you were held up on the road to Pyin Oo Lwin.'

'So that's why he was so quick to hide the kamma-vaca,' said Natalie.

'I'm pretty sure those soldiers were paid to waylay you. But they took what they thought was valuable, not really understanding what they were after.'

'Who'd pay them to hold us up?' asked Natalie.

'The man who I think is behind this,' replied Moss.

'Who is it? Who wanted to stop Natalie from bringing me the kammavaca? Who wants it so badly?' asked Aye Aye.

Moss spoke calmly. 'I believe it is Michaelson. I can't be totally sure, but it's certainly his style.'

'Who is Michaelson?' asked Aye Aye.

Natalie quickly told her that he was a London dealer who had tried to buy the kammavaca from her.

'Well, he's too late,' said the princess. 'And I won't be selling it to anyone, either. How do you know this Michaelson, Moss?'

'I've had dealings with Michaelson. As Natalie knows, I teach Buddhist religion and Buddhist art, so I am often in Asia. Some years ago Michaelson approached me to help him illegally acquire a certain piece of Indian art.'

Seeing Natalie's shocked reaction, Moss held up a hand.

'I never did, but I realised that, although Michaelson is certainly a prestigious dealer, his methods of obtaining some artefacts could be unscrupulous. But I couldn't prove anything. Michaelson persuades people that he is rescuing important pieces, sometimes all that survives from certain cultures, and taking it out of danger before they are gone forever. And people buy his argument, and so he obtains many such pieces illegally.'

'But Moss, that does not explain why he was so

interested in the kammavaca. There was nothing illegal going on there,' said Natalie.

'Well, that is why, when you told me about Michaelson's interest in it, I said nothing, because he was making you a legitimate offer on something that you were legally entitled to sell. But now I know that his interest in the kammavaca was not just because of its interesting provenance. I think it was for another reason entirely.'

'What's that?' asked Natalie. It all seemed surreal. Meeting Moss in the middle of nowhere in Myanmar, hearing about an artefact-smuggling operation and finding out that Michaelson was probably behind the attempts to steal the kammavaca.

'Do you remember that I told you that I had begun to research the antique dealer Ferguson?'

Natalie explained who Ferguson was to Mr P, who was starting to look a bit bewildered by the turn of events.

'He became quite a notorious character in his old age,' continued Moss. 'Back in Britain, he began to tell anyone who would listen about "the piece that got away". Then, quite recently, I discovered there was an actual reference to it.'

'Really?' said Natalie. 'Go on.'

'Ferguson left a lot of papers as well as an unfinished memoir. Evidently, quite some time after he'd sold the kammavaca to your uncle Andrew, he actually came to this monastery by chance. Among the monks he spoke to was an elderly monk who told him about a kammavaca that he had illustrated as a gift for King Thibaw.'

'He met the monk who had done the beautiful paintings?' said Natalie in amazement.

'Yes. When the kammavaca was made the abbot wanted the king to know its origin. So, rather than religious or mythical illustrations, the monk painted specific scenes, including the monastery and the river. But then,

Ferguson recounts, the artist-monk dropped a bombshell. He told Ferguson that different monks were given different pieces of the kammavaca to transcribe so that no one monk except the abbot knew what the full content of the kammavaca was. He said that the abbot had planted a secret in it.'

'Why would the abbot do that?' asked Natalie

'In the hope that the king would have it deciphered when he needed to. Ferguson was convinced that the last gift given to King Thibaw contained, written into it, the whereabouts of something valuable, like a treasure. Of course, when he tried to find Andrew to buy it back, he had already been killed by tribesmen, as we know, and the kammavaca shipped to Australia.'

'But the story of the secret message persisted?' said Natalie.

'In the world of collectors and dealers, it did. Michaelson must have thought that your kammavaca might be the one Ferguson had talked about.'

'Yes, I had lots of good offers for it, but Michaelson always outbid the others,' said Natalie.

'Anyway, that didn't matter since you came to the conclusion that you were going to return it to its rightful owner,' said Moss.

'Do you believe the kammavaca holds the secret about where some treasure could be found?' asked Mr P.

'Ferguson thought it was gold or jewels but I've come to a different conclusion. I think it's something else,' said Moss.

Mr P nodded. 'In Buddhist thought treasure could be nirvana,' he suggested.

'Yes, perhaps. In my family there was always the story that this particular kammavaca held a very important secret, but I have no idea what it is,' said Aye Aye.

'But Moss, if you thought Michaelson was going to

try and steal it from me, why didn't you say something?' Natalie asked.

'It didn't occur to me that he would, but when I heard that you had run into trouble I guessed that Michaelson was the cause. But I don't know how Michaelson knew you were in Myanmar. How did he find out?'

Natalie thought a moment. 'Mark told him. Michaelson sent an email offering more money and Mark emailed him back saying it was too late as I was already in Burma returning the kammavaca to Princess Aye Aye.'

'So that is when he decided to take action. Michaelson must have thought that in Myanmar, where he has lots of contacts, stealing the kammavaca from you would be easy. Luckily Soe Soe and Mr P proved to be very adept at protecting both you and the manuscript.'

'But Moss, if you knew the kammavaca was safe, why have you come?' asked Natalie.

'When I learned via my friend in Yangon whom Soe Soe contacted that you were driving to the monastery to have the kammavaca translated, I just had to come and find out what it said. I also wanted to explain to you in person everything that had happened. I hope you don't mind,' replied Moss.

'I suppose not, if it's all right with Aye Aye. It's her kammavaca now,' said Natalie.

Aye Aye straightened up. 'I have my grandfather's kammavaca, thanks to you all, including you, Moss. I can hardly object to you finding out what it says. Now we have to wait for the abbot and hope that he might be the one to decipher the old Pali script. Since this is where my kammavaca was created, this monastery holds the key to its meaning.'

They walked back to the monastery, hoping to find the abbot. On the way, Natalie turned to Moss. 'How did you get here so quickly?'

'Speed boat from Mandalay. I started travelling as soon as Soe Soe told my friend that you were coming here. I was in India, near Kolkata, a relatively short hop away. I was able to get here in little more than a day. I hope you weren't too surprised.'

'I have to say, when I first saw you walk out of that building a thousand suspicions flashed through my mind.'

'Natalie, I felt a moral obligation to make sure things were all right with your mission. I admired what you wanted to do.'

'Thank you. This has been an extraordinary trip. Quite wonderful.'

Eventually the abbot appeared, strolling slowly and thoughtfully across the open space between the kitchen and the monastery. He looked up and when he saw the small group waiting for him, he nodded and signalled for them to join him as he began slowly ascending the steps to his room.

'He wants us to follow him,' said Moss.

'Mr P, it would be nice if you could translate for me,' whispered Natalie. 'Aye Aye might not want to be distracted by my asking questions all the time.'

'I will be happy to do that, if it is all right with the abbot,' agreed Mr P.

They sat quietly in the room where they had first met the abbot yesterday. The abbot indicated that they should pull out the cushions that were stacked against the walls. Gracefully he sank onto a cushion, folded his legs into the lotus position and laid the kammavaca on the mat before him. Mr P sat slightly behind Natalie and Moss. Aye Aye sat directly opposite the abbot, with her head bowed.

The abbot began to speak. He went on at some length and Mr P whispered to Natalie, 'He is describing how this kammavaca was created here, specifically for King Thibaw, and that different monks worked on each section so the whole was never known by any one monk except the abbot. The young monk who made the paintings became very famous. When the kammavaca was presented to the king, no-one knew he would shortly be forced into exile, except . . .'

Mr P listened to the monotonous timbre of the abbot's voice before continuing: 'Except the old abbot of this monastery. He had seen a time of change coming, and he wanted to give the king some comfort when it would be needed.'

'What does that mean?' whispered Natalie.

Mr P held up his hand as he concentrated on the abbot's words. As the old monk spoke, Aye Aye gave Mr P and Natalie a swift glance, which Natalie couldn't interpret.

The abbot picked up the kammavaca, opened it and read a section, quoting directly. Then he stared at Aye Aye as she absorbed what he'd said.

Mr P turned to Moss and Natalie, his eyes wide, a slightly stunned expression on his face. He spoke slowly, choosing his words carefully. 'It seems to be that the kammavaca holds the prophecy that the future of this country lies in the empowerment of the women of Burma, including the reinstatement of the authority of the nuns. The king and his descendants were entrusted with the scared knowledge that it will be women who will lead the country back to greatness.'

Mr P leaned towards Aye Aye. 'Is that how you understand it? Of course, it is open to interpretation. The abbot at the time the kammavaca was made must have seen the British occupation coming and had a vision that a woman might restore Burma's sovereignty. But now, of course, the prophecy could apply to the overthrow of today's junta.'

Aye Aye nodded. 'It's extraordinary and very powerful. To empower women. You know that Burmese women have always been strong, but to reinstate the nuns' authority, this is a stunning prophecy. That it will be a woman who leads Burma out of darkness. I am thinking of Aung San Suu Kyi.'

'But she's still under house arrest,' said Natalie.

Mr P and Aye Aye exchanged a quick smile.

'But her influence, her selflessness, her devotion to her country and her people gives all of us strength. If she can accept and wait and keep her faith strong, then so can we,' said Aye Aye.

'So there is no message about any hidden riches?' said Natalie. 'Sister Tin Tin Pe will be pleased about the nun's equality.'

'You are right. But I'm not sure the monks will see it this way. It'll be controversial,' said Aye Aye. 'It really is a treasure. What could be more valuable than this? Here we have a manifest, we have hope, we have documentation from our own past showing us the way forward. It will be formidable ammunition when the time comes.'

'What does the abbot think?' asked Natalie, looking at the old monk's impassive face.

Aye Aye asked him and translated his answer for Natalie. 'He says we all share virtues of purity, of morality, of concentration and of wisdom if we follow Buddha's teachings.'

Suddenly the monk lifted his finger and spoke more firmly.

Aye Aye repeated his words. 'There was a prophecy that the sasana will last for five thousand years and that there will be a revival after two thousand five hundred years.' She turned to Natalie and her face lit up. 'And that is the twenty-first century, which is now!'

Mr P was shaking his head. 'This will give much hope to many people. It vindicates The Lady. If this information is told, it will be a crucial moment in our history.'

The abbot picked up the kammavaca, slid it into its box and bowed to Aye Aye, his hands beneath his chin.

She returned his gesture. 'The monks will know when

the time is right to tell of it. For now the kammavaca will be placed somewhere safe.'

Natalie caught her breath, absorbing the importance of the moment. 'Will it be secure?' she whispered.

'They will take it somewhere for safekeeping. It won't be left lying on a shelf here,' said Aye Aye firmly. 'That was always meant to be the fate of this kammavaca. Its message is to be shown when it is needed.'


Each of them was quiet as they walked down the monastery steps towards the river.

Moss, who had been silent up until now, kept shaking his head. 'I can't believe it. To be here, to witness this. Can it remain a secret?' he asked Mr P.

'There will be whispers eventually, I am sure. But that is a good thing, because people will know that there is hope for the future.'

Aye Aye was walking with determination and some pride. 'Democracy might seem a dream now in Myanmar, but it will come.'

'I don't think Michaelson would have offered me forty thousand dollars for the kammavaca, or tried so hard to steal it, if he had realised what it contained,' Natalie said to Moss.

'No,' he replied. 'I'm sure he thought it would deliver him something of monetary value.'

'I think the kammavaca's message is perfect,' said Natalie.

On the landing Natalie thanked Moss for his help before waving him goodbye. She stood in the sun watching the launch speed off into the distance through the sparkling water. She lifted her face to the sky, feeling the heat of the sun after the dim coolness of the shadowy monastery, and closed her eyes. She could hear the flapping wings of a large water bird as it swooped above the surface of the river, the papery rustle of bamboo leaves above her and the splash of the river against the bank. The sounds calmed her tumbling thoughts.

Had she just dreamed everything? Had she really rescued a small object that held a prophecy, a message of hope and a dream for the people of this far-off golden land in which she found herself? She had more than fulfilled the small, impossible dream of completing Uncle Andrew's journey. She had come to a strange land on a vague errand. Yet now she felt as one with this place. She had been able to step far out of her comfort zone with the faith that what she was doing was the right thing. And she had been rewarded.

The full import of the meaning of the kammavaca was still difficult to comprehend. But the rewards of her journey were incalculable. The friends, the beauty of the land, the knowledge she had gained, the inkling of what might yet be to come were wonderful. She had risen to challenges and had many new experiences, she had gained wisdom and compassion and now she knew that her horizons were limitless.

She was ready to return home.

# EPILOGUE

## November 2010

NATALIE'S MOBILE PHONE AND computer were pinging with messages. The house phone rang before she reached her desk.

'She's out! I don't think there's any TV coverage yet. See if you can find it on the radio.' Vicki was almost shouting. 'It's wonderful.'

'Fantastic! Even though it was announced, I didn't think it would happen until she walked outside her gate!' enthused Natalie. 'I must call Thi and Mi Mi!'

By the time Mark walked in the door from work, the children were jumping up and down, infected with their mother's joy at the news that Aung San Suu Kyi had been released from house arrest, although they had little idea what it all meant.

Natalie rushed at Mark and hugged him. 'The Lady is out from house arrest. Isn't it wonderful! This is the start!'

'Yes. A beginning.'

'I mean, it's early days, but this is the first hopeful sign that things are going to change in Myanmar. There're crowds and crowds outside her house.'

Mark looked at Natalie's ecstatic face. 'I'm glad you're glad. That is a pretty big deal. I suppose you'll be getting together with your Burma friends to celebrate?'

'We've been talking. There's a long road ahead. Do you think the prophecy is coming true?'

'I have no idea, Nat, but it's a start,' said Mark softly.


In her new sunroom Natalie looked out the window that faced the canal. She loved the way the light danced in from the bright water and spun rainbows through the glass ornaments lined up along the sill, especially Andrew's little red elephant from May Lin's glass factory in Yangon. She loved their renovated home, and the fact that Mark was now working back on the Gold Coast fulltime. The children were growing and happy. Life was good.

But there was a part of her that didn't bask in the sunshiny life of Queensland's paradise coast. Sometimes, in the crush of traffic jams or the noise of a shopping mall, Natalie would stop and suddenly recall the silent spread of the Bagan plains, sunlight and morning mist slowly revealing the ancient temples. Sometimes other visions of beautiful Burma, modern Myanmar, and its special people, flashed into her mind, making her smile.

She might never go back. But she would be watching and remembering. And hopeful.

# There's more
# to my story online

*Di Morrissey*

Dimorrissey.com          facebook.com/DiMorrissey

Including:
Book trailers and videos of Di,
newsletters, exclusive previews,
reading group notes, event updates
and all of Di's latest news.

**Love talking about books?**
**Find us online at Pan Macmillan Australia**